Praise for Lindsey Duga's
KISS of the ROYAL

"A heart-warming and charming debut. In *Kiss of the Royal*, Lindsey Duga carves out a delightful fantasy adventure wrapped up in finding first love."
—**Sara Wolf,** *NYT* **bestselling author of**
Bring Me Their Hearts

"A timeless tale with a marvelous twist!"
—**Wendy Higgins,** *NYT* **bestselling author**

"An action-packed fantasy filled with richly-drawn characters, page-turning twists, and a steamy romance, *Kiss of the Royal* will capture your heart like a magical kiss."
—**Brenda Drake,** *NYT* **bestselling author of**
the Library Jumpers series

"Full of swoony romance intertwined with non-stop adventure, *Kiss of the Royal* was a delight from start to finish. Lindsey Duga has created a world with fairytale charm and shivers that readers are sure to enjoy."
—**Mindee Arnett, critically acclaimed author of**
Avalon* and *Onyx & Ivory

"Brimming with detailed world building and characters you can't help but fall in love with, *Kiss of the Royal* left me breathless until the very last page, just as any good kiss should!"
—**Amber Mitchell, author of *Garden of Thorns***

KISS
of the
ROYAL

LINDSEY DUGA

Entangled Publishing, LLC
2614 South Timberline Road
Suite 105, PMB 159
Fort Collins, CO 80525
rights@entangledpublishing.com

Entangled Teen is an imprint of Entangled Publishing, LLC.

Visit our website at www.entangledpublishing.com.

Edited by Lydia Sharp
Cover design by Liz Pelletier and Heather Howland
Photography credit: Getty/RomanOkopny
Getty/koosen
Interior design by Toni Kerr

ISBN 978-1-64063-183-0
Ebook ISBN 978-1-64063-184-7

Manufactured in the United States of America
First Edition July 2018

10 9 8 7 6 5 4 3 2 1

entangled teen
an imprint of Entangled Publishing LLC

To Mim and Pap

PART ONE

THE PRINCESS
AND THE HERETIC

And so, with Myriana's sacred Kiss,
the birth of a new race of mortals began.
It is with her power and her sister's—Saevalla's—passed
down generation after generation, that we possess the
sole weapon on earth to vanquish the might
of the Forces of Darkness.

Excerpt text from *The Royal Legion Archival History*

It is with logic and reason that we lead the
kingdoms into an ordered reign.
Perish emotions and vanquish doubts,
for they are tools of heretics and cracks in our armor.
Stay strong, Royals, for we are the Legion,
and we will conquer the Darkness
and see the Wicked Queen put to rest at last.

Excerpt text from *Queen Gardenia Myriana*

CHAPTER ONE

RETURN OF THE PATROL

By the seventh day of constant agony, I wished I hadn't already killed the dwarf who cast this locking curse on me. I wanted the opportunity to kill him again. Slower this time.

Sitting up in bed, I gave my calves a testing flex, and pain shot through them. *Holy Queen.* I clenched the sheets until the ache subsided, then loosened my hold. They still bloody hurt. But smiling through the pain meant I could escape the bed I'd been chained to for the past week.

Unfortunately, Ulfia had been my recovery nurse long enough to see through the facade. She narrowed her eyes and folded her arms across her ample bosom, towering over me. "You don't think I know when you're faking it?" she chided.

"And *you* know I can handle it. I've had a week for the healing process. That's *more* than enough time."

Ulfia scowled but didn't argue my point. I'd been through much worse than a locking curse before, and keeping me in bed a day longer wasn't going to make a difference. I needed to get up, to move, to practice, to get out of this *blasted bed* and be useful.

"*I* will be the one to say whether you are healed or not, princess."

As Ulfia attempted to guide me back onto the pillows, I placed my hands over hers and pushed them off my shoulders.

"I'm in perfect condition, I swear. I could run laps with the recruits until dusk."

"Oh very good, princess, wheeze yourself to death, that'll help us win the war." Ulfia bent over my legs, her soft gray curls falling in curtains over her round face, and started massaging my right calf to find any lasting remnants of the locking curse.

I stared at a spot on the wall, where mineral deposits in the stones had created an interesting pattern that resembled fairy wings, and gritted my teeth while Ulfia probed mercilessly into my muscles. I'd just shifted to watching the dust motes float about lazily in the sunlight when she hit one particular spot that made me hiss out a swear through my teeth.

I truly hated dwarves. And their sneaky curses.

Ulfia looked up, raising an eyebrow, giving me her signature I-told-you-so look. If it were up to her, no Royal would ever see battle again after so much as a bruise.

"The patrol will be at the castle any moment," I said. "I need a report from Kellian before I hit the training fields." It was bad enough I had to miss out on patrol with my partner because the healing Kiss was taking over a week to do its job, but this particular patrol was critical to new intelligence on the enemy. After the eastern kingdom of Raed had reported a horde of goblins casting new curses, the Council sent out an emergency patrol to gather any information about how they could be defeated.

Ulfia gave my calf a small swat. A needling sensation pricked my skin, and I flexed involuntarily, forcing a violent shudder through me. "You'll do no training today," she said. "Did you not hear a word I said, Ivy Myriana? You. Are. Not. Healed. Yet." She tapped my foot with every word.

I opened my mouth to protest again, when a familiar-looking page burst through the door as if he had a witch on his heels.

"Princess Ivy! Your Kiss is needed—the patrol—at the palace gates!"

I stood at once, which was a mistake, because I wobbled and almost fell on Ulfia. Luckily she was a strong old bird and caught me easily by the waist, clucking her tongue in disapproval.

Although she had a tight hold on me, I tried to free myself. "I'm on my way."

"On your way, my fanny," Ulfia snapped. "Come here, boy." She gestured for him to take her place. "The princess is still getting over a locking curse. Be sure you walk with her."

Under Ulfia's glare, the page scurried over to me and tentatively took my waist as I leaned on his shoulder. His face went from white to a ferocious red.

Blue sunlight streamed through stained glass as we made our way down the corridor to the servants' halls, where we'd emerge close to the gates, avoiding the Hall of Ancestors, the grand staircase, and the one-hundred-pound double doors.

I glanced at the page's face again, noting the freckles across his cheeks, not unlike my own, and his name came to me. I'd heard my own page, Bromley, use this boy's name before. "Desren, did they say anything to you? Who needs my Kiss?"

The boy flushed deeper, probably shocked I knew his name. He pushed open the servants' door and helped me through. "I'm afraid I don't know many details, princess. Only that the curse is a bad one. Princess Tulia's Kiss did not work."

At this, I stumbled, and Desren had to tighten his grip to keep me from going down. "*What?* But Tulia is a pure-blood Royal."

His jaw tightened, but he said nothing.

So. I was their last hope. Tulia may be pure, but she wasn't a direct descendant like me.

Nerves rose in me like a thousand bubbles pressing against the cork of a spirit bottle after shaking. *Oh Heavenly Queen*, had they been taken by the same curse we'd gone to investigate? Just how powerful was it?

We emerged into the bright sunlight reflecting off the white-and-caramel-colored stones decorating the pathway to the intricately woven iron gates. Beyond those gates, the beautiful Crown City of Myria sprawled out for miles, with shops, homes, and steeples, creating a rolling expanse of stone and thatched roofs—some structures as old as the castle, some as new as the dwarf attack from last week.

The sky was a brilliant blue, with a few wispy clouds slowly moving from east to west, following the wind's journey. The only thing that marred such beauty was a swirl of dark specks in the distance. For a moment, I considered them to be nothing more than a flock of crows chased off by some farmer, but the specks fluttered about, hovering, rather than scattering away in fear.

"Desren, what does that look like to you?" I pointed to the dark specks.

"You mean the crows, princess?"

"No, they're not—" I stopped, swallowing. They were sparrow harpies—birdlike blood scavengers the size of fairies, with dark, leathery wings. Living shadows. They were never seen in the daylight or without some kind of monster horde to follow and feast on the trail of bodies.

"Milady—the patrol." Desren tugged me gently forward, heading for the gates.

I tore my eyes away from the sparrow harpies, making a mental note to mention them to a Master Mage later. Their strange behavior should be investigated.

Just past the gates, the patrol was coming up the slight

slope of the castle road. Even from here I could make out the blood and slime that coated my comrades' battle armor. As they approached, scratches and bruises came into view. Their exhausted faces and weary eyes evidence of their journey through the night back to Myria. Back home.

My gaze jumped from prince to princess, searching for my partner's face. Ridding myself of Desren's shoulder, I limped toward them as they passed through the gates.

Tulia and Minnow, pure-blood princesses in the Myrian Royal Legion, saw me and dismounted from their horses. Their partners, Edric and Roland, followed suit.

"Ivy," Tulia started, reaching for my arm, but her fingertips only brushed my sleeve as I pushed into the patrol's scattered, battle-weary ranks. Struggling past the tired horses, road dust caught in my throat and the iron scent of blood stung my nose. My stiff legs screamed at me to slow down. Claws seemed to tear at my muscles, but at this point I wasn't sure if it was the remains of the locking curse or the cold, painful fear of the horrid truth.

I couldn't see him.

No, not another one.

Not another prince. Not another partner.

At last I found Kellian's steed. But his rider was not astride. Instead, the brown stallion pulled a cart carrying a body lying across fresh hay and covered with a dark gray cloak. A legionnaire cloak. Kellian's cloak.

Suppressing a moan, my weak legs gave out, and just before the cobbled road came up to meet me, Roland's arms wrapped around my waist and hauled me up.

After my initial shock, a little relief inched into my shoulders. Kellian was alive, at least. Cursed, yes, but alive. Even if it might take him months to recover, I could still save him. I would *not* move on to my sixth partner in four years.

"If you're not healed yet," Roland began, his five-day stubble brushing my ear, "you shouldn't try the Kiss."

I understood Roland's warning but would not heed it. I'd performed dozens of Kisses while drained and exhausted, and not one had been weaker for it. The magic within my Kiss was impossibly strong, despite the traces of some stupid curse.

My hand tightened around his arm. His leather guards were coated in dirt. "I'm healed enough." I gently pushed his arm away and faced the immobile figure on the cart. With a quick prayer, I pulled the cloak from Kellian's face. His brown hair was caked with dried blood, but his face had been cleaned— probably by Tulia or Minnow—showcasing his high cheekbones and sun-kissed skin. He was only two years younger than me, but lying there, seemingly asleep, he had the look of a child. At just fifteen, he was the purest prince in Myria, the only one with enough Royal Magic to match my own.

"How did it happen?" I asked, straightening and waving my hand over his face. Cold radiated from his skin. Definitely a curse of extreme magnitude.

"We were ambushed by the horde of goblins. It was just like the scouts from Raed had said—they came at us with magic we'd never seen before." Minnow's voice, usually so light, much like her soft, petite appearance, was low and trembling. "We barely had time to administer battle Kisses to any of the princes."

"Is that why—"

"No," Minnow said quickly. "I gave one to both Kellian and Roland. Your prince was protected, although…my magic is not as strong as yours."

Because I knew I'd have to miss patrol thanks to the Kiss's healing time for the locking curse, I'd asked Minnow to stay by my partner. If I couldn't be there, a pure-blood princess was the best the Legion could offer. Minnow was strong and capable, but if I'd been there, if Kellian had used *my* Kiss instead, he'd be exhausted now, but awake. Not only because Kisses by one's ordained partner were stronger by the Holy Queen's blessing, but because *my* Kisses were the best. But due to our dwindling numbers, every able Royal was needed on patrol, regardless of having their partner with them. As King Randalph had reminded me when I'd requested Kellian be removed from patrol while I was out, there were other princesses perfectly able to bestow a Kiss—and any Royal's Kiss was better than no Kiss.

Not this time, King Randalph.

"So…" I glanced at Minnow and Roland. "It was this new curse? What was it like?"

"I can show you." Minnow held out two fingers and extended them toward my forehead.

I almost backed away. I didn't want Minnow's memories to become my own and join the rest of my nightmares in which my partners fell with lifeless eyes and blood trickling from their lips. But I had to see this mysterious new curse. I had to find out what my Kiss was up against.

I nodded and closed my eyes. Minnow touched her fingers to my forehead and whispered the words of shared memories. *"Don'na illye min'na."*

My mind fogged, and a forest shimmered into existence, shapes and blurs all hazy in the edges of Minnow's memories. But the thing she meant for me to see was mind-numbingly clear: Kellian, his body glowing with the cobalt flames of battle magic, engaged in a fight with a goblin. Kellian swung his sword, slashing the goblin's face and tearing through its eye, leaving a crude, bloody gash. With a shriek and garbled words, the goblin began to cast a curse. Just as he let the curse fly—vibrant emerald lightning crackling through the goblin's long spindly fingers—Kellian stabbed the goblin in the chest. The goblin dissolved into smoke, the ground alight with green flames. Its curse clung to Kellian's sword and crawled over the metal, reaching the hilt. The green lightning danced over his hands and up his arms, then took over his entire body, shaking him like a puppet. The blue battle magic that had encased Kellian flickered and died as he crashed to the ground.

I reeled back from Minnow's fingertips. Such power…a curse that existed even after a monster's death? I leaned over my prince, feeling the cold roll off him in waves. Time was running out.

I was his only hope. The blood of the great Queen Myriana was his only hope. Blood that ran through my veins. *My* only hope. *I will not lose another partner to the Forces of Darkness. I cannot endure that shame again. That pain…*

I bent closer, my lips hovering over his.

I'll save you, my friend.

With a quick prayer to my ancestor, the living goddess, the first Queen—*O Holy Queen, lend me your strength*—I prepared the strongest spell words in my arsenal for this revival Kiss.

Illye donia.

The words reverberated in my mind as I pressed my lips to his. Even in his comatose state, the Royal magic within Kellian surged forward and reacted with my own. Like flint striking steel, the two sparks created a flame that fed into the spell words. Magic drained out of me, into Kellian, and I nearly collapsed. Lightheaded, I held myself up on the cart long enough to watch silver dust wash over Kellian…then disappear like mist after a hard rain.

I stared in disbelief at Kellian's unmoving body, barely hearing the shocked whispers behind me.

My Kiss had failed.

CHAPTER TWO

IGNORING THE PAIN

I crumpled, my back sliding down the wall of the cart and my tunic snagging on splinters. Almost as soon as my legs touched the cobbled stone road, Roland had me back up.

His hands gripped my arms tight enough to pull me from my shock. "I'm fine," I said quickly, refusing to meet his gaze. "My legs are still a little stiff, that's all." I cleared my throat. "I need someone to give me a full report on the patrol and this new curse. And then—"

With callused fingers, Roland tilted my chin upward, forcing me to look into his dark eyes and equally dark face. "Go rest, Ivy. We'll take care of him."

Take care of him. As in, bring him to the Curse Ward to sleep away his days until his body aged and turned to dust.

Turning away from Roland, I searched Kellian's face, neck, and arms for the slightest twitch to show my Kiss was working. Finally, my gaze landed on the back of his hand. The Mark of Myriana—*my* mark—an ornate crest of holly and ivy curled together in a crown, wrapped around the back of his hand and traveled up his wrist to the base of his palm. The mark appeared burned and smoky—no longer sharp, clear lines as it had once been.

Kellian's mark resided on the back of my own hand. The crest of the Royal House of Elhein was a mountain lion's claw with two swords crossed. It now looked faded and worn, too.

I grabbed his hand, covering the mark, and squeezed it. No response. "Please wake up, Kellian," I murmured.

"What?" Roland asked.

I released Kellian's hand. "Like I said, I'll need a full report on this new dark magic." Remembering Minnow's memories with the mysterious green lightning, my frantic mind jumped from one thought to the next. If I had been there, would I have been able to administer a Kiss to Kellian that could've defeated this curse? Minnow was not his partner, she didn't bear his mark like I did, and therefore could not give him counter-curse Kisses—only simple ones like battle magic Kisses or healing Kisses. Was that it, then? Was I just too late, or was this curse simply too powerful even for the great Myriana's magic? The thought made my gut twist.

"And you'll get that report," Minnow said, reaching for my hands with her usual gentleness, "but not until after you rest."

I almost didn't let her touch me, didn't want anyone to try to console me when I needed no consolation—only an explanation.

But seeing my battle-weary and exhausted comrades, I knew now was not the time. Here they were, worrying about me, when *they* were the ones who needed sleep.

So I let Minnow take my arm. The image of Kellian's body shaking with green lightning played over and over in my head as we trailed behind the patrol into the Hall of Ancestors. The sound of everyone's reverberating footsteps and muted chatter snapped me out of my trance.

"I think I'd rather stay outside. I've been in the infirmary too long," I said, forcing strength into my voice. Even though my legs were still sore and stiff, I needed time alone. To stop the influx of poisonous thoughts already seeping into my subconscious—*I'm a failure, I lost another partner because I'm too weak, I can't uphold the bloodline of Myriana.* These thoughts always came to me in the same voice, one that had haunted me since childhood.

I pushed them away and gave Minnow's hand a reassuring squeeze. "I'm glad you made it back safely."

Minnow still watched me with concern, her sky-blue eyes shiny with unshed tears.

I couldn't let her think Kellian's state was her fault. That was my burden to bear. "You did your best. Thank you for looking after him."

She blinked away the tears. "Ivy…"

"It's you who need rest." I nodded to the other Royals heading for their rooms. "You look like you're about to collapse. Brief me on what you were able to discover on patrol after you've slept."

Minnow gave me a quick hug then shuffled away, her footsteps echoing in the massive hall.

I stared at the lofty ceiling for a moment, seeking refuge from my thoughts. The marble arches of the Hall of Ancestors expanded and met in the middle, like two sides of a rainbow joining in perfect unison. It calmed me to admire the detailed, pearly-white marble statuaries of princes and princesses battling dragons and griffins, of mages dueling witches and warlocks. It was said the stories of all the past Royals were represented here.

Would my stories end up here, too, someday?

The feeling of serenity didn't last. Soon those faceless sculptures taunted me. *"Failure. Useless. Your service in the Legion is over. The war against the Forces of Darkness will carry on without you."*

I had to get out.

I hurried through the Hall then stopped at the steps leading down to the gates. The wall towered over the Crown City of Myria, surrounding the town below with its cobbled walkways and the homes of our subjects.

Their lives were laid out before me. Lives I'd taken an oath to protect.

With that weight on my shoulders, I descended the steps as fast as my sore legs would allow. Slipped through the gaps in the blossoming apple trees, their white petals fluttering in the wind, carrying the scent that always reminded me of apple spiced-honey cakes, I headed for the training grounds. After a week of dormancy, my muscles yearned to work. And my soul ached to prove I wasn't totally worthless.

My heart bled for Kellian. The image of him on the cart, his face left with traces of blood and grime, would follow me forever. Until my own legionnaire cloak covered my lifeless body. He'd been so strong and brave, and *good*. In many ways, I felt like it should've been me on that cart instead of him. He'd trusted me to protect him. To *save* him. But I failed him instead.

And now I was without a partner. Again. Without a prince, I was doomed to spend my days on the training grounds or in my quarters, studying spells for my Kisses but never getting a chance to use them. I prayed it wouldn't happen, that the Royal Council would find me another prince, so I could continue fighting on the battlefields. Where I belong.

I paused in front of a low fence built of brucel wood and copper nails and gingerly stepped over it, using a nearby jerr tree to steady myself. Finally coming upon the fringes of the training grounds, I could just make out the young recruits of princes and princesses sparring. A second group was running laps, and a third was at the archery targets. A breeze rolled over the grounds, rustling the grass like rippling emerald waves.

My legs already ached from my short journey. I tried to

hide my limp as I made my way to the sparring group. Boys fought boys, while the girls practiced defensive moves using shields. As usual. Later, princesses would be taken aside to practice a long-range weapon of their choosing, like longbows, crossbows, or throwing knives. Because *only* princesses had the ability to cast spells after the Kiss, we were each assigned a prince who was able to receive the spell and fight with magically enhanced strength. According to priests, a female Royal's power for spell-casting derived from Queen Myriana, since it was *her* Kiss that had saved King Raed. Therefore, we had to be well protected and prepared by learning spells, defensive moves, and long-range weapons instead of close combat.

Still, there were princesses who practiced swordsmanship relentlessly, simply because they didn't like staying within a protective *Illye* circle, away from the heat and thrill of battle. Princesses like me.

I *wanted* to fight alongside my partner, sharing the sweat and fear of a troll wielding a blood-spattered mace. Though I understood it was to keep me safe, it was frustrating staying behind an *Illye* circle while my partners were out there risking everything.

I headed over to the girls, taking a shield from one I'd taught healing Kisses to only last month. I couldn't recall her name, but I remembered her thin face and black-as-night hair. I flipped the shield to be flat against my forearm, running my fingers over the sharp metal edge. "Hold it like this. Remember, your shield can be a weapon, too. Use the edge to inflect any damage you can. The minute you stop fighting is the minute you admit you're ready to die."

The girl nodded, taking her shield back as I handed it to her. There were dark circles under her eyes, and her neck and cheeks were slick with sweat, but her scowl was most prominent. She was determined to learn more than just how to hide behind wood and metal. I saw my younger self in her. After watching my first partner fall with an ax in his neck, I'd sworn I wouldn't simply cower behind a shield, magical or wooden, when I could've been there with him.

Like I could've been there with Kellian.

I turned away from the girls, toward the boys practicing with their wooden swords. When the nearest prince stumbled after a particularly vicious attack by his partner, I took him by the shoulder, steadying him. He glanced up, his eyes going wide with surprise.

"May I cut in?" I asked.

He blinked then dropped the sword into my outstretched hand.

His sparring partner swallowed, Adam's apple bobbing under his collar. "Princess Ivy?"

"The very same." Slashing the weapon through the air for a practice cut, I stepped in front of the boy whose sword I'd taken. "I'm your new opponent."

"I don't think that's such a—"

I bent my knees and lunged forward with a strike. The young prince just managed to parry my attack and jumped back. I advanced, swinging my sword with a ferocity that made a few observers gasp. They quit their own matches and formed a circle around ours.

My muscles hummed with satisfaction. Action at last.

With every turn and duck, the prince became more unhinged, desperate to save face.

I swung high. He dodged then aimed for my knees. A rookie move. I stepped around him, and his wooden blade missed me by inches. A simple elbow strike to the back of his head had him falling forward onto his stomach.

"Sloppy," I said, the tip of my sword now at the middle of his back. "Focus on your defense. You can't attack if you're dead."

A few of the girls dropped their shields and clapped enthusiastically, while the boys begrudgingly joined in.

As I stepped forward, legs throbbing, and helped the boy up, my feeling of victory faded quickly. This was not the way to make myself feel better about my Kiss failing. Not in winning against a thirteen-year-old boy. Even though I was only four years older than him, with all my experience in battle, it felt more like fifty. Thirteen was young, but he could be younger still. Our numbers were dwindling against the might of the Forces, and soon we'd *have* to bring Royals younger than thirteen into battle and on patrol. At fourteen, I saw a troll's head lopped off its body. I had nightmares for weeks.

But the fact that these boys were going to see battle sooner rather than later would not change, regardless of whether I was using them to vent my own frustrations. They needed to be taught, and I certainly didn't mind being the one to do it.

I turned to the audience of trainees. Swinging the wooden sword onto my shoulder, I called out, "Who's next?"

They avoided eye contact, none of them eager to be knocked to the ground.

I pointed my sword at a tan-skinned prince with bronze hair. "How about you?" He seemed old enough.

"M-me?" The boy glanced around then looked back, face reddening. "I'm only an eighth-blood, princess. I just started training a week ago."

My stomach twisted almost as tightly as when I'd seen Kellian's sleeping face. Besides bringing in younger Royals, we were also recruiting Royals who barely qualified. Princes and princesses who were even less than a quarter of a Royal bloodline. *An eighth-blood.* Those with less Royal blood had less magic—simple as that. So what good were they? Mere fodder for the Wicked Queen's creatures?

I could see a griffin's talons cutting into their small bodies, and a chimera's iron jaws ripping into their flesh and crunching the bone. It made me want to dig a hole in this perfect green grass and vomit.

"Princess Ivy! Milady!"

I dropped my sword, recognizing my page's voice.

Bromley was a skinny fourteen-year-old boy with cropped honey-colored hair. I knew his face better than I knew my own. So when he pushed through the crowd of boys, I could read the anger in his narrowed brown eyes and clenched jaw.

As he came to a stop before me, breathing hard, he glared at the training sword in my hand.

"You're not in bed."

I raised an eyebrow. "Astute observation, Brom."

Like all pure-blood Royals, I'd been assigned an attendant at an early age. Bromley had been given to me when I was eight and he was only five. I'd never really wanted a servant, but I'd wanted a friend.

The edge of Brom's mouth twitched. "Master Gelloren has called for you."

The anxiety I'd just worked so hard to chase away came rushing back. Of course Master Gelloren had already heard about Kellian's fall by the new curse. Of course he'd already heard about my failed Kiss. And of course he'd already want to see me. Because when it rains, the fields flood.

What would Gelloren say? What would he *do*?

I shoved the sword flat against the chest of its owner, and the recruits parted as I made my way through the small crowd. I could no longer deny the pain in my legs, anyway. Probably wouldn't have lasted a minute in another fight.

Bromley hurried to catch up. "What happened?"

I focused my gaze on the jerr trees ahead as we walked. The lines of red leaves began to blur, and I swallowed. "Kellian, he…didn't quite make it. Comatose. Some new curse."

"I…I'm sorry, milady." He paused, the distant clattering of wooden swords and wind whistling through leaves filling the silence. "Who administered the revival Kiss? Maybe you could go and—"

His words hit me like a strike to the gut, and I nearly fell.

"Princess!" Brom caught me, but he wasn't as strong as Ulfia or Roland, so we both stumbled a little, stopping underneath the pleasant shade of the jerr trees.

Brom didn't know it was *my* revival Kiss that hadn't worked, but I couldn't explain what had happened without lashing out. The wound was still too fresh. "I'm fine. Did Master Gelloren tell you what he wants?"

Brom shook his head. "He didn't. But maybe it can wait. You need to be resting. Ulfia told me—"

"The only thing I need right now is to get back out there. I'm going on the next patrol, Bromley, with whatever prince they'll give me." I straightened and started forward.

He tried to catch my arm. "But—"

I wrenched away, kicking up blades of grass as I picked up my pace. "I'll use a half prince. A quarter prince. I don't care! I'll Kiss whoever can get me back out there. They *need* me, Brom."

The Legion did need me—all of Myria did—especially if the young prince I'd just fought and the eighth-blood prince were any indication of how desperate we were. Regardless of whether or not my Kiss had worked against this new super-curse, it was still stronger than any Royal's here. I wouldn't let another prince—young, weak, or otherwise—lose his life when I could be there to stop it. I'd protect them when I couldn't with Kellian.

The wind picked up and tore a few leaves off the jerr trees. They swirled past me as I headed toward the castle, calling me back to their peaceful shade—the only form of shadows and darkness that was good in this world.

CHAPTER THREE

THE AWFUL TRUTH

The living and study quarters for the three Master Mages were located in the northeast tower of the castle. Brom left me at its entrance. If Master Gelloren had *summoned* me, it was a matter he wanted to discuss privately.

I paused in front of his door, taking only a moment to enjoy the sun coming through the stained glass of the western-facing window.

Months ago I would've taken pleasure in visiting Master Gelloren's office. We'd play Basilisk and Mongoose and he'd lead me to believe I'd won, then he'd take all my cards during the last hand. And if we didn't play cards, we'd spend hours poring over maps and talking strategies about patrols and legion troops. He'd always been so warm to me, but lately our conversations had become short and weary. No cards. Not even a cup of shassa root tea.

He certainly wasn't to blame. It was just this never-ending war. More and more troops lost. More and more times Gelloren left in the middle of the night to quell blazes in town with his elemental water magic. More and more Council meetings with the other Master Mages on what to do next.

No wonder he didn't have time for tea or a simple game

of cards. Especially with princesses who kept losing partners.

When I knocked, Master Gelloren's deep voice called, "Come in, Ivy."

I pushed open the heavy wooden door and let it close behind me.

His office was the same as always. Maps of the four kingdoms and elemental charts that only mages could understand decorated the stone walls. A tower of used teacups balanced precariously on the edge of his desk, while piles of books covered almost the entire floor, and somewhere, amid all the clutter, a bird tweeted incessantly.

Master Gelloren sat at his desk, bent over a pile of letters, wearing his usual oversized emerald robe. Judging from the stain on the collar, the wrinkles, and the crumbs of his favorite midnight snack—gingerberry tarts—sprinkled in the robe's folds, he'd probably worked all through the night.

"Take a seat," he instructed without looking up.

I remained standing, watching his quill glide across the parchment.

Eyes still on the letters, he said, "Well, all right then, stand."

"Master, it's not out of disrespect. I just want you to take me seriously."

This time, he did look up. Even though he was one of the older Master Mages, Gelloren hadn't gone fully gray yet. There were still tawny blond streaks in his well-groomed beard and braid. "My dear Ivy, I assure you, I always take you seriously— whether you are sitting down staring daggers at me, or standing up staring daggers at me." He smiled, dabbed his quill, and continued his letter.

Ears tingling with heat at his veiled chastising, I sat, focusing on my knees. Finally, after sealing his letter with wax and placing it on top of other outgoing letters, he straightened and folded his hands inside his robe.

"Regarding Prince Kellian...my deepest condolences."

His words forced the scene from Minnow's memories back into my mind. I pictured the goblin—with a left eye that was horribly mutilated from Kellian's blade—casting its mysterious curse, and green lightning engulfing my prince as the goblin disappeared into smoke.

I looked from the stack of letters on his desk to Gelloren's face. He was watching me with those gray eyes that knew me so well. I didn't have to pretend with him. And I didn't have to tell him how Kellian's loss made me feel. Like the goblin had personally carved out a piece of my heart with its clawlike fingernails.

He knew. Gelloren didn't need tears or whining. He needed me to be strong. Focused.

"My Kiss...didn't..." I cleared my throat. "It didn't work, Master."

Gelloren gave a tiny nod. "And you think that is somehow your fault."

I glanced down at my hands balled up in my lap. I knew this new curse had to be terribly powerful, but even so...my revival Kiss was the best in the four Kingdoms. How could one *goblin*, one of the weakest kinds of dark creatures, have been strong enough to beat me?

"Minnow shared her memories with me," Gelloren said. "It's clear this green lightning is a new curse of great magnitude. Gifted though you may be, Ivy, your power isn't unlimited."

Gelloren would never coddle me. He always told me the truth—no matter how difficult. So I should have felt some relief, but his words made me feel worse. My power was limited, and the Forces were growing unimaginably stronger. How could I feel better about that?

Swallowing, I forced the words out. "Yes, well...I wouldn't want you to think I no longer deserve a partner." I twisted the hem of my tunic, needing something to squeeze. "Because Kellian is no longer able to fight…I would like…"

Just say it, Ivy. Tell him you want another partner, that you want to find the Wicked Queen yourself—that it's your duty.

"You don't need to say it, my dear."

I held my breath. Would this be the moment my career at the Legion came to an end? With no pure princes left in Myria to wield my magic, the Council could argue I should be shipped off to the southern castle of Freida to begin producing heirs, just like my sister, Clover, had been three summers ago. She'd already had a son and was trying for her second.

Gelloren sighed, picking up another letter and unfolding it with his thin fingers.

Could that be a summons from Freida? *Oh, Holy Sisters, I'm only seventeen!* If they sent me there, how long would I be forced to stay? Would the war just get worse and worse until I came back to nothing but blood and ash?

He smoothed out the letter. "You need another partner. I know this."

My shoulders relaxed.

"Kellian's state, while tragic, is no excuse for us not to use Myriana's Mark to its fullest in battle," Gelloren continued.

At the mention of my greatest ancestor and her mark, I drew myself up taller. "Thank you, Master. I was afraid you'd make me retire to Freida."

Master Gelloren placed the letter facedown, leaned back in his chair, and studied me. "No, we need your power now more than ever. The Forces of Darkness are rising to insurmountable numbers. Witches are creating more nests of dark curses, generating more and more goblins, trolls, griffins… and now with curses we have yet to identify."

I nodded, knowing this all too well. Hearing it out loud made me realize I had no reason to fear they'd send me away.

Even if the Council pushed, Gelloren would make them see the awful truth: they could not afford to wait until my children grew up to fight the Forces. What good was it to have Queen Myriana's direct descendants if we didn't use them? Thanks to a carefully constructed family tree, it was *literally* what they had been born to do.

Master Gelloren looked out his study window. "I fear that if we do not do something drastic soon, it won't matter how many heirs we produce. We'll be overpowered."

The bird, still hidden somewhere in his office, stopped singing, as if it sensed the gravity of our conversation.

"I just don't understand, Master Gelloren. How can we be so outnumbered? We are far more adept and trained than we were five hundred years ago. We kill at least fifty creatures every patrol, and yet a hundred more take their place!" The goblin's scarred face flashed again in my mind, and I squeezed the fabric of my tunic until my knuckles turned white.

Master Gelloren stood and walked to his window, staring out at the Royals training below. The sun had fallen behind one of the few clouds in the sky, changing the shadows within the room, giving the office a more sinister atmosphere.

Which reminded me... "Sir, I spotted a swarm of sparrow harpies today, just outside the town limits."

"Yes, I saw them, too. I dispatched a team earlier to investigate."

"What do you think they mean?" In my studies, I'd learned that sparrow harpies spotted during the daytime were a bad omen. Often a harbringer of something evil to come, although I couldn't imagine what. We were already under constant threat.

"I've an idea that I don't feel comfortable sharing yet. I will when the time is right," he said, turning from the window and giving me a familiar smile.

I didn't like that smile. It was one of indulgence that he

wore when I thought I had dealt the winning hand during a game of cards.

"Master…"

"We must continue to fight, and that is all we can do for now, my dear."

"So get me out there." I stood, too. "Please, whatever I have to do—I'll do it. I'll go to chapel every night and recite the sacred prayers, anything. Just find *someone* to be my partner—I don't care who it is."

Gelloren stroked his gold-and-silver streaked beard and maneuvered around a tower of books. "It's not that simple, Ivy. We must find you a partner who can utilize your power for what you're worth. And currently there are no Royals in Myria whom I feel are truly at your level."

"Sir, it doesn't *matter*. Even if he has barely any Royal blood—even if he's a terrible swordsman—I can make up for it." I poured all my passion and all my anger at seeing my partner's comatose body into my words. "I had four princes before Kellian and each one was able to slay beasts three times their size. Telek took down a griffin in a single stroke with the power of one of my Kisses, and Drake slew three dru-goblins *at once*. Master, I was the nine-year-old who, with her first Kiss, was able to cure a village of a drought curse—"

"Enough." Gelloren waved his hand, the sleeve of his robe swishing under his thin wrist. "I know very well what you're capable of, Ivy. Which is why," he said, picking up the letter that lay facedown on his desk and then handing it to me, "I will not allow just *any* prince to be at your side. You must be protected."

For I am a powerful weapon in the Royal Arsenal.

The letter was from a Master Mage of the Saevall Castle in the West. Quickly, I scanned the neat, tiny handwriting, and my knees started to bounce. Not with anxiety or nerves. But with excitement. "They're sending reinforcements? To Myria?"

Gelloren nodded. "I wrote to Saevall last month, explaining that we had lost a few of our best Royals to the Forces. They've responded by sending us a generous reinforcement from their own Legion."

I frowned. "Are you sure they can afford that?"

"We're much worse off than they are."

It was true. Myria was the northernmost kingdom, sitting on the outskirts of the Galedral Forest and the Wu-Hyll Mountains, which were said to be the birthplace of some of the Forces' most powerful creatures.

"I've been told one prince in particular is especially promising," Gelloren continued.

But I stopped listening. I was too busy reading the bottom line of the letter. *Expect their arrival on the morning of the fifteenth day of spring.*

Tomorrow. Help would be arriving tomorrow, along with a prince who could get me back on the battlefield.

CHAPTER
FOUR

REINFORCEMENTS

After taking a pain-relieving potion for my legs from Ulfia, who had done nothing but scowl and mutter something about stubborn idiots while she prepared it, I spent the rest of the day on the training grounds. Bromley had followed to help me spar. Although I'd never asked him to—he gladly attended fighting lessons and trained beside me. At fourteen, he wasn't at full height or strength, but he was quick and a fast learner. Ever since I had threatened to dismiss him from my service for going easy on our fights, our sparring sessions were always interesting, though he rarely won.

Today was no different. I threw my shield up in front of my face as the wooden blade of Brom's practice sword came straight for my head. I shoved against his sword with my shield, and the "blade" thumped down the side. Grunting, I pivoted, my sword swinging toward Brom's side when his shield came down to meet me. Before he could counter, my legs gave way, and I was down on the grass, staring up at the sky and grimacing.

Bromley's head poked into the corner of my vision. "Milady?"

"Blasted son of a wraith." I pounded the pommel of my

sword into the grass.

"Miss Ulfia did say the potion would take away the pain, but not the effects of the curse," Bromley said as he took a seat beside me.

"I know," I muttered, dropping my sword and stretching my fingers out to the sun, releasing the built-up tension. The light around my hand made it hard to see Kellian's mark of partnership, although I knew it was there—seared into my skin until the unbinding ritual was performed. Mentally, I wasn't yet prepared for another, but I'd have to do it.

Removing his mark was like giving up. Giving up another prince and another friend, and admitting I hadn't been strong enough to protect him. And that maybe I would *never* be.

Stop, Ivy. I folded my arm over my eyes, blocking out the sunlight.

"Maybe we should get to supper. I heard there's roasted pheasant with kasper-mint jelly."

"Not hungry," I said, even as my stomach growled.

Brom lay down beside me and sighed. "Did Master Gelloren say you wouldn't be getting another partner? Because you know…maybe now would be a good time to rest. I mean you're just getting out of this locking curse and—"

"No," I said sharply. Brom was always trying to find ways to keep me out of battle. Usually I never got mad at him, because I knew he did it out of worry. But today was not the day to bring up the idea of resting. Not after a failed revival Kiss. "I'll have another partner soon enough."

Bromley shifted on his side, and I peeked at him from under my arm. "Really?" he asked. "Who? Amias?"

I sat up on my elbows, following Bromley's gaze to a group of older princes sparring. Amias was among them, his black hair shining in the late afternoon sun. I could almost smell his sweat. I knew his scent and the heat of his breath too well.

We'd Kissed many times during practices and skirmishes when both of us were in between partners, but the Council had never deemed us compatible.

The biggest reason being that Amias was only a half prince. His mother was a queen, but his father was a blacksmith in the lower towns. This would be reason enough not to be paired with him, but nowadays half princes actually ranked pretty high compared to quarters, eighths—even twelfths. Plus, he was naturally good with a blade—he never worked very hard at it—and with my Kiss, he'd be truly fearsome. It was also no secret that Amias wanted a direct descendant of Myriana at his side to give him more power and prestige.

I lay back down, returning my arm over my eyes. "No. Not Amias. Never Amias." If we became partners it would turn into a competition. Each of us trying to use the other for our own gain. We were too similar, and that was dangerous.

"Roland?"

"Roland and Minnow have been partners for three years, and their partnership is one of the strongest in the Legion. I could never split them up." Partners could be shuffled around for a number of different reasons: princesses were shipped off to Freida, or one too many mistakes in battle caused the Council to question their compatibility, or partners who simply never got up again…like mine. But severing a partnership bond was a painful procedure for both parties, so the Council avoided it when possible.

"The Council could do it to guarantee you a good partner," Brom pushed.

I shook my head. "It doesn't matter, Brom." I lowered my arm and told him about the Saevallans' impending arrival.

"You'll be getting a *Saevallan* prince?" Brom asked with wide eyes.

The castle stretched above us, with its stone towers and

battlements and Myrian flags flapping in the wind. Myria Castle was an ancient structure, but stronger and more formidable than any other in the four kingdoms—even Saevall, the kingdom built from golden sandstone.

"There's no one left here."

Brom went quiet. Then he tugged my sleeve. "Speaking about nothing being left, we might not even make dessert at this point, and I'm dying for some gingerberry tarts."

I smiled for the first time that day and waved my hands toward his face. "Come on then, help me up."

M y quarters were not grand. When I was very young, living with my mother and Clover in the kingdom of Freida, I had a fancy room with velvet drapes and silk embroidered cushions. That was before I started training at the Legion. Since then, I had lived in a quaint room with a bookshelf, a desk, a single bed, a window, and another adjoining room with my bath. The floors were stone, decorated with woven rugs. My only wall ornamentation was a tapestry depicting the Wu-Hyll Mountains, big purple-and-white monstrosities, with the green threads of the Galedral Forest at their base. There was a sunset right behind the mountains, making the purple peaks stand out like sharp shadows against the sunset's warm colors.

It was this tapestry that I was staring at—that I was *always* staring at—when my two younger sisters barged into my quarters.

"Ivy! How are your legs? Is the curse completely gone?" Colette hurried over and hopped onto the foot of my bed, while Robin took a seat in my desk chair.

I smiled at my little sisters and hugged the pillow tighter

to my chest. "Gone enough."

"I'm sorry I didn't come see you earlier. Queen Jocelyn had me going over the spell behind a freezing Kiss." Colette was my half sister from the same mother. With golden hair and deep blue eyes, she kept growing lovelier, and she was only a nine-year-old, just beginning her training at the Legion.

"Those are basic. How could it take you all that time?" Robin asked, flipping her hair over her shoulder.

Colette stuck out her tongue. "Says the princess who can't break a simple binding curse with her Kiss."

Robin went red and pursed her lips. Robin was also my half sister, and Colette's elder full sister. She looked more like our mother with her dark hair and eyes. Unlike Clover and me—we took after our father. After he died in battle, shortly after I was born, the Council assigned our Mother a new breeding partner, and Colette and Robin were born. They were not direct descendants, though, because of their father's bloodline.

"It's late." I gestured at the stars and crescent moon out my window. "Why are you two not in bed?"

Robin rolled her eyes. "Colette wanted to see you. I told her you were fine."

Colette glared at her sister. "What about *you-know-who*?"

I sighed. "His name is Kellian, sister. And while I'll miss him, losing a partner is nothing new." Again, pain needled its way into my chest. It certainly *wasn't* new.

Five partners lost. The shame and guilt were almost too much.

All had been killed in battle. They'd been overwhelmed by beasts, as if they'd had targets on their backs. It had been as if the monsters knew they were the strongest and needed to be taken down first.

My Kiss was to blame for that.

After my third partner had died from two griffins' talons

ripping him to bloody ribbons, I had collapsed before Master Gelloren, sobbing into his lap.

"Why, Master?" I'd said. "Why does this keep happening?"

He had stroked my hair gently, letting me cry, something the Kings and Queens would never have let me do. No weakness. Not ever. "Your Kiss has great power, my dear. It contains the Mark of Myriana. Monsters and curses will always be naturally drawn to its power and seek to destroy it first."

I'd felt nothing but despair. Was that it, then? Were all my partners doomed to carry that mark and its strength and suffer for it?

Maybe Kellian had been strong enough, but now I would never know. He was gone, too. As much as the guilt of losing him weighed me down, I knew it was the Forces who had destroyed my princes—the Forces who deserved to be slaughtered like the monsters they were. And it was the Wicked Queen, the Mother of all those awful creatures, who deserved to crumble to dust—like she would have a long time ago, if not for her unnatural dark power.

"We...we just wanted to see if you were okay," Colette said, pulling me out of the memories threatening to drown me.

"I am." I swallowed, forcing a smile "I will be."

Robin grinned. "Especially now that new meat is on its way to Myria."

"Of course you heard." I rolled my eyes.

"We also heard a certain prince is already picked out *just* for you," Robin said in a singsong voice.

"Yes, well, I *do* need another partner and—"

Robin waved away my words. "I mean, haven't you heard all the *rumors* about him?"

"What are you going on about?" I fiddled with a loose thread on the pillow.

She abandoned her chair, hopping on my bed next to

Colette. "The Swordsman Prince!"

I just stared at her.

Robin sighed in exasperation. "By the wind wisps, sister! You really need to listen to the dinner talk more. There's a new Royal among the Saevallans who's supposed to be the best fighter the four kingdoms have seen in over half a century! He's young but extremely powerful. People say he's already taken down a troll's lair—*by himself*!"

I shrugged. "That's not too impressive."

"No, Ivy, he was *by himself*. There was no princess—no Kiss. Rumor is he's never had a partner before."

I laughed. "That's the most preposterous thing I've ever heard. There's no way a Royal without a Kiss can defeat five trolls by himself."

Robin blushed, no doubt realizing how ridiculous she sounded.

Not wanting to hurt her feelings, I grabbed Robin's hands and squeezed them. "Wouldn't it be amazing if it were true, though? Imagine a man that strong without magic. Imagine what he *could* do with a Kiss…" I lunged for Colette and tickled her sides. "Take down the Evil Mother herself!"

Colette squealed and laughed, pushing Robin between us.

Robin grinned. "There'd be no one like him in all the kingdoms. He'd be a perfect partner for you."

Colette peeked out from behind Robin. "Plus, I bet he's got muscles for days."

At that, I lost it, dissolving into a fit of giggles.

"It's all muscles with you, Lettie." Robin swatted Colette with a pillow. "He's probably tall, to have taken down trolls."

"Why? You can be short and take down trolls!"

"Everyone knows trolls' necks are the weakest, and that's the best way to kill them. How can someone short reach their necks?" Robin argued back.

"They could hop!" Colette protested.

"Oh, would all their leg muscles help them hop?"

"Girls!" I broke free from my laughter and wrapped them both in my arms. It was moments like these when I was thankful I had them in my life. They'd been able to coax a laugh out of me on a day such as this one. "You're talking about my future partner. Now get to bed—both of you. And don't forget your prayers."

They hugged me good night, and when they got to the door, Robin paused. "Whether it's true or not what people say about him, the Mages *are* considering him for your new partner." With that, she shut the door behind her, and I was left chuckling to myself at the idea of my new partner being able to take down a troll's lair "by himself" and having "muscles for days." Even though they were surely exaggerated, the rumors gave me hope for victorious battles to come...but the rest was only childish imagination.

The next morning, I opened the door on Bromley's third knock, and his brown eyes lit with recognition at my attire.

I had exchanged my tunic and boots for my Royal Legion dress and charcoal gray cloak. The gown was made of fine cream fabric with gold thread entwining in intricate designs along the hem and sleeves, with a golden Royal crest over my left breast. In meeting the Saevallan Royals, I had to look the part of Myria's finest.

"Good morning, Brom," I said, stepping into the hallway. The sunrise coming in from the eastern bay windows made the gold piping glitter.

"Good morning, princess." He eyed my fine cloak then

glanced at my red-brown curls that were, as usual, wound into a tight bun. "You look very nice, but you do realize they're not here yet, right?"

I ruffled his honey-colored hair. "When they arrive I don't want to rush to change. Now, why are you grumpy this morning?"

Brom dodged my hand, his cheeks tinged pink. "I'm not grumpy. I just don't see why you're so eager for another partner."

I pulled him close, his cheek pressed against my shoulder. "You know why," I told him softly. When I held him like this, it was like we were kids again, both aching for comfort and safety, and finding it in each other's arms.

Brom said nothing as he pulled away. He was probably the only person within these castle walls, with the exception of Master Gelloren, who knew how badly I craved battle. How badly I wanted to find the Wicked Queen and end this war with *my* magic.

I didn't know if it was possible for the magic of one Royal pair to take down the legendary Mother of the Forces, who'd somehow managed to elude our people for nearly five hundred years, but it was an ambition I'd had since I was young. Find her. Defeat her. Stop her from producing these monsters. Stop us from sending *children* off to war and forcing them to grow up too fast. But she had dark powers that were beyond imagination—powers that had kept her alive far longer than was natural.

I'd once told Brom, when we were both very young, the reason behind my ambition. I'd never regretted telling him, but it was a personal secret that made me feel vulnerable.

"I do know why." His voice was so low I barely heard him. "You won't get her approval, though. Even if you win. I had hoped you'd already realized that yourself, that maybe your reason had changed—"

I looked back at him sharply. "Too far, my friend."

Brom glanced away. He knew he'd crossed the line in mentioning *her*. "My apologies, milady."

Outside the thick stone of the castle, the Myria bells rang. Two, three, four, five times. The Royals from the West had arrived.

At breakfast, I met with Tulia and Minnow. My two friends didn't say a word to me about Kellian's condition, which I appreciated. They knew how hard it was to lose a partner, especially Tulia. Tulia's partner, before Edric, had stumbled into a nest of dark vipers on patrol, and the poison had been too strong for her Kiss to save him.

After I was done pushing the shassa herb eggs and biscuits around my plate, Tulia, Minnow, and I headed for the Hall of Ancestors to greet the reinforcements. The corridors leading to the Hall of Ancestors were strung with garlands of gardenia, giving the air a sweet, intoxicating scent. I brushed my finger against a white petal and smiled appreciatively. It was a thoughtful gesture to have them here today. Gardenia was the name of Saevall's infamous Queen Gardenia Myriana, who had defeated a gray-horned dragon with the power of her Kiss and saved Saevall's Crown City. The servants must have spent all night stringing her namesake up to welcome the western Royals.

Tulia nudged me. "Looks like everyone's excited to see the new Saevallans," she said as we followed a group of whispering and giggling younger princesses wearing lighter gray cloaks, which indicated their Royal-in-training status.

"Well, it *has* been a long time since we've had visitors."

Minnow twirled a long piece of her blond hair. "Not to mention, we're all eager to see…you know…that swordsman everyone's talking about."

At the mention of my new potential partner, a trill of excitement went through me, and I remembered the rumors about him. There had to be some basis of truth to them, otherwise how would they have begun? He *must* be an excellent swordsman. At the same time, though, a smidge of guilt itched me. *How long will this partner last?* I twisted the fabric of my cloak in a futile attempt to wring out my guilt.

Uncurling my fingers, I forced the insecurity down. Master Gelloren believed in me. So did the rest of the Council, otherwise they would not be giving me a new partner. That knowledge should be enough to ease my mind.

We passed through the marble arches into the Hall of Ancestors, where Royals lined the sides, making three neat rows along the walls. I was perfectly happy to stay next to my two friends, but when Master Gelloren entered through the main doors with the other Master Mages, and his gaze flickered toward me, I knew he wanted me up front with him.

For the most part I was treated as every other Royal in the Legion. I was given the same living quarters, ate the same food, took the same classes, risked my life the same as they did. Except for the times when my bloodline was played up. Mages, Council members, and Royals from other kingdoms were all impressed to see a direct descendant of the first true Royals, Queen Myriana and her partner, King Raed.

I gave a swift smile to Tulia and Minnow then broke from the row, following the Master Mages to the head of the Hall. I took my place behind and to the right of Master Gelloren just as the doors opened and distant trumpets sounded.

The thump of boots and the clink of armor filled the Hall of Ancestors as our visitors strode forward. At the head of the Saevall Royals was a tall man with shiny armor and a long scarlet cloak, indicating his Commander rank. He looked to be maybe twenty-five or so, and had a scar down his cheek and startling light eyes.

This must be him. It would make sense that a talented fighter would rank as Commander so young.

Master Gelloren stepped forward, arms wide. "Welcome, Royals of Saevall, to the Crown City of Myria. I am Master Mage Gelloren. We are overwhelmed with gratitude at your presence."

Gelloren bowed deeply, and every Myrian Royal followed suit. Even as I bent low, I couldn't take my eyes off the Commander, the legendary swordsman.

How many battles had he seen? How many dark creatures had he slain? With the power of my Kiss, how many would he yet slay? Together, how vast would our power be?

Surely this man was strong enough to deserve my Kiss. To bear the Mark of Myriana and accept the target on his back.

The Commander stepped forward. "Master Gelloren, thank you for the warm welcome. We are eager to help your Royal Legion any way we can. We happily give our lives to protect the kingdoms from the Forces." His voice was deep and thunderous. It sent bumps of awe crawling across my skin.

Master Gelloren nodded. "Your aid could not come at a more desperate time. Recently, we lost one of our pure Royals, Prince Kellian from the House of Elhein, to an unbreakable curse. Now, Princess Ivy from the grand House of Myriana is without a suitable partner."

I stepped forward, and murmurs rippled through the group of western Royals. The Commander's light eyes jumped to me then back to the Master Mage.

"Princess Ivy is our most powerful princess, and her partner must have the strength of a hundred men. We have heard of the great swordsman from your kingdom, Prince Zachariah, and we are eager to see if their two awesome powers could be combined."

Something like amusement flittered across the Commander's face. "Zach!" he roared.

Strange. Why is he calling his own name? Wait...is he not Zachariah?

There were hurried steps, and Saevallans moved to the side to make way for someone in the very back.

"Oops! Stepped on a cloak—sorry, Fran. Oh, pardon me."

Master Gelloren and I raised our brows at each other.

"Excuse me, Kendra—move, please."

Finally, a young man stepped out from behind the Commander. He was lean and tall-*ish*, but not impressively so. Under an old traveling cloak, his clothes appeared soft and well-worn. He had dark hair, nearly black, but brunette strands shone in the beams of sunlight. I took him to be maybe a couple years older than me. Everything about his appearance, from his drab clothes to his leather armor, said...common. Everything except the fine silver sword attached at his waist, the kind of sword only a Royal would own.

He held up his hand in a small wave, and the kaleidoscope in his hazel eyes danced as if laughing at a joke only he found funny. "Pleased to meet you, I'm Zach."

CHAPTER FIVE

RUMORS AND HISTORY

His introduction was met with silence. I didn't know what to say. This couldn't possibly be right. This simple-looking commoner couldn't be a *prince*. Such a clumsy fellow couldn't be the skilled swordsman rumored to have taken down a troll's lair *by himself*. Could he even unsheathe his sword without fumbling, let alone wield it?

The young man faced us with a big grin. Then his gaze landed on me and, for a split second, his smile faltered. "So, what did you call me for?" He scratched the back of his neck. "My apologies, but I was distracted. Collin had told me this really funny joke. Would you like to hear it? A dwarf, goblin, and troll walk into a tavern and—"

"Zach," the Commander interrupted through gritted teeth, "we were discussing your possible partnership with Princess Ivy."

"Oh." Zachariah blinked then glanced at me. "That's happening *now*? Here?"

Master Gelloren, whom I had never seen surprised, seemed to snap out of his astonishment, blinking a few times. "Prince Zachar—"

"Zach." Oh Holy Queen, he *interrupted* a Master Mage. "Just Zach."

Gelloren recovered and mustered a smile in return. "Of course. Zach," he said as he turned back to me and held out his hand. "This is Her Royal Highness, Princess Ivy Myriana."

I took Gelloren's hand and stepped up next to him, giving Zach another long look. Where were his "muscles for days"?

Appearances could be deceiving, I supposed, determined not to lose hope. My own didn't offer much regality, in popular opinion—too many freckles. And my hair, curly with pretty autumn shades, frizzed too easily.

"Prince Zach." I dipped my head as I offered the typical Legion princess curtsy, grabbing the hem of my dress with my right hand and crossing my left fist over my chest. "Thank you for journeying all this way."

"My pleasure." Zach was smiling again when I returned my gaze, but this time the smile was much smaller, and somehow softer.

Gelloren gave my shoulder a squeeze and addressed Zach. "If your skills prove worthy of Princess Ivy's power, then you will be bound as Royal partners."

I could feel the pride in the Master's gesture and words, despite all that had happened yesterday. I held my head a little higher.

"So I've been told." Zach frowned, glancing warily at his Commander. "I'm honored that you think so highly of me, but I—"

Suddenly the Commander grabbed Zach's collar, choking off his words, and jerked him backward. "Master Mage, we are weary from our journey. Perhaps we could rest and eat first, then discuss the partnership."

It was a reasonable request, but I'd hoped to get some kind of verbal agreement of our partnership, at the very least. If the interruption had surprised Gelloren, he didn't let it show.

"Yes, of course." With a small wave of his hand, the trumpets sounded again.

The voices within the Hall of Ancestors rang out as one: "Long Live the Royals! The Light against the Darkness!" Then Myria's Royals trickled back into the adjoining corridors.

I barely muttered the words along with them, my eyes still on Zach. He didn't seem enthused about our partnership at all.

Not that I expected princes to fall over themselves for me, but I'd anticipated receiving more than mild curiosity... or... Had he been disappointed? Disappointed as I had been?

The idea that I could be dissatisfied in him, but he couldn't be in me, struck me like a physical blow. Not only was that unfair, but also hypocritical and rude. I had to give him another chance—at least learn more about him before deciding how I felt.

Gelloren turned back to the Saevallan Royals. "Princess Ivy will lead you to the feast." He nodded to me and then left with the other Master Mages, robes swishing as they went.

I held out my arm in the direction of the northwest corridor. "You're in for a treat," I said with a smile. "The strawberries in Myria are the best in all the land, and they're in season."

Zach winked at me. "I love strawberries. Strawberry sugar cake, strawberry cordials—"

"Return to your position." The Commander pointed toward the back of his company.

"Yes, sir, Lord Commander," Zach called over his shoulder, still grinning as he headed to the back. The Saevallan Royals parted for him but none looked especially pleased to do so. From the rolls of their eyes, it seemed almost as if...they were embarrassed by him. But wasn't he their champion? Their prized Swordsman Prince?

"And tell Collin if he has the bad manners to run his lewd mouth during a formal reception," the Commander barked, "then he can spend the next one shoveling horse—" He clamped his lips and turned back to me. "Pardon me, princess."

I laughed. "We're all soldiers. I'm sure I've said far worse at one time or another. Now, this way please, Prince…"

"Weldan. Prince Commander Weldan of the House of Zale," he said as I led them out of the Hall of Ancestors. "I must say, it is an honor to meet one of your bloodline. A pure descendant of the Royal Founders."

"It is we who should be honored, Commander. Our numbers have been drastically decreasing. Your reinforcements mean everything and more to us."

"We are all on the same side, princess. There's no need for thanks."

I smiled, liking Weldan more with every step, every word. "Yet you still have it."

He nodded, but his expression darkened. "I'm sorry to hear about your prince."

Kellian's inert form after my failed Kiss flitted through my mind, and my smile vanished. The same image had kept me up almost all night last night, along with memories of Kellian. My fingers curled around my cloak, squeezing. "Yes, it…will be difficult to replace him."

Weldan sighed and shook his head. "I've heard of your capabilities, princess, and I believe it would be difficult to match anyone to your standards."

I opened my mouth to reply when a large *crash* sounded from behind us.

Everyone looked back to see Zach sprawled out on the floor with an ancient suit of armor lying in pieces around him. A girl stood over him, her face flushed in anger.

"Watch where you're going, you—"

"Kendra!" The Commander's voice was sharp, and the girl quickly straightened.

Zach half picked himself up onto his elbows. "No, go ahead. What were you going to say? Something about my dashing good looks?"

Kendra rounded on him, but Weldan intervened again. "Zach, enough."

With a scowl, she strode over Zach, stepping on his back as she did so, pushing him to the floor.

Zach let out a puff of air. "Now who's not watching where they're going?" he called after her.

"Get up and pray that suit isn't damaged," Weldan snapped.

"It's fine," I told Weldan, although I knew for a fact that the suit came from the Battle of Galliore during the great griffin invasion. "It's just an old decoration." How had he crashed into it walking down such a wide corridor? Could anyone be so clumsy?

Weldan continued forward without another glance at Zach. I followed him, watching Zach over my shoulder, who was now picking up the pieces of armor. His movements were fluid and graceful as he plucked up the heavy pieces and set them aside—certainly not movements of someone who would've knocked it over in the first place.

We came to the dining hall. The training grounds outside were visible through tall open windows bordered by maroon curtains sporting the Legion emblem. The Saevallans shed their heavy armor and cloaks and handed them off to the array of servants before heading to the long brucel-wood tables. In no time, Weldan and I were left standing alone, watching the rest of his Royals served plates piled with hot quail eggs and brien-peppered sausage, herb and honey bread with mint yogurt, and fresh strawberries topped with sugar cream.

I gestured to the end of a table, and we sat across from each other.

"To be honest, princess, there are few in the entire land

who could be worthy of bearing the Mark of Myriana." Weldan nodded in thanks to a servant who brought him a goblet and a plate of steaming food. "But..." He began, pausing to take a sip from his cup, "if anyone has the raw skills, it *is* Zach."

So I'd heard. It was still hard to rectify the unbelievable rumors of the magnificent warrior with a man who laughed at crude jokes and tripped over hall decorations. "You mean the one who just dismembered a suit of armor?" I said with a teasing smile.

"Well, to be fair, he was probably pushed."

I blinked. "Why?"

"Kendra is always finding an excuse to pick a fight with him. They have a history."

"They were partners, then?"

"Oh Heavenly Queen, no. They'd probably kill each other before they even *noticed* the monsters. Besides...Kendra is my partner."

I felt a twinge of disappointment. If Zach turned out to be a bad match for me, I would've liked to have had Weldan as a possible option. He was much more the warrior I'd imagined.

"Sometimes I joke that they're jealous of each other. They both try to monopolize my attention." Weldan chuckled. "But Kendra has problems with...well, you can see that Zach is a tad unorthodox."

I watched Zach enter the dining hall, holding the suit of armor's helmet under his arm. With the stealth of a thief, he swiped a plate of fruit off a passing servant's tray and replaced it with the helmet. He plucked an orange off the stolen plate and tossed it into the air, then caught it while dodging and grabbing a chunk of sourdough bread from another servant's tray. He sauntered over to a table, sat by himself, and began to peel the orange.

It seemed strange to me that a young man who had acted

so clumsily before, pushing through his comrades and being manhandled by his Commander, moved about with such finesse now. Was it all a facade?

"Yes, I can see that," I said. "Truthfully, it looks like he just walked in off the streets."

Weldan took a bite of toasted herb bread dripping with mulberry jelly. He chewed slowly and swallowed. "Actually, he did. He came to us, claiming his birthright as a half prince. He may be uncouth and annoying, but he's a good man and a loyal friend. Though he's never respected authority, which doesn't make it easy on me as his acting Commander." Weldan rolled his eyes. "But mark my words, Zach is the one you need. He is, in fact, a legendary swordsman. The rumors you have heard of him are all painfully true."

It had been fun to entertain the idea of a warrior like that with my sisters, but now it was getting ridiculous. I leaned forward, raising a brow. "Oh come on, Prince Weldan, you and I both know that—"

"Excuse me, princess," Weldan began, "I hate to interrupt, but I just remembered that I must send a carrier bird to report to the Council at Saevall that we made it here safely."

"Of course." I motioned to a servant, and the young maid hurried to our table. "Please take the Commander to the aviary and see that he has the rest of his meal sent to his room."

The servant curtsied, and Weldan thanked me, strolling off after the maid, his long scarlet cloak trailing behind him.

Sighing, I stared at the table, my eyes tracing the intricate swirl designs in the wood. The fact that Weldan had vouched for Zach's strength was a good sign. However, his insistence that such rumors were true was discreditable.

I was still staring at the wood as a single bright-red strawberry rolled into my view. I looked up.

Zach had taken Weldan's place with the stealth and silence

of a thief, and he was watching me with yet another smile, a plate of fruit in front of him. "You're right. I've never had better," he said, taking a bite of a strawberry.

"I'm glad you like them." Sitting so close, I took in details I hadn't noticed during our introductions. His hair was kept short, not a single strand falling into his hazel eyes, and windswept to the side, the color of the darkest leather saddle. He had the beginnings of a beard, with an odd streak of bare skin along his jaw. I wondered if it was because of a scar.

"So what was my Royal Commander saying about me?" Zach asked, raising an eyebrow.

My mouth almost twitched into a smile. "He told me you are…unorthodox."

Zach's grin stretched. "To say the least, princess."

"But also that you are a legendary swordsman."

"Did he now?" Zach leaned back and folded his arms, his grin falling slightly.

I realized now I could put all those rumors to bed. After all, their very source sat right before me. Glancing around at the rest of the western Royals, I made sure they were still engaged in their meals and conversations. I wanted to hear this directly from Zach, with no interjections from anyone else. I wanted the truth.

"Prince Zach—"

"Just Zach."

Having me drop his title was a definite indication he hadn't been in the Legion for long. His commoner upbringing must be deeply ingrained. "Zach, there are some fairly…*amazing* rumors about your skills. I was wondering if any of them were true."

Zach snorted and shook his head. "You'll have to be more specific. Which rumors?" He bit into another strawberry.

"Did you really take a troll's lair down by yourself? Absent partner?"

Zach stared at me, chewing slowly. Finally, he swallowed and said, "You've heard about me, but I know next to nothing about you."

"No one's told you about me?" I asked, too surprised to be annoyed that he evaded a question he'd invited me to ask.

"I didn't say that." He placed the strawberry stem back on his plate. "It's just that I don't take much stock in rumors. I prefer to get to know the person myself."

The smirk told me he wasn't just referring to the rumors about me—but of course now I was curious as to what he'd heard. Was that his way of telling me I shouldn't believe all the rumors about him?

"Milady, if you don't finish eating soon you'll be late for your class."

I glanced up to see Brom standing next to the table.

"Sacred Sisters," I muttered. I'd forgotten that I'd swapped a class with Tulia so she could rest after returning from patrol. I stood and gave a short bow to Zach. "Apologies, Pri—Zach. I have a class to teach. I hope to see you at supper."

Zach smiled and went back to his food. With one last glance at my potential partner, who was now leaning over and swiping a chocolate croissant off an unsuspecting Kendra's plate, I suppressed a small giggle, and followed Brom out of the dining hall.

The moment I entered the classroom I unfastened my cloak and tossed it onto the back of the lecturer's chair. It wasn't often that the Legion princesses or princes taught classes, since most of the time we were either training or out on assignment, but the Mages felt it was important for the young recruits to learn from their superiors and establish a bond well before the battlefield.

With a glance at the young princess recruits and their looks of reverence, I found I quite agreed.

"Princess Tulia is resting from her time out on patrol, so she requested I fill in for her." I scanned the students' faces as they sat in neat rows behind finely polished wooden desks. The girls in this class were all under ten years old. "Good morning, ladies."

At once, the princesses stood and curtsied in the same manner I had greeted Zach. "Good morning, Princess Ivy," they said in unison.

"Let us begin with prayer. Would one brave princess like to lead us?"

A few timid hands rose into the air, and I picked the smallest. The little girl bowed her head and clasped her hands across her stomach. We all copied her prayer stance.

"O Sacred Sisters, daughters of holly and thistle." Her words started shaky but grew stronger as she continued. "Help us ignite the magic of our brethren and guide us through the darkness with your divine light. It is with your blood that we stand strong. And it is by your blood that we reign."

"Long live the Royals," the class said in unison, "the Light against the Darkness."

"Thank you, princess," I said to her with a smile. "Everyone may sit."

Roughly a dozen girls all slid back into their chairs.

I glanced at the lesson plan Tulia had left on the desk. "You're on History? How long have you been here?" History was something Mages taught. The Legion princesses offered more hands-on lessons, which I intended to do.

A princess with ebony skin raised her hand. "Seven days, Your Highness."

Tulia hadn't mentioned that her class would be the newest recruits, and I was surprised I hadn't recognized any. Then again, a week ago I was on patrol and got hit with the dwarf's locking curse. It just now occurred to me that I had missed the spring initiation ceremony. It wasn't so important anymore, though, since a new ceremony was held at the beginning of every season now instead of annually.

I sighed. It had been a long time since I'd taught the basics. "All right. Who wants to recite the story of our founders?"

No one moved. I placed my hands on my hips. "Don't be shy. Anyone who's been to chapel knows the story." Chapels throughout the four kingdoms had beautiful stained glass and paintings of the story of Myriana and Saevalla. Even if the girls had never read a history textbook, our religious teachings made sure they knew of our holy queens' origins.

The girls exchanged glances before one with short blond hair stood, tugging on the hems of her sleeves.

"Go ahead," I said with a small dip of my chin.

"Long ago, before the Royal Legion existed," she began, "before queens, kings, princesses, and princes ruled the four kingdoms, there lived a lonely old woman in the great northern forests. Her cabin sat alone at the base of the Wu-Hyll Mountains. She was called Maid Freida. Having lived by herself for many years, she longed for children."

The cadence and eloquence of how the young girl spoke surprised me. Part of me wondered if she had been around the Romantica, and if she had picked up their alluring way of telling stories. I hoped not. The Romantica's heretical teachings of Love were woven into their stories, songs, and plays. A small child being around the Romantica's influences, even in innocent settings like festivals, could have long-lasting detrimental effects, especially for a Royal. Any knowledge or belief in Romantica ways needed to be rectified immediately with the Legion's teachings.

Then again, the girl could just have a natural talent for storytelling.

"One cold morning," the little girl continued, "while Maid Freida was picking up branches, she heard an infant crying. Then two infants…"

My eyes slipped closed as I listened, transported back in time to when I was no more than five years old and spent my days in a luxurious bedroom with satin pillows and curtains. I sat huddled in the lap of my sister, Clover, her arms draped over my shoulders and her chin resting atop my head. Her scent of vanilla and cinnamon tickled my nose.

My sister's voice melded with that of the young princess's, and soon it was Clover telling me the story again…

"She followed the cries to find two bundles of red-cheeked babes sheltered under bushes of holly and thistle. Maid Freida took them home to her cabin and raised the two girls as her own. She named them Myriana Holly and Saevalla Thistle."

I reached up and tugged one of Clover's dark tresses. "And that's why we're also named after flora."

Clover's light fingers danced over the bridge of freckles across my nose. "That's right, little wisp, we bear her name as our surname, and as direct descendants we're named after flora. Now, will you let me finish the story?"

I giggled and swatted her hand away. She caught my small fingers and squeezed them, then continued the story I'd already heard a thousand times.

"One day, Myriana and Saevalla came across a young hunter traveling through the woods. He told them his name was Raed and he was on his way to the dwarven mines to trade his fine animal skins for jewels the dwarves mined deep within the Wu-Hyll Mountains. Although Myriana and Saevalla begged Raed not to go, he left them with crowns of flowers for their hair and continued on his way."

I whimpered in Clover's lap, and she laughed softly,

brushing the hair from my forehead. "Would you like me to stop?" she asked.

"No, keep going," I pleaded.

"One winter's night, a hideous beast came to Maid Freida's cabin. But the beast meant no harm, and he collapsed from exhaustion on their doorstep. Together, the girls and Maid Freida brought the beast in, fed him, and nursed him to health.

"Through the winter months the beast stayed with them and sometimes wove together crowns of holly and thistle for their hair. One day, when Myriana was out gathering herbs, she found the shredded cloak of the hunter, Raed, not far from the entrance to the dwarven caves. Remembering the flower crowns he'd woven, Myriana realized that the dwarves must have placed a curse on Raed, turning him into a beast.

"Desperate to save Raed and seek vengeance against the dwarves, Myriana journeyed to the mines within the Wu-Hyll Mountains. Her sister, Saevalla, ever protective of Myriana, went with her, and—"

"I'd go, Clover," I interrupted, pressing my back into my sister's chest. "Like Saevalla, I'd go with you."

Clover leaned over me and kissed my forehead. "I know, Ivy. I'd do the same for you. That's what sisters do."

I shot a glance at the locked door to our bedroom. Our mother was still away. We were still safe. I looked up at Clover. "Then what happened?"

"Raed followed the two of them to the mines and arrived just as a dwarf was about to attack them with a great ax," Clover continued. "He jumped in to save the sisters and was gravely wounded. It was then that Myriana bestowed upon him the first Kiss that—"

Giggles erupted around me, and I was brought back to the present, back to the classroom full of princesses.

I pulled myself out of the remnants of my memory and

smiled at my students. "What? You don't think kissing a beast's snout would be pleasant?"

The giggling escalated to laughter, and I motioned for them to calm down. I flicked my hand back to the princess. "Keep going... You're doing great."

The girl beamed. "Myriana's sacred Kiss held power unlike anything humans or mages had ever seen. Her Kiss turned the beast back into a man and gave him the strength of ten men. With the power of her Kiss, he was able to slay the dwarf."

I gestured for the girl to take a seat. "Well done, princess." She was an excellent storyteller, like Clover, and I felt guilty for thinking she grew up around Romantica. She didn't even mention the True Love's Kiss version that the Romantica cults liked to spread. Then again, even recruits should know to never utter such blasphemy. "Now, who can finish the story?"

Another princess with brown ringlets stood. "Myriana, Saevalla, and Raed took the dwarves' treasure and built the kingdom of Myria, establishing themselves as the first Royals and founders of the Legion. To continue the magic in their bloodline, Myriana and Raed produced an heir."

The girl paused, hesitating. It was common for everyone to avoid the next part of our history. Not many liked discussing the origin of the Wicked Queen. But it was important to never forget the evil we were up against.

"Continue," I said.

Emboldened, the girl threw back her shoulders. "The brothers of the dwarf that King Raed had slain stole the first heir. As the ultimate act of revenge, the dwarves cursed the baby princess so terribly that she became a creature of darkness herself—the Evil Queen."

The young princesses shifted uncomfortably in their seats.

"To protect the lands against the Evil Queen, Myriana and Raed produced more heirs with their power, and, to add more soldiers to the war, Raed and Saevalla also produced heirs blessed with the same power."

"And the other lands?"

"Under Myriana's teachings, other lands used the Kiss to drive back wicked creatures and establish their own kingdoms." The girl cleared her throat. "For five centuries, the Legion has ruled throughout the Lands, keeping the Forces of Darkness at bay, protecting the people and teaching its subjects to make decisions through logic and reason, not emotions."

"And how do we teach them?" I prompted.

"We lead by example."

I indicated that the girl could sit back down. "Correct. We practice what we preach, girls. As Queen Gardenia Myriana once said, perish emotions and vanquish doubts, and we will drive out the Forces. Which brings us back to why we're all here: monsters. Our five-hundred-year war against the Evil Queen and her Forces of Darkness. Now, you are all princess recruits, but one day you will be full Royals of the Legion and follow your princes into battles against goblins, trolls, witches, dragons, wraiths, griffins…" I paused and looked at their nervous faces. One girl in the front row looked to be only seven years old. She had a large bruise under her eye, perhaps from her first sparring class. I crossed to her desk, took her hand, and gently pulled her up. "…but it is with *your* power, *your* Kiss, that we stand a chance against these creatures. What's your name, princess?"

"Gertrude," the girl said in a high voice.

"Gertrude, do you know how Kisses work?"

The girl looked away, cheeks red.

"It's perfectly all right if you don't. Many in the villages do not." I guided Gertrude to the front of the class and sat her on the front desk, and then I turned to the rest of the class. "The first thing you must understand about Kissing is that it works *only* between two Royals. Royal Magic exists in every Royal, but it lies dormant. A Kiss is what unlocks the magic in the Royal and allows one *or* the other to use that power."

Every girl in the room stared at me with rapt attention. I remembered my own eagerness when I was their age. My desperation to prove myself...to one person in particular.

"It acts as a catalyst that unleashes the magic," I continued, "but a kiss alone does not make it a Royal Kiss. You must learn the spells to make them either battle Kisses, healing Kisses, counter-curse Kisses, and so on. Does that make sense?"

They all nodded.

"Now, remember, only princesses can actually cast the spells, so we get the delightful task of memorizing them all while the boys get to play with wooden sticks." I flitted my hand toward the window, where the training grounds expanded below. "While it's true that we may not *have* to learn swordsmanship, we must help our princes as best we can—which is why I urge all of you to learn more than how to shoot an arrow. You never know when your life, or the life of your partner, will depend on close-range combat.

"But putting that aside"—I turned back to Gertrude—"let's see a demonstration. One of the basic Kisses a princess first learns is how to heal her prince. The words are *Illye Menda.*" I brushed back Gertrude's hair and Kissed her cheek, my lips brushing the tender spot of her bruise, while my mind spoke the spell words.

I felt Gertrude's magic, soft and fluttering like a baby bird, rise up to meet mine, fierce and powerful like a dragon. Using just a tiny sliver of my magic, I healed the bruise. Eyes wide, Gertrude pressed her fingertips below her eye where the bruise had been.

The other girls all *ooh*ed as Gertrude hurried back to her chair.

"All right, moving on. Let's try—"

My words were cut off by the sound of the door opening at the back of the classroom. It was Tulia, her dress wrinkled and her short brown hair disheveled, with Bromley at her heels. She walked briskly down the classroom aisle to meet me, her cloak flying behind her.

Yawning, she said, "I have to teach after all. *Your* page was sent to wake *me* up and take *you* to meet Master Gelloren."

I raised my eyebrows. "Is it that urgent?"

"Apparently so. Get going, then."

Grabbing my cloak, I waved to the girls and followed Bromley out. Just as the door was closing I heard Tulia say, "Get out your books," and the girls responded with moans.

"Sorry, Tulia," I murmured with a small smile.

When I turned toward the Tower of Mages, Bromley grabbed my elbow. "Master Gelloren is with the Council."

My heart skipped. Surely it had to be about Zach. But why would they need me? Thanks to my pure ancestry, I had little choice in partners. Not like half princesses, or even Minnow and Tulia, who got much more of a say in choosing their princes than I ever had. The Council had never hesitated to assign me a partner without my opinion before.

Then again, we'd never had a Royal quite like this legendary swordsman in Myria before, either.

CHAPTER SIX

THE COUNCIL'S DEBATE

The Council met in a large circular room located almost directly behind the Hall of Ancestors. Tapestries of past Royals decorated the walls, and above a round table with cushioned mahogany chairs was a large stained-glass window that filtered red, gold, green, and blue sunlight.

Out of the three Master Mages who resided in Myria's castle, Gelloren was the oldest and wisest, and therefore had high standing with the Council. He had taught almost all the current Council members, so there was no one they trusted more.

I entered through the large brucel doors, the wood carved into images of faceless Royals and fierce dragons. Conversation halted at my entrance, and all gazes turned to me.

"Princess Ivy, come in," Master Gelloren said.

The table was not full. At least four members were missing. The Royal Council was made of princes and princesses who had been appointed by the Master Mages to a seat in their kingdom's Council. Once a member of the Council, their titles changed to king or queen. While each kingdom had its own Council, it was always a symbol of great prestige to be a part of the Myrian Council, since it was the founder of the Legion.

"Princess," said King Randalph as he stood, his wooden chair squeaking on the marble floor, "our condolences on losing Prince Kellian."

Instinctively, I clasped my right hand, the hand that still bore Kellian's fading mark. "Thank you, Your Majesty."

"Your severing ritual is scheduled this afternoon, is it not?" Queen Jocelyn asked.

I ignored the sharp stab of pain. *So soon.* "Yes, Your Majesty."

"So you will be prepared to accept the mark of another in a few days' time?"

My pulse quickened. "Of course, my Queen."

"Then what are *your* thoughts on Prince Zachariah?" King Randalph asked.

I licked my lips. "It's hard for me to say, Your Majesty. I have yet to see what he can do with my own eyes."

The Council members exchanged looks, and the room fell into an uncomfortable silence. Such gravity could not just be because they'd heard my potential partner was a little uncouth.

Queen Jocelyn leaned forward. "We must be wary of prejudice, Randalph. We must think of what is best for the Legion…the whole Kingdom."

"I am well aware, Jocelyn. But his bloodline…"

I approached the table, gripping the back of an empty chair. "If I may ask, Council, what *about* his bloodline? I was told by Prince Weldan that he's half. He may not be a pure Royal, but if his skills are as good as they say, then it shouldn't matter."

King Randalph waved away my words. "And what of the *other* half of his bloodline?"

I frowned. "I'm not sure I follow."

"His father was Prince Abram from the House of Jindor, and his mother, well, we're not quite sure of her name."

"How could you not know her name?"

King Randalph lowered into his chair and folded his arms. "She was not recognized by the Royal Council of Saevall, and they forbade Prince Abram from ever seeing her again."

"But…why?"

"She was a Romantica."

My hands slipped off the chair I had been leaning on, and I almost fell forward. Embarrassed, I caught myself and eased into the chair in front of me. "A Romantica…" I spoke the word carefully. As if it was some sort of evil curse I shouldn't utter.

In a way, it *was* like a curse. Romantica claimed that our ancestors Myriana, Saevalla, and Raed were nothing special, that they were not the first of a new superior race with the unique power to vanquish darkness. Instead, they believed their Kiss was born from True Love, a magic in itself—a preposterous idea. I certainly was not "in love" with anyone, and yet my Kisses were the most powerful in Myria.

Romantica also practiced primitive traditions like marriage and courting. They even claimed sex was more than just a release or a way to continue the bloodline. Instead, they claimed it was the ultimate act of Love, when in reality it was nothing more than the manifestation of Lust.

Lust was a powerful force that was necessary to continue Royal bloodlines, and something much easier to understand than the Romantica's Love. Lust was a physical human reaction, a real, tangible thing that could not be denied. Romantica simply mistook Lust for Love.

The truth was this: Love was nothing more than an illusion. Utter nonsense.

I twisted my hands in my lap. "Are you certain he's truly…?"

"Yes, it would seem that Zachariah was raised by his mother until she was killed by a griffin that attacked their village," King Randalph said. "At a young age, he disappeared from the village and returned only a year ago, claiming his Royal birthright to join the Legion."

"I can't believe we're even debating this." King Krowe leaned back with a look of disgust on his face. "He's the son of a Romantica heretic. Who can say his allegiance even lies with the Legion?"

I often disagreed with King Krowe, but here, I could see his point. Romantica had been a thorn in the Legion's side too many times, making us expend resources we could've used to battle the Forces. Whole Romantica villages declared independence from the Legion, and Royals were sent to put down rebellions. There was even one case where extremists had tried to kidnap Royal recruits.

"If Prince Zachariah wanted to spy on the Legion, he would've taken measures to rise in the ranks," Queen Kallina said. "Commander Prince Weldan has vouched for him, and he claims there's no one in Saevall who has killed as many monsters as Zachariah in so short a time."

"A griffin *did* kill his mother. He's probably trying to avenge her," Queen Jocelyn pointed out.

"And even if that *weren't* the case, he's still willing to lay down his life to fight the Forces." Kallina placed her elbows on the table and intertwined her fingers. "We've never looked down on the status of the non-Royal's side of the bloodline before."

That was true. Royals were always pairing with commoners to keep bloodlines fresh. If they didn't, the Royal gene pool would become more like a puddle.

"Perhaps…but a Romantica?" King Krowe scoffed. "I'd go so far as to say heretic blood cancels out Royal blood."

Queen Jocelyn scowled. "It doesn't work that way, and you know it. If Zachariah's father was a prince, then he has the power. No exceptions."

"Still, Jocelyn—"

"Enough." The sharp voice of King Helios cut through the air. As the oldest member of the Council, and the most revered, any time he spoke, people listened.

He was also my grandfather.

"Here's the truth of the matter," he said, "we are *desperate.* The Dark Forces are growing, and we are shrinking. We need every Royal we can get. We cannot push away his help and ignore the fact that he is known to be a powerful swordsman— with abilities we have not seen for over half a century—just because his mother belonged to a cult. Yes, the Romantica have made enemies of us in the past, but we mustn't forget the face of the *true* enemy. Dismissing his abilities would be prideful and stupid, knowing what we must face."

Complete. Silence.

Then they all nodded, even King Krowe.

"My King, I know times are hard," I said, "but what will we face? I feel as if I'm missing something."

King Helios looked me in the eye. "We've received word from farther north that an alarming amount of darkness is gathering and festering within a cave in the Wu-Hyll Mountains. We believe it is the manifestation of an egg."

Fear enclosed my heart, and I struggled to keep my breath even.

"The egg of a Sable Dragon," he said.

I lost the feeling in my legs even though I was sitting. "H-how do you know for sure?"

"There have been many dark signs," Master Gelloren said. "Signs I have been following closely."

"The sparrow harpies," I muttered. I'd been right—they *were* an omen.

"It's the same as the signs from a hundred years ago, when the last Sable Dragon was born. Swarms of sparrow harpies in broad daylight," he said, giving me a nod, "thunderstorms with black lightning, flowers within the chapel wilting…and, of course the most obvious—the drastic increase of monster attacks. The good news is it's still only an egg. We will know all too well once it does hatch."

"How soon do you think it will be?" I asked.

"I can't be exact, but if I'm reading the omens correctly, I would say we have a little less than a month. Dragons are vulnerable as babies, but they reach adulthood quickly. And when that happens, it will be nearly unstoppable."

Besides the Wicked Queen, the Mother of the Forces, the Sable Dragon was the most powerful evil creature to have walked the earth. Its massive body was said to be covered in obsidian, and its flames…black. I had heard stories of the years that a Sable Dragon terrorized the lands. Many, many Royals and their subjects had lost their lives. It was said an entire Legion perished in the time it took to kill the beast, and thousands more innocents as well.

"Which is why we must send out a very small group to kill the dragon before it reaches adulthood. Preferably before it even hatches," King Helios said, leaning to where the multicolored light from the stained glass dyed his white hair red and violet.

"But…shouldn't we send as many as possible?" I asked.

Master Gelloren shook his head. "Even a group the size of a patrol would attract too many dark creatures. It's best if only a pair of Royals sneak into the mountains, destroy the egg before it hatches, and get out without attracting any more beasts. Not only that, but a large group could alert the Evil Queen's spies. With her prized son bound to hatch, she's sure to be on the lookout for any Royals questing to destroy it."

It was then, as Gelloren's gaze met mine, that I realized

why they were telling me this. This secret was kept to prevent raising alarm throughout the Legion and the kingdom. The only reason *I* was being told was because they wanted me to…

I stood so violently my chair wobbled. "I accept."

My grandfather avoided my gaze. "Dear princess, we have not asked anything of you."

"Yet," I finished for him. "And you have my answer anyway."

An icy ball of fear weighed in my gut. It was so cold I thought it would freeze my insides. But at the same time, something much more powerful burned inside me. In my chest, melting that block of ice, were flames fueled by anger and passion. Anger at the Dark Forces for taking down Kellian, and passion to protect my Kingdom and its people.

But can you do it, Ivy? You? A princess with five lost partners?

I was a direct descendant of Myriana. I *could* do this. My Kiss was the Mark of Myriana—and as dangerous as that was, killing four out of five partners and leaving the other in a coma, it had also saved *hundreds* of lives with its power. Now, it would have to save hundreds of thousands.

I cleared my throat. "I will go, my King. I'd do anything to protect our kingdom."

"Princess Ivy, your bravery and loyalty are of no question. You are no doubt the most powerful princess in the Legion, but you are in need of a prince," King Randalph said, "and we have not yet officially decided on Zachariah. Nor do we know if he would be willing to accept this perilous mission."

"King Helios has made more than a strong enough point," Queen Jocelyn said. "We need this prince if his skills are as good as they say."

"Then we must test them." King Krowe drummed his fingers on the table.

"It could be tricky," Randalph said. "Romantica spawn though he may be, he's still a member of the Saevallan Royals.

It would be rude to insult our guests by demanding a test."

Krowe smiled, making his dark beard twitch. "Oh, not to worry. I have an idea."

I wasn't allowed to hear the idea, having been dismissed only a few seconds later. They ushered me out the door, and I found Bromley waiting for me in the hall.

I motioned for him to follow me, and he was silent for maybe a minute before the pestering started. "C'mon, what'd they say?"

"Didn't have your ear pressed against the door, Brom?" I teased.

He scowled. "Last time I did that, Master Gelloren cast an itching spell on my ear so bad I had to cover it with paste."

I laughed.

"Are you going to tell me, then?"

I waited until we were out of the castle and halfway between the gardens and the training grounds before I pulled him behind a willa blossom tree and told him everything in a low whisper.

Bromley backed away, eyes wide, mouth open. "A *Sable* Dragon?"

Knowing I could trust Bromley with this news, I nodded. I trusted him with my life.

"And you said you'd go, didn't you?"

"It's my *duty*, Bromley."

"To fight, not to die," he shot back.

I laid a hand on his cheek. "Brom, I taught a class of little girls today. One of them was *seven*. You know what they did? They giggled at the idea of kissing a beast's snout. That's what they should be doing—giggling and playing, not picking up a shield or learning spells to kill monsters. Maybe going after this dragon is a step toward that future."

Bromley sighed. "I just…I just don't want it to be you. Does it have to be you?"

My heart swelled, and I threw my arms around his shoulders, squeezing him tightly. For a moment, he was stiff, but then he melted into the hug.

Brom was more than my page, or even my best friend—he was my brother. We'd grown up together. What I felt for him was like the bond I shared with my sisters. Romantica would call it Familial Love, and though we refused to use the word "Love," Royals believed in the bond between families quite deeply. It was this bond that had allowed us to come together and rule—knowing our bloodlines and where we came from was everything.

Even though Brom wasn't related by blood, that didn't stop me from treating him and caring for him like an older sister would.

"It has to be someone," I whispered, "and I want it to be me."

Brom leaned away. "Your severing ritual is in a few hours. Do you want me to be there?"

"No, I— It's okay. I'll be fine." My shaky voice betrayed my confidence, but I gave him a smile anyway. He frowned but didn't push further.

A few hours later, I knelt next to Kellian's body, gripping his hand but unable to look at him. Holding on to him was like holding a marble statue—cold, lifeless, stiff.

Ulfia was with other patients, and only Master Gelloren sat with me now. No one else needed to be here. Unlike a partnership bonding ritual, a severing ritual was not something anyone wanted to witness.

Gelloren stared at Kellian's face. The Master Mage looked two hundred years old in that moment, ancient and tired. He murmured a prayer to Myriana and Saevalla then looked to me. "Are you ready, my dear?"

I squeezed Kellian's icy hand and brought it to my lips, whispering, "I'm sorry, my friend."

I nodded numbly, and Master Gelloren started the spell. I couldn't hear the words—it was like he was speaking from a great distance. But it didn't matter what he was saying. All that mattered was that I'd failed Kellian.

Purple flames ignited around our hands. They burned just enough to make me suffer for leaving him.

Now it was my turn. To sever the bond of partnership, I had to let go of his hand. It *sounded* easy, but the truth was the pain was insurmountable. Beads of sweat gathered at my temples as I gritted my teeth and groaned, releasing his hand. As our hands separated, the marks on the backs of them burned away in the fire.

The back of my hand was now blank. I was partnerless once more.

The flames fizzled out, and I gasped, cradling my burning hand to my chest and rolling over onto the floor. For a few dizzying moments, I hoped that was the worst of it, but it never was. I grabbed the bucket next to me and emptied my stomach. I retched and coughed and ached all over.

Gelloren handed me a damp cloth and helped me to a bed next to Kellian's. I buried my face deep in the pillows, the cloth cool against the back of my neck, and let my body scream in pain.

The priests and mages had theories about why the severing ritual was so painful. Some said the link forged by magic was like a physical limb that was being severed. Others said that it was just the release of magic that caused our bodies to weaken to the point of exhaustion. I had my own theory. I believed it was a punishment. It was like Myriana was punishing us for being the survivor, or not being strong enough to protect each other, or for simply…giving up.

Master Gelloren gently laid his palm on my back. "It is as the Holy Queen would have it, Princess Ivy. She can see you are meant to move forward."

He was trying to console me, but I didn't like the idea that Queen Myriana would let Kellian die simply because I was meant to move on. The very idea of it made me want to cry and scream and stab things.

I rolled over, away from Kellian, and stared at my blank hand. Already the pain was receding, and soon I'd have another's mark. One I hoped to keep for much longer, if not forever.

What would Zach's mark look like?

The Saevallan Royals had traveled all night to arrive in the morning, so they had eaten breakfast, then slept half the day, and now were back at the dining hall for supper.

While they'd slept, the castle had exploded with gossip. And all of it had to do with Prince Zachariah. Or Zach, as everyone had started calling him. Most princesses seemed smitten by him—apparently his rugged appearance and mischievous smile made him daring and…enigmatic.

It almost made me wonder if there were two Zachs. How could one person be so many different things?

After sleeping the rest of the afternoon away in the infirmary, I had managed to shake off Ulfia, who'd wanted to check me from head to toe, and headed down to supper. I sat with Tulia and Minnow, our gazes occasionally flitting to the table where Zachariah, Prince Weldan, and a few other Saevallans sat.

"So what do you think, Ivy?" Tulia asked. "Is he partner material?"

"I think he's gorgeous." Robin slipped onto the bench next to me, her eyes glued to Zach.

"Is *your* name Ivy?" I elbowed my sister, then shrugged and said, "I've barely talked to him, but he seems…" Our brief interaction, the way he'd smirked at me from across a plate of strawberries, came to mind. "Tricky."

Robin, Tulia, and Minnow stared at me.

"Tricky?" Tulia raised an eyebrow.

"Just…more than what he seems. I can't get a read on him." There was his Romantica lineage, but I wasn't sure if that was something I was allowed to tell others yet. And I wouldn't add to the gossip pool.

"I agree. He's mysterious and rather intimidating, isn't he?" Minnow said.

"I don't know about intimidating," I muttered, thinking of the suit of armor incident.

"Well, I mean, he hasn't had a princess and is still so powerful? So legendary. If that's not intimidating, what is?"

"Exactly!" Robin leaned forward. "There's even a story going around about a time he took down a chimera—no battle magic at all!"

Recalling Zach's words about rumors, I frowned. "Robin, I keep telling you—"

I was interrupted by the banging of a heavy wooden door. Amias burst through the doors, a sword at his side, looking broad-shouldered and as imposing as ever. The black hair that fell into his eyes made his appearance even more striking. "Out of the way!" he roared to a few younger Royals. Amias stormed to the table next to us, where Zachariah sat calmly eating his dinner.

"Oy!" he shouted, planting his boot on the table and

sneering. "You're the *legendary* swordsman, are you?" The other Saevallans moved away from the table, rolling their eyes, as if this kind of thing happened all the time with Zach.

Zach didn't look up.

"Oy. *Oy!* Up, you bastard."

"Prince Amias!" I shouted, standing. "You will treat our guests with respect!"

"Respect? Ha! Don't make me laugh, Ivy. Respect for this heretic? For this son of a Romantica hag?"

There was a collective intake of breath throughout the dining hall, and a stunned silence followed. Like I suspected, him being a Romantica had not been one of those rumors flying about. More than likely, the Saevallans hadn't been keeping Zach's mother a secret on purpose, but it probably wasn't something they advocated, either. So, assuming that no Saevallan Royal had told Amias, then who had?

As all eyes locked on him, Zach simply kept chewing his tarrow-spiced duck.

"That's right." Amias raised his voice even louder. "The one the Council has chosen to partner with Princess Ivy Myriana, a direct heir of Queen Myriana, is a *Romantica.*"

At this, there were more gasps.

My jaw clenched tight, fingers curling into my palm. How dare Amias use me as an excuse for his outrage, when it was clearly petty jealousy. This was not the first time Amias had tried to interfere with my partnerships. He'd gone to his uncle, King Krowe, and told an elaborate story about how Kellian had consumed too much dwarven liquor, when Kellian had food poisoning instead—the reason behind his poor stomach a "mystery."

It was why the Legion taught that logic and reason, not emotions, should govern our actions. We should lead by example. Always.

And yet, I couldn't help being curious to see how this played out. What would Zach do when his bloodline was attacked? Was he ashamed to be born of a heretic? I wondered if that was why he was so skilled—that he trained so hard to overcome his parentage and the prejudice that came with it.

Zach took a sip from his goblet, then looked up and smiled at Amias. "I don't mean to offend, but is there something you need from me? You're ruining my meal."

Amias leaned forward. "Why? Don't want everyone to know about your heretic mother?"

"Ah, no, it's not that." Zach reached for a piece of bread. "It's just your foul breath. It's making it hard to hold down the delicious food."

Silence.

Then Amias roared, grabbing the table and upending it.

Zach was fast. He lifted his plate and his goblet and slid back as the table and all the other dishes crashed to the ground.

I covered my mouth. This was beyond jealousy. I'd never seen Amias act like this.

He turned on Zach. "Romantica scum! You don't deserve her!"

Zach tilted his head. "Don't deserve who?"

Irritation, and maybe a little disappointment, prickled under my skin. Did he not remember meeting me at all?

Then Zach's face lit up. "Oh! The princess with the freckles who likes strawberries! You mean her, right?"

My cheeks warmed. *That's* what he remembered? Seas of Glyll, did he *have* to remember my freckles?

Amias let loose another roar, but this time I rushed to stop him. "Back *away*, Amias!" I commanded, planting myself between them. Zach was going to keep on baiting him until one of them put a table through a window. I could almost hear the glass shattering and the wood crashing to the ground below.

"He insulted you, Ivy!" Amias reached for his sword.

"*I* didn't hear any insult. And you insult us all if you draw your blade in front of our guests. Now back down."

Amias did not advance, but neither did he step back.

"So the problem is…" Behind me, Zach placed his dishes on the table closest to him and stood. "I'm not worthy of her. Is that correct?" he said, jabbing his thumb at me.

Amias narrowed his gray eyes.

Zach looked me up and down, and I felt myself blush again. "That could very well be true."

Amias's hand on his sword slackened, just slightly.

"*But*," the Swordsman Prince went on with a smirk, "I think the important thing here is I'm more worthy than *you.*"

Not even my words could stop Amias now. He lunged for Zach, forgetting about the sword—forgetting about everything, apparently.

"Amias!" A voice boomed throughout the dining hall, echoing off the walls. It was a voice that made Amias stop, and very few could. Amias whirled to face King Krowe, who now stood on the steps of the hall, looking grand with his gold crown and sapphire cloak.

"Calm yourself, nephew," he commanded.

Amias straightened, his fists curled at his sides. "Uncle, this heretic can't be Princess Ivy's partner. He shouldn't even be eating at our tables."

"That is not for you to decide," King Krowe said. "It is the Council's decision. As it is for all partnerships, we must take *everything* into consideration." Krowe glared at his nephew in a way that made me conclude Amias must have gone to the Council to ask for my partnership *again*. Despite him already having Matilda, a half princess, for a partner, and that the Council had already refused to bind us twice before.

"For the good of the kingdom," Krowe continued, "the

prince with the most skill should be paired with Queen Myriana's direct descendant. And seeing as he's the best swordsman here—"

"*I* am the best swordsman here!" Amias yelled.

"Perhaps you *were*," Zach said calmly.

Rage built in Amias's face like never before. I thought he might actually explode. He unsheathed his sword and pointed it straight at Zach's chest. "I could *kill* you."

"You could try." Zach's eyes narrowed, turning cold and sharp, at last looking like the cutthroat warrior he was rumored to be.

This new persona gave me chills—of either fear or excitement. It was impossible to tell which.

"Let me try, then." Amias pressed the tip of his blade to Zach's chest. "Let us see who's better. Who the worthy one really is."

Zach stared at the blade's point for a moment before he brought two fingers to the side of the sword and moved it away from his chest, as if it were no more lethal than a blade of grass. "Fine, I accept your challenge."

King Krowe clapped. "Grand! A duel, then. Tomorrow at dawn!"

At that moment it was obvious he had been the puppet master pulling Amias's strings. He was the one who let Zach's parentage slip out. So *this* had been his brilliant idea.

Amias slowly lowered his sword, still fuming, and Zach merely turned around, sat at the table where his food was, and continued eating.

I stood there, wringing my napkin in my hands, annoyed but not surprised. A duel was the perfect way to test Zach's strength without offending the Saevallans as our guests. Logically, I knew it was a good plan, but it didn't *feel* like an evaluation or a test. It felt like a competition for *me*. And I didn't like being viewed as a prize to be won.

But if this was what I had to endure to get the legendary swordsman as a partner, to go after the Sable Dragon egg, and to one day find and defeat the Evil Queen, then I would sit and be considered a prize. And as for the victor, I would reward him with my Kiss.

CHAPTER SEVEN

A FIERY DUEL

Everyone greeted dawn in the arena of the training grounds the next day. I doubted a single person within the castle was *not* either sitting on the slopes of the hill up to the castle or under the red leaves of the jerr trees.

The murmur of the crowd was low, as if they were speaking in hushed voices for fear of waking the still-sleeping sun, their tongues placing bets. Who would win? A proper prince who was big and strong and naturally good with a blade? Or the legendary swordsman with a heretic's blood? Fires glowed around the edges to light the grounds. It was so early that even the Myrial bells had not yet chimed.

The Council and the Mages sat on chairs within the carved-out indention of the hill. As I passed them to stand next to Tulia and Minnow, I heard a few of them quietly congratulating King Krowe on his brilliant manipulation of his nephew.

"Best use my nephew's outrage to our advantage," he muttered to Queen Jocelyn.

Despite my aggravation at being a prize, I couldn't have agreed more. I was eager to see Zach's skills in action. To see for myself if he was worthy of Myriana's Mark.

With the morning air so chilly, I was wrapped in my gray

cloak, wearing a handsome navy blue dress underneath. My hair was done in a bun, as usual, except for a few wisps of curl that always escaped if there was a breeze.

"I see Amias is as ready as ever," whispered Minnow, leaning closer to me. She also wore her gray cloak, and her blond hair was fastened in braids.

Amias stood at the base of the hill, strapping on his armor and testing out his sword arm.

"Question is," Tulia said on Minnow's other side, "where is his opponent?"

It was nearly dawn, and Zach was nowhere to be seen. A few minutes ago, Master Gelloren had sent a page to fetch him from his room.

"Is Zach usually late?" I asked Prince Weldan, who stood next to me in his scarlet cloak.

Weldan shrugged. "He's usually the first to arrive for training and missions. But even though he's been in plenty of fights, he's never been challenged like this before. He's probably not taking it too seriously."

"Too seriously?" Tulia leaned in. "Amias is the best swordsman we have. Zach better take it seriously or he'll end up with his head on the grass and no body attached."

Weldan's lips twitched upward. "We'll see."

Tulia made a mocking sound just as all heads turned toward the castle steps, where a young page was descending with a yawning Zachariah trailing behind. Zach wore only a tunic and pants, no armor except wrist guards, and his sword at his side. When he reached the middle of the grounds, he called up, "My apologies! I hadn't realized that dawn meant *dawn.*"

Master Gelloren smiled. "Good to have you join us, Zach. Would you like a moment to warm up?"

Zach began stretching, first his neck, then his arms and legs. "Not necessary," he said.

He probably had just rolled out of bed. All he did was a few stretches and he was ready for a duel?

Master Gelloren nodded to me, and I made my way down the hill, my cloak and the hem of my dress rustling across the grass, collecting the morning dew.

"Good morning," Zach said cheerfully when I reached him and Amias.

Though I'd seen him smile before, after witnessing the cold way he'd faced Amias and accepted his challenge, his smile felt different now. I was much more aware of it.

"Good morning," I replied politely. "Do you need to hear the rules of the duel?"

"I'm afraid so. I've never been in a formal one like this before," Zach said. Amias drew his sword.

"They're simple. You will each receive a battle Kiss to increase your speed, strength, and skill. The prince who yields first, loses. Are you both ready?"

Zach nodded. Amias swung his sword, then hooked it back on his belt. He held out his hand. My last Kiss with a prince had been Kellian's failed revival Kiss, and a brief twinge of fear pricked my insides that this one wouldn't work, either.

I took his hand, and with a few steps, closed the distance between us. He bent his head down and Kissed me.

As his lips touched mine, the words of the battle spell—*Silen proderr Natalya*—echoed in my mind, and I felt my magic, beckoned by his Kiss, pull from my chest and leave me, rising up to meet Amias's. His magic, rough and unyielding like unrefined steel, seized mine, and the familiar weakening sensation passed through me. Had it been a stronger spell, it would have cost me more, because Amias always drew so much of my magic. My other partners never acted so greedy. But at least I knew now that my Kiss was still as powerful as always.

Amias released me, his entire body glowing blue as the battle magic pulsed around him gently, enhancing his body and preparing him for the fight.

"As expected from your lips, Ivy, I am invincible. Imagine what we could produce in the bedchamber." Amias gave a ravenous smirk.

Revulsion rose in me, turning to nausea. I hated the way Amias looked at me as if I was just a power arsenal, but his sexual innuendos were the worst. As if I would actually agree to lying with him. I prayed that when I was finally sent to Freida he would not become the father of any of my children.

It was with that thought I realized I was rooting for Zach, a complete stranger and the son of a heretic. Lesser of two evils, I supposed.

I turned to Zach, studying him for the second time. I recalled my sister's words—*I think he's gorgeous.* I wouldn't have said "gorgeous," but he was good-looking. Originally he seemed lanky, but he was actually lithe and strong, toned but not burdened by huge muscles that would slow him down. His face, without his goofy smile, was slim, all angles—attractive but not in an obvious pretty-boy way.

Before I'd gotten close, he grabbed my shoulder. "No enhancement required, but thank you."

I blinked. "What?"

Zach glanced at the sunrise. Dawn was now pouring over the land like spilled honey, slow, sweet, and shiny. In the distance, the Myrial bells began to chime. "I won't be needing your Kiss, princess."

"Don't be daft." I leaned forward.

He leaned backward. "Again, not to offend, but I can beat him without your magic."

"You're really serious, aren't you?"

Zach just smiled at me.

Anger blew up inside me like dwarven liquor tossed in a fire. Such arrogance! Did he truly think he was good enough to stand up to *my* magic? Without aid?

Folding my arms, I stepped away. "You could easily die. You'll be of no use to us then."

Zach chuckled. "Your concern is flattering, Your Highness, but I'll be fine."

As I returned to the Council members, a murmur rippled through the crowd.

"Ivy, what is the meaning of this?" my grandfather called from his chair.

"He does not wish for a Kiss, Your Majesty," I answered.

"He does not—that's ridiculous!"

"He would not accept it." Out of the corner of my eye, I noticed Weldan lift his eyes skyward, as if he'd expected this.

Amias, still pulsing blue with my magic, watched the Council, waiting their approval. Was this even allowed?

"We cannot force it on him," King Helios said, then gestured to the trumpeter. The boy blew his horn, signaling the start of the duel.

Amias withdrew his sword and held it aloft in front of him. The blue haze of my magic engulfing him swallowed up the blade as well.

I glanced at Zach. He had drawn his sword but held it casually at his side.

Surely Amias wouldn't kill him? No, Master Gelloren would stop him before that happened. But I did know this: there was no way he could win. Our partnership would be over before it had begun.

Amias started for him, running across the grass, leaving a trail of blue mist. He was fast with my magic, inhumanly so. And strong, too—like a bull charging its enemy.

Zach didn't move. Even when Amias was only five feet

away, Zach stood still. Seconds before Amias brought his sword down, Zach pivoted in a sharp turn and slammed the pommel of his sword into the back of Amias's head. Amias went down, his face diving into the ground.

The crowd gasped and many cried out. I clenched my fists, my lips parting in amazement.

Any regular person sustaining a blow like that wouldn't be able to get up, at least not right away, but Amias was protected by my magic. He picked himself up, spitting grass, and turned back to Zach. Even from this distance I could hear the growl rip through his throat like a wild animal. He went for Zach again, the aura around him glowing brighter.

An upward cut. A dodge from Zach. A sideways turn and slash, then Zach finally let his blade meet Amias's. The weight had to be intense. With the magical strength Amias possessed, it must've been like holding against the weight of a griffin. Shockingly, Zach held strong. Then he slammed his knee up into his opponent's gut. Amias choked and doubled over. Zach hit the hilt of his sword into Amias's head, and he again went down.

Far from defeated, Amias lumbered to his feet, swinging at Zach's shins. Zach, with one hand on Amias's shoulder, jumped and flipped over his foe's back and landed behind, kicking Amias back to the grass. Keeping his boot on Amias's back and his sword pointed to Amias's throat, he said, "Yield."

Amias let out a roar, and the glowing mist raged into blue flames. He pushed up from the ground, causing Zach to teeter off-balance. Amias slashed outward, and Zach only had time to throw his own sword up in defense. But the strength of my magic was too much—it sent Zach flying backward into the dirt.

The crowd roared their approval. I tried to hide a smile. *You aren't fighting against normal magic, swordsman, you're fighting against the great Myriana's.*

Zach sprang to his feet, squaring his shoulders and bending his knees. Then Amias, using the full extent of my power, was at him again. Zach barely kept up with the strength and speed of the magically enhanced prince. Clashes of metal against metal rang through the arena. The young men fought like beasts with inhuman speed.

Then Amias made a fatal mistake—it was a stupid one, too. Zach ducked to escape an upward cut, and Amias threw his arms up to deliver a blow, leaving his chest wide open. Zach shot up, grabbed the front of Amias's armor, and pressed the side of his blade against his opponent's neck. "Yield!" This time it was a shout. A demand.

Amias froze then dropped his sword. The arena was deadly silent. Zach kept his blade at Amias's throat for just a few more moments before lowering it. Then he turned away.

But Amias was not done. He kicked Zach square in the back, and with the battle magic still enhancing his strength, it sent Zach flying into a lit torch at the edge of the training area. The torch went down and rolled across the grass. Flames spread as Zach heaved himself up.

Before I could stop myself, I was sprinting down the steps and onto the grounds.

Zach was running as well, his sword pointed at Amias like a jousting stick.

The flames climbed up the white bark of the jerr trees.

Zach met Amias's sword with the sound of a lightning strike. Amias staggered, and Zach reeled back, then slammed the pommel of his sword into the vulnerable part of Amias's temple. Amias crumpled, the blue magic that encased him snuffed out like a candle.

When I finally reached the two of them, breathing hard as the fire swarmed up into the red leaves of the trees, Amias was unconscious.

Zach glanced over his shoulder at me. "I hate sore losers."

I could do nothing but stare at the swordsman.

He had won.

Not only had he won against Amias, but he had won against *me*. He had faced my magic absolutely *powerless* and won.

CHAPTER EIGHT

AT THE WALL

"You...you just..."

Zach looked at the rising flames. "Oh, no." He scratched the back of his head. "Bloody idiot ruined the lovely trees."

"Not the fire!" He looked back at me in surprise, and I tried to calm myself. "How did you...?"

Master Gelloren came up beside me, robes billowing. With a flick of his wrist, the fire extinguished and smoke filled the air.

"Zach, your reputation precedes you," he said, moving his hands back inside the sleeves of his robe. "That was quite impressive."

"Glad you enjoyed the show. I don't suppose breakfast is ready?" Zach swung his sword onto his shoulder. "That really worked up an appetite."

"Of course. I'll have a page show you the way."

"Actually, Master, I don't mind taking him," I said, forcing a pleasant smile to my lips.

"Very well, then," Gelloren said, fixing me with that questioning look he'd often give me over a hand of cards. No doubt he'd been under the impression that I'd be furious, since Zach had managed to defeat my Kiss so easily, and I certainly was, but seeing Zach's skill… I'd have to put aside my pride. We needed him.

Ignoring Gelloren's look, I gestured for Zach to follow me.

He paused before I led him away, turning to look back at the trees. "I am sorry about the trees, though."

Smoke rose from the burned leaves—once so red and full of life, they were now black and just a breeze away from ash.

"They'll grow back. That's the beauty of trees."

Zach looked back at me. "Well said, princess."

We made our way up the steps to the castle, passing Royals and gaping servants, through the giant double doors toward the dining hall, following the beautiful, sweet-smelling garlands of gardenia. Zach trailed his fingertips across the creamy white petals, as I had, and said, "That was a beautiful sunrise this morning."

"I heard the West has the most amazing sunsets. Is it true the kingdom of Saevall looks as if it's engulfed in the sun's flames?" I asked.

Zach shrugged. "Like I said, rumors are always a bit exaggerated, but I guess it does, at just the right time."

"Rumors are not always exaggerated." Though I wasn't going so far as to say I believed that he'd defeated a troll's lair by himself without a Kiss, I *could* believe that he'd been able to survive without a partner until now.

There was a pause. "Ah, I assume you're referring to the rumors surrounding me, then?"

"After a fight like that, you can't possibly deny your skill."

"Oh, I wasn't going to."

At this, I whirled around. He nearly ran into me, my face almost colliding with his collarbone. I took a step back. "I want you as my partner."

I hadn't expected to say it in quite this way, or even so soon, but it had been the reason I'd offered to take him to breakfast—to ask him with my *own* words, not Gelloren's or the Council's. With his raw skills and my power, we could take down the Sable Dragon. There wasn't a doubt in my mind now. Though I was still angry that he'd defeated my Kiss almost effortlessly, my excitement at the prospect of what we could do surpassed everything else.

Zach's eyebrows flew up into his dark brown hair. Then he recovered, smirking slightly. "I thought that had already been decided."

"Your fight with Amias was a test orchestrated by the Council—you passed. But besides that, *you* must consent to the partnership."

"That so?"

I raised an eyebrow. "Yes, obviously. Partnering with someone means linking your magic reservoir to theirs. It requires a great commitment and, once made, cannot easily be broken. It's not something to be taken lightly. We can't force anyone into it, nor should we."

Zach tilted his head, as if considering the idea. "It rather sounds like marriage."

I drew back, appalled at his comparison to the archaic Romantica tradition. But his Romantica mother had raised him...maybe he didn't know better. "It's nothing like marriage," I said flatly.

"Either way, no thanks." Zach slipped around me and continued walking.

For a moment, I remained there, frozen in disbelief. Then I spun around and hurried after him. "*Excuse* me?" I grabbed his arm, stopping him.

Zach covered my hand with his, right where Kellian's mark would've been. I felt the urge to suddenly rip it away but didn't.

Zach's fingers were callused but still gentle somehow. "I appreciate the offer, but I'm better on my own."

I didn't know what to say. I hadn't even considered he might say no.

He plucked my hand off his arm and started walking again. I darted in front of him, forcing him to a halt once more. "No one is better on their own," I snapped. "Think of how powerful you could be with my magic—how many more dark creatures you could kill."

He looked down at me. "I can kill plenty now, thanks." He tried again to move around, but I placed my hand on his chest, applying enough pressure to keep him back.

"What did you even come here for, then?"

"Contrary to your belief, the world does not revolve around you, princess. I came to Myria to help with the war, *not* to be your partner. We were already two days away before Gelloren's bird arrived with the message that he wanted to pair us up. I'd be here even if your partner was still conscious."

"Do you really not understand what partnering with me means?" I poked him hard in the chest. "If we were partners, you'd be granted more than just simple battle Kisses. The combination of our magic could unlock complicated, powerful spells. You'd save thousands with my help."

Zach sighed. "Please move aside so I can get my breakfast, princess. I've already dealt with one hardheaded Myrian today."

"Don't act all high and mighty just because you defeated Amias. You're arrogant if you think you can survive in the northern lands without the Kiss. We have dark creatures such as you've never seen before. It's *you* who's the stubborn one. That will get you killed up here."

Zach stared at me as I breathed in and out heavily, my hands curled into fists. Then he moved in close, his hand under my chin, pulling my face near his—I had no time to react.

"Seems like you're awfully eager to kiss me, Ivy. Why don't we just cut to the chase?"

Before I could stop myself, I raised my fist. Zach caught it just like he did everything else—effortlessly.

His hand closed around my fist. "Have to admit, I'm impressed."

I glared at him, his fingers pressing into the part where Kellian's crest had been. It was one thing to deal with Amias's insinuations, but it was quite another to attempt a powerless kiss on a princess. It was an action of Lust, and it was insulting.

It was common for princes and princesses to appease their appetites driven by Lust, but I had never partaken in any partnership that wasn't completely professional.

I had no patience for anything but training. Let others succumb to the power of Lust. To me, it was a distraction that led to vulnerable emotions. Depending on how greatly it affected a person, it was often just as evil as the monsters we battled.

Finally he let go of my fist, and I jerked away. He seemed completely unfazed. "Was that truly necessary? Come now, my breath has to be better than *Amias's*."

He'd been teasing me. He'd had no intention of actually kissing me.

His demeanor now was cool, confident, even…suave.

What happened to the awkward, easygoing fellow? The prince who complimented my freckles? How could that same person try to kiss me off the battlefield? Who was this man who could be two people at once—the blundering fool then the smooth and graceful warrior?

Perhaps it was exactly as he wanted it. People would underestimate him, thus making it easier for him to strike. Like a baby basilisk viper. Small and innocuous, but its venom deadly.

Or maybe he wanted to drive me away with his teasing. I

hated how well it had worked.

"I think I can find my own way to breakfast," Zach said.

He brushed past me, and I let him go, afraid that if I stayed with him any longer I'd want to stab him with his own stupid sword.

For the better part of the day, I sulked in my room. First, Zachariah had defeated my power in one simple duel. It made my stomach churn with anger and embarrassment. Next, he had turned down my proposal of partnership. Finally, he had teased me with suggesting a kiss *off* the battlefield and implied *I* was the one who wanted it.

Perhaps that was the most insulting thing of all.

I threw my pillow against the tapestry, sending ripples through the fabric, then flung myself back on the bed and winced. My hair was still in a bun, and it hurt my neck. Irritated, I tugged my curls out of their nest and let them fall around my shoulders.

Amias had once surrendered to Lust and kissed me on the edge of the castle grounds, at night with the torches lit around us. I could still remember the smell of his wine-soaked breath. He had tilted my head back and seized my mouth roughly with his lips—so similar to his battle Kisses, I almost couldn't tell the difference. But there *was* a difference. A slight hum in his throat, a change in his breathing, a change in mine. The magic that usually rose in my chest after meeting another Royal's lips lay dormant. But another feeling traveled down my spine, into my limbs, my hips and legs, locking me in place.

Then he had opened his mouth and demanded more.

Greedy. He was always so greedy. I couldn't stand the feel of his tongue on mine. I hated the emptiness I felt inside, the absence of magic within that sort of kiss.

I had pushed him away. Told him that if he ever tried that again, I'd stab an arrow into his eye.

I'd almost punched Zach, and he hadn't even kissed me—
only entertained the thought.

There were many things the Legion did that I wished I
could change. For one, I wished princesses were treated less
like arsenals and more like the soldiers we were trained to
be. And another, I wished we had more say in when we'd be
shipped off to Freida to produce heirs. But I could make my
peace with both those things because it was for the good of
the Legion, the kingdoms, and the people.

But I refused to be used as a plaything to satisfy a prince's
Lust.

Clenching my fists, I got up from my bed and headed for
the door. Now was as good a time as any to research the Sable
Dragon. With Zach or without, I was going after that egg.

Myria's library smelled of wood and leather. Even though
every book was ancient, the librarians would recopy the fifty
oldest books into new leather-bound books each year. The
texts themselves might have been old, but the cavernous room
never smelled that way.

"North back wall, behind the colonnade," I muttered to
myself as I walked through the stacks. I was fairly certain
that was the section I was looking for. The library was vast,
and I spent most of my free time on the training grounds. I
didn't have the patience for studying the ancient texts more
than necessary.

Thinking I'd found the correct book, I leafed through the
pages. It wasn't until I noticed a large diagramed picture of the
three enchantments surrounding a curse on an amulet that I
realized I was in the wrong section.

"Cursed amulets. Useless." I tucked the book back in its

spot and tried the next stack. Finally I remembered that the section on dark creatures was to the *left* of the colonnade, and I was able to find the book in moments.

As I slid the book from the shelf, I found Zach's face staring at me from the other side.

I gave a yelp and dropped the heavy book, the spine hitting my foot. I let out a string of curses under my breath.

"You curse like a bartender at a sleazy tavern," Zach said, struggling not to laugh.

"That was your fault. Who hides behind a bookshelf? What are you, a child?"

Zach just grinned, hands in his pockets.

"How did you find me?"

He shrugged. "Bribed a servant."

I waited for him to offer more, and when he didn't, I gave a frustrated sigh. "Okay, *why* did you bribe a servant?"

"So they'd tell me where you were."

I started to push past him, but he planted his arm on the shelf, halting me. "Troll's breath, you can't take a joke, can you? I wanted to apologize."

"For?"

"Implying I would kiss you. I suppose that was out of line."

"You suppose?"

"I didn't mean any harm by it."

"It was offensive."

"Do you not know how apologies work?"

I noticed he'd shaved since this morning, and it made him look younger. It reminded me that, although I certainly hadn't found what he did funny, he probably thought it had been harmless. Just as I had joked around with my sisters in imagining the perfect Swordsman Prince.

"All right, I accept your apology. Though I'm not sure why you're apologizing, since I doubt you came to me with a sudden change of mind about being my partner."

Zach broke our gaze, his hazel eyes flitting to the book at my feet. "Even if we're not going to be partners, that doesn't mean I want you to hate me."

His words caught me off guard, and I searched for a reply. Of course I didn't hate him—it was far too strong a word. But yes, I had been angry.

He stooped to pick up my fallen book and read the title. *"The Forces' Darkest Children."*

I reached for it, but he stepped back, away from my grasp. "Why do you have this?"

"None of your concern." I paused a beat. "Why? Have you read it before?"

"I've read a lot about monsters. This book is supposed to contain the worst of the worst. What are you looking for?"

He started to flip through the pages, and I yanked it out of his hands. "Zachariah, did you think I wanted you as my partner for just *any* battle? I assure you, if it were only the next patrol I was up against, I could manage with Amias."

Zach narrowed his eyes.

"I see," he said slowly, then turned and left without so much as a good-bye.

I stood there, the book in my hands, staring after him. Was *he* angry with *me* now? I wasn't sure what I could've said to offend him, but I also knew the tension between us was so precarious, even my self-righteous tone might've made him leave.

Well, I couldn't worry about that now. I had research to conduct.

Under the stained glass of the north wall I found a window seat and pulled my legs up so the book rested against my thighs. I flipped past the section on wraiths and stopped on dragons. The last dragon in the book was the Sable Dragon. There was little information about it. It was said that it had killed the people who knew most about it and the recorded text was only stories passed down and not actual accounts.

If I were to destroy it, though, I had to start somewhere. My hands tightened around the edges of the book, and I started to read.

The Sable Dragon is born of evil—shadows, darkness, wickedness from the hearts of men.

I sped through the details of how the darkness accumulated and the different omens associated with it—all signs Gelloren had mentioned. When it came to the section on its shell and skin, I slowed down, looking for weaknesses.

The shell is made from the hardest substance known on earth. No blade can pierce it. At the time of hatching, the dragon is most susceptible. According to King Yolan, descendant of the Second King, the dragon is made of obsidian, with the ability to produce black flames. The flames burn the coldest ice, all while the victim is tortured by every horrid emotion and feeling that plagues this world. To induce even more suffering on its victims, the flames burn much more slowly than normal fire. Its only vulnerable spot is its mouth, where the very flames are produced.

The text was terrifying but nothing I hadn't expected. I knew of two other Sable Dragons preceding this one. And though this egg didn't necessarily mean the dragon, if hatched, would be worse than the other two, it could still mean the end of the Legion. We were weaker than the Legion who had defeated the other dragons two hundred—even one hundred—years ago. The state the Legion was in now would not be able to hold up against a monster such as a Sable Dragon. All to say, I *had* to get to that dragon before it hatched.

"You'll need this, too."

I tore my attention from the text and looked up.

Bathed in blue and purple from the light shining through stained glass, Bromley stood above me, holding out another book. *Kisses of Dragon Slayers: Volume Nine.*

I'd read volumes one through seven a couple of years back, before my first mission to slay a Bronze Dragon, but Master Gelloren had told me I needn't bother with the last two volumes, since they held spells to kill dragons that had long since been extinct.

I took the book and flipped to the back.

"A servant told me I could find you here," Brom said.

"New rule: no servant is permitted to tell anyone where I am," I muttered, flipping another page.

"You weren't at lunch or dinner, so I figured you wanted to get a head start after seeing Prince Zach fight."

I didn't reply. Bromley assumed I'd be going with Zach to kill the Sable Dragon. Well, he was half right. I was going, just not with Zach. I'd find another partner. Maybe another Saevallan. Or, Heavenly Queen forbid, I'd even get Amias if I was that desperate—maybe the Council would make an exception because of the tight deadline. Whoever it was, I was certain my power alone could beat the dragon.

I found the spell. It was long and intricate. More than five dozen syllables, all with unique pronunciation and rhythm. *Of course* it had to be complicated. The higher the risk, the greater the price.

"Do you think *she* ever slayed a dragon?" Brom asked, staring up at the stained glass.

I stood, both books in my arms, and turned to look at the stained glass as well.

It was of Queen Myriana.

Her image stood at least fifteen feet tall, with indigo-colored hair, white skin, and a beautiful blue dress. Roses, thorns, and ivy entwined in her hair and around her dress and arms. While holding a sword, she stood back to back with the Wicked Queen, who was wrapped in a violet cloak and holding a staff of gnarled wood. It was a beautiful juxtaposition. Like two sides of the moon, one blackened by shadows, the other illuminated by the sun. They were also both mothers. Myriana, mother to the first generation of Royals, and the Wicked Queen, mother to the Forces of Darkness.

Usually whenever I admired this stained glass, I focused on Myriana, but today the sun seemed to be shining directly behind the Evil Queen, bathing us in violet. The staff was beautifully designed with swirls of ancient dark symbols, but I knew that was merely an artist's choice. The truth was we didn't even know if she *had* a staff, much less what it looked like.

The historical texts had always been cryptic about the Evil Queen and her past. It was also extremely annoying to run into ripped or warped pages of history books whenever the text got close to her origins.

Even the version the young princess told in the classroom was said to have been mostly fabricated by bits and pieces of rumors from over five centuries ago. The Royals accepted that they were mother and daughter—that Myriana's firstborn had been stolen and cursed into a hellish oblivion. How could anything, or anyone, take away an innocent baby and turn her into something so wicked and twisted...so terrifyingly evil that new monsters and curses were born by nothing more than her thought or nightmare?

Tearing my gaze away from the cloaked queen, I refocused on Brom's question. "Oh, I'm sure she fought many dragons. Maybe not a Sable—"

My words were drowned out by the tolling of the Myrial bells, then three sharp horn blasts, one after the other.

A breach.

I shoved the books into Brom's arms. "Copy page 354 of the *Dragon Slayers* volume for the spell. I have to go!"

The librarians didn't say a word as I ran through their

precious stacks. They knew I was running to join the fight. Even without a partner, I had to help stop whatever monster had breached our walls.

Down in the armory, it was ordered, calm…routine. Younger Royals strapped armor to the older Royals. Princesses slung quivers of arrows to their backs and fastened wrist guards as they stood under shelves and racks of weapons upon weapons. Swords, shields, rapiers, daggers, staffs, longbows, crossbows, maces, and axes all hung neatly on gray stone walls stretching high into rafters of dark brucel wood.

Tulia and Minnow were already loaded with shields and their preferred weapons—Tulia with a collection of throwing daggers, Minnow with a crossbow. I hurried to my friends and grabbed a sword and a smaller, easier-to-move shield.

"Any report yet?" I asked, strapping the shield to my left arm.

Tulia shook her head. "Just the three horns. It's probably a horde. We're waiting for the scouts now, and then we're to set out."

I grimaced at the word "horde." She was probably right— no single monster was stupid enough to attack Myria's walls, but they gained courage in numbers.

The double wooden doors banged open, and two running scouts sped through, stopping to report to Roland and Edric. Then Roland pointed to six pairs of half princes and princesses and signaled for them to depart. They were outside before Edric had even crossed to Tulia, Minnow, and me.

His face didn't look quite so strained now, but there were still signs of fatigue in his gait—just like Minnow and Tulia, he was still tired from their week-long patrol.

"The good news is the breach is contained. The Royals on the wall were the first to respond, so they have a good handle on it." Edric nodded to Tulia. "But we should hurry, just in case."

Minnow and Tulia started off with their partners, but I grabbed Edric's arm. "And what of me? Don't tell me you expect me to stay behind."

Edric shrugged off my arm. "You don't have a partner yet."

I winced at his tone. So matter-of-fact. "What of the Saevallans?"

Roland tugged on his sword belt. "Many of them are already at the wall."

"Then I'm going as well." I couldn't stand the thought of being left behind, especially when our reinforcements were out there risking their lives for a city they didn't call home.

"Don't be a fool, Ivy. No one will be able to protect you out there."

He was right. It was a stupid, brainless thing to do. But I couldn't just sit back, waiting on my comrades to come home. I couldn't see Minnow or Tulia in the Curse Ward next to Kellian. I *needed* to go out there. Prince or no prince.

"I don't need protection. I can stay in the *Illye* circle."

"You can't stay in there unless you've been Kissed. You know that," Edric snapped.

"Then Kiss me." I reached for his neck, but he drew back.

"No, Ivy. I'm not going to help you get yourself killed." With that, he pushed my arms away and stomped through the doors of the armory.

Five Royals passed me before I snapped out of it.

I grabbed Matilda, Amias's partner, and squeezed her arm. "I need a favor."

Matilda blinked. She didn't particularly like me—especially since her partner was always trying to leave her for me, but she also wasn't about to turn down the direct descendant of

Myriana. "Yes, Your Highness?"

"I need a battle Kiss." If I wanted to go out and actually *fight*—to see if all those sword lessons were worth something, I needed a princess to cast the battle spell on me. A prince's Kiss wouldn't work this time, since princes couldn't cast spells.

Matilda glanced to the doors, to the sounds of hooves thundering away. "I don't think…"

"I'll tell no one. No matter what happens, you won't be blamed."

Still, she hesitated.

"Or, I could take Amias away from you, and you'd be left with a weaker partner or a spot at Freida." I hated to threaten her—but I was desperate.

Matilda didn't pause this time. She grabbed my shoulders and Kissed me. Her magic was like the paws of a cat, small pinpoints of pressure. I could tell when she spoke the battle words—*Silen proderr Natalya*—because then I could draw the magic out of her, as Amias had done to me just this morning. I took only a sliver of hers, because I could draw from my own magic now. Blue flames danced across my skin, even though I felt nothing but a soft, warm sensation.

When our lips parted, she glared at me. "I hope my spell is good enough for the great Ivy Myriana," she snarled.

I drew myself up, flexing my arm muscles, feeling the power and strength course through me. "It'll do."

Twilight had just begun to show on the eastern horizon, in the direction of the breached wall. It was no coincidence. Monsters preferred attacking in shadows and darkness. Perhaps by hitting us at sundown they thought they would surprise us.

But they would never truly be able to catch us completely

off guard, thanks to our Sense. Royals could *feel* the power of darkness closing in. A stony feeling, like a heavy shadow, settled over our chests as evil creatures got closer. During the partnership ritual, where marks were exchanged, the mage performed a spell that allowed princesses to take the prince's Sense. That way the prince could fight freely, without the weight of the darkness pressing against him like a second, heavier gravity.

The fact that the princesses had to be the ones to bear the burden of the Sense's weight was not necessarily fair, but, like everything else, it was logical. The Legion argued that the princesses weren't the ones outside the protective *Illye* circle, engaging the monsters in close combat. And the Legion ruled by logic.

I had pushed the feeling down, as I had been trained to, but as I sat astride my mare, Lorena, I let the shadow loose. It settled across my chest like a breastplate, heavy with cold and fear. Its intensity told me it was, in fact, a horde of creatures. They were not particularly strong monsters, but there were many.

I swallowed and balled the feeling back into my chest, smothering it. It served me no purpose now. I knew where the enemy was and knew the extent of its power. I could not let the darkness grab hold of me, or I would never be able to move. Instead, I focused on the strength from the pulsing blue magic that surrounded me. It had been a long time since I'd felt the battle magic myself—only in training scenarios, never on an actual battlefield. This would be interesting.

I urged Lorena forward.

Rubble lay half a mile away from the forty-foot wall. Something big must have broken through to send debris so far. My horse picked her way through the rocks, and when I could go faster by foot, I dismounted and ran toward the battle, my legs stronger now with my enhanced battle magic. It made me grateful the locking curse was long gone. Up ahead, wooden buildings were on fire, and a whole roof had been caved in by a large boulder.

Oh, Sacred Sisters, I prayed, *please let there be no more innocent lives lost. Please, Queen Myriana, protect my people.*

Royals helped injured villagers out from under burning logs. Two children, their clothes covered in soot and ash, huddled behind a rock with a prince guarding them with his sword.

The fight was at its peak. Princes, lit with the blue flames of battle magic, fought against dwarves with axes. Princesses crowded together in a silvery protective dome of magic as they fired out arrows with longbows and crossbows.

Saevallans were also in the fray, fighting like rabid dogs against wolves. Their bronze armor glinted in the setting sun. Weldan was among them, also alight with blue magic.

His scarlet cloak flew behind him as he leaped onto a pile of rubble and drove his sword into a troll's neck. The troll fell with the power of a chopped brucel tree and shook the ground at my feet. Its giant body disintegrated into black smoke, and the ground where it had fallen ignited in green flames, burning all the grass and turning the earth into something that death itself had touched.

"Ivy!"

My name came from within the *Illye* circle, and I glanced back to see Minnow standing at the edge, her crossbow at her side, waving at me. But I ignored her. She'd tell me to get within the circle to stay safe. Not this time. Not when villagers could still be hurt and not when I could actually do something about it. After weeks of lying in bed while my partner had gone on without me, I could finally fight again—I had battle magic now. The blue fire pulsed around me, and strength and power surged through me like lightning.

I had to do this. No, I *wanted* to do this.

I unsheathed my sword and headed into the smoke.

The first thing I encountered was a goblin. Its bald head and big ears swiveled around to me, scaly gray arms following with a large spiked hammer in its hands.

"*Yek ut Mukk!*"

Die, Royal scum.

I sneered at his words. "*Out Nerak!*"

Not today.

I ducked low to avoid the swing and stabbed my sword into its tender feet. The creature reared back and screamed, half its cry drowned out by other sounds of battle. While it was distracted with pain, I drove my shoulder into its gut, forcing it to the ground. With a wild feeling of victory, I stabbed the goblin in the chest. The creature went up in black smoke and scorched the earth with a surge of green flames.

My nerves flew like ash on the wind. I killed a monster, without a partner to hide behind. With Matilda's spell and my own reservoir of magic, I alone was powerful enough.

"Ivy!"

It was Edric this time, no doubt furious I went against his order. I barely glanced his way, and instead, ran the other direction, into the plumes of smoke.

I drew in a breath as the smoke around me cleared. Fire and debris were everywhere, while a gaping hole in the wall revealed rolling lands shadowed in twilight. I sent out another prayer to the wind, shuddering at the thought of undergoing another breach while civilians lay in their beds, weak and vulnerable.

Thankfully, though, we were winning. Much faster than usual.

And that was for one reason.

Zach.

The half-royal, half-heretic prince dodged and slashed through dwarf, goblin, and troll as if they were nothing. He moved like something out of the gates of the afterlife. And what was more?

He was free of blue flames. No one had Kissed him.

Perhaps there hadn't been time to administer him one, or he wanted to prove that he didn't need it…but there he was, slaying monsters in one blow.

After seeing him fight this morning, I shouldn't have been surprised, but deep down, I didn't truly believe it. Because I'd guessed that, like I had, he'd at least take a simple battle Kiss against an *entire* horde of monsters.

Yet, clearly, he was doing fine without.

His footwork was fast and light, his sword strokes sharp and ruthless, and the way he rolled and dodged—it was if he'd been trained by barbarians. His style was undisciplined and wild, yet completely effective.

As eager to see more of his fighting as I was to kill another monster, I rushed past a burning stable and clashed swords with a dwarf.

He'd taste the blue flames of my blade, just as the goblin had.

The dwarf's beard was oily and black, his skin was gray, and his eyes were liquid amber. He growled and slashed his sword down. I was slow with my shield, and the sword nicked my shoulder, dousing the blade with crimson blood. He brought the sword to his mouth and licked it.

Breathing through the fiery pain in my shoulder, I took a step back as the dwarf howled with delight. "Myriana's pure heir. My lucky night." With crazy eyes, he lowered his sword and charged at me again.

I raised my shield and tried to parry his blow, but he had

tasted my blood and was crazed by the idea of killing Myriana Holly's direct descendant. Still, I wasn't the princess with the best sword skills in the Legion for nothing, and I had my battle magic. With my shield raised to stop any more blows from above, I dropped to the ground, diving between the dwarf's legs and coming up from behind. I swung at his undefended back just as he rotated and brought his arm up to stop my sword.

It went halfway through his arm. If it had been a goblin, the blade would've sliced clean through, but dwarves' skin was a lot tougher, thicker.

I wrenched my sword out of his flesh and moved to stab his heart, but the ground rumbled under my feet. In horror I looked at the black blood spilled on the ground, then back up.

The dwarf's beard twitched as he smiled.

Dwarf blood magic. *Holy Queen, no.*

The earth moved, and rubble rose around my ankles, rocks digging into my shins and locking me into place. Oh Sweet Sisters, I couldn't move my legs.

He wanted my death to be slow and agonizing. He lashed out at my thigh.

The cut was deep, blood gushing from the wound and soaking my trousers. With the loss of my blood, so came the loss of battle magic. It flickered and died.

Seeing the flow of blood, and my body without its protective shield, he ran his gray tongue over his top whiskers.

I trembled. Without my magic, how could I win? I raised my shield and gritted my teeth, blood pumping painfully from my pounding heart.

As the dwarf tossed my shield aside and nicked another wound on my ribs before knocking me to my back, I prayed to the Sisters to save me from my own stupidity.

I realized the confidence I'd felt when killing that goblin had been foolish. How could I have been so arrogant to believe my Kiss was worth the power of two? The Legion gave us partners for a reason: so we could protect each other, watch each other's backs. Kellian was gone because I, his partner, hadn't been there.

And as much as he needed me then, I needed him now.

The dwarf raised his sword above his head and brought it down. The blade stopped a breath away as a sword's tip emerged in a bloody hole through the dwarf's broad chest.

The body crumbled to dust.

Zach stood over me, his sword bathed in what looked like ink. His expression was not battle-hardened or one of anger as I had expected it to be. He looked at me with amusement, maybe even a little curiosity.

He said the same thing he'd said in the corridor. "Have to admit, I'm impressed."

CHAPTER NINE

ANTLERS OF THE STAG

'd told Zach I wasn't looking to impress anyone, but when he offered me his arm, I accepted it. He helped me to a safer location and lowered me to a large wooden beam, then he dropped to his knees and inspected the gash on my thigh.

The battle was pretty much over. Smoke rose to the first signs of stars, and the *Illye* circle cleared as the princesses emerged from its protection.

Zach ripped off a piece of my dress and pressed it against the wound to stop the flow of blood. I gritted my teeth and winced. "Sorry," he breathed, touching a gentle hand to my knee. "You'll need to get this cleaned up. It's pretty deep. Stitches, too."

"Are you daft?" I cradled my head, woozy from blood loss. "Just Kiss me."

Zach leaned back, frowning. "This really should be cleaned first, princess."

It was just a simple healing Kiss, but I was in no mood to argue with him, so when a prince passed, I stopped him.

"Christopher?" I said.

He stopped. "Princess Ivy."

At his side was a young woman with a swollen belly. Her

cheeks were covered in streaks, her tears having left clean tracks through the soot and ash. She was surely a victim of the attack, but she seemed to have escaped mostly unscathed, save for the cut on her arm, and, since she was obviously pregnant it was a double miracle.

I beckoned Christopher toward me and, without question, he pressed his lips to mine. His magic rose up, strong and steady like a horse's gallop, and met mine. I spoke the healing spell in my head, and the gash on my thigh, and the nicks on my arm, shoulder, and ribs healed cleanly. Though I felt much better, I wished the healing Kiss also replenished blood, but I'd have to wait for my body to produce it.

With the last bit of the spell, I took the arm of the maiden, touched my lips to her wound, and it healed instantly.

"Thank you, princess," she said.

"You're welcome. You were very lucky to get away with only a scratch."

Christopher bent down to whisper in my ear, "It was a bloody miracle. She was found under the rubble of a collapsed house, with the bodies of the rest of her family. She *should* be dead."

As they left, I sent a quick prayer to Myriana that the poor girl wouldn't have to raise the child all on her own.

I looked back to Zach, who was watching Christopher and the pregnant girl walk away with pulled brows and a tight jaw— an expression that held both anger and somehow…regret?

Before I could question him, he was already disappearing into the final remnants of smoke.

· · ·

After making sure *all* the creatures had been slain and Tulia had promised to bring Lorena back to the stables, I was whisked to the castle on the back of Edric's horse. Waves of anger rolled off him as we rode, but I was too weak to care. I leaned my head against his back, glad to be away from the smoke that stung my eyes and burned my throat.

Edric had to lift me off his horse, and Brom helped me up the stone steps into the Hall of Ancestors with the rest of the Royals trickling in. Most veered into the western halls, where they'd get cleaned up, see to any healing, and rest before the celebration feast. Any victory was reason enough to celebrate nowadays.

I yearned to follow them, but when I noticed Brom was leading me toward the center of the Hall, I stood up straighter and supported more of my own weight, preparing myself for a lecture from the Master Mages. Surely word of my solo act and Zach's rescue had reached them.

But what I saw standing on the elevated platform at the end of the Hall made me want to turn around and face a *dozen* dwarves instead.

Amid the Council, Weldan, Kendra, Zach, and the Master Mages, was a woman with long dark hair and a maroon dress. She stopped talking to Master Gelloren as she caught sight of me, and her eyes narrowed.

The bones under my skin froze as if I'd just swallowed icicles.

Oh my Queen, why is she here? Now of all moments? When did she leave Freida?

The southern kingdom was practically a month's journey away. They must have received a letter signaling her arrival. Why had no one told me? Did the Council enjoy watching me sweat?

As much as every fiber in me wanted to turn and run, I let

go of Bromley and mounted the platform. The Council and the Mages stopped talking as I stood in front of the woman in the maroon dress.

"Mother," I said softly. "It is good to see you."

Queen Dahlia Myriana took one look at my smoke-stained dress, my dirty face and arms, and the dried blood, and her perfect red lips twisted into a grimace. She raised her arm and backhanded me across the face.

My head whipped to the side, but by some miracle I didn't stumble. I stayed upright, tasting blood in my mouth. My ears started ringing.

I glanced at the Saevallans, the Council, and the mages, out of sheer embarrassment. None of them looked especially surprised, except Zach. His mouth was open in shock, and I just had time to notice Weldan's hand on his arm before I dropped my head in shame.

"I wish I could say the same, child." My mother's cold voice dripped with disdain. "Imagine my displeasure when, within the hour of my arrival, I was told that my own flesh and blood shamed me not once, but twice."

I was used to the words, but her tone was worse than usual. I had embarrassed her with my recklessness, and she was making sure I paid for it…in front of everyone.

"First, losing *another* partner, and then you risk Myriana's magic by tossing your life to the winds of fate? I would ask what you were thinking, but obviously you weren't. Entering a battle without an *Illye* shield…without a partner to protect you. Tell me, child, do you wish to taint the name of Myriana? Or mine?"

"No, my Queen." I dipped my head even lower.

There was shuffling next to me, but I didn't dare look up to see where it came from.

I could feel my mother's cold eyes on me as her voice

echoed across the hall. "I return with news of the Wicked Queen's whereabouts to find my Legion suffering from my own daughter's selfishness and carelessness. How many does Kellian make? Five? Six?"

I jerked my head to the side, as if she'd struck me again—she might as well have. From the corner of my eye, I noticed Zach's fists curled at his sides.

"Did he die like Telek?" she asked.

My heart cracked. As I struggled to push down tears, I silently begged her to stop.

"A sword through his chest because his battle magic had run out and you were off fighting a lowly creature instead of staying by his side?"

Pain ripped through every nerve ending in my body. Telek's death haunted me to this day. Master Gelloren spent months coaxing me to fight again afterward, telling me it hadn't been my fault. I'd chosen to protect Minnow, who had fallen before a troll, instead of watching over Telek. His blood was on my hands. *Sisters, forgive me.*

"Perhaps you're ready to finally join the other princesses at Freida. Maybe we might find the one thing you're truly good at."

I closed my eyes and took a slow, deep breath, the world dimming around me.

As painful and harsh as my mother's words were, they were true. I had been prideful to think I could've taken on a horde attack without a partner. Time and again I was faced with the downfall of another partner, and the darkest parts of my heart—the parts with my mother's voice—told me that it wasn't the Mark of Myriana's fault, but mine. It had always been mine.

I didn't deserve another partner, let alone a chance to go after the Sable Dragon.

For a moment, I couldn't breathe. Insecurity drowning me,

clawing at my throat…

"I'm afraid she can't join them just yet."

I raised my head. Zach stood to my side, a step in front of me. It was a foolish thought, yet it seemed almost as if he was trying to shield me.

Queen Dahlia raised one eyebrow. "Ah, the legendary swordsman I've heard *so* much about. And why can't she, Prince Zachariah?"

"Because Princess Ivy has agreed to be my partner."

If the Hall hadn't already been quiet, it went dead silent now. I struggled to keep my face neutral, even though inside I was tearing my hair out in confusion.

What in the name of the Holy Queen?

My mother folded her arms. "You were in the battle and rescued her from her stupidity, and yet you would have my daughter as your princess?"

I tried not to wince, and it came out as a twitch.

"I would. If she'll still have me." He cast a glance back at me, and the ghost of a smile traveled over his lips.

I opened and closed my mouth like an idiot, completely stunned. What was more surprising? Zach's sudden change of mind wasn't the thing that had me speechless. He'd pulled me out of a dark, bottomless pit of self-hatred and loneliness my mother's words always stirred within me.

No one had ever stood up to Queen Dahlia before—she was the Queen Heir of Myriana. It simply wasn't done. And no one had stood up to her, especially, on my behalf. But this prince had, and from our past interactions I couldn't fathom why.

"I say we discuss this after the feast," Master Gelloren said, at last interrupting an awkward silence.

"An excellent idea," King Helios said, then gestured to my mother—his daughter—to come with him. Dahlia cast another disgusted look my way and followed her father.

Since Zach had consented to the partnership, only the approval of the Council was needed now. Did the Council even want me with Zach after all my mother had said? I hated to admit it, but Zach with his heretic bloodline wasn't even as much a risk as a princess who didn't stand by her prince.

With the show over, the rest of the Council and the Saevallans started out of the Hall.

But Zach didn't leave. He stayed next to me, and in a low voice, said, "May I walk you to your room?"

I swallowed, the shame still burning on my skin. "I can manage, but thank you."

"I'd like to speak with you."

"All right, then." I allowed myself to take Zach's outstretched arm. Partly because I needed it, and partly because my mother was still watching and she needed to see that Zach and I were serious about being partners.

We walked down the corridors, silent. Bromley trailed after us for a while, but when I realized Zach wasn't going to talk with Brom around, I dismissed my page. With a scowl, he vanished into the entrance of a servants' corridor hidden behind a tapestry.

"You want to tell me why you suddenly changed your mind?" I finally asked. When he stayed silent for a few more paces, I said the words that made my voice crack. "Please don't tell me you were trying to be chivalrous by protecting me from my mother. I don't need anyone's protection from her." *No matter how great it felt.*

Zach stopped mid-stride, his elbow tightened, squeezing my arm against his ribs. His hazel eyes bored into me, a gaze so intense I found it hard to swallow. To do anything but stare right back. "I know you don't."

His words settled over me like a blanket. They were

genuine. Earnest. The truest words he'd spoken to me, it felt like.

"Gelloren told me about the Sable Dragon."

I dropped my gaze, curling my fingers around the fabric of his sleeve. So that's why he'd suddenly rushed off while we were in the library. He saw the book and made inferences from my previous words. *"Did you think I wanted you as my partner for just any battle?"*

I looked up at him. "And you want to go."

Slowly, his grin came back, and I couldn't believe this was the godlike fighter I'd seen drenched in blood amid the smoke and fires less than an hour ago.

"It sounds like the adventure of a lifetime," he said.

I dropped his arm and leaned against the wall. We watched each other carefully, scrutinizing. Me, with a frown, and Zach, with a smile.

"You're using me," I said. "You want to go after the dragon, and you know I'm your ticket."

Zach tilted his head, the smile still there. "Tell me, princess, how is that any different than you wanting me for your benefit?"

I wasn't happy with the way he phrased it, but it was true. I did want him. He had unprecedented skill.

A mutually beneficial relationship.

So why was I so wary? Why did I not trust that charming smile?

I had no other option. If they were to take my mission away from me—especially after the verbal lashing my mother had given me—because I had yet to find a partner, I'd never forgive myself. And even if I did have someone else to take, none could compare to the prince who stood before me.

And, though it made me feel weak and vulnerable, I remembered him standing in front of me, facing my mother. A human shield to the poison of her words seeping into my skin and nestling into my heart and mind.

"Very well. If the Council agrees, let us be partners."

Without another word, Zach took my arm again—continuing his gesture of support. Already, he was treating me like a partner should.

We walked the rest of the way to my room in silence, and as soon as I was behind the safety of my door, I slid to the ground and pulled my knees to my chest, letting the sobs come.

I wept for Kellian and Telek. I wept for *all* my partners. And I wept for myself.

My mother hated me with every fiber of her being.

With her voice echoing in my ears, I stayed on the floor and sobbed until Bromley came to get me for the Council meeting.

Even after my mother's hurtful speech, the Council agreed to my partnership with Zach. Thankfully, I was still the purest princess in the Legion with the only Kiss powerful enough to take down the Sable Dragon. And after seeing Zach defeat Amias and hearing of his skills at the wall, they were more than satisfied he was a good match. In fact, they never once mentioned his heretic blood.

Master Gelloren took Zach's hand and mine then pressed them together, wrapping them in a garland of ivy. During the partnership ritual, the mages had a variety of holy plants to choose from, but since I was a pure descendant, they used the flora for which I was named. They believed it invoked a deeper bond between our magic and Kisses.

"With this sacred flora, I bind Princess Ivy of the Great House of Myriana and Prince Zachariah of the House of Jindor together as Royal Partners serving in the Holy Sisters' names.

With this contract, the partners accept each other's burdens and share each other's magic, growing stronger and more powerful with every shared Kiss." Master Gelloren tightened the ivy around our hands, and Zach's fingers twitched against mine.

My mother sat at the Council table, watching the small ceremony with narrowed eyes and pursed lips.

"*Illye holiend miyan oshantu.*" At the partners' spell words, the ivy burst into purple flames, singeing our hands and wrists.

Amid the purple flames, it felt like an invisible quill was etching each other's marks onto our skin. It burned and stung, but still, we didn't let go. If anything, we held on tighter as the clean spell lines were drawn.

A crown of holly and garlands of ivy curled magically around the back of Zach's hand and down his wrist. It ended at the base of his palm, like all the other Marks of Myriana. Zach's mark was a bracelet of branches ending on the back of my hand in elegant stag antlers.

Zach ripped his hand from mine as soon as the flames disappeared, his face flushed.

I wished he hadn't, though. Princes who had partners before knew that once the partnership ritual had been completed, the princess would be weakened by taking on the Sense of the prince, like a wraith was standing on her shoulders. The words "the partners accept each other's burdens" was quite literal when it came to princesses.

Perhaps if I hadn't suffered from blood loss earlier in the evening, I would've been able to stay standing. But the burden of Zach's Sense hit me full force, and I crumpled to the floor.

"Hey—" Zach dropped to one knee and grabbed my shoulders. "Ivy, are you okay?"

Embarrassed, I tried to pull away, but he held tight. "I'm fine—this is normal."

Zach's brow furrowed. "Normal? Why don't I feel it, too?"

I looked past Zach's worried face to Gelloren. The Master Mage just raised his eyebrows. "Never had a partner, indeed," he muttered.

"I took your Sense," I explained. "So you don't have to worry about it while fighting."

Zach squeezed my shoulders. "What?" he hissed through gritted teeth.

I was surprised at his intensity and placed my hand on his bent knee. "It's okay. That's what princesses do for their princes."

Zach glanced at my hand that bore his mark and quickly stood. "That's not what I signed up for," he said, glaring at the Council, then at Weldan, perhaps angry at his friend for not fully explaining the terms of the partnership bond.

The Commander looked out the window, avoiding Zach's angry gaze.

Zach walked to a candelabrum by the door and aimed a swift kick at it. Metal clashed to the ground, the candles rolling across the floor now void of flames. "No one told me giving her my mark meant she'd be *stealing* my Sense!" he shouted, then flung the door open and left.

Silence followed his exit. The Council members looked to Weldan, as if expecting an explanation. Weldan kept his gaze trained out the window.

I got to my feet, now steady, and nodded to Gelloren, an indication that we could proceed. Though I was more than a little surprised at Zach's outburst, I could also understand it—he'd just lost a natural part of himself without consent. But there was little I could do about it now that there was no way of giving his Sense back—until our partnership bond was severed through either ritual or death.

The finality of that thought struck me in a way I hadn't

anticipated. We were partners now. Zach was my sixth prince. While I was both excited at the prospect of having a powerful warrior as a partner, I was also completely terrified. What if I lost him, too? I didn't think I'd be able to handle that. And more, what if I returned to Myria a failure? With no prince, and the dragon hatched, coming to destroy us all.

It wouldn't matter then if I didn't return with Zach. We'd all be gone soon, anyway. Flecks in a sea of ashes.

Gelloren turned to my mother and shook out his sleeves, letting them fall over his hands. "Queen Dahlia, what news do you bring us?"

My mother looked away from me. "The eastern kingdom of Raed requires an investigation in their forests. They had a sighting of the Wicked Queen."

When had the Council of Freida given Queen Dahlia approval to seek out the Wicked Queen? It must have been more than a few months ago, since she had been to Raed, as well.

Then again, I shouldn't have been surprised. Dahlia's thoughts had always been consumed with the legend about the Mother of the Forces. She was obsessed with her for reasons my sisters and I never tried to understand. They were the only real conversations. *"Someday, child, I will find the soulless old crone. I will find her and tear her apart. I will see where her power comes from, and we will finally end this wretched war."*

Mother would often look down at me through curtains of her dark hair if I failed at a spell or combat move, and whisper words dripping with disdain. *"Useless child. Pray the dwarves don't steal* you *away. Though it might save me the trouble of worrying about whether you'll live or die."* Sometimes they were just musings she would voice out loud. *"I wonder if the Holy Queen ever felt responsible for giving birth to a daughter so weak she allowed herself to be turned into a walking demon."* But often they would make her sound somewhat unhinged.

It was hard to differentiate my childhood memories of her from my nightmares.

Seeing her there sitting among the Council, next to her father, talking about the Evil Queen, I remembered Brom's words the other day. Was I going after the dragon just to prove my worth to my mother?

The meeting ended, and I barely noticed. Gelloren stopped both Weldan and me from leaving and requested we meet with Zach to review the details of the journey to the egg. Weldan promised to drag Zach to the strategy room after lunch tomorrow, since we were supposed to leave the very next day after that.

Mother didn't look at me again. This time, I welcomed her dismissal. I had a new partner, more skilled than the others before him. It was time to shed the doubts she piled on me and finally prove her wrong.

The next morning, Brom told me she had left at dawn.

I opened the door wider, and Brom entered my room, shutting the door quietly behind him. I walked to the wall where my tapestry hung and sat on the floor, holding my knees.

Outside, a thunderstorm raged. Lightning flashed outside my window, and thunder shook the castle like an earthquake.

I didn't mind the sound of the rain. It had a calming effect. Part of me was relieved she was gone, but the larger part still ached, knowing how little she cared. How little she even wanted to see me.

Brom sat beside me, and I leaned my head on his skinny shoulder.

It had been our ritual as children. Every time my mother

would break me, Brom would be there, offering me his silent, supportive presence. Every time Brom would grow homesick for his parents who had died the day before he became my page, I would be there, offering my warm, gentle hand.

"I'm coming with you," he said.

I smiled against his shoulder. I didn't have to ask what he meant.

I knew, and he knew I knew.

CHAPTER TEN

PREPARATIONS

"**Y**our wounds have healed nicely from the battle, milady," Ulfia said as she brushed her fingers across the pink skin on my thigh where the gash had been. "As expected of your Kiss."

I only nodded—I couldn't bring myself to feel anything but nerves for our departure tomorrow. After I'd finished packing, I lingered in my room until Brom had persuaded—forced—me to visit Ulfia to check on my wounds just in case.

"I've got some salve for that bruise," Ulfia said, eyeing the purple mark on my cheek, courtesy of my mother.

"It's fine. Don't trouble yourself," I tried to protest as she glided to the cabinet.

Ulfia's salves worked wonders but always smelled abhorrent. Nine times out of ten, Kisses healed most wounds, but the magic wasn't always perfect. Sometimes they required a little help and a little time. Like the locking curse that had plagued me, they could take weeks, sometimes months, to fully disappear.

"Nonsense." She rummaged in the cabinet for a while, as I stared out the window and tried not to think about Kellian being in the Curse Ward next to me.

"Found it!"

"I'll take that," someone cut in.

At the new voice, I tore my gaze from the window.

Zach stood in the doorway, holding the jar of salve.

My nerves doubled at his sudden appearance, and I jerked down the hem of my dress to cover my exposed thigh.

"Oh, but—" Ulfia began, and Zach produced one of his disarming smiles.

"I'm her partner now. I've got to get used to doing things like this, right?"

While I glared at Zach, Ulfia pursed her lips and left the room, even though no one had asked her to.

"How'd you find me? Bribe another servant?"

Zach ignored me, unscrewing the lid on the jar then dipping his fingers into the mint, shassa root salve. "Tilt your head."

I didn't. I just stared at him. "I can put on my own salve."

"Difficult to do without a mirror. Move your hair." When I still didn't budge, he added, "Please."

Sighing, I brushed the wisps of curls away from my cheek. At the touch of his fingertips coated with the salve, I almost shivered—because the salve was cold.

This close, I could see my mark on his hand. His sleeve covered most of it, but the pattern of ivy peeked out on his wrist.

He rubbed the salve on more gently than I thought possible, given how tender the bruise was. I thought briefly about asking for a Kiss to heal it, but yesterday he refused to give me a Kiss to heal a bloody gash, so I doubted he'd give it up to heal a bruise.

"You should've told me."

"What?" I finally looked at his face. I was right: underneath the beard he had a faint scar on his jaw and another on his cheek. A thousand colors speckled his hazel eyes.

"About you taking the Sense," he clarified, carefully setting down the salve on the bedside table. "I would've never… It's not fair that you…"

"Is it my responsibility to tell you things you should already know?"

He made a *tch* sound with his tongue.

"It's what's done," I said. "You'll thank me later."

"I won't."

Zach placed both his hands on either side of me. With him so close I had to lean back to avoid the touch of his forehead. He lowered his gaze to my legs, and his hand hovered over my thigh, right where the gash had been. The air was tight between us, as his gaze went from my legs to focus on my face, lingering on the bruise that still stained my cheek.

"I'm worried." He lifted my hand that bore his mark and traced the stag's antlers with his thumb. "Without my Sense, I'm going to be fighting blind."

My heartbeat was racing, and I feared he could hear it, or feel my pulse in the wrist he held. "You have me for that now," I said softly.

"Goodness, are we intruding?"

I peered around Zach's shoulder to find Master Gelloren and Amias—of all people—standing there.

Zach quickly moved away, and in three strides he was out of the room. Amias glared at me, then at Zach retreating down the hall. His face reddened, and he, too, walked away.

Gelloren tilted his head, a small grin almost hidden underneath his whiskers. "Popular today, aren't you?"

"What did Amias want?" I asked.

"I believe he'd heard about your partnership with Zach. But perhaps he wanted to appeal to your…er…non-warrior side."

I folded my arms, scowling. "I'm pretty sure I don't have one."

Gelloren wisely didn't comment. He strode forward and

inspected the bruise Zach had finished rubbing salve on. "About your mother… She's harsh only because she cares."

No, a small voice spoke inside me, *she has never cared. Never about me.*

"You know, Ivy, we wouldn't have told you about the dragon if we didn't think you could beat it."

I stared at Master Gelloren's calm, familiar face. In many ways, he felt like more of a grandfather to me than King Helios ever did. "I know."

"And now with Zach… Well, let's just say that after seeing him fight, I feel much better letting you go."

I nodded.

Master Gelloren dug into the folds of his robe and pulled out a small silver compact, with intricate designs of flowers and ivy—appropriate. Touching it made my fingers tingle.

I popped it open and gasped. "A magic mirror."

Magic mirrors were rare and powerful. It took a lot of work and effort for a mage to create one, but once made they could be used for many things. They could show anything your heart wanted to see, act as a communication portal, show scenes and memories from the past, and sometimes witches and mages trapped spirits and magical creatures within the glass.

"It's so we don't lose contact," Master Gelloren said. "You can talk to me anytime."

"Thank you, Master." I closed the compact, the silver grooves of ivy pressing into my palm.

After lunch, I met with Weldan in one of the strategy rooms we used for war planning. It had everything we needed, namely, maps. Maps of all the roads throughout Myria, way up into the Galedral Forest, maps of the Fields of Galliore, and the islands in the Seas of Glyll, and the best routes to take to get to Raed, Freida, and Saevall.

Zach was late. This seemed to be a habit for him.

While hunched over a map of the Galedral Forest, I glared at the door. "Is he even coming?"

"He'll be here," Weldan assured me, passing me a sanded stone to hold down the other corner of the paper that kept curling over my fingers. "But listen, Ivy, there's something I've been meaning to talk to you about. Zach comes off as irresponsible and hardheaded and rather...tactless, but he's a good man."

I remembered a similar conversation from the first day we'd met, at breakfast. "So you've told me."

"Yes, well—"

The door banged open, and Zach strode in. "Couldn't find the bloody room," he said, before either Weldan or I had a chance to question him.

Zach studied the map I was looking at over my shoulder. "Why do we have to do this anyway? Don't you know the way, Ivy?"

"Not by heart," I said with a frown. "I'll need a map until we get to the mountains. Then I'll be close enough to use my Sense to guide us to the egg."

The map was suddenly ripped out from under my nose. "Are you saying that if I still had my Sense I'd be able to find this dragon myself?" Zach's voice was dangerously low.

Weldan sighed. "Zach—"

He threw up a hand to silence the Commander then glared at me, waiting for *my* answer.

Still remembering his reaction upon learning about his stolen Sense, I chose my words carefully. "You could've. But it would've taken you much longer. Now that I've absorbed yours, I'll be more sensitive to it, and we'll find the dragon's egg faster."

Zach tossed the map back onto the table, grumbling to himself.

"You would've known this if you'd ever had a partner," I said under my breath.

Zach walked over to the other side of the table and sat down in one of the large armchairs. "Never really needed one."

"You're so arrogant."

"Pot calling the kettle black, Highness."

I almost chucked a paperweight at his head. "At least I don't try to fight without a Kiss." Then a thought struck me—a thought so ludicrous it hadn't occurred to me before now. "Does this mean you've *never* been Kissed?"

Zach chuckled and kicked up his boots onto the table. "Oh, I didn't say that."

"Enough," Weldan snapped, pulling out another map of the surrounding villages. "Let's focus, shall we?"

I scowled at Zach, and he smirked right back.

Yes, Prince Weldan, tactless indeed.

Though it was late spring, the dark morning was cold enough to see our breath as we saddled our horses. The stables smelled of fresh hay and oranges.

Zach was already prepared. He had his steed—a deep chocolate horse I heard him call Vel—saddled, fed, and laden with packs from the cooks. Weldan stood with him, and they talked in low voices. Though I desperately wanted to hear what they were saying, I busied myself with checking my gear and prepping my own treasured horse, Lorena.

After rubbing down her dappled gray coat, I turned to Bromley. "All ready?"

"Yes, milady," Bromley said, dressed finely in the dark green cloak I'd given him for his fourteenth birthday.

We took our horses by the reins and led them up to the front of the stables, joining Zach and Weldan.

"Good morning, Princess Ivy," Weldan greeted warmly.

"Good morning, Commander Weldan. Thank you for seeing us off."

He gave a nod. "Of course. I wish you the best of luck, and please be careful."

"Thank you, Commander. We'll be careful."

It was then Zach noticed Bromley, and he grinned widely. "Ivy's page is joining as well, then? What's your name?"

"Bromley, sir."

"Let's see your weapon, Bromley."

While Zach went to inspect Bromley's crossbow, Weldan pulled me aside.

"Remember what I said. Zach is a good man. He'd never let anything happen to you. You have to believe that." The way Weldan focused on me, his light eyes seemed to have been carved from stone.

I frowned. "It's not really me I'm worried about. We have a mission—"

"Ivy." A hand grabbed my upper arm, tugging me back.

I looked up. "Amias? What are you doing here?"

His expression was as serious as I'd ever seen it. "I have to talk to you."

"I'm talking to the Commander."

"No, we're done," Weldan said gruffly, his gaze on Zach, who was astride his horse and staring at the three of us.

"Commander—" I started, but he quickly headed out of the stables, following Zach and Brom. Feeling as if I'd been abandoned, I turned back to Amias, trying to keep my annoyance at bay.

"What is it, Amias?"

"Don't go with him." His hand on my arm tightened.

I blinked. "I have to."

"You're Ivy Myriana—you can do whatever you like."

If only that were true. I raised my hand, showing Zach's mark etched onto my skin. "He's my partner."

"But he doesn't have to be. You can appeal to the Council. It could be *us* going off together on a"—his face twisted into a scowl—"secret mission."

So his uncle didn't tell him where Zach and I were going. Good.

"We've been through this." I peeled his fingers off my arm. "And you've stepped aside as I've gotten other partners before. Why are you so adamant now?"

"I don't trust him."

I sighed. "Of course you don't."

"I'm serious. There's something about him."

"Don't play the Romantica card again. It didn't help you last time. It won't help you this time, either. I have to go."

"Ivy—" Amias's fingers brushed my cheek.

"Let's get going," Zach's voice broke in. "It's almost dawn."

I looked to the entrance of the stables to see Zach astride his horse, expression blank.

"Good-bye, Amias," I said.

He dropped his hand as I turned and swung myself up onto Lorena.

We left Amias inside the stables as our horses *clip-clopped* over the stone, passing in front of the main steps to Myria Castle. A small crowd stood on the steps, watching us go. There were no trumpets or waving hands, just a solemn salute and farewell, as was customary on most mission departures.

Colette and Robin were standing with Minnow and Tulia, sporting brave smiles. I had told my younger sisters last night that I was leaving with Zach, but not about my true mission. I hadn't wanted them to worry. Nor did I tell them that our mother had been here and had not even wanted to see them.

We made our way through the gates onto the cobbled stone of the town's streets, with the sweet scent of willa blossom trees carried on the early morning breeze.

CHAPTER ELEVEN

THE FORBIDDEN TOPIC

We had reached the outer gates of the Crown City at first light and now, almost to the end of the first day, we'd already been through two of the larger villages of Myria.

"Your kingdom is quite vast, princess," Zach remarked as we passed yet another farm.

"Is Saevall much smaller?"

"In populace? About the same I guess. But in land we fall short. I have to hand it to you Myrians. You may need reinforcements, but it's no wonder, with all this land you protect."

"Well, we can't ask our subjects to uproot their homes or livelihoods."

"Your Legion has my respect," he said, lifting his face skyward to watch a hawk circle above us.

I raised an eyebrow. "We didn't have it before?"

"The idiot who interrupted my dinner left a bad taste in my mouth."

Remembering Amias's rude words, I said, "I *am* sorry about that. He shouldn't have acted the way he did and...said what he said."

Zach shrugged. "I'm used to that kind of talk."

"It doesn't irritate you?"

Zach patted his horse's neck. "Once upon a time it did. But not anymore. Besides, he seemed more jealous than anything."

That was true. "Amias has always wanted to be my partner. He craves the power that my Kiss brings him."

Zach leaned closer to me from astride his horse. He smelled of fresh hay and shassa root tea. "You sure that's the only thing he craves?"

My muscles locked up, remembering that night on the training grounds, with the torches and the change in Amias's breathing when he kissed me. "What are you saying?"

Zach smirked. "You two were awfully close in the stables, that's all."

Anger coursed through me, anger at Amias for making Zach think we'd been engaging in any Lustful actions, and anger at Zach for thinking that I'd be distracted on the morning of my most important mission yet. I tightened my grip on Lorena's reins and gave her a kick that sent her careening in front of Zach's horse.

"Whoa, Vel," Zach commanded, his horse sidestepping then coming to a halt. Brom stopped ahead of us.

"I don't appreciate your tone *or* your insinuation."

"And what insinuation is that?"

"That Amias seeks *a different* kind of partnership. That he and I are—" Heat crept up my neck. I cleared my throat. "*Sexual* partners."

Zach simply stared at me, perhaps watching the redness crawl up my neck onto my face. "My apologies. That's none of my business."

"No, it's not. And you'd be wrong anyway," I snapped. "I don't have time for petty desires."

"Petty? My dear princess, it's only human nature. But even if you two *were* only…'sexual partners,' why was he so possessive of you? The man was ready to run me through."

"How should I know? Men are territorial about women they…" I trailed off. Zach's intense gaze made the heat in my cheeks worsen.

"Men aren't territorial about every woman they bed. Only some," Zach pushed.

"I have *never* bedded Amias," I hissed, almost lifting myself off Lorena's back. "His jealousy doesn't have anything to do with Lust. I *told* you, he—"

"Wanted your magic, yes." Zach maneuvered his horse around Lorena. "Agree to disagree, I guess."

"Don't insult me." I gritted my teeth. "I know what you're implying. If Amias possesses Lustful intentions toward me—which I'm not saying he does—that's all it is. What you're saying Amias might feel for me is…"

Zach looked back at me, silently daring me to say the word hanging in the air.

So I did. "Blasphemous."

"That's really what you think?" There was something in the way his eyes held mine, unwavering, and his jaw so tight, that drew chills. It was accepting Amias's challenge all over again.

I didn't let the look intimidate me. This was the talk of a Romantica. I shouldn't have been surprised, considering what his mother had been, but *he* wasn't a Romantica. He'd joined the Legion, committed to our beliefs and our laws. He was a Royal.

"I *know* it."

Zach stared at me for a moment longer then grinned. "Yes, of course. Blasphemy. It was worth it to see your face, princess. You could fry an egg on those cheeks."

He'd been teasing me again. I wasn't sure if I was relieved or even angrier.

"Of course, if all that *were* true," he added, "then I feel sorry for Amias."

...

When we came to a forest, a miniature one by most Northern standards, we made camp. It was sundown, and Zach and I both agreed it was best not to travel at night. In fact, it was practically the only thing we'd agreed on all day.

Once our fire was strong and we had eaten for the evening, I offered to take the first watch, which Zach and Brom gratefully accepted. They fell asleep easily. As the fire came close to dying, I fed it more wood but struggled to keep my eyes open, so I moved closer to Zach to wake him.

I studied his sleeping face for a moment. He was very different from Kellian. His features were sharper, less rounded from youth, and gruffer, like he had seen and experienced things that aged him. Still, though, he *did* look a bit like a child. Then again, most people looked younger as they slept.

I placed my hand on his arm and was about to shake him, when his eyes snapped open. He moved in reflex, and before I could stop him, his hand was at my throat. He didn't squeeze, just held it. I swallowed and didn't dare move.

When his eyes focused on mine and recognition flitted across them, he retracted his hand. "Sorry."

"I didn't mean to startle you." I instinctively touched my throat, even though I knew there'd be no bruise.

Zach sat next to the fire and dropped another log into the flames. "Nothing you need to apologize for—it's just a trained reaction."

I moved to my spot next to Bromley and lay down in my bedroll, using my arm as a pillow. "Where *did* you do your training? I heard it wasn't at the Legion in Saevall."

"No, it wasn't."

I waited for him to continue, but he didn't. Fine. I'd figure it out later—one way or another. We'd be spending a lot of time traveling together. I turned away from the fire to face the darkness of the woods and closed my eyes.

"You Royals think you're the only fighters in the land. The only ones willing to lay down their lives," he said softly.

I wanted to reply that since civilians didn't have magic, they had no business throwing away their lives when we could protect them, but sleep pulled me under, and I had no strength left to fight it.

The second day of our journey was not that much different than our first. Without incident, we traveled along the path, heading north toward the great Wu-Hyll Mountains. Though the farther we ventured from the walls of Myria, the less likely our luck would last. With the Forces' creatures able to smell our magical Royal blood, it was a good thing we had kept our party so small—even with just one more Royal we would've already been attacked by now.

Worse yet, the darkening sky made it easier for monsters to venture out in the day.

The thought kept me on edge. Zach, however, seemed perfectly at ease. He would ride next to Bromley, giving him tips on riding, on swordplay, even on hunting. But his conversations with me didn't progress much. They always ended in some kind of disagreement. As the day wore on, eventually we reached a point where no more than one or two lines at a time were said between us. I wasn't sure which was worse, a heated conversation like we had yesterday, or none at all.

That night he offered to take the first watch, and Bromley

and I played a game to see who would take the second.

It was an old children's game Brom had taught me after he became my page. I'd never known many games growing up—even Gelloren had to show me how to play cards—so I cherished the few that Brom had brought into my life.

The game, called Bac-Chat, started with the two of us holding each other's hands as tightly as we could, then we would count to five. On five, we would release each other and make symbols with our hands that represented one of the five structures in the game: a blacksmith forge, an apothecary, a castle, a chapel, and a tavern. The person who finished their structure and grabbed the other's hands first, won.

I'd attempted a castle—index, pinky, and thumbs pressed together, with the knuckles of the two middle fingers touching—but Brom grabbed my fingertips after pulling off a brilliant blacksmith forge.

"Ha! Bac-Chat!" Brom said, squeezing my hands.

I groaned.

Zach watched us, and his pointed gaze felt almost too familiar to me now, but he stayed silent, content to observe. In the back of my mind, I couldn't help but wonder what he thought about Brom and me, since we did not have a normal Royal-servant relationship.

"Best two out of three?" I suggested.

"Not a chance. Give it up. You lost." Brom grinned, settling down in his bedroll.

I hated having second watch, as it meant two two-hour naps instead of a nice, long four-hour doze. But I fell asleep quickly, and before I knew it, a hand was on my arm, shaking me.

"Ivy," Zach's voice whispered in the darkness. "Ivy."

I opened one eye, and his face swam into view. "Time already?" I asked blearily.

"No, it's… You were talking in your sleep."

I sat up, my braid dropping over my shoulder. "What did I say?"

It was a bad habit I had, talking in my sleep, but I usually didn't do it unless I was under a lot of stress. Not that traveling to prevent a fearsome dragon from hatching and scorching the world wasn't stressful.

Zach looked away. "It…uh…I couldn't quite understand you. You were muttering."

I frowned at his discomfort. Once, Brom told me I had called for Mother. Another time I had called for Clover. It seemed as if I was always calling for someone.

It was then I remembered my dream. The goblin with the gash across its eye. Green lightning shaking Kellian's body like a puppet. My lips on cold ones…

"Was I calling for Kellian?" I asked, tossing my cloak aside that I had somehow wrapped myself in.

Zach ran a hand over his hair. "I believe so, yes. And… someone else named Telek."

Telek, too? Must've been because my mother had mentioned him. His death would never relinquish its hold on me. "They were both my partners."

"Yes, I'd heard, when your mother…" He trailed off, his gaze drifting to the fire. His voice was low, solemn. But he didn't need to pity me—they were only dreams, nightmares I didn't often remember.

He studied my mark on his hand, at the holly and ivy intertwined together and wrapping around him. "It must've been hard…to lose those partners. You must've cared for them a great deal."

I frowned. Based on our previous conversation with him suggesting Amias harbored *feelings* for me, I wondered if he was implying the same thing about the others.

"No more than I would a friend or comrade," I said.

He shook his head. "You talk to me as if I don't know the laws against Love."

"There are no laws."

"Aren't there?" He stood, the firelight at his back making his face shadowed and unreadable.

Perhaps to a Romantica it seemed that way. Especially when the Legion sometimes persecuted them for such primitive practices like courtship and marriage.

"There cannot be laws against something that doesn't exist," I replied evenly.

"Never mind, Ivy, go back to sleep."

I stood, too. "No, you're not going to brush it off this time. What are you trying to say—or *not* say?"

"Fine, *I'll* go to sleep."

"Zach—" I reached for his arm but tripped over something and pitched forward. Zach caught me, wrapping an arm around my waist, and held me up as I leaned forward over his arm. I glanced down at what had tripped me—his cloak. Not mine. I hadn't noticed it before, but he must have strewn it across me as an extra blanket when I slept.

"All right there?" His voice came from above, and I detangled myself from the cloak at my feet and turned in his arms. We froze for a few seconds before we hurriedly detached ourselves from each other. It was such an awkward moment that neither one of us said anything.

As the silence stretched on, a nervous giggle escaped my lips. Catching his eye, the snicker escalated into laughter. Soon both of us were smothering laughter so as not to wake Brom.

"By the wind wisps," I breathed, straightening and running a hand through my now wayward curls, "I've never felt so clumsy. Is this how you feel all the time?"

Zach grinned. "I knew you'd throw that whole suit of

armor mess in my face eventually. Would you believe me if I said I was pushed?"

Just as Weldan had said. I was beginning to pick out certain truths from all the mysteries of Zach, and he was definitely not the clumsy sort. "Absolutely not," I teased. "Especially knowing you have an extra-long cloak to trip over." I picked it up and held it out to him. "Thank you for…letting me borrow it. And for catching me."

Zach took his cloak and met my eyes. "You don't need to do that."

"Do what?"

"Thank me. That's what partners do, right?"

Something strange moved inside me. Almost like my magic was stirring, not rising up as it did, but moving downward, building an uncomfortable pressure.

"I'll take the watch now," I said. I wouldn't be able to sleep anyway.

CHAPTER TWELVE

THE SLIGHT PROBLEM

I awoke to Bromley shaking me, because there was no morning light to alert my mind that night had passed. The clouds above were dark and heavy, completely blocking the sun.

The fire had already been extinguished, and Zach was by the horses, adjusting their bridles and attaching our packs to their saddles. Our conversation last night hadn't necessarily brought us any closer. If anything, it had confused me even more. The way he was talking, it was as if he really was a Romantica, and not just the son of one. But he was a Royal of the Legion. He had joined the Saevallans willingly. He had come to Myria to help us fight.

Perhaps I was just paranoid.

He handed me a piece of bread and cheese folded into a napkin. "Can you eat your breakfast on the road? We should get going."

I stuck the parcel between my teeth and hauled myself up onto my horse. "How far do you think we can make it today? The next village?"

"If the weather permits, I hope so." Zach frowned. "We're moving too slowly for my taste," he muttered under his breath.

"What exactly do you mean by that?"

He avoided my gaze. "Nothing."

"Are you implying we're slowing you down?" I snapped.

"What's wrong with you? Why do you take everything as a personal attack?"

"I wouldn't have to if it didn't so obviously sound like one."

"For the love of—I wasn't *attacking* you. I just meant I'd be going a lot faster on my own."

"Uh, excuse me…" Brom tried to cut in.

"And there it is again," I said, ignoring Brom. "I'm so tired of your arrogance."

Zach swung up onto his horse. "*I'm* arrogant? Look in a magic mirror lately?"

I squeezed my breakfast so hard the bread crumbled. "There's also something called respect that we try to practice. Maybe you should learn some of that."

"And who will teach me? Certainly not you." Zach scoffed. "I thought that's what Royals were supposed to be good at— leading by example."

"Give it a rest!" Brom finally yelled, chucking a pinecone at Zach's back. "Both of you."

That shut us up. There's nothing worse than being called out by someone younger than you.

Zach and I exchanged uncomfortable glances, but we kept our conversations and attitudes civil well into the afternoon.

The landscape we traveled had changed in the past two days. Though the land was still mostly fields and plains, I could tell we were approaching another forest due to the small copses of trees. True to the morning, the sky remained overcast, and it put me on edge. That, and being two days away from the Crown City's walls. Deep in my chest I could feel the Forces' power stronger the farther we got from the castle.

Midday we came to a plowed field nearby a village. In the distance we heard the screeching of a crow. Lorena trotted forward nervously.

I felt it, too. Shadows stretched across my chest like a tight, uncomfortable corset. Resting my hand over my heart, I said, "Something's close."

Seeing my pale face, Zach cursed. "This really *is* like being blind."

I chose not to comment. Now was not the time to argue about me "stealing" his Sense.

Zach turned his horse around, its hooves agitating the dirt. He searched everywhere—the fields to the southwest, and the trees to the northeast.

It was Bromley who spotted it first. "The skies—"

His words were cut off by a shriek. What I'd first thought was a crow must have been the distant screech of a griffin. It appeared small in the sky, but it was diving toward us at an impossible speed, growing larger by the second. Possessing the powerful, lean body of a mountain cat and the head and wings of an eagle, the griffin was a deadly creature both on the ground and in the sky.

"Spread out!" Zach cried, brandishing his sword.

Bromley dashed off to the left and I to the right, grabbing my sword and raising it, ready to defend myself. As Brom's horse galloped on, he drew up his crossbow, aiming.

But the beast was still diving much too fast, headed straight for Zach. He urged his horse to go south, likely in an attempt to get under the griffin instead of ahead of it. The griffin pulled up at the last moment, screaming and raising its giant talons. With a great flap of its black wings, it dove for Zach again. Except the monster had lost nearly all of its momentum, making it easy for Zach to catch its front talons with his sword. Inches from Zach's face, the monstrous beak snapped and clicked, squawking with a deafening sound.

I turned to Brom. "If you see an opening, take it." Then I

kicked Lorena into a hard gallop, racing toward my partner and the monster. *Have to get closer.*

Vel whinnied and snorted as the griffin attacked his rider. Then Zach reared back and head-butted the griffin. It let out an earsplitting shriek of pain, shaking its beak and beating its wings as Zach tried to gain leverage over it.

The griffin was not as easy to kill as dwarves, trolls, and goblins. The beast had one very important advantage: wings. That was why four or five Royals were needed to take one down. They were strong, vicious, and could attack from above, leaving even a warrior as skillful as Zach always on the defensive.

Brom's arrow just barely missed its flank. Gaining ground, I unhooked my shield from Lorena's saddle as she galloped toward them, then I took aim and threw the shield. It whirled through the air like a disc, hitting the beast's wing, and knocking it off-balance. Zach seized the opening and went for its neck, but the griffin beat its wings and took to the sky again.

"Zach!" I reached for him, my hand outstretched and waiting. There was a simple Kiss I could bestow upon him that would render the griffin's wings useless for a few minutes, allowing us to attack on the ground.

Zach reached for my hand, bewildered, half his attention on the beast and the other half on me. When our horses drew close, my hand found his, and I pulled myself to him, the spell already forming in my mind, magic coursing through me, ready to be used.

Zach pulled back. "No, Ivy, don't."

"What—"

We both turned at the sound of the griffin's wings as it dove for Bromley. Another of Brom's arrows whizzed through the air. Zach let go of my hand, turned his horse, and headed for the griffin. Zach's hand that held mine seconds before produced three knives. Three—two—then one—the knives flew skyward to hit the griffin's furry flank. With another piercing cry, the beast rose into the clouds.

I watched, sword loose in my hand and my mind racing. *What in the Fields of Galliore is he thinking?*

Maybe...maybe he just hadn't been ready for it. Maybe he was determined to continue showing off to prove he never needed a partner. I kicked my heels, and Lorena took off after Zach, who had stopped by Brom and was dismounting.

I pulled up next to them and jumped down from Lorena as Zach handed Vel's reins to Brom. "Watch him," he said.

"What are you doing?" I asked him, my eyes on the griffin circling above.

Zach hefted his shield onto his arm. "Protect the horses with Brom. We don't want the griffin wounding one of them."

I grabbed his arm. "I don't mean the horses. There's a Kiss we can—"

Zach tore away and ran across the fields, his boots kicking up bits of grass and dirt.

I swore and handed Brom Lorena's reins. "This is insane." Then I grabbed Brom's crossbow.

The griffin rose higher then tipped downward, beak first, streaking toward Zach's lone figure like a meteorite about to hit the earth.

Zach stood his ground, shield up, preparing for impact.

I couldn't believe it. He was going to try withstanding a griffin's dive?

No. Cold hands, cold like Kellian's, grabbed my heart and squeezed. *We've only just started, and I'm going to lose him.*

The griffin was close now, talons extended. I couldn't watch another partner fall. Hoisting the crossbow at eye level, I took aim and shot the arrow into its wing. The griffin gave a shriek of agony. It dipped and flopped about, then steadied itself and flew higher and higher, up into the dark clouds, then northward, away from us.

As the griffin became a speck in the sky, Zach turned on me, fury darkening his eyes and drawing his brows together. He sheathed his sword and stomped over, yelling, "Why did you aim for the wing?"

He was angry for a good reason. When the wing of a griffin is hit, the monster retreats to heal, then comes back to terrorize villagers after a couple of days, deadlier than ever.

But I was angry, too. "Because we couldn't have beaten it anyway!"

"You don't know that!"

"I do." I tossed the crossbow on the ground. "Better to have it run off than kill us, all because of your stupid pride."

"Pride?" Zach halted. "You think I didn't use the Royal's Kiss because of my *pride*?"

"You wanted to prove you could beat the griffin on your own." The wind blew at my cloak and wisps of my hair. Zach's bangs swept off his forehead, revealing a faint white scar near his hairline.

"It has nothing to do with me wanting to prove anything," he said, jaw set and eyes locked on mine. "I will *never* Kiss you."

The words resounded inside my chest like the Myrial bells. He had refused my Kiss before—once, at the beginning of the fight with Amias, then the healing Kiss after the battle on the wall breach. But...but we were partners now. There was no reason for him to refuse me any longer.

The whole purpose of our partnership was to use our Kiss to defeat the dragon.

He had to know this. He had to understand this. I hadn't heard him right. It was the wind. "What...what did you say?"

"I will never use the Royal's Kiss, Ivy. You Royals have forgotten its true magic."

A physical shock ripped through me, and my legs nearly gave way.

He really was a Romantica.

A heretic.

And I was bound to him.

Despite everything else, the first thing I thought about was my mother. *Holy Sisters*, what would she say if she knew I had a heretic for a partner? *"As expected of your worthlessness."*

Bromley approached us, leading the other horses. He looked from me to Zach in confusion.

"Surely…*surely* you must be joking," I said in a hoarse whisper.

"*Troll's breath.*" Zach shook his head. "Yes, Ivy, I didn't Kiss you to defeat the griffin all because of a *joke*. I enjoy laughing in the face of death."

"You can't…you can't truly be a…"

"Don't give me that look. You knew very well what I was. You all did. I made no secret of my bloodline," he growled.

"Being born to one and choosing to follow their ways are two different things. Up until this moment, you led us all to believe you were a *Royal*. You came to Saevall's Legion. You told us you wanted to protect the Lands." My voice shook. How could we have been so naive to believe a Romantica would never try to disguise himself as a Royal?

"I *do* want to protect the Lands—battle the Forces." Zach crossed to his horse, yanking the reins away from Brom and hoisting himself onto Vel. He leaned down to look at me, his eyes narrowed. "They killed my mother. There's nothing I want more. But I'm not willing to give up my morals to—"

"*Morals?*" I cried, my voice shrill now. I felt Brom's hand on my shoulder, no doubt trying to calm me down, but I shook him off. "The Romantica cult is nothing but a group of fools with misguided beliefs and nonsensical ideas."

"They're not misguided!" Zach roared. "And so help me, princess, if you refer to Love as nonsense one more time—"

"You'll what?" I dared. "Now is not the time to believe in myths, *Prince* Zachariah. We are members of the Legion on a mission to defeat the darkest threat the world has faced in a century. *True Love's Kiss* is a story told by cult-believers—not Royals—because it's a bloody fairy tale!"

Zach pounded his fist onto the pommel of his saddle, causing his horse to toss his head. "I don't care what you believe, or what you think *I* believe, but I refuse to use a kiss as a weapon."

"It *is* a weapon! It's been used as one for almost five hundred years. It's how we defeat the dark creatures. It's a catalyst—the end of a spell!"

"Then you've been wrong for five hundred years." Zach turned his horse and started north, toward the village in the distance.

I grabbed the crossbow off the ground, mounted Lorena, and rode ahead, pulling up in front of him. "This partnership is useless if you refuse to Kiss me."

Zach laughed without humor. "What are you going to do? Turn around and ride two days back to find another partner? The Sable Dragon could be fully grown by the time you finally reach it."

"I never said I would get a new partner. I'm saying you're as useless without me as I am without you because you don't know how to sever our bond. As long as you still have my mark, I have your Sense. Good luck trying to find the dragon without it."

Zach's eyes narrowed. "I'll wander the whole mountain range if I have to."

"Now who's wasting time?" I retorted. "If you wanted so badly to go after that dragon by yourself, then why didn't you just leave without me? Why bother becoming my partner first?"

"Because I couldn't just let—" Zach's face suddenly tinged red. He turned his horse away. "Figured I'd last longer with you to help, especially after you *stole* my Sense, but now I'm willing to test my luck." Then he glanced back over his shoulder. "Face it, Ivy. Even without your Kiss, I'm still a stronger partner than any other prince you could choose. But if you'd rather have someone to Kiss, then I'll find this dragon alone. Sense or no Sense."

CHAPTER THIRTEEN

THE DECISION

Zachariah was no Royal. He was a liar and a fraud. He'd never had any intention of Kissing me from the start. Yet he had agreed to be my partner to go after the Sable Dragon. Everything was so clear now. Why he'd never had a partner. Why he'd never performed a Kiss with me.

Zach continued down the field, leaving Bromley and me behind. Brom looked at me with a question in his eyes: *what now?*

I didn't know.

A large part of me wanted to do the very thing Zach told me was impossible: return to Myria, find a new prince, and start over. But Master Gelloren had said we probably had no more than a month, and a week had already gone by since then. By the time I turned around, found a partner, and reached the egg, it could be too late. Even if I did contact Gelloren through the magic mirror and had him send Amias, or someone else, we would need a mage to perform the separation ritual between Zach and me, *and* the partnership ritual between a new prince and me, which would take yet more time. The *worst* thing, though, was Zach was right—there were none as good as him. So was my only option to continue on with Zach and hope he would eventually give in and Kiss me?

The closer we got to the Wu-Hyll Mountains, the more danger we were sure to face. I would have dismissed this only a couple of days ago out of sheer confidence in my abilities to protect myself. But the only reason I was alive was because Zach had saved me from the dwarf, and I still had the remnants of the bruise, courtesy of my mother, to remind me of my sore miscalculation. No, I had more than just a bruise. I had memories of my other partners, too. No matter what Gelloren said, no matter if they had the Mark of Myriana, I'd been their *partner*, sworn to watch their back, and I had their fate—their blood—on my hands.

I swallowed and rubbed my eyes.

Could I really trust our little party to defeat all the creatures of the Forces and walk away unscathed, without the aid of magic?

No, I couldn't. But it was either that or return home a failure.

Just like my mother predicted. She'd told me time and time again that I failed her. Failed at upholding Myriana's signature flawless white skin and luscious dark hair—with my freckles and ruddy curls, I couldn't be further from my grand ancestor. And I'd failed at bringing my partners home, alive and safe. She never let me forget it.

Zach rode farther away. Bromley cleared his throat.

I couldn't return home without the dragon's egg destroyed. I couldn't let my mother be right again. Not this time.

More than that, if there was even the slightest chance I had of protecting young recruits from seeing battles, I'd take it.

I squeezed my reins, the leather making a grinding sound in my palms. He was going to Kiss me, one way or another. I'd convince him. I would make him see that his beliefs were nothing but ridiculous fairy-tale ideals.

I cued Lorena into a fast trot after Zach. Bromley followed.

When we caught up, I brought my horse close to Zach's. He gave me a sideways glance but said nothing.

"We can reach the village by dusk," I said, nodding toward the distant houses and barns, my voice as gruff as possible to hide any emotion. I didn't want him to think his betrayal had wounded me. Even if it *had*, that wasn't the reason I felt my throat getting tighter. It was from a sudden rush of crushing guilt. Now that the battle was over and I could think clearly, I regretted my impulsive decision to shoot the griffin in the wing. Everyone knew wounding the wings was the easiest way to force a griffin to retreat, but it was also the surest way to guarantee the deaths of innocents two days later. Maybe Zach could've killed it without a Kiss. But I'd been too rattled. Too scared for him. Scared and with no faith in what seemed impossible.

Zach's shoulders relaxed slightly. "Looks like it."

"We'll be staying the night."

"I assumed so."

"Because we need to kill that griffin." I didn't want him to think I regretted my decision, because it'd make me feel vulnerable, like his anger at me was more justified than mine. Yet at the same time, I didn't want him to think I was selfish enough not to care about the villagers whose lives we just doomed. Whose lives *I* just doomed.

There was a short pause, then, "Finally, something we agree on."

The village was small, with houses, stables, and shops that spanned just a half-mile radius. When we approached the dusty road, paved by various slabs of rock worn by feet and time, two guards approached us. They wore rusty chain mail, and dark green shields were slung across their backs. Both middle-aged men. Both looking exhausted and defeated.

"So you saw the griffin, did you?"

It wasn't much of a greeting, but judging from the looks on their faces, I couldn't blame them. I nodded and swung off my horse. "Yes, I'm sorry to say we didn't kill it. But we will."

The guard, the one who had spoken, waved me off. "I know Royals on a mission when I see them. I'm sure you need to be on your way." He grimaced. "We can handle one griffin."

I shook my head as Zach and Brom dismounted. "We're here to help. It's my fault it flew off. I had a clumsy shot."

I caught Zach's eye. There was something different in his gaze, but I couldn't tell what it was.

The two guards bowed, their chain mail clinking. "Thank you, milady. My name is Lynel and this is Toreck."

The other guard, the younger one, bowed again and said, "We're very honored to receive Royals in our humble village."

I dipped my head. "My name is Ivy Myriana. This is my page, Bromley, and my partner, Prince Zachariah."

Zach stretched out his hand to Lynel and smiled. "Zach, if you don't mind."

Lynel shook it, looking a bit confused, probably because Royals never shook hands with civilians, then he turned to Toreck. "Why don't you show Bromley to the stables—get these horses fed and watered."

Toreck nodded and took Vel's reins from Zach. Bromley led Lorena and his horse, following Toreck toward a stable at the far end of the dusty road.

"We really are honored to have you both here," Lynel said with a tired smile. "Come, come, I'll make sure you have full plates and nice warm beds for the night."

As Lynel led us to one of the larger houses, Zach leaned over my shoulder, speaking quietly. "A clumsy shot, was it?"

I turned my head and noticed how close he was. I could see the flecks of both emerald and amber in his eyes. "Would you rather I tell him the truth—that you refused to use a Royal's Kiss and I had to drive it off?"

"That's up to you, but what they think of it won't change my mind."

"If I thought it would, I would've said it."

"You know, Ivy…" Zach's hand brushed mine, and I couldn't tell if it was on purpose or not. "I think you understand me more than you'd like to let on."

My ears grew hot. "You flatter yourself. It just means I'm no stranger to men dumber than a bridge troll."

Zach's laughter was so loud I couldn't help but smile with him, even when Lynel glanced back at us with a raised brow.

Because the village had no inn, Lynel brought us to his house. His ancestors had been the founders of the village, so his house was the biggest. It had two stories and a brick chimney, and the high roof was made of brucel wood. One of his partners, Patrice, showed us to two rooms they kept tidy and vacant for travelers, and told us she would have baths drawn and a warm meal ready.

"You really don't have to go to all the trouble," I insisted, standing in the doorway to my room as Patrice took up the tiny hallway, one of her little ones clinging to her apron and staring up at me in awe.

Patrice, with her round face and lovely blue eyes, shook her head and waved her hands. "I won't hear another word of it, princess. You are welcome guests. We are honored to host Royals in our home."

Desperation surged through my gut. I *would* protect these people from the griffin. *No matter what.*

"We're really grateful to you, ma'am," Zach said, coming up behind her.

Patrice smiled. "Dinner will be along shortly. I'll come and fetch you."

"I'll help prepare," I said, removing my cloak and rolling up my sleeves.

"That won't be necessary, princess," Patrice said hurriedly.

"Don't be silly. I don't mind." I started to follow her, when Zach caught my bare arm.

He brought his face close to my ear and muttered, "I'm going to take a look around the village and see if I can get some information about the griffin attacks. They might know where the nest is located."

"Good idea. We've got less than forty hours before the griffin's wing heals and it can attack, so the quicker we find its nest, the better," I said softly. Not to mention our own deadline to find the dragon. "But why are you whispering?"

"Just wanted to get a closer look at those freckles." He winked.

I ripped my arm from his grasp and turned on my heel, all but running after Patrice.

An hour and a half later, Patrice covered the stewpot for it to simmer and then banished me from the kitchen. I was about to check on Brom at the stables when small hands caught the edges of my tunic. Children had gathered around me. They were as quiet as kitten's paws—I hadn't even heard them enter the kitchen.

"Hello there," I said, kneeling to smile at each of them.

"Jordan, Colleen, Priscilla, leave Princess Ivy alone. She has things to do," Patrice chastised them.

"Oh, I don't mind. I adore children," I said with a laugh as the youngest tugged at my hair and pulled it from its wrap. "It must be good to have all these helpers. Do Lynel's other partners live here as well?" It was common for village founders to have quite a few partners to produce heirs to take their place later, so what Patrice said next surprised me.

"Oh, it's just me. These little ones are all mine." There was pride in her voice.

"That's…rare," I said, not wanting to offend her by how strange I found it. The toddler now had my braid and was beginning to unwind it with his tiny hands.

Patrice smiled. "It may seem odd to you, but we're quite far from the Crown City, and we live much simpler lives out here in the outskirts of Myria. Often your first partner is all you need. Plus, the more children, the more mouths to feed."

I couldn't argue with that.

"I have another baby sleeping upstairs, only a month old. My oldest daughter is watching over her," Patrice said proudly, stroking the hair of the smallest girl.

"Congratulations," I said.

"Thank you. He is quite the miracle."

I found the choice of words odd, but I didn't inquire further. After playing with the children for another half hour, I went to check on Brom. He'd yet to emerge from the stables.

The sun had just dipped below the horizon, and the last streaks of red, violet, and orange were barely visible over the rolling fields framed by the villagers' houses. Glad to see the clouds gone, at least for now, I took a moment to admire the colors before I headed past a few shops, to find the village stables.

People were wrapping up for the evening, putting their farming tools in their sheds, bringing in firewood for dinner, closing shops, and sweeping their storefronts. It was a gentle, quiet village, and once again I felt a stab of fear for them. *No. We'll find the griffin and kill it. We still have time. There's no need to panic.*

In the stables, Brom was shoveling straw into our horses' stalls.

Leaning against a wooden beam and bringing my hand to the nose of a pretty black mare, I said, "Can you believe him?"

Bromley stopped and just shrugged, then went back to pitching the straw.

"That's it? That's your whole response?" I said in disbelief. The horse nudged my palm, and I trailed my fingers over her soft snout.

He stopped and drew the pitchfork onto his shoulder. "I agree it's not ideal—"

"Ideal?" I scoffed. "Try a catastrophe. Brom, he tricked us. He agreed to be my partner, knowing what he was expected to do, then backed out."

Brom gave me a sheepish look. "Technically he didn't back out. He's still *here*. He's still going after the dragon."

"To what avail? We'll die before we even get there if we don't use the power of the Kiss. The entire point of our partnership is to use the magic of the Royals. One can't work without the other—you know this."

It was Kellian being on his own all over again. It was me going into battle without a partner, with the dwarf standing over me about to drive his sword through...

Solo acts didn't work. I had enough proof.

"I know, but what can we do? Go back?"

I patted the mare's neck. She blinked her large brown eyes and snorted. "No, we'll continue on. We have to. But I'm not giving up. He *will* Kiss me. And we'll share the most powerful Kiss the Forces have ever seen."

CHAPTER FOURTEEN

THE GRIFFIN'S NEST

The stew smelled heavenly. Combined with cinnamon-buttered bread, it made the perfect meal after three days of dried, salted meat and cheese. Once we had eaten, Patrice and Lynel's children cleared away the table and left us to share a drink.

Zach had his mug filled with ale but had yet to touch a drop.

"So when did the griffin attacks start?" he asked, tearing off another chunk of cinnamon bread.

A heavy silence fell over the table, and Zach and I exchanged worried glances. Patrice reached over and grabbed her partner's hand. Lynel placed his other hand on top of hers. "About a month ago. It showed up at the barn at the edge of the village, out of nowhere. It killed my brother and nephews. Patrice was the only survivor."

The devastation and fear on Patrice's face made it feel like the griffin had its talons in my heart, piercing it and making it bleed.

"I still can't believe it just left me alone. I think the Holy Queen must've been watching over me. She wanted our baby son to be born." Patrice laid a hand on her stomach.

Her previous words made sense now. That's why she'd

called her baby a miracle. Because they had both survived the griffin's wrath.

Lynel took another swig of ale before answering. "After that attack, it scorched our western crops and chased all the game from the forest. We think it made its nest in there, though to be honest, we haven't investigated." He looked down at the table in guilt.

It was nothing to be ashamed of—the griffin was a powerful dark creature, as dangerous as it was bloodthirsty. Civilians stood no chance against their large claws and beaks.

Zach nodded to me, subtly, confirming what he'd told me just before dinner. After asking around, the villagers had all said something similar—that the griffin always went off in the direction of the northeastern forest. We'd also discussed the merits of going to the nest directly, hopefully to catch the bird in the midst of healing, rather than waiting for it to attack the village, so innocent lives wouldn't be lost.

"We'll leave at first light for the forest," I said, leaning over to touch Lynel's shoulder.

Lynel smiled. "Thank you, milady. Your kindness knows no bounds."

I smiled back and caught Zach's eyes across the table, but he quickly looked away.

In my room, I snuggled into the cool comfort of clean sheets. After sleeping under cloaks in the forest, I was more than appreciative of the bed. Still, sleep didn't come easily. Lying in an unfamiliar room, alone, was harder than on the leafy forest floor under a sea of stars next to Brom.

Tonight, I was more uncomfortable than usual. Zach and Brom were in the next room. I knew that and yet, I couldn't escape the echo of the griffin's screech. It had been foolish of me to shoot that arrow. I'd been pushing down the guilt of it for the whole evening, but now I let it settle over me like a second quilt. Not only had I put lives in danger, but also we would waste a whole day tracking down the nest and slaying the creature. I had panicked—terrified we couldn't defeat it without my magic. Was I being too cocky, thinking that way?

No. For once, I'm not the cocky one.

It was Zach. Thinking he could slay the beast without my help. I didn't care what the stories said—no man had the strength or skill to take down a troll's lair by himself. With that griffin streaking toward him like a comet, he would've been driven into the ground.

And yet, I remembered how he fought at the breach in the wall. How his sword dripped with blood.

Maybe I should've trusted him to kill the griffin. He certainly was capable—I'd wanted him as my partner for that reason. But there was a difference in trusting someone and possessing blind faith. I rubbed my cheek against the pillow and felt the ache of the bruise my mother left me, and along with it, the terror I'd felt with the dwarf's magic keeping me in place, waiting for the taste of his blade. How foolish I'd been.

That wasn't going to happen again. I couldn't let myself make the same mistakes with Zach as I had with my other partners. I'd watch his back, and he'd watch mine, linked with the power of our Kiss.

I rubbed the heels of my hands against my eyes. As I rolled over and faced the door, I noticed amber light emanating from inside my pack. Slipping out of bed and padding across the wooden floor, I crouched and opened the bag. The light turned to a soft glow as my fingers closed around the enchanted compact mirror. I clicked the latch, and it popped open. Blinking against the onslaught of amber light, I heard my name.

"Ivy?" The voice of the Master Mage was soft and brought comfort.

My eyes now accustomed to the light, I could see Gelloren's

face within the glass. "I'm here."

He smiled, his beard twitching. "How has your journey been? Where are you?"

"A village in between forests. They've given us lodging and food for the night."

Gelloren nodded. "How many days' ride from the mountains?"

"I can't be certain. Five? Maybe more."

"How is your new partner? Pulling his weight, I'm sure?"

My fingers tightened around the compact, and the engraved ivy of the mirror pressed so hard into my palms I knew it would leave the pattern on my skin. Now was the time to tell him. Tell him that Zach refused to Kiss me. That this mission was as hopeless as it was impossible. But what then? As Zach had reminded me, we had already come so far, and it would be a waste of time to turn back now. Even if I did, who else was as skilled as Zachariah?

"Yes, Master Gelloren, he's quite strong."

"Oh, so you've had a need for the Kiss?"

I cursed myself for walking into that. I tried to keep my face neutral. "We had a run-in with a griffin, that's all."

"How did your magic affect him?" The eagerness and curiosity in the mage's voice was clear.

I fiddled with the hem of my undershirt. "The Kiss wasn't necessary. We managed to drive it off with arrows. But Master, it's late. I should…"

"Yes, yes, get some sleep. I'll contact you again in two nights. I hope you will have made more progress, Ivy. The signs grow ever more alarming. We had yet another storm—the ice froze an entire field of crops—and another flock of sparrow harpies was spotted just beyond the wall. The fate of Myria and the other kingdoms rests in your and Zach's hands."

...

A soft knocking on my door woke me. Stumbling out of bed, I cast a quick glance at the window. It was still dark outside, but the pale hint of dawn nudged the horizon. I groaned, massaging my temples. *Not good, Ivy.* How unlike me to sleep late on a mission.

Thinking it was Brom, I pulled the door open without throwing on a cloak. Zach stood in the doorway, dressed and ready, his hair damp.

"Good morning," he said with a smile, glancing at my long undershirt and bare legs.

I resisted the urge to cover myself. It was my own fault for answering the door indecently dressed. "I'm coming," I said sharply.

"No rush. Brom just went to fetch the horses."

I pulled the door closer, half shutting him out. "Call him Bromley. You don't know him well enough to act so familiar."

Zach gave me another one of his amused smiles. "I disagree. We shared a room. We're plenty familiar."

I pressed my lips together to keep from smiling.

"Besides, he doesn't mind."

"He's just being polite."

"Don't worry, princess, I'm sure he still loves you more."

"I'm getting dressed now," I declared, and shut the door in his face.

"Too bad," I heard him say through the wood.

I almost flung the door open and whacked him on the back of his head with my shield, but decided I needed him conscious. So instead, I pulled on my tunic and pants, then laced up my vest and boots. After fixing my hair into a braided bun, I shouldered my pack and made my way through the quiet house and out into the chilly morning.

Brom had our horses waiting. Zach was already astride and checking the knives fitted into the saddle. Lynel and his family were outside, along with Toreck and two other men. I took Patrice's hands and thanked her, but she insisted on a tight hug. Patrice's arms were warm, and she smelled like freshly baked bread and earthy herbs—I realized then that this must be what being hugged by a mother was like. Safe and comforting. I reveled in it for a few precious moments.

Then Patrice drew back, took a pack of food from one of her children, and handed it to me. "It's not much, but…"

"It's more than enough," I said, taking the bundle and tucking it into my saddlebag. Then I turned to Lynel, Toreck, and the two other men.

Before I could say anything, Toreck said, "Don't worry. We'll be accompanying you only as far as the edge of the wood. Your partner made it clear he doesn't want us along for the fight."

Zach avoided my eyes as he continued to check his daggers.

Toreck's jaw was tight and his brow furrowed. I didn't want any civilians with us, either. If things went badly, their blood would be on our hands. But I wondered what Zach had said to offend him so much.

"We're very grateful for your bravery," I said with a nod to the other men as well, "but we want all of you to return to your children."

Toreck uncrossed his arms and hooked his thumbs in his belt. "Yes, well, best be off."

As the men led the way on their horses, I rode Lorena next to Zach. "Just what did you say to them?"

Zach scowled. "Nothing that wasn't true."

"Oh, of course. You insulted them by saying they'd get in the way."

His silence was all I needed.

"*Sacred Sisters*, you could've been a little more gracious. Was it as offensive as the way you acted with me yesterday?" I rubbed my forehead and sighed. "What is it with you and not accepting help?"

Zach twisted in his saddle and raised his eyebrows. "You're one to talk, princess. Who was the one who went onto the battlefield *by herself* just a few days ago?"

"That's not the same. Not accepting help when it is given and not having help *offered* is completely different." I poked him hard in the arm. "Besides, I remember asking you to be my partner that morning, and you refused."

That shut him up. All the way to the forest, the two of us brooded.

When we reached the tree line, we dismounted, and Lynel and his friends promised they'd watch the horses. We thanked them, then Bromley, Zach, and I started into the forest. The path was small and clear, and as the hour passed, the trees got thicker. The sun rose, but instead of getting lighter, it got darker, and there were no sounds of stirring animals. We were nearing the heart of the forest.

Zach cursed and muttered something under his breath, something that sounded like, "Nothing—there's nothing. Why do princes sign up for this willingly?"

For a moment I thought his comment was in reference to the ever-growing darkness, but then I realized he meant his Sense. He wouldn't be able to feel anything of the griffin or its nest.

But I could feel it. I could feel it twofold.

The sickness that only the proximity of the Dark Forces could bring made my knees weak and my head light, but my limbs were heavy as if shadows were crawling into my blood and weighing it down. Usually I hid the feeling fairly well, but I must have looked sicker than I imagined, because Zach gripped my upper arm.

His cheek was next to my ear, and his hand on my arm seemed bigger than I had imagined it would be. Not that I had done much imagining.

"Getting close?"

Instead of nodding, because the action would make my head ache, I said, "Yes."

"Why didn't you feel this bad when the griffin came up on us yesterday? Is it because of *my* Sense?" There was a twinge of anger in his voice—he really wasn't going to let that go.

"Part of it. But the nest of a monster is the source of the Darkness that gathered there to create it. It's stronger and heavier than the beast itself. It's the origin of the curse that it was born from." My brows pulled together in confusion as I regarded him. "Why don't you know? Every Royal knows that."

Zach shrugged as he pulled a branch away for me, his other hand still grasping my arm. "I didn't spend my time in a classroom, learning like everyone else. Every waking second I was in battle training. You think I came out of the womb swinging a sword? I practiced, Ivy."

"Never said you didn't." I stepped over a fallen branch to avoid the crunch of breaking wood.

Zach smiled. "Don't think I'm a natural, then?"

"Never said that, either."

"Then what *do* you think?"

"I think you have to be a born natural and have practiced day in and day out to be able to defeat my magic."

"You think you're that powerful, do you?"

"You would be, too, if you—"

Zach squeezed my arm and came to a halt, forcing me to stop. "Your face just got about five times paler. We're almost there."

He was right. It felt awful, like I needed to cough up whatever dark shadow had passed over my lungs.

Brom unhooked his crossbow from his back, and I followed his example, tugging on my wrist shield before drawing my sword.

Zach drew his sword, scanning the forest canopy. "What are you feeling? Where is it?"

I took a soft but labored breath and raised my arm to the north. "That way… Higher… More shadows."

"About how long would you say we have before it knows we're here?"

"I'm sure it already knows we're close." I gestured to Zach and then to myself. "It can smell our Royal blood. Neither of us has an advantage."

Zach smirked. "Good. I like a level playing field." He glanced back at Brom. "How good are you at climbing trees?"

Brom squared his shoulders. "I can manage."

I raised an eyebrow at my page, but he just nodded. There weren't a lot of trees on the castle grounds to practice climbing, but if Brom said he could do it, I trusted him.

"Move from tree to tree, shooting arrows. I want to see if we can get some clue to where the griffin could be," Zach said, frowning up at the dense canopy. The foliage was so thick only pricks of sunshine sparkled like tiny stars. "Ivy and I will keep moving on the ground, maybe draw it out somehow. We sure as hell won't be able to attack it *in* its nest."

Without another word, already accepting Zach's leadership, Brom started up the nearest tree. I watched wearily until he was halfway up before I turned to Zach. Just as he started to move northward, I grabbed his arm.

"Zach, we should Ki—"

"I *said* no. I've got a plan."

I struggled not to raise my voice. To keep it calm, negotiable.

"You're taking unnecessary risks. We could kill this griffin easily, and you know it. This is foolishness."

Obviously appealing to his logical side hadn't worked. Maybe I needed to try a different tactic. Maybe appeal to a *different* side of him. A side where thoughts had nothing to do with it because it was all about contact.

I slid my hand up his arm, onto his shoulder, and leaned in to him.

He stiffened under my touch.

"I don't want to fail before we destroy the egg. There're too many people depending on this mission. On *us.*" At the last word, I pulled closer, my lips brushing his ear. If he turned his head even slightly our mouths would meet.

He jerked away, but not before I felt a shiver run through him.

Son of a witch.

"Zach, please. I need you to stay with me. I'm too—" The word *weak* caught in my throat. It was something I wasn't used to admitting.

"Just stay back." His voice was low, dangerous, and almost as dark as the creature we were about to face.

Then he disappeared into the dense growth.

I stood there for a moment then hurried after him, my voice louder than it should have been. "Zach—at least let me help. We can—"

Pain ripped through my abdomen, forcing me to stumble and catch myself.

I coughed and sucked in a breath. The scent of the forest was gone, replaced with the smell of death and decay. Above, there was a *boom* like muffled thunder of a distant storm. It held power and heavy, concentrated energy.

I looked up and there it was. The nest was a thick mass of swirling, smoky darkness. Rotting black branches and vines curled together to form a misshapen ball.

There was a shuffling above. Rustling of dried leaves, snapping of rotting bark, flapping of feathers. At that moment, Brom released an arrow. It sliced through tangles of thick foliage and lodged itself into the nest.

The griffin sprang from the nest in a swirl of inky smoke and copper feathers. Blackened branches fell to the forest floor as the beast dive-bombed, rocketing toward me like a shooting star across the leaf-strewn sky. It seemed bigger today, with glistening black-and-copper wings and fur, glowing red eyes, and a bronze beak open wide, shrieking its awful cry.

I barely had time to drop my sword and raise my shield with both arms before the griffin's talons dug deep into my shield. Wood splinters, feathers, and leaves swirled in a mini-hurricane around me. My arm was sure to be ripped to shreds if the beak didn't pierce my neck first. All I could do was defensive maneuvers, ducking and dodging away from the beak and daggerlike talons.

Perhaps if the griffin were more like a lion and less like a squawking bird I'd have more of a chance in close quarters. But there was little I could do with its wings beating on either side and its claws tearing at me. And the smell... Its stench was that of a rotting corpse.

The griffin screeched and gave one final squeeze of its talons, breaking my shield. Wood went everywhere, and I struggled to breathe through the panic and darkness in my lungs. I'd been through dozens of nests before, felt the Sense weigh heavily on me, but this time was different—I was alone with no sign of my partner. I didn't even have the strength or reflexes to launch a counterattack. I could only throw myself backward, against the trunk of a dead oak.

The griffin let loose another squawk and dove, its beak going straight for my chest, and I had no energy to stop it.

At the last possible moment, Zach emerged from the foliage, blocking the griffin's beak with his sword. Bronze and metal clashed, the sound ringing through the forest.

In his haste to get to me, Zach had slid with one knee on the ground and was now struggling under the griffin at an awkward angle. The monster slashed at Zach with its talons and delivered fresh, deep scratches down his arm. Zach let out a roar as the bird jerked its head back, and knocked the sword out of his grip.

The sword skidded over dead leaves. Recovering, I unsheathed a dagger from my thigh and leaped forward, driving it deep into one of the griffin's red eyes. It screamed in rage and reared up on its hind legs. Too late, I realized its talons were coming right down on my throat.

Before it could tear into my neck, Zach pushed off the ground in a whirl of leaves and feathers and shoved me back into the tree, hard. The talons...the talons found his chest instead.

Bronze claws tore into Zach's chest, and I screamed.

"*NO!*"

I sprang upward and drove the dagger into the breast of the bird, catching Zach as he began to fall back. It wouldn't kill the griffin, but maybe it would buy me a moment or two.

My arms were already slick with blood pouring from Zach's wounds, and every inch of me screamed in pain and deep, overwhelming despair. His blood was too warm. Too full of life. This couldn't be happening. Not another one.

Only this time, it wasn't because of me. It was *for* me.

His body slumped against mine, and his head fell back over my arm, hazel eyes growing darker by the second.

"No, no, no," I whispered as I cradled his face, my hand trembling.

Lips coated in blood, Zach tried to open his mouth but

couldn't do so more than a slit. His eyes focused on mine for only a moment before they fluttered closed.

I couldn't breathe—couldn't think. "*Zach, Zach, Zach.*"

As my body moved on its own, bringing him slowly to my lap, the griffin and its nest burst into orbs of golden light. Like a star had exploded in the forest, illuminating the dark crevices and chasing out the shadows.

I yelled and buried my face into Zach's shoulder at the sudden brilliance.

When I raised my head, the gold glow from the griffin's body had descended on Zach's mangled chest and covered it like a liquid gold salve. It shone with the blinding radiance of the sun. I shielded my eyes against the onslaught of light and struggled to blink against the miniature supernova.

Zach shuddered and rolled to the side, on his hands and knees, breathing hard as the golden orbs drifted up into the trees.

I scrambled forward, pressing my hand on his bare chest.

His chest that was completely healed.

He stared at me, pale and gasping for breath—but alive.

Impossibly alive.

What in the name of the Royal Sisters had just happened?

CHAPTER FIFTEEN

BIRTH OF A HERETIC

A s the gold light dissolved, revealing the normal shadows of a thick forest, we stared at each other in shock. I brought a hand to his face, felt his breath on my palm and the stubble on his jaw, then let my fingers stroke his neck, noting his strong, pounding pulse.

Alive. He was completely alive. Relieved knowing this one truth, I took a shuddering breath then grabbed his tattered shirt in my fists. "What *was* that? Has that ever happened to you before?"

My movement made Zach fall back on his elbows, bringing me down with him. "No—it's never—no!"

Halfway on top of him, a million things ran through my mind. It had been magic—but caused by what? There was no mage. No Kiss. I'd never even *thought* a spell.

"You've never seen it before? Merciful Queen, what did you *do*?"

Zach's shocked face suddenly hardened. He took my shoulders and moved me off him. "I saved your life."

"Yes, but—"

"Don't I deserve a thank-you?" He stood, brushing dead leaves off his pants.

"Hey!" I leaped to my feet. "I wouldn't have needed saving if you hadn't *left* me, or at the very least, included me in your plan, if you even had one. I'm your *partner*, you can't—"

Just then, Brom crashed through the branches and bent over, resting his hands on his knees, gasping. "There—you—are—gold—explosion."

I grabbed Brom's shoulder. "That was the griffin." Then I launched into an explanation.

With every word Brom's eyes grew wider, but as soon as I was done, Zach nudged both of us forward. "C'mon, plenty of time to discuss this later. Let's get out of this bloody forest."

Brom shot me a look, and I merely shook my head. If Zach cared so little about the mysterious gold magic, I'd talk to Bromley about it later.

Escaping the shadows of the forest and feeling the sun and wind on my clammy skin felt good. When we retrieved the horses from Lynel and his comrades, the men immediately began asking questions about the mysterious gold light. Apparently it had been so bright, so powerful, that they'd seen it even at the edge of the woods. Instead of admitting we had no idea what had caused it, I ended up telling them it was a rare form of magic that destroyed the griffin, which wasn't a *lie*.

The men all bowed, overjoyed, and kissed my hands in gratitude. Zach just nodded and shook their hands.

Once they were gone, Zach pulled a spare tunic from his bags, reminding me that I should change my bloodied shirt as well. I grabbed a clean one out of my pack and stepped behind Lorena to change. As I shed the ruined tunic, I called to Zach, "Are you really all right? The talons…they went deep."

"See for yourself."

Peeking over my horse, I watched Zach lift the shredded shirt above his head, revealing his bare chest and defined abs.

It felt like my whole face went up in flames. Luckily

his shirt was covering his face, so he didn't see how badly I blushed. Beyond his muscled torso, I couldn't help but notice the remnants of dried blood on his chest that hadn't come off when the magic—whatever it was—healed him. I remembered him standing, intercepting the talons that had been meant for me...

Forgetting I was half dressed, in only a thin chemise, I crossed to him, clutching the clean tunic to my chest as my other hand traced the dried blood on his bare chest. While I'd had princes save me before, they'd always worn my magic, a protective shell. None had ever sacrificed their *life* for me.

The very idea of it was overwhelming. There were many scars under the dried blood. Scars that could've been so easily prevented by Kisses. Yet he chose to endure the long and painful process of natural healing. Why? For what? His belief in something that didn't exist?

Zach removed his shirt entirely.

I glanced up at him. He was staring at my bare shoulders, then he dropped his gaze to my hand on his chest, the hand that bore his mark.

Realizing how inappropriate this was, I swallowed and started to withdraw my hand.

He caught my fingers and wrapped them in his hand. "Stop."

Now, even my ears were hot. "Stop what?"

"Thinking what you're thinking."

"You don't know what I'm thinking."

"Don't I? I made my choice, and I don't regret it."

My gaze shot upward. "Yes, because by some miracle you're still alive."

"Then let us be thankful for the miracle."

"What you did was stupid and reckless," I muttered, squeezing the hand that wrapped around my own. "But...thank you. For saving my life."

Zach shook his head with a sad smile. "Don't worry, it won't happen again."

"What won't?" I asked. "Saving my life?"

"No." The muscles in his jaw tightened, and his hand gripped a little tighter. "Putting you in a position where I had to do that in the first place."

I lowered my gaze to his collarbone, finding yet another scar. It was long—nearly six inches. "And what position was that?"

"You. Alone. I won't do that again."

A foreign feeling stretched from my stomach into my limbs. It was like a hundred wind wisps were trapped inside me, fluttering and flying about, riding the currents of my bloodstream.

Still holding my hand to his chest, he traced a darkening bruise on my wrist where my shield had broken. "It's not that I think you're weak. You're the strongest princess I've ever met. But I'm not used to anyone suffering the consequences of my decisions. I've…always fought alone."

How ironic that I never had. Except for just a few days ago at the breach in the wall. Still, considering my past, I wasn't the best person to teach him about partnership.

"Um, I hate to interrupt," Brom said, having finished attaching his crossbow to his saddlebags, "but shouldn't we get moving?"

I ripped my fingers out of Zach's hand and retreated behind Lorena. Before I finished dressing, I threw him a rag. "Wipe off the blood. You don't want another ruined tunic."

"Gladly," Zach said, rubbing at his chest. He pulled a new shirt over his head, then vaulted onto his horse and started Vel off at a steady canter.

Brom hung back with me as we mounted and urged our horses into a trot.

He glanced at me. "You know…"

"Don't."

"I've never seen you go that red. And men have been bare-chested in front of you before."

I grimaced. "He surprised me. That's all."

Bromley smiled but didn't say anything else.

He was right not to push, because those thoughts were dangerous. If I admitted to myself I found Zach attractive and had enjoyed the feel of his arms while in the forest, it was admitting that I felt…Lust.

That kind of distraction was inexcusable for a mission as important as this one. *Maybe* if we didn't have a Sable Dragon to destroy, and *maybe* if Zach wasn't a Romantica who believed feelings of Lust were only a precursor to *Love*, then…

I shook my head.

It was possible I might've tasted the feeling of Lust when Amias had kissed me that night…but the feeling of losing grip, of succumbing to anything, had terrified me.

I certainly wasn't going to allow myself to feel anything such as that for Zach.

Amias was always so rough, holding me in a way that felt demanding and consuming, while Zach… I could almost feel him tracing the bruise on my wrist from moments before, and again the one on my cheek left by my mother. It had been tender and warm…two things that were even more dangerous.

We rode hard all day in an attempt to make up for lost time. It was also a good excuse to avoid Zach and the tension that still sizzled between us.

At dusk, the terrain had changed from rolling hills to thick trees spaced widely apart over flat land. We dismounted to give

our horses rest and kept walking, hoping to reach the outskirts
of the next forest before we stopped for the night.

As we entered the wood, with its wide, well-traveled
paths and large old trees, I marveled at the fading sun shining
through the mangled branches. It reminded me of the gold
specks that were the final remnants of the griffin.

Brom and I had discussed ideas of what it could have been,
but none seemed plausible.

It perplexed me. Yet it was more than that... It disturbed
me. For one, I had never seen a monster do that, not in all the
many creatures I'd faced and battles I'd fought. They had all
either dissolved into black smoke as the ground burned at
their feet, or they crumbled like dry clay. It couldn't be the
type of monster, either, because I'd helped take down plenty
of griffins, and none of them had ever done that.

Entrapped in my thoughts, I didn't notice my pace slow.
Soon I was walking right next to Zach, with Bromley some
distance ahead.

I wanted to avoid an awkward silence while walking next
to each other, but I felt suddenly speeding up would be too
obvious.

It was also the easy way out. If I wanted to defeat this
dragon with his help, with our Kiss, I needed us to be *real*
partners.

I cleared my throat. "So are we going to talk about what
happened in the forest?"

"I told you: I don't know what happened with the gold—"

"Not that. Well, yes that, but also...it was a close call back
there. You could've died. You almost *did*. If you would've—"

"I'm *not* going to Kiss you, Ivy," Zach snapped.

"Sacred Sisters," I breathed through my teeth. "Yes, you've
made that abundantly clear, thank you. I was talking about
you just running off, leaving me."

"I told you, it won't happen again. But besides that…I had a plan."

"Which you should've included me in."

"I was going to, but you wouldn't shut up about the Kiss."

"I just wanted you to understand we were taking an unnecessary risk."

Zach stiffened, his fingers tensing on his horse's bridle. "Oh, you mean by trying to manipulate me? Actually, I think the word is *seduce* me into Kissing you."

My pulse quickened, in either anger or embarrassment, I wasn't sure, but I couldn't let it drop. "I did what I thought would save us—and it would have, by the way."

Zach let out a dry laugh and shook his head. "How typical of you Royals. You even use *Lust* as a weapon. How do you sleep at night, knowing you toy with people's emotions?"

"And how typical of you Romantica. Running when people need you," I spat. "Your speed is legendary—could it be because you spent most of your life running?"

The words had been out of my mouth for less than a second before I realized I had said something terribly wrong. Zach suddenly halted. There was a rigidness in every muscle of his body, and his eyes were wide with horror. At least, I thought that's what it was, but the emotion was gone too quickly to be sure, replaced instead with a look I'd seen on my own reflection many times: regret.

I reached for him, wanting to correct whatever I'd said wrong. "Zach—"

"No."

It was one word, but it said so much. It was no to my apology. No to anything else I could say. No to me.

I retracted my hand and slowed, with his rejection forming a solid barrier between us.

•••

The next hour or two, until the sun went down and we could progress no farther into the woods without the aid of a torch, we traveled in complete silence. Bromley, bless him, seemed to sense that sour words had been exchanged, and Zach was in a dark mood because of it—a mood Brom understood not to interrupt.

I knew better than to try speaking to him, too, mostly because I guessed he wasn't ready to hear any apologies. Plus, bringing it up around Bromley felt awkward. In truth, during those achingly long minutes of silent travel, I agonized over what I'd said. What did I know about his past? What did I know about all those scars? I hadn't meant for it to turn so personal.

When we found a good spot to make camp, we started our usual ritual of feeding the horses, getting the fire going, and pulling out the provisions, all with barely a word passed among the three of us. Anything that needed to be discussed, Zach's answers were short, and anything he needed to say, he directed at Bromley. He didn't even look at me. Not once.

My stomach rolled and frothed with guilt as I fed Lorena her dinner. She chewed the oats from my hand and seemed pleased to find bits of dried orange peels mixed in—her very favorite. But even Lorena's ticklish nose as she searched for more citrus didn't make me smile.

After we had eaten, Bromley jumped up from his spot by the fire. "I think I'll go get some more firewood."

It was painfully obvious he was dying to escape the tension. That, or he wanted to give us an excuse to talk and sort things out. I doubted that was a good idea.

"We have plenty of wood." I gestured to the pile of dry wood stacked nearby.

"Then I'll go find a stream for fresh water." He left without even grabbing a flask. Couldn't say I blamed him.

Zach sat across from the fire, sharpening one of his many knives. He paused, inspecting it, the orange and red flames reflecting in the silver blade.

It took several moments and a few deep breathing exercises for me to rise. I moved around the fire and took a seat next to him, making Zach twitch and nick his finger on the blade.

Cursing softly, he stuck his thumb in his mouth. He pulled it out to examine it, but blood rose to the surface immediately. As he went to suck on it again, I instinctively caught his hand and brought his finger toward my lips.

Then I stopped. Healing his wounds by a Kiss was not what he wanted. I released his hand, tore a small strip of fabric from the end of my sleeve and wrapped the end of his finger. I squeezed, applying pressure to the wound.

Throughout the whole process, Zach hadn't moved or said a word, but I could feel his eyes on me.

"No Kiss?"

"You said no," I whispered, barely audible over the sound of the crackling flames.

He didn't reply. I thought he'd jerk his finger out of my hand, but he left it there.

I stole a peek at his face. His mouth was set in a thin line, but his brow was no longer furrowed, giving him a look of cool indifference rather than anger or hurt.

"I'm sorry, Zach, I know what I said upset you."

Still, he remained silent.

"I just wanted you to know how sorry I am. Everything I've seen of you says running is the last thing you'd ever do. Whatever the situation, if given the opportunity, I know you'd stay and fight. You'd stay to protect the people you...you love."

Or think you love.

Zach tapped his other fingers on his knee.

Well, it was hopeless. Perhaps tomorrow he'd be in a better mood. I started to release his finger when Zach caught my palm with his whole hand and squeezed it. Mystified, I watched him, afraid to take my eyes away, hoping he would offer some kind of hint about his thoughts.

"Do you know why I was born?" he asked.

I opened my mouth then closed it again, completely blank as to how to respond. Zach was indeed a rare breed. Romanticas and Royals never crossed paths, unless it was to put down a rebellion, and even then, a Royal wouldn't usually go near a Romantica for fear of being branded a heretic themselves and stripped of their Royal title.

I thought he'd continue, as if it was a rhetorical question, but he waited for me to respond.

"It was…an accident, I suppose?"

"That's what most people suspect. But that's not what my mother told me." Zach leaned back and glanced skyward. There were no stars or a moon to be seen, only the shadows of trees, and beyond that, blackness. "Have you ever been to a theater, princess?"

I shook my head. I'd heard of them, though. Apparently they were a Romantica tradition—a house where they told stories and sang ballads, almost always about Love.

"Oh, they're amazing. Maybe after all this is over, I'll take you to one." Then he briefly closed his eyes, like he was steeling himself. "My mother worked at one. She sang beautifully and told stories in a way that made you feel like you were really there. But her best talent was just sitting with the guests and… talking. She made you feel like you were the most important person in the world, like there was only you and your dreams and nothing else mattered.

"My father was a prince passing through the town with his patrol. He and a few others visited the theater, and he met my mother. Her own mother had died just the day before, but she tried to be herself anyway, hiding her grief behind a pretty smile while serving food and drink.

"But my father…he noticed somehow. He pulled her aside and asked what was wrong. He'd seen her the other night, and tonight she was…different. To have a complete stranger see through her mask—it made my mother open her heart to him. Once she did, it didn't take her long to fall in love with him. As for my father, at first, he claimed to not love her, but he returned to her almost every night to be with her. It wasn't until he discovered she was pregnant that he finally realized…"

Swept up in Zach's words, I couldn't look away from his face.

His mouth twitched into a tiny smile. "My father became a heretic, too. He married her in secret, and when the Legion found out, they sent him on a solo suicide mission. But my mother talked about him all the time. She said every day she was away from him was painful." Zach stayed quiet for a long time then looked at me. "Such desperation… Have you ever felt that, Ivy?"

Again, my voice locked in my throat. No, I hadn't felt such a thing. It was preposterous, and yet I couldn't bring myself to say it. Perhaps it was because of the intensity with which his eyes held mine, and I could *feel* desperation in them.

It was unheard of—a Royal wanting to marry a Romantica. Was this even true? Or a lie told by Zach's mother to ease the pain of his father's disappearance?

Zach seemed to read my thoughts. "I'm not naive. This could very well be a lie to help me think better of a father I never knew. But even if it was, doesn't that mean something? That my mother still loved him so deeply as to lie for him? Even for me? Maybe it wasn't mutual, but that doesn't mean it wasn't real."

"I've never seen such a thing," I said at last. My throat felt dry after staying silent.

Zach placed a few more pieces of wood into the fire, and sparks flew upward. "No, I don't suppose you have. Your kind is bred, isn't it?"

Although I wasn't happy about the term, I couldn't deny its truth. I was a product of intricate breeding, of careful calculation and manipulation of genes to produce the most powerful Kisses of the Legion. I was a pure-bred Royal. My parents may not have even felt Lust for each other. They had entered the bedchamber with a goal, a purpose.

But a noble one—to produce an heir capable of fighting the Dark Forces and defending the four kingdoms. As for my mother, she saw every one of her children as soldiers, bred to help her find and destroy the Evil Queen. And it was what I wanted, too. I fought to end this war. To keep those little girls in Tulia's class away from goblins and griffins.

Zach smiled and said, "But it seems the end result was well worth it." He paused. "You're a smart, resourceful, and beautiful princess. I can't deny that."

The fire before us was too hot. It made even my palms sweaty.

"Don't forget 'infuriating,'" I added.

Zach laughed, and I realized I had missed his laugh and easy smile in just that short amount of time. "And that."

"Zach, what I said…I said out of anger, and fear. You scared me when you ran off." I'd been alone without a partner, just like at the wall, with the dwarf about to kill me and Kellian gone, with no one watching my back.

"Ivy…"

"Even if you won't Kiss me, you have to learn to trust me. We're still partners."

"And *you* have to trust *me*. Trust me when I say I can protect you without the Kiss, that we can defeat the dragon without it."

I opened my mouth, but Zach raised his hand to stop me.

"You can't change what I believe, no matter what you say or do. I will always believe kisses are not weapons. They were *never* meant to be weapons."

"The safety of the kingdom should be placed before anyone's personal beliefs," I said.

"Give me a chance."

"You're no good to me dead, Zach."

"I don't plan on dying, Ivy."

"You almost did today."

"But I didn't."

This was hopeless. We were going around in circles. But we had accomplished one good thing: Zach was talking to me again—and not just that. He'd told me something very personal. If he continued to warm up to me, perhaps I could convince him to see my side.

I held up my index finger. "One chance," I said, with the tiniest hint of a smile.

"Fair enough." Zach reached over and took my hand. Intertwining our fingers, he brought them up to his lips and kissed the back of my hand, where his mark rested.

His lips were warm and smooth. As shocked as I was, I prayed I didn't noticeably tremble. A part of me wanted to jerk my hand away, remembering Brom's comments regarding Zach's bare chest earlier.

"You smell like citrus."

I tried to push down a shiver at his words, but I couldn't. He had to have felt it. "That's Lorena. She…she likes orange peels."

He smiled against my skin. "She and I have something in common, then."

He lowered our hands from his lips but didn't let go. As his gaze lifted to my face, the trees and the campfire turned into blurs of color—shades of orange, red, green, violet, and brown—around us. And while the rest of the world's details dimmed, his face seemed strangely in sharp focus, so clear, so crystal.

"That's not…it doesn't…" I fumbled, unable to form a real sentence. Luckily I was spared any further struggling when the sound of footsteps crunching alerted us to Bromley's approach, and Zach released my hand. I scooted away and immediately felt silly. Why was I acting like we were about to be caught doing something we shouldn't?

Zach stood as Bromley entered our little camp. "Seas of Glyll, you're loud, Brom. I've got to teach you to move through the woods without awaking every creature within a mile."

Bromley caught my eye and grinned. "That might be a good idea."

Zach clapped Brom's shoulder. "I'll take the first watch. You two get some rest."

After clearing my head of any residual *blurriness*, I settled into my bundle and turned away from the fire, reaching into the pockets of my cloak and pulling out a folded piece of paper with the spell Brom had copied for me. I reread the spell over and over because, despite our conversation, I knew there was no way we could destroy the dragon without the Kiss. I trusted him to protect one princess, but how could he protect all the kingdoms from the greatest monster the world had ever known?

CHAPTER SIXTEEN

AN UNEXPECTED HEROINE

I woke up coughing. A shadow had fallen over my lungs, my Sense burning with the threat of another dark creature. But this feeling…was more like a mist than a heavy rain. I'd felt it many times on patrol—I knew what it was.

My cough woke Zach, and he shot to his feet, one hand at his sword. When he realized there was no immediate threat, he crouched beside me.

"What's wrong? Is there something coming?"

"It's just sparrow harpies. A whole flock of them. Must be close."

At my words, Brom, who'd been keeping watch, made a face of disgust. "I hate those things. Any way we can avoid them?"

I frowned. "We shouldn't waste time trying to feel around the flock with my Sense."

Zach looked from me to Brom. "Sparrow harpies? I thought they only came out at night."

I nodded. "Usually they do, but sparrow harpies during the daylight is a sign that a powerful dark force is gathering, like—"

"Like a Sable Dragon egg. Got it." Zach sighed. He held out his hands, and I took them, letting him help me to my feet. "Are you okay to—"

"Of course I am. They're only sparrow harpies." I wondered if him leaving me alone with the griffin had really shaken him.

"Are you sure? I could—"

"Zach, it's not like I don't appreciate all the attention, but I'm used to carrying this burden, remember? You're my *sixth* partner."

At that, he dropped my hands, the tips of his ears tingeing pink. "Right. Of course."

In no time, we were on our way through the forest again. Although Zach made no move to touch me, I felt his gaze flicker to me every once in a while. I was a little ashamed at the way the nerves in my stomach fluttered when I caught him staring, or the way I kept revisiting my hands in his. But then a healthy dose of fear would ripple through me—fear of losing grip—and I'd feel like myself again.

Two hours later, we heard the flapping of wings. Hundreds of them, if not thousands. In fact, it sounded more like buzzing.

The three of us simultaneously dismounted. We went forward on foot a few more paces, then Zach stopped. "Should we tether the horses?"

I hesitated. "Sparrow harpies don't touch the living. The horses won't like them, but if the harpies are feasting on something, we can't wait out the swarm."

"There's no way to drive them off?"

"None that you would agree to," I muttered.

"Okay, then the horses come with us." Zach moved forward. I scowled but didn't object.

The buzzing was impossibly loud now. It pounded in my ears and echoed in my brain, rattling my teeth.

The sky was thick with harpies. Great swarms of black bat-winged creatures the size of sparrows—if sparrows were lumpy and grotesque. They had tiny heads and flimsy arms and legs, their black leathery wings supporting their weight that mostly came from their gargantuan stomachs. Some hovered, some dove down, and some zipped through the air like flies, their wings a blur.

In the middle of the forest was a large meadow, and spread across it was...a massacre.

Corpses littered the tall grass, flattening the growth with gore and blood. It wasn't people—thank the Queen—but it was a herd of red rowan deer. The majestic creatures had been slaughtered by some dark creature, but it was hard to tell how they'd been killed, since the sparrow harpies had pecked their carcasses down to their silver bones. Whatever creature killed them had to be fast to catch them—possibly griffins from the air or serpents from the tall grass.

The harpies dove and buzzed and burrowed into the deer flesh but paid us no attention. Sparrow harpies lived only for the scent of death and fresh blood, not the healthy or the living. They were scavengers.

Tears sprang to my eyes. The metallic scent of blood and decaying flesh lingered on the air. But the sight was worse. Red rowan deer were sacred creatures, so they were rarely hunted, and when they were, every part of their bodies was used—their fur, meat, silver antlers, and bones, which were made into many great Legion weapons. But more than anything, they were sweet, gentle creatures. It was said their breath in the cold winter air formed the wind wisps that traveled to the Seas of Glyll.

It was a tragedy beyond words. I pressed my palms to my eyes, tears clinging to my hands, and swallowed a few more times. Brom turned away and gagged. Zach stood slightly ahead, gripping Vel's reins and staring at the massacre with a clenched jaw, a slight sheen to his pale skin. After a moment of silence, he said, "Let's go."

I stopped halfway across the meadow, my boots coated

with blood and mud, sparrow harpies buzzing relentlessly, and bowed my head, offering a silent prayer to the Holy Queens. My whispered words were carried away by the wind, over the meadows and away from the Sable Dragon's dark omens.

Two hours later, the forest had grown so thick, light had all but disappeared, and yet another shadow had fallen over my lungs and heart. Fighting down a wave of nausea, I lowered my head and breathed in Lorena's mane, which still smelled of the stables back home, and watched the dark green foliage on the ground pass by at a slow trot. As the nausea receded, the shadow over my lungs tightened, squeezing air from my chest.

"Something's close," I whispered.

Zach turned in his saddle. "From what direction?"

"Southeast, I think."

"How many?" His hands clenched and unclenched on his reins. Not for the first time, I wondered if he was angry that *he* no longer felt the Sense or that *I* felt it *double*.

"Either a lot of small things, or one big thing, and it's coming fast."

Zach withdrew a dagger from his belt. "Off the horses."

Brom and I obeyed. Brom grasped his shield and withdrew his crossbow from his saddlebag. I grasped the hilt of my sword, missing my own shield thanks to the fight with the griffin and feeling naked without it.

We moved as quietly as possible through the forest. I listened hard, but more than anything, I felt. I dug deep into the reservoirs of my Royal magic and pushed out my Sense — reaching like arms into the trees around us. In the air there was nothing sinister, but perhaps… I pushed my Sense down,

down to the forest floor, and it was then—to the east and moving steadily—I felt a dark presence.

"It's in the growth." I touched Zach's elbow. "The grass."

Zach swore. "Back on your horses."

This time I didn't obey, because Zach hadn't moved.

For a second, I was tempted to mention the Kiss, but I knew by now that neither logic nor seduction worked on him. Instead of arguing, though, I needed to make him trust me more. But how?

By doing this his way. I just hoped it wouldn't get us killed.

"And you?" I said.

"I can't kill whatever *it* is on my horse, can I?" he snapped.

"Why do you think the responsibility falls on you alone?" I jabbed a finger toward his chest. "We're here, too." I gestured to Brom, who had remained on the ground with me.

Zach's gaze shifted from me to Brom, as if he was considering our worth.

"Let us help fight. Or would you rather repeat the griffin incident?"

At last he met my eyes, and I could see I'd trapped him.

Before Zach could agree, the sound of shuffling through leaves and underbrush reached my ears. No, smoother than a shuffle. Like a slither.

"Serpents," I whispered. Likely the same ones that had taken down the herd of red rowan deer—and now they were out for more blood.

At that, Zach hoisted me up onto my saddle faster than I would've thought possible and drew a second dagger from his belt.

The slithering grew louder, and each breath I took became more labored. Before I could shout a warning, something from the undergrowth launched itself into the air.

The serpent practically flew, propelling its long body toward me. It was a basilisk viper, known by the gray and green branch-like pattern of its scales and its pupil-free yellow eyes.

Zach was already there, twisting around like a snake himself, thrusting his dagger through a swift upward cut and lopping the viper's head clean off. It fell to the earth and crumbled into dust as more slithering whispered through the forest.

Our horses tossed their heads, their hooves dancing in panic. "Any ideas?" I shouted. From the sound, it must be close to twenty vipers.

"Just cover me. Brom, give Ivy your shield and shoot anything in the grass that moves."

As Brom tossed me his shield and loaded his crossbow, I pleaded with Zach. "Please, you need—"

"What I *need*"—he threw another dagger at the forest floor a few yards away, and a hiss escaped—"is a way to get rid of all the growth."

The vipers were closing in, their hissing and slithering now at an impossible volume. Brom shot arrows at any rustle while Zach and I threw daggers, but it was impossible to tell if we hit anything.

Another basilisk rocketed through the air, and Zach threw his dagger, pinning the snake to a tree. Just as I flung another dagger, Lorena whinnied and reared up. It was all I could do to grip her sides tight enough not to fall from her back. The snakes were now at her hooves.

Or at least I thought they were. Not serpents, but flames, nipped at her hooves. Zach and Brom gave shouts of surprise and jumped from foot to foot, fire now spreading from their feet and burning the undergrowth to ash. It spread rapidly in a perfect circle, destroying all forms of plant life in its wake and leaving only the bare soil. And twenty angry basilisk vipers.

This couldn't be a natural fire.

I turned in my saddle, looking for the source of magic. Surely it wasn't Zach. He seemed just as surprised about the flames. Could it be from the same source as the griffin's golden demise?

With all the grass and growth burned away, Zach whipped about like a leaf in the wind, slicing and throwing. I watched, open-mouthed, as bits of serpent were tossed into the air. Brom and I helped, but it was nothing compared to Zach's intense killing spree. There were a couple of times when serpents had nearly gotten me, but Zach hacked them to bits.

Once the dust of the vipers' corpses settled and the darkness lifted from my lungs, the forest was silent, interrupted only by a slight rustling. Where was it coming from? The ground had been scorched in a perfect circle around us.

Zach looked up, and I followed suit.

To the east, in a high brucel tree, was a young woman. She was crouched on a wide and sturdy-looking branch, half her body shielded by leaves and branches. She would have been well-hidden, but her vibrant blue robe gave her away.

For a few moments, no one moved or spoke. Zach glanced at me, and I mouthed, "*Mage.*"

She must be. With elemental magic like that—so controlled and precise.

"Greetings, lady," Zach called, cupping a hand over his mouth. "Do we have you to thank for that magic?"

She straightened, the hem of her azure robe sweeping across the leaves and bark. Her hair was as black as a raven's wing, falling in beautiful waves down to her elbows, and her skin as white as snow.

I felt a pang of envy. Even with her up in a tree I could see how flawless her skin was. *Unlike mine,* I thought irritably, always aware of my freckles, forever a mockery of my great ancestor's beautiful skin. Something my mother never let me forget.

Seeing her there, with the light behind her and her dark hair a sharp contrast against the bright green leaves, reminded me of the stained glass depiction of Queen Myriana in the library. How similar they looked.

"Fantastic deduction, prince," the mage said. "Did you also solve the mystery of why the world goes dark when the sun goes down?"

Zach threw back his head and laughed. It was the same easy laugh he'd given me the day in the village. Still chuckling, Zach hooked his daggers on his belt. "Fair enough, mage."

At his carefree laughter, irritation squeezed the nerves in my neck, making my shoulders hunch. It wasn't just that he was laughing so easily with this beautiful woman, but it was also irritation at myself for being annoyed to begin with.

"Who are you?" the woman asked.

I dismounted Lorena. "My name is Ivy Myriana, direct descendant of Queen Myriana and Royal Princess of the Legion of Myria."

"I wasn't talking to *you*, princess," she said sharply, her head snapping from me back to Zach. "I was talking to the wraith disguised as a swordsman."

Zach raised his eyebrows. "A wraith, eh? Is that a compliment?"

Ignoring his remark, I placed a hand on his shoulder. "This is my partner, Prince Zachariah of the kingdom of—"

The mage jumped from the tree, landing gracefully with leaves showering down around her. Placing her hands on her hips, she squinted at Zach. "*You're* the Swordsman Prince from the West?"

Zach shrugged. "You were expecting someone taller, weren't you?"

I rolled my eyes. "Don't mind him. A troll stepped on his head when he was a baby."

The female mage just ignored us. "That can't be," she said. "I heard he doesn't take partners. That he's a prince without a princess."

"Ah, well, this is a *special* arrangement." Zach's eyes lingered on me.

Special. I quickly looked away.

"Hmm," was her only response.

There was an awkward pause between the four of us, and it was then, as I began looking all around, I noticed that something was missing.

Zach's hand wrapped around my side, startling me with both its suddenness and intimacy. "Ivy? What is it? Do you feel okay?"

I shouldn't have been pleased at the gentleness in his voice or the tenderness in his touch—but I couldn't stop the smile.

Placing my hand over his, I squeezed his fingers. "I'm okay. Promise." I shifted my gaze back to the mage, as Zach withdrew his arm. "I was just wondering… Where's your master?"

The mage looked at me with a contemplative frown. "My master?"

I folded my arms. "You're very young to be traveling alone and using your magic without a master to help you."

It took many years for young mages to fully control all their elemental powers, and this girl couldn't have been more than a few years older than me.

The mage smirked, twisting two pale fingers into a wavy curl that lay over her shoulder. "You needn't worry, princess."

As she spoke, I could've sworn her eyes grew a shade darker, but it might've been a cloud passing over the sun.

"My master is very close."

I looked to the trees again but felt silly. There was no one there. "What are you and your master doing so far north?"

The mage shouldered a light bag I only just noticed she carried. "Heard a rumor of a witch passing through these parts."

I raised my eyebrows. "And you didn't tell the Legion so they could investigate?"

"What's the point of possessing these powers if not to help those who need it?" She turned on her heel. "Now, I believe I've answered enough of your questions, while you've barely answered mine. I'll be off."

Affronted, I almost pointed out that all she'd really asked was why Zach had chosen me as a partner and no one else, which now seemed rather personal, but I didn't. She *had* just saved us. "Wait," I said. "Lady Mage, if you…if you wouldn't mind, I have a favor to ask of you."

She turned only halfway back, her gaze flickering to Brom, who was watching her with fascination, then back to Zach and me. "So ask it, then."

Ignoring her haughty tone, I pointed in the direction we'd come. "A herd of red rowan deer were brought down by these basilisk vipers, and now their bodies are being picked apart by sparrow harpies. I was wondering if you could…help their souls find peace."

The mage regarded me, her blue eyes fixed on my own.

Before I could say another word, she nodded, then raised her hand above her head and brought it down in a quick slicing motion.

Wind ripped through the trees with the force of a gale on the seas. Zach, Brom, and I threw up our arms against the wind and the onslaught of thousands of leaves. When we looked up, she was gone.

"Show-off," I muttered.

We picked up our thrown daggers and loosed arrows and started once again through the forest. Not long after, we smelled smoke on the breeze. We turned and looked back. Sure enough, thick black smoke was rising above the treetops from the direction of the meadow. The sparrow harpies dissipated like ash in the wind, leaving the souls of the great deer to find peace in the magical flames.

CHAPTER SEVENTEEN

INCOMING STORM

We moved through the forest at a steady pace, even though the terrain was slowly changing and collecting more hills. By heading north for the mountains, occasionally drifting east when we'd catch our bearings from the sun's position through the trees, we covered a lot of ground. Then the thunder started.

It came fast, low and threatening, like a second canopy above our heads, pressing in on the leaves and branches of the forest.

I cursed, stopping Lorena and patting her muzzle as the third rumble of thunder boomed around us. "This isn't a normal storm."

Zach scowled over his shoulder. "Don't tell me…another blasted sign?"

I nodded. "We need to find shelter. Fast."

"I could scout ahead and look for a cave," Bromley offered, already dismounting.

I knew Brom was a good scout—the other princes and members of the hunting parties often bragged about his skills—but still, my stomach dropped at the idea. Not only was the magical storm itself dangerous, but also it interfered with my

Sense, preventing me from noticing a dark creature roaming about.

I bit my bottom lip to stop myself from forbidding him.

Zach caught my eye, then swung down from his horse. "No offense, Brom, but I've got longer legs—I'm pretty sure I can move faster."

As he handed me Vel's reins I gave him a grateful smile, briefly squeezing his fingertips. Zach returned my smile, then tossed his hood over his short brown hair and hurried into the forest, his hand lashing out at trees with a dagger, marking his trail.

Brom and I continued forward but at a much slower pace, listening to the sounds of the forest and the incoming storm. We were only minutes away from the onslaught of rain. I just prayed the black lightning would wait till we found shelter. Unlike regular lightning, where fires would ignite, black lightning hit the earth with subzero temperatures, freezing every living thing and cracking open the earth. Entire crop seasons were ruined, and people starved. The ice rupturing the ground caused earthquakes, and when the ice thawed, there would be flooding. It was one devastation after the next.

Which was why we needed to find a cave soon. Black lightning never struck stone. Nothing to kill there.

"I should be out there, not him," Brom said after a particularly large thunderclap. "He should be *here* with *you*, princess. To protect you."

"I can take care of myself, Bromley," I said gently.

He met my eyes. It was the same look he'd given me when I teased that I'd put a goblin in his closet when he was a child— one of real fear. Had those vipers terrified him more than he'd let on? Had the griffin? I had been so concerned with the thunder that I hadn't noticed how quiet he had become after the attack.

We got down from our horses so we could travel side by side.

"Those serpents," he said, "they almost got you. Several times. But he saved you from them…effortlessly. The griffin, too. I wasn't there, but I saw the blood on Zach—he *saved* you. What if we're attacked again? I can't protect you like he can."

I halted the horses and glanced at the sky. "It's not your job to protect me, Brom."

"Which is why it should be *me* out there!" Bromley shouted.

I took a step back, shocked. Bromley had never yelled at me so forcefully before.

Color drained from Brom's face, and he fell at my feet. "I'm so sorry, milady. Please forgive me."

Oh, Brom. My sisters were dear to me, but Brom was more like family than anyone else, and I knew he felt the same about me. We worried about each other.

I dropped to my knees and placed my arms around his shoulders, pulling him close. "Zach offered to go because he saw I wanted you with me. I was scared for you, Brom. I didn't want you out in the forest alone."

Bromley said nothing, but his hands dug deeply into the earth.

I pressed my cheek against the top of his head. "I know it's selfish, but I couldn't bear it if anything happened to you."

Bromley moved his head up, bumping my cheek and looking me in the eyes. "Me, too. I couldn't stand to see you… You're…you're the only family I have."

I smiled and kissed his forehead. "You're my family, too."

He brushed away my kiss like an embarrassed little brother. "What happened between you and Zach? Last night, I mean, when I left?"

The question was so sudden that it threw me off guard. "Well I…I had said something unbelievably rude to him, then

I apologized, and we came to a sort of…agreement."

Brom's lips pulled to the side in a half smirk. "I can tell something happened. You two seemed—"

A crack of lightning drowned out his voice. Black veins ripped through the gray sky, and several yards away an entire cluster of trees went white with ice, the ground shaking under our feet as the trees' roots froze as well. We quickly stood and grabbed the horses' bridles, stroking their noses to keep them calm. As if triggered by the black lightning, rain fell in large pellets. We threw up our hoods and kept moving in the direction of Zach's trail marks. Just when we were freezing and soaked to the bone, a cloaked figure emerged through the rain. I hoped it was Zach, but I drew my sword just in case.

The figure signaled, and my heart fluttered with relief. Not only was Zach safe—he had found shelter.

We had to pass through a waterfall to get to the small cave, but it didn't matter, since we were soaked anyway. The cliff the waterfall came from wasn't very high, but it made me anxious all the same. The Wu-Hyll Mountains were getting closer, which meant the egg was, too.

Zach had already explored most of the cave, but he stuck close by me, ready to respond if I felt the presence of the Forces. But I felt nothing, only damp and chill from the freezing rain.

After we started a fire, we took turns using the dark depth of the cave to change out of our soaked clothes into semi-dry ones from our bags. Then we ate and settled by the flames. I offered to take the first watch, and almost as soon as our shifts were decided, Bromley fell asleep.

Zach sat next to me this time, both our bodies facing the cave's entrance where the horses huddled under the mouth, away from the waterfall. I was much more aware of his presence than the last few times we sat around the fire. No, rather, I was just as aware as before, but the feeling was different. I was… nervous? Anxious? No, neither of those, although similar. It was something I couldn't name or explain.

"Thank you," I said at last.

"For what?" he asked, laying out his knives and cleaning them of the vipers' blood.

"For scouting instead of Bromley."

He shrugged. "I didn't want him out there alone, either."

I sighed. "He was angry at me. He said *you* should've stayed with me, that you could protect me and he couldn't."

"Ivy, don't do this. Bromley was just a little shaken from the attack, that's all. He's worried about you."

"Yes, the vipers scared him, and without that mage, things could've been much worse."

Zach stopped cleaning his dagger and focused on the fire. "Who was she?"

"I have no idea. She's never been to Myria before, that's for sure."

"She seems skilled."

"Especially for one so young." My nerves slid away as we fell into an easy rhythm of conversation. "Usually it takes many, many years for mages to perfect elemental magic like that. Even more strange, she's wandering about without a master."

Zach went back to cleaning. "She said her master was close by."

"Even if that were true—which I'm not convinced it was— she still shouldn't be able to exert that level of control over her magic."

"Why not?"

"Mages are different from Royals in that they don't need a trigger for their magic. And, also unlike Royals, their magic doesn't specifically repel the Darkness. They're born with only the ability to control the elements."

"I knew that," he muttered.

"There are three Master Mages for each kingdom, and they advise the Royal Council of kings and queens," I continued, ignoring his interruption. "Each Master Mage takes on at least one apprentice mage every five years. Because it's difficult to control their own power, they need a master to learn from and to keep their abilities in check. But she was able to perform that fire magic on her own, with no master in sight."

Zach's brow furrowed. "Then you think she's dangerous?"

"Not necessarily. She must be very skilled to control fire like that—to have it burn in a perfect circle. So I doubt she'll be accidentally burning down villages any time soon."

Zach snapped his fingers. "That's why you asked her to burn the rowan deer. Because you knew she had enough control for the fire not to spread."

"That, and I couldn't stand the idea of those poor creatures being..." My voice trailed off, lost in the sounds of the pounding water and crackling fire.

"I understand." Zach's voice was low, somber, but still comforting somehow. He put away his daggers and picked up his sword next.

I remembered the griffin knocking that same sword out of his hand, and how, without a weapon, Zach had stood up against the griffin's talons to save me. Then the golden light...

"Do you think that mage has been following us?"

Zach paused his cleaning and pursed his lips.

"Maybe she was the one who killed the griffin. It had to have been vanquished by magic. There's no other explanation."

He frowned, staring at the sword, and remained silent.

"But then again, that certainly wasn't elemental magic. I've never—"

"You just said it's odd for a mage as young as she is to be so powerful," he said. "Maybe she has a different kind of magic, as well."

I wrung out my wet hair. "Maybe." But even that didn't add up. Mage magic was elemental. It had always been that way. There was also the fact that the mage had been in the forest with us, and none of us noticed she was there. Yes, she'd been stealthy in the trees during the viper attack, but it still seemed unlikely.

I studied Zach. The tightness in his jaw made it clear he wasn't eager to discuss the idea anymore, so I switched topics. "Look, back there with the vipers…"

He sighed, and the tension in the cave grew. He suspected I was going to say that we wouldn't have needed the mage's help if he would've just Kissed me.

I remembered what Brom said, that Zach and I seemed different around each other today. More civil. Closer, even. I couldn't ruin that.

"Yes?" Zach asked.

Shocking even myself, I reached over and touched his hand, my fingers brushing his inner wrist. I swore I felt his pulse speed up, but I couldn't be sure.

"You saved me quite a few times back there. Thank you." Our hands felt too hot, and I wasn't sure it had anything to do with the proximity of the fire. It was a different kind of heat.

Zach twisted his wrist and caught my fingers in his palm and gripped them. "You're welcome."

I couldn't move my hand away, and it wasn't because he was holding it tightly. After a few moments, he let go and began tracing his fingertips along my palm. I was entranced with the feeling. His fingers, though callused, seemed so gentle against my skin as he trailed them down my wrist and back up to my knuckles. The garlands of my mark bent and twisted in movement with his hand as a tingling feeling spread up my arm, into my throat, and down my chest. I wasn't sure what he was doing or what his purpose was, but I didn't want him to stop the strange rushing sensation flowing through me. His index finger stopped over my pounding pulse, and his eyes locked onto mine.

His fingers pressed just a little harder into my skin, as if he were tugging me into him. I drew close, curious of the sensation that was spreading from my arm to my whole body.

Then a loud snore echoed off the cave's walls, and Zach and I both jumped, our hands breaking apart, breaths sharp and quick.

We glanced behind us to find Brom snoring, softer now.

But the...whatever it was...was gone, and Zach packed up his knives and sheathed his sword without another word, then settled in for sleep.

My curiosity fled, replaced by familiar logic. That feeling between us was too intoxicating, too addictive. Dangerous. I had the sudden urge to stick my arm in the chilling waterfall in hopes of getting rid of Zach's fiery warmth in my hand.

PART TWO

THE QUEEN AND HER DESCENDANTS

Born under holly
Born under thistle
Nestled in blankets of snow

A girl of the moon
A girl of the sun
Together they play and they grow

Deep in the forests
And in golden fields
A brave young hunter is met

A maiden of love
A maiden of hate
Three can never sing a duet

Excerpt from a Romantica ballad

CHAPTER EIGHTEEN

THE ROMANTICA'S TALE

When the clouds finally dispersed midafternoon the next day, we set out moving west to get back to our main trail. Zach led us through the trees and brush with ease, barely glancing at the marks he had made. It was as if he already knew this forest like the back of his hand.

As we traveled we could see the devastation from last night's storm. Ice in one form or another seemed to be everywhere—sheets of it on the bark, icicles hanging from branches—and huge cracks where the ground had split apart, showing frozen roots, so we had to go out of our way several times. I just hoped the storm had stayed in the forest and not moved on to any nearby villages.

"I'm really getting sick of these trees," I muttered, brushing aside a branch. "How much more of this forest, you think?"

Brom plucked our map from one of his saddlebags. He unfurled it and sighed. "At least another day."

"If we're lucky, we'll come across one of the cleared areas by nightfall," Zach said without looking back.

Brom handed the map to me so I could double-check, and with just a glance, I saw he was right. The forest we were in took up a large portion of the middle of the map, stretching from east to west with tidy illustrated trees to show the wooded areas. There were small patches of the forest without the tree drawings—small but definitely there. "Yes, there're a few ahead." I traced my finger across the map and paused at a small cluster of houses. "Those must be the areas this village uses for lumber."

As I leaned over to tuck the map back into Brom's saddle-bag, I muttered to him, "I'm surprised he remembers that from our meeting with Commander Weldan. He was hardly paying attention."

"I heard that," he called back.

Brom and I laughed.

Zach tilted his head to the sky. "With no trees overhead, it looks like we'll get to see the stars tonight."

Clear skies at last—perhaps even a sliver of the new moon. Though my enthusiasm for the vast night sky made the day and our travels just grow longer. I felt my mind drift several times as we passed tree after tree.

"Where do you think she came from? What kingdom, I mean?" I asked Brom when we had stopped to give the horses a chance to drink from the nearby stream. It was early evening, and the trees were at last beginning to thin.

"The mage? I've never seen her in Myria." Brom shrugged. "I haven't heard any rumors about a young female mage, either."

"She's definitely been west," Zach piped in, washing his hands in the stream and splashing water onto his face. He winced. "That's freezing."

"The streams come from the mountains, so they're practically all melted snow." I went over to him with a clean cloth and brushed it against his face as he reached for it. Our hands touched, and we both flinched—the memory from last night on *my* mind, at least.

"Why do you think she's from Saevall?" I asked, pushing

past the awkward moment.

"I didn't say she's *from* there. If I had to guess, I'd say she's from Raed."

My mother had just come from Raed with news that the Wicked Queen had last been sighted there. Maybe the mage knew something about the Sable Dragon, which was why she was so far north. But that was unlikely. Few people could decipher omens from regular dark activity, let alone understand what those signs meant.

"She's been west, at least, because she's heard of me," Zach said.

Brom filled up his flask and tilted his chin in thought. "But many people from across the kingdoms have heard of the Swordsman Prince."

"Yes, but few *know* that I fight without a partner. That's a rare piece of information that's often rumored but never confirmed."

"Why? Do you not want people to know of your one-man crusade for True Love?" I asked.

He chuckled. "It wasn't my idea. It was Weldan's." Zach handed me back the now-damp cloth. "Weldan fought for me at the Saevallan Council to allow me into their Legion. They weren't pleased about it, especially when they learned I was the son of a Romantica. They didn't trust me, but Weldan argued on my behalf."

"Did he know that you were…?" I asked.

"A Romantica? I never told him outright, but I think he suspected. Even so…Weldan cares more about killing monsters than bloodlines. He saw I could fight and wanted me in the Legion. Somewhere down the line, I think we became friends. Hard to believe, right?" he said with a crooked grin.

I recalled the conflicting way Weldan treated Zach— in front of his men, harsh and irritated, but alone with me, he'd spoken of Zach with reverence and confidence. I could sympathize with Weldan's plight. He couldn't show favoritism to friends, especially if those friends excelled above all others and were heretics.

"Not so hard to believe," I said with a wink.

Zach raised his eyebrows and glanced away, rubbing the back of his neck. "Anyway, once I proved myself on the battlefield, the Council didn't need any more convincing. Of course, when they found out I wouldn't take a partner, they almost threw me out. But Weldan said I should at least be allowed access to the information about the Forces provided by the Legion's sources, with the stipulation that I keep quiet about my...*opinions*."

"Does Weldan share your opinions?"

Zach stared off into the trees thoughtfully. "No, but he does respect them."

Only a few days ago the jab would've ruffled my feathers, but now I could tell he didn't mean it to be offensive. Strange, that we could talk about this topic without either of us getting irrationally angry.

Him, because he believed he'd won the argument.

And me, because I knew it to be only a temporary truce. I still planned to get his Kiss.

B y dusk we had come across several tree stumps, evidence of the nearby village. It made our pace faster, but mostly it was just a relief to travel without branches brushing my arms, legs, and head.

It was when the sun was finally shining its last rays — great streaks of yellow and orange across the sky — that Zach stopped

and raised his arm, pointing toward the horizon. "Smoke. There.
Do you see it?"

It was faint. A subtle white haze drifting above the trees.
It wasn't too far away, either, perhaps a little over a mile.

"A village?" I asked.

He squinted at the smoke. "Looks like it's coming from
a large open fire, maybe even a bonfire. Unusual for a village.
The mage again? She could've looped ahead of us...outrun
the storm."

"Don't think so. Mage fire smoke usually gives off a coppery
tint," I said.

"Troll's breath," Zach cursed, dropping his gaze from the
smoke to the sparse woods around us. "It's directly in our path.
If we go around it, it could add another two hours out of the
way, and we need to stop for the night." He looked to Brom
and me. "It's probably nothing I can't handle."

"Could be bandits," I pointed out.

Zach smirked. "Like I said, nothing I can't handle."

Remembering his complete and total victory over Amias,
I couldn't argue with him. I rolled my eyes anyway. "What a
pompous prince."

Zach laughed loudly, and a buzz of happiness went through
me.

The smoke grew as we traveled, as if its masters were
feeding the flames with triple the amount of wood it had
started with. The sweet burning smell tickled my nose, and
in its fragrance I could detect the aroma of pork and wild
pheasant. My mouth watered. It had been a while since we'd
stayed at the village with Patrice's delicious stew.

Once we heard voices, the crackle of the fire, and faint
music, Zach made us stop, and we dismounted. "Stay here.
I'll be back."

I grasped his wrist. "Be careful, they could—"

Zach placed two fingers on my lips. "I appreciate you worrying about me, but I'll be fine."

I pushed his hand away. "Get on, then," I snapped, ignoring the way my pulse had quickened. "I'm starving."

Zach disappeared into the gloom of the trees, and Bromley and I barely waited for more than five minutes before Zach came back, not nearly as surreptitiously as before.

"It's a band of entertainers—perfectly harmless."

"Entertainers…" I threw my arm out in front of Brom as he stepped forward. Narrowing my eyes at Zach, I said quietly, "You mean Romantica."

No response. Neither of us moved. With a sigh, Zach finally said, "They're good people, Ivy. We don't need to tell them we're Royals."

"You mean *one* of us is a Royal," I shot back.

Zach's jaw tightened. "They're *good* people."

The story about his mother came back to me. The pain in his eyes when he'd talked of his past and his people. They certainly weren't *evil*. Just misguided. But I wasn't going to make the mistake of insulting Zach again.

"I never said they weren't. I'm just… They're different. How do I even go about talking to them?"

Zach took my hand. "Like you're talking to me, only less snooty."

I broke into a grin. "I can't promise anything if they're even half as obnoxious as you."

Zach laughed and unfastened my cloak, turning it inside out so the Legion crest was no longer visible, and then he tugged me along. Bromley trailed after us with the horses.

We came to the edge of the woods, and I had to stifle my gasp at the scene before me. Instead of a simple campsite, it was practically a festival, complete with tables piled high with food freshly cooked over their glorious fire, musicians playing on flutes and fiddles and beating on stretched skins, and colorfully dressed characters chatting, eating, and dancing. Their canopied wagons of blue, red, and purple were parked in a circle around the fire, and their horses—even a few goats— were tethered in a grassier area, grazing.

Looking at the festive scene, the devout Royal in me prayed the priests would never find out about this. They would want me to perform a dozen rites to rid myself of their heretic germs.

"So what did you tell them?" I whispered to Zach as a few Romantica waved to us—a young teenage boy and two older men.

"I fed them a story of how we're traveling to the village for trade." Zach waved back and led us over.

The older man, dressed in a deep-purple tunic, gray pants, and a vest woven with crimson and indigo threads, spread his arms and smiled—I guessed he did. It was hard to tell with his big black beard. "Welcome, travelers—friends! Young maiden." With a flourish, he grabbed my hand and planted a swift, scratchy kiss on my knuckles. "My name is Jiaza, and this is my brother, Pan, and my son, Kiaza. It's a delight to have you at our feast. Come, come, there's plenty. Kiaza, take their horses and get them watered."

Jiaza, still grasping my hand, brought me to the women with giant steaming pots and chunks of meat roasted on sticks. In no time, the smiling, busty Romantica women had laden us with food. Immediately Brom took a bite of his meat, and I followed suit. The savory juices of the pheasant, bursting with flavors of shassa root, frezz berries, lemon pepper, and other hidden herbs, consumed my senses, and it was all I could do to not gobble it down while standing.

Jiaza led me to a spot near the fire and sat across from me. "So," he began, rubbing his hands together, "traveling north, eh? Whereabouts you three from?"

"Myria's Crown City," I answered before taking a large bite of pheasant.

"Ah, good honest folk down there, but not much for celebrating! Too many fighters. If you ask me, it's all the Legion's fault." Jiaza nodded knowingly.

"No one asked yeh, yeh old coot," a voice said from behind.

Laughter rippled through the little circle, but Jiaza ignored them and winked at me. "Lovely women, though, yeah? Now, what're you looking to trade?"

I chewed faster to answer, but before I even swallowed, one of the women who had served the food sat next to me and drew an arm around my shoulders. "Hush, Jiaza, the poor dears are just about starved for a decent meal. Let them eat! They can suffer your interrogation after their stomachs are full."

The woman, who introduced herself as Yana, was Jiaza's wife and insisted I have second helpings. She even gave Bromley thirds, mostly because he was too nice to say no. Yana was a heavyset woman with thick dark-brown hair that was braided with beads and red threads. Her attire was simpler than that of her daughters and nieces, and much more concealing.

The younger Romantica girls wore surprisingly little for the northern climate, with bangles and shiny metals on their wrists, ankles, and collarbones to reflect the firelight when they danced. And there always seemed to be at least one of them dancing. They moved like firebirds, diving into the flames, spreading their sparkling silk wings and swooping away. I had never seen dances such as these. Only Royal waltzes at the castle. This Romantica dancing was foreign and mesmerizing.

I could understand why Zach would enjoy watching the dancing girls, because I was captivated by them, too.

Yet, I did not like it.

Nor did I like when they flitted around him, touching his

arms and whispering into his ear, pulling him closer to the fire for a dance.

I ignored them, pretending not to see and not to care. No, I wasn't pretending—I really *didn't* care. What would be the point? I had no reason to be irritated. None whatsoever.

"Maid, what troubles you? Do you wish to dance?"

A young man with curly black hair and a golden crystal dangling from his ear stood before me, his hand outstretched. His brown eyes reflected the firelight.

"Wish to...? Oh, no—I'm fine." I laughed nervously, scooting away from the smell of smoke that clung to his hair and clothes. Not that it was a bad smell. It was sweet. "Besides, I can't dance."

"Nonsense." The man grasped my hand and tugged. "Everyone can dance!"

"Not this one." Another hand caught the man's wrist and pulled it away from me. Zach smiled as he stepped in front of me and dropped his hold on the Romantica. "Believe me, she'll step on your toes out there."

The man shrugged and returned to the ring around the fire, clapping to the music's rhythm.

The night air was chilly, but the heat in my cheeks and neck warmed my body all over. "I'd step on *your* toes," I muttered as we took seats on a bench together.

"You could *try*." He laughed. "But I'm an excellent dancer. Maybe I'll show you."

"I might enjoy that. Remind me the next time we're not on a dangerous mission surrounded by dark curses."

Jiaza, who had been drinking deeply from his cup, suddenly stopped and bent forward. "You two ran into a curse?"

Zach and I glanced at each other. Inwardly, I kicked myself. What was I thinking, bringing up this talk in front of Romantica?

But the bearded man didn't wait for our reply. He shook his head and took another swig. "More curses. More creatures. When will it end?" Then he reared back and threw his cup into the fire, the flames sparking angrily.

"Jiaza!" Yana hit her husband with a cleaning rag that hung from her belt. "That was a good mug!"

"Bah! What good are mugs if we're attacked nearly every week?" Jiaza grumbled, clearly drunk.

Yana sighed and turned to Zach, Brom, and me. "I'm sorry about that, my dears. We're just frustrated. We've had some rough days. And after seeing the last cursed village…"

"Cursed village?" I asked.

"Yes, it's just north of here. It's a terrible disease, started by some witch's curse, no doubt. Things were so bad we didn't even stop long enough for water from their well. Poor villagers are suffering, but being so far from Myria, they haven't had any Royals check on them."

"Royals!" Jiaza roared suddenly, squeezing his beefy fists together. "Good riddance! We're better off without them!"

I bit my lip, suppressing a retort. It wasn't as if I didn't already know how Romantica viewed us.

"But Royals help us," Brom said, glancing at me.

We didn't just help them. We fought for them. *Died* for them. And yet here was this ungrateful…*heretic*— Zach squeezed my arm, and I refocused.

Jiaza's features were now slumped, the light in his eyes no longer there. "Oh, sure, they help where they can. But really, lad, they're just cleaning up their own mess."

This time Zach's squeeze couldn't stop me from speaking up. "What's *that* supposed to mean?"

Yana pursed her lips and smoothed her worn, ruffled skirt. Jiaza raised a bushy eyebrow. "Why, the tale, maiden. *The* Tale. Of Queen Myriana and her sister, Saevalla."

I stiffened. The history of my ancestors was not a campfire story to be told over drinks. It was something to be read, studied. It was not just a *tale*.

Brom leaned forward with wide eyes. "What do you mean, cleaning up their mess?"

Jiaza stroked his beard. "I'm surprised yeh haven't heard it, lad. Well then, let ole Jiaza tell you the story the kingdoms don't have in their books. Yeh see, they don't want yeh thinking it's their fault. They want yeh to believe the Legion is our savior—"

"Jiaza, don't yeh say another word against the Royals. They're honest young sirs and ladies putting their lives on the line every day. They deserve our respect," Yana said.

I felt a rush of gratitude toward the woman, which was just as well, seeing as how I was inches from punching her husband.

"Aye, aye, yeh right." Jiaza nodded slowly, and his eyes seemed to focus a little more, as if he were sobering up. "Nevertheless, we have our stories and they have theirs, eh? Oh it's similar enough, mind yeh. Myriana Holly, hair as black as a starless night with lips the color of holly berries..."

Jiaza went on to recount the history I knew so well I could tell it in my sleep. I was reminded of the young princess in my class only a week ago reciting the same story. At least, it had *started* the same way...

"...driven by his deep feelings for Myriana, the beast put himself between her and the dwarf's ax, sacrificing himself to save his true love."

I snorted, but no one seemed to notice.

"The beast fell with a great *boom* that was said to have shaken the forest and emptied the trees of their leaves. But like her sister, Saevalla had also fallen in love with Raed, and through anger and grief, drew her dagger and plunged it into the dwarf's heart—"

"Saevalla did no such thing!" I said, appalled. All eyes turned on me. "Myriana kissed the beast out of gratitude, and with her power, Raed turned back into a human with enough power to kill the dwarf."

Jiaza lifted one eyebrow and regarded me. "Aye, maiden, that is what's in the Royals' history books. But the truth"—he shook his head—"the truth is far more twisted."

I pursed my lips, not wishing to hear any more of these awful Romantica tales, but Zach kept his grip on my arm.

"The *truth* is that *both* sisters had fallen in love with the beast," Jiaza said.

"Must've been *some* beast!" joked a man with short hair and a goatee.

"Hush, Tico, let him tell the story," said a girl.

"While Saevalla stood over the dwarf's corpse, shaking with tears," Jiaza boomed, drowning out the others, "Myriana kissed her beloved Raed and this *True Love's Kiss* turned the beast back into the hunter."

Tico walked behind us, stroking his goatee and grinning. "Myriana and Saevalla were overjoyed to have their beloved back," he said, deepening his voice to impersonate Jiaza, and pausing for dramatic effect. "Except…he loved but *one* sister." He leaned in between Zach and me, his dark eyes catching mine. "He asked Myriana to marry him. She accepted, knowing her sister loved the man, too. The jealousy and hate within Saevalla grew dark and twisted."

Jiaza picked the story back up. "And when Myriana's and Raed's first child was born, Saevalla stole the child away into the night."

This time, the girl—the same girl who had hushed Tico before—drew her knees up to her chest and continued. "She went to the six brothers of the dwarf whom she had slain and told them an awful lie—that it was Myriana's husband—*her own beloved*—who had killed their brother. Saevalla then handed over her niece to the dwarves as a peace offering and payment to help her seek revenge upon her sister and Raed."

"Eager for the same vengeance, the dwarves granted her more than a curse." Tico slipped his arm around Zach's shoulders and mine and drew us closer, lowering his voice to a fierce whisper. "They granted her all their powers, sacrificing their own lives in the process, to turn her into something more evil than anything that had ever walked this earth. Saevalla was consumed by the darkness in their souls and turned into the Wicked Queen—Mistress and Mother of the Forces. With the dwarves' powers, she gave rise to an entire army…to the Forces of Darkness."

"No!" I yelled, standing so suddenly that Tico nearly toppled backward. Everyone looked at me in surprise. "Lies! None of you even—"

Zach squeezed my arm, and I tore from his grasp and stormed away. I kicked up leaves and dirt as I practically ran from the fire and the sounds of Romantica merriment, back into the forest.

I shook my head violently, as if the story I had just heard would simply fall from my ears. What terrible lies. Saevalla would've never done such a thing to her sister. And everything had happened because of Love? All the jealousy and hate…it was nonsense. This was why the Romantica were dangerous. They dwelled too much on emotion and allowed it to rule their thoughts, their actions, their very *lives*. Not only that, but they threw around lies about the Legion's true origins. The Royal Three had discovered they were a different breed of mortals— not mages, but still holding unique magic. Romantica liked to think they were simply mortals and nothing special. But they were wrong. They'd had magic that had never existed before and produced heirs, hoping the magic would continue through their bloodline. And it did.

I was proof. All the Royals were proof.

The smells of the food and fire disappeared and were replaced with the crisp scent of pine and brucel. Branches tugged at my clothes and stung my skin as I hurried into the forest, but the stinging in my eyes was much worse.

Why did Jiaza's version bother me so much? Was it because Zach probably believed in this awful, twisted version of Myriana and Saevalla? It tore up my insides. How could the Romantica think that of us? That the Royals' ancestors were the cause of all this darkness?

A hand grabbed my shoulder, and I whirled around. It was Zach, his face drawn tight with concern. "Ivy—"

"You—you believe this tale as well, don't you? This—this horrid *lie*?" I batted his hand away from my shoulder.

Zach took hold of my forearms instead. "Ivy, who knows what truly happened? It was five hundred years ago!"

"I don't care how long ago it was. It matters! They think *we're* the reason they're suffering—how could they think that? And how *dare* they say that about Saevalla? She was loyal to her sister, she would've never—" I was so angry I could barely complete sentences.

Zach slid his hands down to my wrists and intertwined our fingers. With his touch I felt a sudden rush in my blood, remembering last night by the fire. It both shocked and calmed me.

"Ivy." His voice was soft. "It's just a story...a legend. Nothing more than that. And besides, what you do—what you *fight* for—is much more important than what a few entertainers think." Zach placed his hands on my cheeks, his fingertips brushing my hair. "Think about the dragon. Remember the destruction it will bring, and forgive their words. What you and I believe...isn't important. It's what we *do* to help these lands that really counts."

The raging storm inside me died down to a gentle breeze. Slowly, I nodded.

Zach smiled and moved his hands to my hair tied in a tight bun. "Now," he murmured. With a quick tug, he removed the ribbon, and my hair tumbled down around my shoulders. "Let's have some fun."

CHAPTER NINETEEN

DISTRACTED

Zach pulled me back toward the Romantica camp. Back to the fire and the music and the dancing...back to the lies. But Zach was right. It was just *their* story. So what if they believed in something different than I did? I'd always known about their blasphemous version, but hearing it...well, it changed nothing.

With my anger disappearing like the smoke rising to the stars, I let Zach pull me into the firelight. The little band of musicians struck up a tune that was fast and upbeat, and although I didn't know any real steps, I was eager to join in.

On the other side of the fire, Jiaza stood with Tico. He raised his new mug of ale, as if in apology for upsetting me. Part of me was tempted to return and apologize myself, but that would mean leaving Zach's hand and the beat of the music. I wasn't willing to give that up.

I looked back at Zach, and he was watching me. Half his face cloaked in shadow and the other—amber and gold.

"No time like the present," Zach said, and before I could ask what he meant, he spun me around and pulled me close, my back against his chest with one arm around my waist. Like this, I could feel the rhythm with which he danced. As quickly as Zach had pulled me in, he pushed me out and twirled me.

My feet stepped in time to the claps, and before I knew it, I was dancing. Perhaps not perfectly or gracefully, but it didn't matter. The only thing that mattered was the feeling that came with it. It was pure exhilaration. Right then, all the constricting rules and expectations slid off me. The sweet smoke from the fire filled my hair and tunic, and I was whisked away by its wild scent. And by the wild gleam in Zach's eyes.

Then the beats changed, and there was a lighthearted shout from the Romantica in unison. Dancers suddenly started trading partners, winding their way around the fire, linking arms and twisting, then letting go and linking again.

A stranger grabbed my arm and pulled me forward. It was all I could do not to stumble. Then a woman grasped my arm, twisted around, and moved past me in a blur. Dancer after dancer took my arms and pulled past me, weaving in and out like a figure eight. Amazingly, I managed to keep up and follow their folk dance. It was exciting, but I was acutely aware of Zach's absence.

The music changed tempo and the partner-switching stopped. I was left with a young man with curly hair and a crystal earring — the same man from earlier.

He winked at me. "Looks like I get that dance after all, eh, maid?"

Caught up in the atmosphere, I laughed. "Yes, it seems I've gotten better."

Although I didn't step on his toes, I wasn't nearly as graceful as I had felt with Zach. As soon as the thought entered my mind, annoyance surfaced for comparing everything to him.

Then I caught sight of Zach, and the irritation escalated. A girl hung on his arm, batting her long lashes.

Distracted, I missed a step and tripped over my own feet. I expected to stumble, even hit the ground, but instead strong arms looped about my waist and twirled me back around.

The man grinned as his hand traveled up the small of my back, then between my shoulder blades. "You were doing so well."

I tried to inch away, but the pressure on my back increased. I frowned, not liking that look in his eyes. It reminded me of Amias when I was about to bestow a Kiss on him.

But the man merely grinned again. "Up for another dance, maid? I could teach you more."

"Tempting," I said, forcing a laugh. "But I should get back to my companions. We have to leave early tomorrow."

The Romantica raised an eyebrow and looked over my shoulder meaningfully. "Something tells me one of them might be staying up rather late."

Confused, I followed his gaze.

The Romantica girl had Zach's cheeks in her hands, his lips pressed to hers.

I watched, the music fading into a muted buzz, as Zach jerked away, his gaze catching mine. Those hazel eyes widened, and his mouth popped open. He took a step forward, but I was already turning away, my hair whipping about and falling down my other shoulder, reminding me of only minutes ago when his fingertips had been in it. This time, I ran.

His footfalls pounded behind me, and I begged my legs to take me farther into the forest, away from the deafening music and suffocating smoke.

He had kissed a girl he'd known less time than me. A girl whose lips created no magic. After all that talk about kisses being special—about Love.

He was a Romantica, and so was she. Maybe that was reason enough. Maybe he truly hated me for what I was and for what *I* believed in. Maybe that was the real reason he wouldn't Kiss me. Still, I thought kisses meant more to him than just a passing stranger's whims.

When had I become someone who struggled with the difference between a kiss and a Kiss?

The thought nearly knocked the wind out of me. The feelings that were tailspinning out of control made no sense to my logically driven mind. Zach could flirt, kiss, or even bed anyone he wanted—it wasn't for me to judge or dictate. Yet, the fact that he'd so easily kiss another girl, while he wouldn't Kiss me even to save others—for a much greater purpose— made me so angry and hurt and *jealous*, I couldn't see straight.

"Ivy! Please! You don't understand!" His voice called to me through the crashing of bushes and slashing of branches.

"Don't come near me!"

An arm wrapped around my waist, pulling me to him, and I swiveled around, pushing hard against his chest. He stumbled back, raising his hands as if in innocence. But he was far from it.

"What you saw—"

My hands curled into fists. "Save it. You don't have to explain anything to me."

"Ivy, I didn't kiss her!"

"Really, so what was *that*? Wiping a crumb off her lips *with yours*?" Anger made my voice shake, but in my times of being furious with Zach, the feelings here were different.

At this point I couldn't face them.

"*She* kissed *me*!"

I raked my hands through my wild hair, pushing it away from my face. "*I've* tried to Kiss you, Zach. And every time, you've stopped me."

Zach glanced away.

"And now the prince stays quiet. You'll kiss some stranger, but you won't Kiss me, your partner…to *save* people. But you know what? It's fine."

I turned to go again, but Zach gripped my wrist. "It meant

nothing. It was just one kiss."

That stung worse than anything he could've said. "You think that makes it better? Zach, our Kisses are to *save* people, to keep us alive to kill more monsters. Don't you get it? You'd rather kiss her when it means *nothing* than—I mean, am I *so* detestable to you that—?" I forced myself to stop before the tears came in full force.

I dropped my gaze to the dark forest floor, unable to look at him.

There it was. The real crux of it. Maybe what I feared the most. That he didn't like me. At all. Maybe I'd been reading the signs between us wrong—after all, I'd had no real experience with Lust of my own—but I'd thought at least there'd been some attraction there. But when he'd kiss another girl so easily…

I reached up and tugged at the roots of my hair, my head spinning with poisonous thoughts. *Merciful Sisters, I hate this. I hate feeling pathetic. Like a failure. Usually it's only my mother who makes me feel like this.* The tears suddenly went away, replaced by anger. I wouldn't let a man cripple me this way—it was enough that my mother did.

When I looked back up, Zach was staring at me, real pain in his eyes, as if I'd stabbed him with his own dagger. "*No*. No, Ivy, how could you think that?"

I hugged my arms. "You haven't given me a reason *not* to."

"I was distracted… She caught me off guard."

My laugh was bitter. "Troll's breath, Zachariah, what in the Fields of Galliore could have distracted you so much?"

He opened his mouth then closed it.

Nothing. No excuse to give.

We stood like that for a long time, with only starlight raining down on us. We were in one of the clearings, free from towering branches that obscured the sky. I'd wanted to see the stars, but now, after this, the view would seem tainted.

Dancing, laughing, only minutes ago. What was wrong with the two of us? Why couldn't we get along? Like real partners?

That's all we were—partners. Nothing between us except this mission. This dragon.

"This changes nothing. You still refuse to Kiss me. But I need you for the dragon. Let's get out of this forest. I just want to sleep." In one swift movement I gathered up my curls and tied them back again. I brushed past Zach and heard him turn around to follow me to the campsite. He remained silent, but I could imagine the look on his face, and it was one I wanted to forget.

The next morning, I woke next to Bromley. I couldn't remember much after standing in the forest under the stars. I vaguely recalled pulling Brom away from more Romantica food and tales and settling down to sleep, but after everything, the details were hazy.

The sun was just peeking over the horizon, so the world was still mostly shadows. Zach was by the horses, saddling up and getting ready to go. I touched Brom's arm and he sat up, rubbed his eyes, and got to his feet. I was a little slower.

"Go on, help him," I said to Brom, gesturing at Zach. "I'm coming."

I rolled up our wraps and fit them into our bag, which I then slung over my shoulder. I stopped briefly by Jiaza and Yana's wagon. With a sleepy smile, Jiaza raised his hand in parting.

Though I still hadn't forgotten his tale of lies, I remembered what Zach had said: *they are good people*. I smiled and raised my hand as well, in thanks.

The silence on the road was not tense, like so many of our other post-fight silences, just melancholy and uncomfortable. Bromley didn't seem to notice, or if he did, he gave no indication. Then again, Brom had a knack for reading my emotions, so he probably knew something had happened. However, neither Zach nor I acted rude to each other. In fact, we were civil. By speaking politely and using small gestures, it was as though we were strangers working together.

Which was far worse than hostility.

At noon we stopped for some leftover roasted meat Yana had packed for us last night. We were passing through wooded areas, but the trees and their branches were thinner. So rather than the woods being bathed in shadows highlighted by flecks of intruding sunlight, it was all golden. The sun seemed so close to us, its light bouncing off the shiny leaves, making everything glow with a hazy yellow hue.

Its beauty was not lost on me, but in the back of my mind I felt disconnected. From Zach, from Brom, from my mission altogether. I thought of the female mage and wondered again if the golden magic had been hers. Zach hadn't seemed to care much, while Brom shared my skepticism.

I was so consumed in my thoughts that I hadn't even noticed Zach leave. When Brom caught me looking around for him, he said, "He went to get water."

"Right," I muttered, stroking Lorena's neck. She huffed and tossed her head.

"You two had another fight?" Bromley asked.

Sighing, I turned to face my friend, and Lorena nudged my back with her nose. "I don't get it, Brom—why can't we get along? We're supposed to be partners…but then he goes and…" I let out a frustrated groan and went back to my horse.

"He goes and…?"

I hesitated. I didn't want to bring Brom into the middle of

this, but on the other hand, I wanted to tell someone. Maybe I was looking for some consolation. "Last night a girl... Well, he let something happen, and he said it was because he was distracted."

Brom merely stared at me, waiting for me to continue.

"But—but that's ridiculous, right? I mean, come on, distracted? He slices snakes as they jump through air. His reflexes are better than a werecat's. I mean, really, what on earth could have distracted him to lower his guard that much?"

At this, Brom rolled his eyes and went back to rubbing down his horse.

"What?" I asked.

"I'm tempted to let you figure it out for yourself."

I was surprised at his freshness. "Tell me. You know the fate of Myria—and possibly the other four kingdoms—rests on this mission. On our partnership."

Brom paused, resting his arms and chin on his horse's saddle, and smirked. "It's you."

"What?"

"He was distracted by *you.*"

His words settled in. Before my mind could comprehend them, my feet were already moving in the direction of the stream.

My whole body rang with a weird sort of inner hum, as if the speed at which my thoughts were flying actually created a kind of noise.

I had to know. I couldn't stand another minute of only *hoping* Bromley was right—that Zach was distracted by me. Could Zach have been watching me last night? Dancing with that Romantica man within *very* close proximity? If he had been watching, maybe he'd lowered his guard so much that the girl had managed to plant a kiss on him when I couldn't...

Zach stood from the bank of the stream as I came to a

stop, realizing how careless I'd been—crashing through the woods like that.

"Ivy?"

"You were distracted," I said, then pressed my lips together. I forced the next words out. "You didn't mean to kiss her."

Zach glanced around, like he expected someone else to come traipsing out of the woods. Finally he said, "I was distracted, and I didn't *want* to kiss her."

"It's not that you'd rather…" I trailed off. I couldn't finish it.

Zach's confusion cleared, and he smiled softly. "When I said it didn't mean anything, it wasn't meant to hurt you. I wanted you to understand that I…I kiss only girls I like. And I kiss only for my own feelings. Never as a weapon. I'm sorry, Ivy, I just can't do that." He walked to me. "But not Kissing you has *nothing* to do with how I feel…I mean, who you are."

My heart thudded heavily, racing in a way it had never done before. Not when Amias kissed me under the torchlight and not even when Zach had taken off his shirt. "I suppose I believe you," I whispered.

Zach reached up and traced a thumb across my cheek, over my freckles. "How come you believe me now?"

"I have to believe my partner."

"Wise decision. Besides, if I were to kiss someone, it wouldn't have been like that."

I couldn't move. My body was heavy, like pounds of iron. "Oh really? And what would it have been like?"

Zach chuckled. "Nice try."

"No, really, we're not on the battlefield. I'm only curious."

He regarded me for a few seconds then took a step closer. When he did, all my senses heightened. Slowly, he placed his marked hand on my hip then slid it up to my waist, then my ribcage. His fingers moved against the fabric of my tunic, feeling my ribs and rubbing my skin underneath. His other hand grasped my wrist, and his fingers curled around, resting on my palm. Our chests were practically touching.

"You ever had a *real* kiss, princess?"

I swallowed, unable to answer.

Zach's hand moved up. His fingers touched the back of my neck, applying just the right amount of pressure so I tilted my head up ever so slightly. His thumb brushed my jaw and, against my will, my eyes closed.

He squeezed my side gently. My lungs shuddered for a breath under his hand. When I felt his own breath on my lips, something inside me crashed against my bones, like the waves of the Sea of Glyll surging upon the rocks by Freida Castle.

But there was nothing more.

He dropped his head to my shoulder. His forehead rested on my heated skin.

I willed my eyes to open as he drew away slowly. His face, then his chest, then his arms, until he held only my fingertips, then he let those fall as well.

Zach said nothing, but his eyes were not teasing as I thought they would be. His lips were pressed into a thin line, and his jaw was clenched. He avoided my gaze as he moved past me, footsteps pounding against the ground like the Romantica drums.

He was usually so light on his feet.

I squeezed my eyes shut, let out another breath, and raised my hand to my cheek, then to my forehead, kneading my temples.

Erase it, Ivy. That didn't happen. It didn't.

I had faced trolls, witches, dwarves, goblins, griffins, wraiths, and stared Darkness in the face without stumbling, but standing here, in this golden forest, I was truly shaken.

CHAPTER TWENTY

A FAMILIAR FACE

It took several splashes of cold water on my face to clear my head enough to start back. On the way, I tried to chase away thoughts the freezing water hadn't dismissed. But nothing in the world could cure what I was feeling now. I was desperate to act normal, as though my entire being hadn't just been stripped away and twisted into something I didn't recognize.

Who was this girl who became weak-kneed? This princess who swooned in the arms of a man? This weakling who gave in to Lust?

I'd never thought I would bend to Lust's will so easily, submitting to petty emotions like jealousy, which the Legion taught so severely to evade. It disgusted me that I couldn't touch him without feeling a ripple of pleasure and dizziness shoot through me. And worst of all, I had stood there ready to give in to a kiss off the battlefield. A kiss I'd vowed never to trouble myself with until I was sent to Freida.

It was painfully apparent that one *glance* from Zach was more exciting to me than any Kiss I'd ever shared with another prince.

The truth of it all made me want to roll into a ball, cowering on the forest floor until winter came and snow hid me from the rest of the world.

More disgraceful still, I was *disappointed*. Disappointed Zach had not followed through with his kiss. Why had he backed away? Did he somehow believe I would lure magic from him if we tried? He needn't have worried. I hadn't been able to summon normal words—let alone a *spell*.

Shame burned through a wall in my stomach. How could I even call myself a princess of the Legion?

"Milady!"

Bromley jogged toward me, concern etched on his features. I wondered how long I had been washing my face.

"Sorry," I responded on reflex. Zach was already on his horse, his face turned away, careful not to look me in the eye. "I—got a little lost."

Bromley didn't question it, but his pursed lips showed he didn't buy the obvious lie. I was just glad he kept quiet. I had nothing left in me to lie again.

The village to the north of the woods was much larger than the other village we'd passed through, but quieter.

The houses and shops of the village were made of beautiful sanded wood, a testament to their trade and the surrounding forest. In the middle of the square was a handsome old cobblestone well. To the north was a large structure with many windows and painted accents of red, green, and blue. It was either the Town Hall or perhaps a tavern that served as the general meeting area for the residents. Spanning to the east and west were shops with colorful wooden signs and houses lined up neatly, each with little spice gardens or some kind of vegetable patch.

"It's quiet," Zach commented, winding the reins of his steed in one hand and scanning the surroundings.

"It's barely dusk. Someone should be out and about, right?" Brom said.

I nodded. "I don't even hear any animals." Then it came to me. Yana had said they'd avoided a village under a curse. With my mind on…other things, I had completely forgotten.

My Sense was vacant in the face of a witch's curse—only a slight feeling of nausea—so I had no clue what kind of curse we were up against.

A door opened across the square, and a small child emerged then quickly shut the door behind her. Gathering her skirts, she scampered down the house's little path and into the spice garden out front. She fell to her knees and started rooting through the garden with speed, almost in a panic.

I let go of Lorena's reins and hurried toward her. Not wanting to frighten her, I slowed about twenty paces away. "Hello? Little miss?"

The child looked up, clutching a bundle of weeds to her chest. Her face was smeared with either dirt or soot, and her fair hair was bundled up in a bun, like mine. Her eyes were wide with fright, and I felt guilty for scaring her. "I won't hurt you," I said, holding out my hands.

Zach came up behind me, but I remained focused on the little girl. "I just want to know if we can help."

The girl's bottom lip trembled, yet she kept quiet.

"Can you tell me what's wrong?"

Her large eyes darted from me to Zach.

"Why is this place so quiet?" I tried again.

The girl dug her hands in the earth, pulled out some roots, and then bolted back inside, stumbling on the way, then latched the door.

"A curse," Zach said softly.

"The one Yana mentioned," I agreed.

Zach and I looked at each other, our eyes meeting for the first time since that moment in the woods. We both had the same thought: what curse was it?

He nodded to the central structure. "Shall we?"

As our little party approached, I admired its architecture. The darkest, richest wood of the oldest trees had been used for the building. It was impressive for a town almost a week's journey from regular trade routes. Beautifully carved designs decorated the outer edges of the windows and doors. Above the large oak double doors hung a sign that read PELKEN'S TOWN TAVERN.

I balled my fists in preparation for what lay beyond those doors.

Zach rapped his knuckles on the wood, and the sound echoed into the empty square. We waited. There was nothing. He glanced at me then knocked again, harder.

Before his fourth knock, the door opened, and a woman with dark hair and sunken eyes glowered at us from behind a crack. "I heard yeh the first time," she snapped in her heavy northern accent. "Yeh think it's easy to drop what I'm doing to answer a blasted knock? Come in 'ere yehselves if yeh've got a death wish."

Zach lowered his hand awkwardly. "I'm sorry, we didn't mean—"

"What's going on here?" I interrupted.

The woman opened the door all the way to reveal a slightly swollen belly. "Travelers. Far south?"

Her pregnant belly made me pause, but I quickly answered, "As far as the Crown City."

Her sharp eyes darted to my cloak, and seeing the Legion crest, instantly her persona changed. She brought a hand to her stomach and leaned against the doorframe. "Blessed Mounts of Wu-Hyll, yeh're from the castle?"

By the wind wisps. I should've thought this through. Now this woman was eyeing me with a look I had seen many times, a look I usually reveled in—one of hope. She hoped we were Royals able to lift the curse on their village with a Kiss.

There were at least two problems with this: one, we didn't have long until the dragon hatched, and two, even if we took the time to investigate what kind of curse it was, and what kind of Kiss was required, Zach would refuse.

Still, I couldn't lie to this woman and watch the hope shatter in her eyes.

"Yes." I straightened. "My name is Ivy Myriana, a princess of the Royal Legion. This is my page, Bromley, and my partner, Prince Zachariah. Please, tell us what's happened here."

The woman beckoned us inside, sniffing and fighting back tears. "Thank the sacred wisps." She wiped at a stray tear. "Princess, we're under a curse. People are fallin' ill every day. Practically everyone is infected. It's been so long since a Royal from the Legion came this far, I hadn't dared hope. She's been a blessing to us, o' course, but she's no Royal—"

"I'm sorry," I interrupted as Zach, Brom, and I stepped into the cavernous hall. "*She?* Who's she?"

Before the woman could answer, a voice from above rang through the hall.

"Look who decided to show up."

The entrance hall was sectioned off into an east and west wing, but north of the hall was a winding staircase, the top floor cut off from view by large wooden beams crisscrossing over the high ceiling.

Together, Zach and I stepped to the foot of the stairs and looked up.

Leaning over the rail, black hair curling down and deep azure robe rolled at the sleeves, was the female mage.

CHAPTER TWENTY-ONE

THE CURSE OF VENERA

In one hand she held a damp rag, and in the other she balanced a steaming pot, probably containing a stew full of medicinal herbs. She smiled down at us like we were old friends.

We were silent as she made her way down the stairs. The mage handed her cauldron to the pregnant woman. "Rochet, I've given this to all the sick upstairs. It should help ease their pain. Can you give it to the rest so I can inform the prince and princess of the type of sickness?"

Rochet nodded. "Of course, thank yeh, Lady Millennia." She took the pot then crossed into the east wing, her footsteps echoing on the hardwood floor.

"So your name is Millennia," I said.

Her smile disappeared, and a scrutinizing look took its place. "I figured you were only a day behind me. Got caught in the storm, did you?"

I almost asked how she'd been able to evade it when she'd been at least two hours behind us after getting rid of the sparrow harpies, but I decided there were more important things to be concerned about.

"Where's your master?" I asked for the second time.

She ignored the question and continued, "Although I have

to admit, I had only *half* hoped you'd pass by this village."

"And what do you mean by that?" I asked, my hands on my hips.

"I meant only that you, like all other Royals, would want to cure this village the easy way—with a Kiss."

I bristled. "Easy way? A counter-curse Kiss is not *easy*. It takes years of study to master the spells for every sickness, and once administered—" I stopped myself from saying the rest: that it leaves a princess almost incapacitated. I didn't want Zach to use that as another excuse not to Kiss me later.

Millennia moved close to Zach, narrowing her deep blue eyes. "So the rumors I heard weren't true. You're *not* a Romantica, since you've obviously allied yourself with a Royal. It's disappointing to me that you took a partner."

"Oh." Zach blinked. "I pray you'll forgive me, milady. After all, everything I've ever done in my miserable life was so I wouldn't be a *disappointment* to you."

Brom snorted and quickly tried to cover it up with a cough.

"Funny," Millennia said with a scowl, then her gaze flickered to me. "I'd hoped one of us might be able to infiltrate their twisted army and still uphold our beliefs, but seems I was wrong."

"Millennia," I said, surprised. "You're a Romantica?" I didn't know Romantica mages even existed.

She rolled her eyes. "Yes, princess. What will you do? Tattle on me?"

"Is that why you don't have a master?" I asked.

"Despite what your arrogant Legion would have you believe, there *are* Romantica mages, and I *do* have a master, but no, she's not here. If you haven't noticed, I am gifted. I don't need a tutor every moment of every day."

Perhaps the Romantica had their mages on a longer leash than Royals. Even so, it was odd. Then I heard coughing from above, and with a pang of guilt I realized now was not the time to interrogate this girl about her eccentricities. "Tell me about the sickness. We want to help."

Millennia took a step back and shook out her sleeves. She regarded me for a moment and sighed. "Follow me."

With a glance at one another, we followed Millennia down the east wing. It was a wide hallway that would've smelled of cedar but now smelled of decay and death and got worse the farther we walked. Millennia spoke over our footsteps. "According to Rochet, a mysterious traveler came to the village about a week ago, asking for a room. The traveler took the room and disappeared the next morning, leaving traces of ol'yen ash."

"A witch," I said. The skin of witches was dry and flaky, which made them shed something that looked and smelled like ash. Then I remembered, when we first met her, Millennia had said she'd been going after a witch. "Is she the one you were searching for?"

Millennia gave a short nod, keeping up her brisk pace. "Had to be. The villagers hoped the witch had only passed through the town, slept in a room, ate a hot meal, took water from the well, and that's it. They didn't think they'd done anything to offend the witch, but as it turned out, during one of their days chopping wood they had come across a garden of dark herbs and uprooted it, worried it would attract beasts."

"The garden was the witch's," I groaned.

"So naturally, the old crone took her vengeance. And the next morning after she left, some of the villagers started fainting with a high fever, then large purple blotches starting appearing on their feet, paralyzing them."

"When the blotches reach their chest, it restricts the lungs and puts them in a deep sleep," I continued, "but when it reaches their heart…"

"How long does it usually take to reach their heart?" Zach asked.

"Depending on the strength of the person, the curse can last a whole month before reaching the lungs. But once it reaches the lungs, they have only twenty-four hours," Millennia said as we came to another large set of double doors.

"The Curse of Venera," I murmured. Although it was a terrible curse, part of me was relieved it was not an airborne sickness. Instead, the Curse of Venera was spread through a poison of some sort. More than likely it was in the villagers' food supply or the clothes they wore.

"Not a pretty curse. And a very powerful one." Millennia wrenched open the doors, and we were slammed with a terrible stench. The smell of rotting skin made my eyes water. I wanted to hold my breath, but I knew it wouldn't help.

Brom staggered back and covered his nose and mouth. Zach grimaced, brought a fist to his mouth, and coughed.

Rochet and a few other villagers went from bed to bed in the giant meeting hall. Based on the number of houses outside, it had to be at least a fifth of the villagers lying in this room, simply hanging on and waiting until they found the sweet release of death.

"These aren't even the worst-off patients. Those with the curse in their lungs are upstairs," Millennia said, her voice thick. "I was able to whip up a stew to ease their pain, but my knowledge of medicinal herbs goes only so far."

Millennia turned and led us out of the meeting-room-turned-infirmary.

"If you knew about this cursed village why didn't you tell us when we first met?" I asked.

Millennia scowled, folding her arms inside her robes. "I *didn't* know, princess. Like I told you, I was following a witch, that's all. I can burn a witch with my mage fire, but I can't very well burn an entire village to cure what the witch left behind, can I?"

I pursed my lips, still mystified a mage would be going after a witch by herself, but the stench in the room and the coughing reminded me again—now was not the time.

I scanned the length of the hall. "How many have died so far?"

"Ten. Gone and burned," Millennia answered.

"Are you sure the worst are upstairs?"

"That we know of. Many may be staying in their homes and trying to take care of themselves, wanting privacy as they rot."

Her words sounded heartless, but she spoke the truth—they *were* rotting.

"I'd like to see the worst patient you have up there—to make my own assessment."

She held up her hands and gave me a look of indifference. "I understand, but I advise you, princess, to be quick in whatever you decide. These people don't have long."

My gaze shot to Zach, who was looking at the sea of beds, each holding a victim of the Curse of Venera.

I turned to Brom, who had gone a little green, and instructed him to shadow Rochet, doing whatever she needed him to. Then Millennia told me where to find the worst patient—an eight-year-old girl at the end of the east hall, upstairs, last door on the left. Apparently she had slipped into the deep sleep yesterday. She had less than three hours to live.

Zach followed me up the steps and down the hall. What would he say when he saw the true effects of the curse? Surely there'd be no shred of doubt in his mind that Kissing me was the right thing to do.

When it came to a curse like this, there wasn't time for arguments about personal beliefs.

We reached the end of the hallway and came to the door.

I touched the brass handle, feeling the cold metal under my fingers and knowing the heat of the feverish skin I would soon be feeling.

Zach's hand wrapped around mine. His body leaned in to my back, his face centimeters from my ear. "I know what you're thinking, Ivy," he said softly. "And I want to save these people as much as you do."

"Then you know what we have to do."

Silence behind me.

I glanced over my shoulder. Zach still stared at the door handle.

"Zach…"

He refused to meet my eyes, and that refusal—it was all I needed to see.

My heart, and the hope I'd had that he'd put his own beliefs aside for the greater good, shattered. Shaking my head, I shook off his hand, opened the door, and slipped into the room. Ignoring the stench, I crossed to the bed and leaned over to inspect the girl's face. She looked younger than eight.

This was why I hated curses. I hated the way they caused pain and suffering until the very end, until the victims were practically begging for death. I'd seen curses, inspected them, and broke them with my Kiss, but I'd treated every one like a simple problem to be solved. An obstacle to overcome. It was better to view them calmly, logically, like I'd been taught. But that was just an excuse. An excuse for my own traumatized past.

I felt the girl's head with the back of my hand. As I'd imagined, she was burning up. After moving down the covers, I pulled up her tunic, revealing her cursed chest. Huge purple blotches, varying in shades, covered her torso. Darker, rougher spots showed where the decay had completely taken hold of her skin. I wanted to cover my mouth and nose, but I forced myself to confirm that it was indeed the Curse of Venera. I had seen this curse once before. It had been far south of the Crown City in a tiny village, where a witch had placed the curse because the villagers had killed her pet griffin—of course, the griffin had eaten a child, but that hardly mattered to the witch. We managed to save only a few survivors, and the princess who had performed the counter-curse Kiss, since I hadn't yet learned that complicated of a spell for such a powerful curse, had used so much of her magic that she was bedridden for a week.

Surely I wouldn't be that greatly affected. For one, the princess had been only a half Royal. Being not only a pure Royal, but also a direct descendant of Myriana, it shouldn't take that much of my strength. Hopefully.

"I've never seen a curse like this," Zach said from above, staring at the girl with empty, tired eyes, and his jaw clenched, as if he were bracing himself.

I rolled the poor girl's covers back up and said nothing.

Silence stretched in the room. I knew there was a battle raging inside him, and it was one I was likely going to win, but I took no pleasure from it. Even though it had been my goal to have him finally give in, I wasn't happy that *this* was the way to convince him. He had been so earnest that night in front of the fire. He believed in True Love with all his heart.

Have you ever loved someone so desperately?

Zach knelt by the girl's bed and rested his hands by her legs, his fingers aimlessly picking at the blanket that lay over her. "You're certain it'll work?"

There had been a few occasions, though rare, that a counter-curse Kiss had not succeeded. The village had been left to rot and ruin, and there was absolutely nothing to be done. But those curses had been too late to catch and were doomed from the start. There was hope in this village. And with me...well, I was certain Myriana's magic would work.

I nodded. "I have no doubt."

Zach glanced at me then back at the girl.

"I take it you haven't encountered too many curses in Saevall?"

He shook his head. "No. I was always fighting monsters."

Gently, I laid my hand on his shoulder and squeezed. "You can't put your sword through a disease."

He looked at my hand, his gaze tracing the stag's antlers across my skin. I couldn't imagine I'd ever want to console him for finally agreeing to Kiss me, but the expression on his face was one of both pain and regret, and it wasn't something I ever wanted to see on Zach or anyone.

But I needed him. This little girl needed him.

I had to make sure he was going to give in.

"My first Kiss broke a drought curse on a village," I said softly.

Zach looked up at me, his brows drawn together.

"I was just nine years old, but I still remember the starving villagers. They'd walked around like skeletons. A child—a toddler—had collapsed at my feet because she hadn't eaten in almost two days." I closed my eyes, almost seeing the same little girl in front of me. "I'd cried that day. I was terrified, not because of the villagers, not because their behavior scared me, but because I feared I wouldn't be able to save them."

I could feel Zach's gaze on me, but I kept my eyes closed. The memories, however old, remained fresh, replaying in my head like a magic mirror had trapped them.

"My mother had slapped me when I started to cry. She told me these people didn't have time for my weakness. I stopped crying, and I Kissed the thirteen-year-old prince whose name I can't even remember now."

In retrospect, maybe I should've known it had all been a test. My mother could've performed the Kiss easily, but the

Council had wanted true proof that I was my father's child, since my mother had been known to sleep with many men. They could've performed an heir test, but my mother had insisted on testing my power, angry that the council of Freida didn't trust her.

When my Kiss worked, my mother had murmured, "That's my girl."

It was that day I realized how desperately I wanted to please this strong yet cruel woman who told me these people didn't have time for weakness or failure.

Finally, I opened my eyes, transported away from the dying village of my memories to yet another one.

Zach's jaw was clenched, but I could see the sadness in his eyes—the face of someone yielding.

"It's not about us, Zach," I whispered. "Not our morals. Not our beliefs. It's about them. It's *always* been about protecting them."

So much of my time at the Legion was about battle. Victory. Success. Pleasing my mother. But I knew there was more to this war than just proving my mother wrong. Or possessing the most powerful partner and Kiss. It was about stopping the Forces from destroying innocent lives—from leaving them hollow, dried-up husks or walking corpses.

Zach nodded stiffly. His voice was hoarse as he said, "All right. Tell me what to do."

Both relief and sadness raged within me. I hadn't wanted it to be like this. He should've understood another way. Believed in me and trusted me, not been coerced by a sickness such as this. I leaned over and grasped Zach's hands. "I'm sorry, but it's the only way."

"Ahem." Millennia cleared her throat from the doorway, and Zach and I both turned to her. "That's not true," she said. "There is another way."

CHAPTER TWENTY-TWO

OUT OF TIME

"Excuse me?" I said, standing.

"I said there's another way." Millennia crossed her arms.

"And I'm sure I misheard you. There's no other way to break this type of curse."

"You know that's not true. You just don't want your precious prince to find out."

I felt Zach's eyes boring into the back of my head.

"What's she talking about, Ivy?"

I bit my lip.

"Ivy."

I made a sound between a groan and a growl in my throat. "It is, and it isn't," I muttered. "True, I mean." Then I took a deep breath and turned to face him. He stared at me as if I had just betrayed him. The look cut through me, but I pushed forward. "Technically, there *is* another way to break the curse, *but* we wouldn't be able to break it even if we tried. It's practically impossible. We have less than three hours before this girl loses her life, and I don't want to waste time running around looking for an amulet."

"Amulet?" Zach asked.

He's not going to let this go. "Curses need an object as a medium—something that binds the magic to this world. Most witches' curses use jewels as mediums, and many reside in jewelry of some kind. The Curse of Venera is usually transferred to an amulet."

"You knew all this and didn't say anything." Anger coated his voice now.

I threw my hands up. "There's nothing to be done! A witch curses the amulet and hides it in the village. Even if we knew where it was hidden, there are dark enchantments guarding it."

"What sort of enchantments?" he asked.

A trill of fear crawled up my spine, and I shivered. I tried to hide it by running a hand over my hair, pushing back loose strands that had fallen out of my bun.

Dark enchantments were like stepping into evil itself. They were unnatural and ripped away coherent thought and your sense of right and wrong. The few classes I'd had on them, where we had to experience various types of enchantments, left me with nightmares.

Recalling the cursed amulet book I'd picked up by accident when looking for information on the Sable Dragon, I recited: "Three enchantments, each dealing with a powerful emotion that consumes you. If you get lost in the emotion, there's no way to pull you out—you'll be stuck in the same state, and die there." I hugged my arms. "Don't you see? It'd be suicide to try retrieving it. Besides, it's been so long since someone actually broke a cursed jewel—well, it might not even work. Not only that, it could be anywhere. And it's too dangerous. Who knows what's protecting it?"

"Ivy, we've got to try."

"Why? Are your own beliefs so important that you're willing to risk the lives of these people? Of this little girl?" I pointed at the girl in the bed. She was so young—still with so much ahead of her, and Zach wanted to risk her life for his blasted principles.

Not to mention I'd been seconds away from getting that Kiss, which would have made him see our power could defeat the Sable Dragon as well.

Zach turned to Millennia. "Give us a moment?"

Millennia frowned. "We should get going if you—"

I jumped in. "We?"

"Obviously I'll go, too. It was my idea." Millennia regarded me with a cold stare. "I may be a mage, but this one"—she pointed to Zach—"is the muscle. One person can't do this alone. I was helping the villagers until you arrived. I can do no more for them now except go after the amulet."

"I see. So you saved us in the forest, saw what Zach could do, and decided to wait and use him later? Well, you can forget it. Find your own prince."

"I don't want just any prince," snapped Millennia. "I want *your* prince."

Like back at the Romantica camp, I felt the disgusting emotion of jealousy crawl into my throat and down my arms, making my hands shake. I wished she'd phrased that another way.

"One who's willing to see that there are alternatives to solving everything with a Kiss," she clarified. "We'll find this amulet, and you can have him back," she said with a flick of her hand.

I struggled not to shout, not to wake the other diseased patients, making my voice strained and rough. "You're insane. Did you not hear what I just said? Even if you did find that amulet, you wouldn't be able to break the enchantments in time."

"Let me make this clear to you, princess: I don't give a goblin's toenail if you want to stick your tongue down your prince's throat. Just don't use a curse as an excuse to do it."

It was as if she'd slapped me. I started toward her, fists clenched, but Zach stepped in front of me and took me by the shoulders, forcing me to take a few steps back. He turned to Millennia. "Leave."

Millennia glared at me then stepped out of the room and closed the door behind her.

As soon as the door snapped shut, I knocked Zach's hands away from my shoulders and growled. Like an animal. What was happening to me?

Zach stared at the door. "I had hoped when the day came for two women to fight over me, it'd be over something completely different."

"You think this is funny?"

"No." Zach faced me. His eyes were focused on me, but it was almost like he was looking through me, at the girl on the bed behind us.

Then, without warning, he pulled me into a tight embrace. "I'm scared, Ivy," he said in a whisper, his lips on my ear. "Of this curse, of everything…of losing that little girl over there, or any other innocent life. But…this isn't just about me being a Romantica. It's bigger than that."

My eyes widened at his embrace. He'd never held me like this before. Actually, I don't think any of my partners ever had. And just like that, my anger dissolved. Millennia's words felt a lifetime away. I gently tugged on the back of his shirt. "What're you talking about?"

He pulled far enough away to look into my eyes. "For a long time, a small group of Romantica have…well, they've developed certain theories. They think the Royal's Kiss causes more harm than good."

The warmth of his arms faded, and I forced a laugh. "That's ridiculous." I started to move back, but Zach held my arms tightly.

"I won't lie to you... We don't have any proof. But let me ask you this: why does the earth burn when a creature is killed by the magic of a Kiss? Isn't that unnatural? Without Royal magic they simply crumble to dust. When they're killed with a Kiss, the surrounding earth looks decayed. Dead."

"And?"

"Whenever you've lifted a curse on a village, what happens to everyone? Are they all healed perfectly, or are they left with scars and disfigurements?"

"Surviving a curse comes with a price. They're lucky to be alive."

"Some die anyway, don't they?"

"That's just the way it is. You're looking for a *miracle*. And you're right—this isn't proof. And it's not good enough to risk their lives on chance."

"But that's what we'd be doing anyway. Even if we Kiss, there's no guarantee this girl will live. And you know that. Just give me three hours, Ivy." He took my hands and tugged me closer, again wrapping his arms around me like a warm wool cloak. "You said partners trusted each other."

It felt as if my heart were being twisted in two. "That's... that's not fair," I muttered.

Millennia came in without knocking. She seemed unfazed by Zach holding me. "We need to get moving."

Zach nodded and drew away. "I'm coming."

I gripped his wrist. "The enchantments will *kill* you. *Please* don't do this."

"Three hours." Zach brushed my cheek with the back of his knuckles. "Give me that, and I swear I'll come back for that Kiss."

"And if you die? What then? This isn't a griffin you can slay or a troll you can strangle," I hissed. "Then nothing can save this village, or the rest of the kingdoms for that matter."

"What's *that* supposed to mean?" Millennia interrupted.

We both ignored her. Zach tucked a piece of loose hair behind my ear. "I won't die. I'll come back."

I blew out a breath. "You're right—you won't. I'm going with you."

As we were heading downstairs, Rochet was coming up. "Oh, we've moved your things into one of the rooms and—where are you all going?"

I gave the woman's shoulder a tight squeeze. "I need you to do a few things for me." I glanced at her pregnant belly. "Are you all right to do that?" The poor woman was probably already worked to the bone, and she had to be close to her due date, too.

She waved her hand dismissively. "Don't worry about me, Your Highness."

"Gather every person who's able to start combing their houses. And the people here, too, tell them to search for an amulet, but also have them report if they feel anything strange."

"Strange in what way?"

"Anything. A flinch, a pain, a sharp prick in their joints. If they get suddenly cold or feel sad or their brain becomes foggy, I want to know. No, actually, have them tell Bromley first, then he will report to me."

Then I turned to Millennia. "How good is your earth magic?"

Millennia smirked. "It's excellent."

"I need you to upturn as much soil as you can. The witch could have buried it, causing the amulet's power to seep into the roots in their gardens."

"How deep?"

"Probably no more than a foot."

"How is the Curse of Venera spread?" Zach asked.

"It's not an airborne disease. Which means it's probably located in a place people frequent often, somewhere they could have come in contact with anything that might've absorbed the amulet's power," I explained.

"I'll check the butcher's shop then. The apothecary after." Zach grabbed my hand, squeezed it, and then hurried down the steps after Millennia.

I turned to Rochet. "Can you take me to the room where the witch stayed?"

Rochet led me to the far end of the east wing of the tavern. It was just like any other room, only dustier. I had a feeling no one wanted to sleep here after a witch had. Rochet hovered near the threshold as I scanned the walls and furniture, my hand grazing the quilted bedspread and the cedar wood of the armoire.

My Sense didn't work on the amulet—cursed items were cloaked and enchanted by witches to prevent Royals from using their Sense to locate them—so instead I moved around slowly, trying to notice any strange feeling—an itch, a throb of pain, a confusing emotion.

But it was difficult for me to separate my real emotions from possible fake ones—especially when anger and jealousy at Millennia, and frustration and disappointment about Zach, kept me so distracted.

"I'll hurry and tell everyone to start searching," Rochet said.

"Yes, thank you." Then a thought hit me, and I stopped her. "Wait—Rochet, have you developed any symptoms at all?"

She shook her head. "No, Your Highness. None yet."

It was strange. If ten people had already died and the curse had already worked so far into so many people, then it was likely she'd start to show *some* kind of symptoms.

"Is there any place that you *haven't* been?" I asked.

Rochet frowned. "In the past week? I don't think so. I've visited almost every house and shop delivering Millennia's herbal soup."

Oh well, it's never that easy. "I see. Thank you."

After she left, I went back to my search. I still rather hoped we never found the amulet. I didn't want to go near any dark enchantments. Wasn't going after the Sable Dragon enough?

A sound from outside interrupted my search, and I rushed to the window. The earth churned as soil was overturned, as if invisible shovels and pickaxes were attacking the ground. Millennia stood in the middle of the square, her arms raised.

I went back to searching, and after another ten minutes of checking the room and shuffling around the furniture, I had to concede it wasn't there. If I were close, I would've slipped into one of its enchantments.

Racing out of the room and down the stairs, I burst through the meeting hall's doors, calling for Brom. "Anything?"

Brom looked up from a spot near the back. "Nothing."

I spent the next half hour hurrying through the tavern, trying as hard as I could to clear my emotions and recognize any magical enchantment. At the last room, I headed outside and stopped on the steps, scanning the shops facing the main square. Where would many people go?

The bells on top of the chapel at the far end tolled out. Two hours.

That could be it…the chapel. Everyone went to the chapel to pray.

Although the witch wouldn't have been able to just walk into the chapel, she could've controlled a villager so they could stow the amulet inside.

My feet pounded over the stones as I ran toward the chapel, echoing my heartbeat and the Romantica drums that still thrummed in my head.

Their chapel was small and built of wood, ornately carved. I threw open the doors and ran, breathless, down the main aisle that led to the dais. It was covered with dead plants. Withered and brown.

I stopped before two wooden statues of the Holy Sisters. Their faces, once so gorgeously carved and sanded, were black and warped as if the wood itself was dying.

A violent shudder passed through me, and I sent a prayer to my ancestors. *Help these people, Myriana. And forgive me for what I'm about to do.*

Then I started ripping up the dead plants. They crumbled in my hands. I turned to the pews and moved through them all, shoving aside all emotion, drawing on my Legion training to feel...nothing.

The bells tolled above me. One and a half hours left.

Swearing, I left the chapel. I'd covered every corner and felt nothing.

Zach emerged from the butcher's shop across the square and ran into the apothecary. Millennia paused her magic and wiped her brow with her sleeve, then moved on to another patch of earth and raised her hands.

Their efforts were futile. I knew this, and yet I couldn't help feeling terribly anxious. Briefly I wondered what Master Gelloren would think of me now—working with not one but *two* Romantica to break enchantments of the cursed amulet. The practice was so archaic and risky that I could almost hear Gelloren yelling at me for being illogical. I could almost *feel* my mother's hand across my cheek for wasting precious time. The idea of her seeing me now, and being so appalled that she'd either faint or feed me to a nest of basilisk vipers, was almost funny.

But she wasn't here, thank the Holy Queen. Yet...even if she were...my partner told me to trust him, and if he was going to trust me, then I had to trust him, too.

I ran to the stables.

One hour left. Nothing in the stables.

Forty-five minutes left. Nothing in the apothecary.

Thirty minutes left. Nothing in the villagers' homes.

Twenty minutes before our deadline, I climbed the steps to the little girl's room. She had twenty minutes left to live. I had minutes to Kiss Zach and perform the spell to try to save her and the rest of this cursed village. The scent of decay was overwhelming within the girl's room. Tears filled my eyes, first from the stench and then from the sadness. This girl was literally rotting away while still breathing.

I prayed Zach was on his way. That he'd given up. "It could be anywhere," I muttered. Perhaps I was trying to make myself feel better even though I knew from the beginning how fruitless the search would be.

Yes, it could be anywhere, since the curse could be easily absorbed by almost anything the amulet came in contact with. But the witch had come by only a week ago, so for the curse to affect this many people in that short amount of time, almost everyone would need access to…

"The villagers had hoped that the witch had only passed through the town, slept in a room, ate a hot meal, and took water from the well, and that's it."

I spun toward the window, my gaze locking on the small cobblestone structure in the middle of the square.

"The well," I whispered, taking off at a dead run. "It's in the well!"

CHAPTER TWENTY-THREE

THREE ENCHANTMENTS

Arriving at the well, I slowed to a jog then stopped about ten paces away. I tried extending my Sense, reaching out to latch onto the Force of Darkness, but nothing came to me except…calmness. The tension in my muscles eased, my head stopped spinning with thoughts. It was so peaceful here. I felt like lounging on the ground and staring up at the passing clouds without a care in the world.

My head was foggy, as if the rest of me could just drift away on a breeze. I stared at the well ahead of me and tried to remember what I had been thinking. Had I been thirsty? *What am I doing?* It was too difficult to remember. *Maybe I should just give up. Just lie down right here and take a nap.* I walked to the edge of the well and leaned against it, slid down its side, pressing my skin against its stone surface and closing my eyes. The sun felt wonderful, and the breeze was perfect. In fact—everything was perfect.

"Ivy?"

I heard my name from across the square and opened my eyes. Zach was on the doorstep of some poor soul's house.

Seeing him, hearing his voice, yanked me back to reality. This was the first enchantment. It made me at ease, made me think the exact opposite of what I had been thinking: the amulet was here.

I couldn't move, my body relaxed from the weight of the spell, but I had to reach Zach before my mind was captured by serenity once more.

"Zach! It's here! It's in the—"

A black tendril of water wrapped itself around my head, covering my mouth. It was like a slimy black tentacle, freezing my cheeks and lips as it jerked me over the wall of the well and into its depths. Dimly, I heard Zach scream my name as wind roared in my ears. My back slammed into the water and shock ripped through my spine, knocking the wind out of me. I submerged, my heavy clothes dragging me as if I were sliding down a tube made of ice, pulling at me. I screamed, but black water filled my mouth and choked me.

Drowning. I was drowning in this cursed water. It had come to life and taken me down—either from sensing my magical blood or the threat to its existence.

I tried thrashing in the water and kicking up to the surface, but it was not normal water. It clung to me like rich, sticky honey, dragging me, restraining me, binding me. The harder I yanked and kicked, the tighter it pulled.

I screamed for Zach in my head. But somehow I knew he was already coming for me, like he had come for me in the forest with the griffin, like he had stepped in when my mother was ripping me apart after the battle at the wall. He'd told her he wanted to be my partner. Just when I thought I'd been drowning from grief and self-doubt, he pulled me up. So I knew that at any moment, he would pull me free from this cursed water.

Zach.

His name brought me comfort. The water around me lost its pull, and it became easier to move. My panic wasn't as strong, although fear was still there. I moved slowly but didn't try to breathe, not yet.

I kicked, and the water gave way to lighter consistency. My head broke the surface, and I gasped, blinking.

Now that I wasn't drowning or consumed with panic, I was able to think clearly. Zach wouldn't be coming for me. He was smarter than that—he'd get me out another way.

Then I heard a splash next to me.

Or maybe not.

He had jumped in to save me. Although he shouldn't have—as dangerous and stupid as it was—I was happy he had. The thought was incredibly selfish and illogical, but I couldn't stop myself from thinking it, just like I couldn't stop the sun from setting.

At once, he started to sink, made worse by his thrashing. He was consumed, as I had been, by the enchantment. I wrenched my arms free from the water, even though they screamed at me, and hooked them under his arms, trying to haul him up. I couldn't. The cursed water was dragging him down. So I did the unthinkable—I ducked back under the water.

My senses were clogged, and ice gripped my limbs and insides. Still, I held on to Zach, clutching his head to my shoulder, burying my cheek in his short hair. His arms wrapped around me, like it was the most natural thing in the world, his palms resting on my shoulder blades and his forearms wrapped against my ribs. Together, we kicked, and our heads broke the surface.

We gasped and retched, our bodies heaving and convulsing together, but we never let go of each other.

"Where is it?" Zach gasped, his voice above my shoulder.

I blinked and tried to focus on the light from above. Distantly, Millennia's calls drifted down to us. But she was too far up.

I coughed again. "In the water—it has to be at the bottom."

The panic once again crept up my throat like the water lapping against my neck and jaw. As it did, the water squeezed itself around me, pulling me back down. "We'll drown."

Zach tightened his grip around me. "We won't. We'll make it."

His heart thrummed steadily against his chest, and I willed my pulse to mirror his. The water loosened once again.

He pressed his forehead into my shoulder, hugged me, and then looked down into the black water. "There's a rope around my waist. Tug on it if I stay down too long. Okay?"

I felt around for the rope in the water, my numb fingers grasping it. "All right."

He stared hard at me, and for a moment I thought— hoped—he was about to kiss me, but then he dove under. The inky black water splashed onto my face as I began counting seconds.

Thirty went by, and I heaved on the rope. He came up, coughing and shaking his head.

"Nothing."

Before I could stop him, he went under again, and I started counting.

I let forty pass by, then yanked hard. No response. Panic seized me, and the water felt like clay baked in the sun. I tugged and tugged.

There was nothing.

"No—" I sucked in a breath and dove. Expecting total blackness, my eyes stung by the sudden onslaught of bright green light. Floating, illuminated by something small and green, was Zach. His eyes were open and staring at the jewel at the bottom floor of the well. His hand was outstretched, fingertips touching the cursed emerald, while his entire body was encased in some kind of green glow.

Three enchantments dealing with three powerful emotions. The first had been peace, the second, panic, and the third... I had no way of knowing until I touched that jewel. If I did, I'd be sucked into the same enchantment Zach was now battling. Defeat the last enchantment, just like we'd beaten the water by pushing down our panic, and we'd break the curse.

Before I reached out to touch the jewel, knowing there was never a question of leaving Zach there, the only comfort was that we wouldn't drown. The jewel's curse would suspend us in time, keeping us there forever unless we defeated it.

But the little girl didn't have forever. She had maybe ten minutes.

I squeezed my eyes shut, reached through the clinging, mud-like water, and my fingertips grazed the cool surface of the emerald.

The chill in my bones forced my eyes open, and I shuddered. The world was black but growing lighter by the second, changing from midnight to charcoal, then to the color of hazy smoke. I blinked and pushed myself up onto my hands and knees.

Where was I?

With focus, my brain cleared. Zach and I were stuck inside the final enchantment. Our real bodies were floating in that black liquid, trapped. Everything here was a projection, not truly real.

The gray around me had faded into a blurred scene, like looking through a foggy window. I was in a field with an orange hue, as if the world were stuck in the autumn season, the ground growing cold under my hands.

"Zach?" I called out, scanning the umber landscape, desperate to find him.

Not ten paces in front of me was a young boy. He was breathing hard as if he'd just sprinted a mile. He stared through me, hazel eyes wide with terror, his brown hair swept away from his forehead by a rush of wind.

Then there was a great black blur and a splash of red. A woman suddenly lay next to me, blood pouring onto the dying grass.

The boy fell to his knees, screaming…screaming.

Under the screaming I caught the dying woman's final word: "Zach."

The blurriness shifted around me and then I was inside a tiny dirty house. The same young boy was huddled on the middle of the floor, shaking.

My heart went out to him. This emotion was all too familiar to me. An overwhelming oppression that I knew well from my childhood. A feeling that made even the smallest movements seem as though the sky was collapsing.

Loneliness.

I stared at the child on the grimy floor, his lone figure small and weak, then gently touched his back. "Zach."

The child stopped shaking, his back still to me.

Kneeling next to him, I prayed I would find the right words to save him. At that moment, I wasn't even thinking about the enchantment and how to break it. All I could think of was how to console a boy whose mother had just died before him.

"I know it hurts." My voice was barely a whisper as my fingertips brushed the thin fabric of his tunic. It was worn, washed over and over again by the hands of someone who had loved him. "And it feels like there's no one else in the world…"

I thought of all the times I had to be logical. To be strong. Did it ever help, or did it only bury the pain and let it fester?

"But you can't give up." My fingers curled into his shirt. "It'll get better. Not tomorrow. But it will. I promise. Because

I'll be with you soon."

At my last word, the world around me twisted, but not before I caught a glimpse of the boy's surprised face as he looked over his shoulder and stared at me.

Now I was sitting at a large desk, in a chair that was much too big for me, with my feet dangling above the floor. Everything was much crisper than before, like a brand new oil painting. With a throb of sharp pain, recognizing the maps on the wall and the books on the shelves, I knew this must be *my* memory. This office was forever ingrained in my mind, as much as I wanted to forget it.

I lifted myself up to look at the papers on my mother's desk. She was writing spell words, a practice I'd seen her do many times to help with memorization. They were all long and complicated, and I struggled to read them, to sound them out, hoping to feel the tingle of magic on my tongue.

Maybe if I memorized this spell I could surprise her. She'd be proud of me.

But I was too small, and I had to stand on the chair to see the top of the spell. As I tried to lean over farther, I accidentally knocked over a bottle of ink, and it spilled black across the table. I let out a squeal of fear and desperately tried to stop the ink from running down the wood and onto the plush cream carpet. Frantic and fumbling, I used my hands, but it only made it worse. I scrambled to open drawers—maybe there was a rag I could use.

But I froze as I caught sight of a beautiful white velvet box within the top drawer. It was so pretty, my little fingers couldn't be stopped from picking it up and opening it, covering it in black stains that would never be removed.

I managed only a glimpse of a beautiful silver ring within the box before a shriek froze me in place.

My mother stood in the doorway, shaking with rage. She

ran to me, snatched the box from my fingers, squeezed my cheeks together with one hand and hissed, "Foolish, *useless*, clumsy child. Get out."

She grabbed my arm, her nails digging into my skin, and dragged me to the door—I was so scared I was sobbing heavily already. "The only reason you are alive is because the Council promised me you'd be useful. You've yet to prove them right." Then she almost threw me into the hallway. "Get out!"

I scrambled over the carpet to reach for the closing door, my mother's furious face red with anger and her eyes...her eyes full of tears?

I tried to slide my hand in—to stop her from shutting me out. Shutting out another daughter she never wanted. Another daughter who had been born from an ordered conception.

Don't close it. Don't leave me alone.

Just before the door slammed, a large hand pulled mine out of the way. "Don't let your fingers get caught."

The words came as if from a great distance, across the Seas of Glyll, trying to reach me on my island of solitude.

My loneliness was a mother who saw her daughters as tools. Weapons.

I knew that, to her, the world of Royals was nothing but a plague of responsibilities and sacrifice. She fulfilled her duties, had gotten pregnant with each prince the council threw at her, and risked her life fighting the Forces as any queen should. But she hated the kingdom's walls and her title that felt more like a collar. Even more so, she couldn't stand to look at her daughters, the products of those nights she was forced to endure.

The only reason I was born was to be a soldier in the Legion's army. In my mother's army. If I failed at anything, I'd no longer be necessary. She never wanted me, and now she'd never need me.

Don't try to feel anything, and you won't get hurt. Don't expect anything, and you won't be disappointed.

"You're wanted, Ivy." A voice cut through my mantra. The mantra that had helped me survive years at the Legion. "For just being you."

It was Zach's voice.

The world around us shattered.

Like the emerald jewel at the center of the amulet.

A brilliant gold flash. Zach and I were under cold but now-clear water. The jewel was in fragments, each piece of emerald shining a brilliant golden light.

Zach tugged at my wrist and we kicked upward, our heads breaking the surface and our mouths sucking in the glorious air.

I opened my eyes and couldn't believe what I saw. Showers of gold fell around us like it was raining liquid fragments of the sun. It fell into the well, creating ripples. The gold rain hit my cheeks and my hair. Dazed, I looked at Zach.

He was beaming at me, treading water, gold light illuminating his wet face.

CHAPTER TWENTY-FOUR

THE SWORDSMAN'S THEORY

The entire village seemed to have gathered around the well as Zach and I were pulled from its icy waters. Millennia and Bromley were the first to grasp our wet hands and pull us over the wooden ledge. Bromley squeezed my hand so hard I thought my fingers would break off. Zach still had hold of my upper arm.

I was numb.

My mind barely registered the growing crowd of villagers as they emerged from their homes, some staggering as they adjusted to walking after days in bed. Rochet hugged me tightly, tears flowing down her cheeks. One old woman dropped to her knees and grabbed my other hand, kissing it.

But I was oblivious to everything except the gold rain that fell from the sky. The brightness reminded me of the miniature gold explosion that happened in the forest with the griffin. And like with Zach's fatal wound suddenly healed, a miracle had happened here.

The curse was broken. The sick were cured.

In my life, I had seen eleven curses lifted from villages. In all those times, never before had I seen golden rain afterward. When a curse was broken by a Royal's Kiss, the sickness just went away. Never anything elaborate. It just…stopped, leaving its patients disabled and disfigured, as Zach had said. It never *healed*, not like this.

Everything about this was different. The atmosphere was light, the air felt clean, and even the healthy looked healthier. Almost like the entire village had been reborn.

The difference was more than astounding…it was unbelievable.

As people pressed against us, I leaned in to Zach, and he wrapped his arm around my shoulders. He pushed past them all, practically dragging me. Bromley and Millennia hurried after us while I stumbled along.

Zach was steady in his gait and clearly not as shaken as I was. In fact, it was almost as if…almost as if he'd *known* this would happen. Which was ridiculous—how could he? But if he had, it would explain why he'd been so desperate to go after the amulet once he knew of it, rather than Kiss me.

Zach shook off the parade of villagers and helped me upstairs to one of the rooms Rochet had prepared for us.

He lowered me onto the bed as Bromley rushed forward. "Milady, are you all right?" he asked, covering me with a blanket. But Millennia stopped him.

"The princess needs dry clothes or she'll catch a cold. Get out, both of you."

Neither Zach nor Brom protested. Zach swung his bag over his wet shoulder. With a glance back at me, he closed the door behind him and Brom.

Millennia knelt and opened my bag, shifting my clothes around, then shoved it away. She dug into a large cabinet and pulled out a cream dress with a faded pattern on it. It was loose and thin, but it was also dry and clean.

"What's wrong with my c-clothes?"

"They smell of smoke." Millennia helped me out of my

clothes and into the dress. Then she sat and started braiding my hair without a word.

"I'm sorry," she said while her fingers wove in and out of my wet locks.

I tensed. "For what?"

"For…saying what I said earlier." When she finished my braid, she laid a hand on my shoulder. "I was wrong about you two. You're different from other Royals. You actually care about people, and I…I don't think you would actually use a curse as an excuse to…"

I drew away, her previous words coming back to me like the ache of an old wound. I'd been so consumed with finding the amulet, breaking the enchantments, and the golden rain, that I'd forgotten what she'd said about my motivations to Kiss Zach.

The worst of it being there was a part of me that wondered if what she'd said was true. And if it was, how could I bear the shame? Using monsters or curses as an excuse…it was beyond contemptible.

I couldn't afford to think about it. If I did, I'd start to second-guess everything, and I had a dragon to defeat. Like my mother said, there was no time for doubt or weakness.

"What are you doing here?" I asked finally.

"I told you: I was looking for the witch, and I—"

"No," I said sharply. "I don't believe you. Your master just leaving you alone, you happening to be after a witch that places a curse on a village. You run into us, not once but twice. What are you *really* looking for?"

Millennia stood so fast the old bed rocked me backward into the wall. She played with a curl hanging around her shoulders, twisting it in her pale fingers as she faced away from me and stared out the window. "My master can read the signs just as well as any of your Royal mages can. There's something dark brewing in these mountains, and we're looking for it."

My pulse jumped. Could Millennia and her master know about the Sable Dragon, too?

"It?" I asked.

Her face still set toward the window, fingers twisting her curl, she said, "Get some rest, princess. You've been through quite the ordeal."

Before I could inquire further, she crossed to the door and opened it. Zach met her, his hand poised to knock. They both took a step back. "Sorry," Zach said.

Millennia rubbed her temple. "Don't be. I was just about to leave." She turned back to me and smiled. "Thank you, both of you, for saving this village." She gave a small bow, bending slightly at the waist, then left.

I returned her smile but made a mental note to ask her more in the morning about what she and her master knew.

Zach hovered awkwardly in the doorway, wearing dry clothes but his hair still wet.

"Where's Brom?" I asked, breaking the silence.

"Getting something to warm you up." Zach sat down next to me on the bed.

There were a million things I wanted to say. What was the golden rain? What did he really suspect was the cause of it? Had he seen something like this before? Was it connected to the golden explosion of light when the griffin had died?

I wanted to ask him everything, but he beat me to it.

"That was your mom."

Because of the enchantment, he had seen my childhood memories of my mother. Before, I might've felt shame that he had seen something so personal and intimate, but knowing he had been through the same pain of loneliness, I didn't.

"I could say the same."

He winced. "Yes. But you first. If you want to talk, I'm listening."

After what he'd seen, he might as well hear the rest of it. "When I arrived at the Legion in Myria, I heard many stories about the great Queen Dahlia. My mother was famous…for things both good and bad. Apparently, she was a rebellious youth in her time at the Legion. She skipped patrol, she escaped the castle, and spent nights at the taverns. There was even a rumor that she went to a Romantica camp. But she was powerful. Her Mark of Myriana made all her partners practically invincible, so the Legion put up with her.

"When it came time to send her to Freida, she tried to run away—with a man. He was rumored a commoner, and the Council wouldn't allow her to waste time or children with a man of no magical blood. They didn't get far. A wraith came upon them, and my mother had no partner to Kiss. No Royal to help her beat the wraith. The Royal party sent after her managed to save *her* just in time, but the man had already died in her arms. After that, everything changed. She went straight to Freida, and nine months later, Clover was born. She hated the Legion for making her fight and sleep with men who were practically strangers, but she hated the Forces more. Every one of her children she gave birth to was a duty, an obligation, but also another soldier to take down the Forces. So she was that much harder on us.

"If I wasn't perfect at everything, she'd tell me I brought her shame. That I'd never be strong enough to save people, to destroy the Forces. But I was just a child—I wasn't perfect. I was clumsy sometimes and got hurt, so I cried, and she was never around to give me even one healing Kiss."

My eyes burned. My throat itched.

"She shut you out often?"

"An understatement. Anyway, she's obsessed with finding the Wicked Queen. It's a vendetta. If it wasn't for the Queen there'd be no Forces. No wraiths to take away the man she'd tried to run away with. No need for Royals to continue breeding like rabbits. No reason for my mother to give up her freedom." I tugged at my braid. "It could be that she just hates me. Not even that she hates what I represent. Just…*me*—" My voice caught. I'd never said these words aloud before.

Wringing the thin dress in my hands, I remembered what Brom had said back in Myria. What he'd said after I told him he knew why I had to fight.

You won't get her approval. Even if you win.

Deep down, I knew Brom was right. There was too much bad blood between the two of us for my mother to ever truly be proud of me. But maybe if I killed this dragon. Killed the Evil Queen and ended the war, she'd stop being obsessed with perfection, with being Myriana's pure descendant. Maybe she'd just see…me. Not as a Royal. Not as a weapon against the Forces. But just as me. As her daughter. It was exactly as Zach had said back in the well. I wanted her to want me for just being me.

Zach's fingers brushed his mark on my hand, and I let go of the fabric, leaving it wrinkled. His fingers entwined in mine and squeezed.

I swallowed and said softly, "But *your* mother… I'm so sorry…"

"It's in the past."

"You were running," I whispered, remembering the sweat on the boy's skin and his labored breathing. Perhaps my cruel words about him running from a fight had been all too true.

Zach ran a hand through his hair. "I was always scared as a kid. A coward, really. But I was also the only half Royal in our Romantica village, so whenever there was a dark monster near, I could feel it."

I bit my lip. "The Sense."

Zach nodded. "I was the only one with the Sense, and

whenever it settled over my chest, it felt like I couldn't breathe. I was terrified. When the griffin came—I'd never felt anything like that. So I just...I ran. I ran out of the house without thinking. Mom chased after me, and because I'd run, she was attacked..."

"You were barely six years old. You can't possibly blame yourself."

"I used to. And it was why I vowed to get stronger. I joined a rebel group of Romantica and trained. It was they who taught me there might be more to the Royals' magic. That it..."

He trailed off, shooting me a wary glance, as if he wanted to take back the words.

My head throbbed, as if warning me that I didn't want to hear what he had to say. "Tell me everything, Zach."

His eyes flickered to the sunset outside the window. The magical rain had stopped, but the sunset illuminated our room in a golden light. It reminded me of the forest that morning, when he had nearly kissed me.

Zach faced me and placed his hands on the pillows and sheets on either side of me. "Lie back, princess." He leaned in, trapping me.

He was so close—and getting closer—my elbows slipped back onto the pillows. He came down with me, his lips pressed into the bare skin of my shoulder.

"I promise to tell you everything. After you sleep." The feel of his lips brushing against my shoulder was so overwhelming that I let myself fall into the pillows as his broad chest hovered just a breath away from mine.

Before I could wrap my arm around him, he shifted to prop himself up on his elbow, then looked down at me. "You really saved me back there, Ivy."

I willed my pounding heart to slow. "Nothing you wouldn't have done for me."

He lowered his face into the pillow, right above my shoulder. "You held me in that water"—his voice was muffled—"and I knew everything was okay somehow."

My hands moved up into his hair. Feeling the wet strands between my fingers, I longed to bring his lips to mine.

Lust.

Zach lifted himself off and lay on his side. I rolled over to face him, our knees touching. He inched closer, wrapping our hands together, our foreheads meeting. "Go to sleep, princess."

I moved closer until my face was between his neck and the pillows. "Will I be awoken by a kiss?"

Zach chuckled, and I felt the vibrations in his throat and chest. "We'll see."

I let myself relax in his arms. I'd been only *half* teasing.

M uch to my disappointment, I did not receive a kiss. Zach was sleeping, his arms still around me, when I woke in the wee hours of the morning.

Briefly, I considered kissing him awake like I'd wanted, but then thought better of it.

It was finally something I didn't want to force.

My head whirled from the realization.

Whether it was a kiss of Lust or a Royal's Kiss, it should be something he chose. I wanted him to trust me enough as a partner to believe that our power could save people.

If it were a kiss of Lust, I shouldn't have to second-guess his attraction to me any longer. Whether it was through flirting while riding, a dance by a bonfire, or an almost-kiss in the forest, I needed to know once and for all if he wanted what I wanted.

But how could I ever swallow my pride and just ask him?

Carefully, I leaned over him to find a bowl of cold stew on the floor. Bromley must've come to drop it off. I groaned, knowing he would've found Zach and me sleeping practically on top of each other. I could almost picture Brom's smug face, as if to say, *told you so.* As I moved back, Zach stirred and flinched, sitting up, causing me to lose my balance and fall over his knees.

"What the—" Zach smoothed back his unruly hair when he saw the early morning darkness outside. "I didn't mean to fall asleep."

"Well, you did… We both did." I picked myself up. With a clear head I realized how foggy my mind had been last night and just how much the proximity of his body caused me to feel dizzy with desire. "We should get moving."

Zach wiped at the freckles on my cheek. "Easy there, Your Highness. I promised you I'd talk. Don't you want to know?"

I wanted to know everything, but Zach was so close to me I couldn't think straight. I needed a clear mind when he told me about the golden magic.

His eyes were locked on mine. His fingertips brushed my jaw, and heat rose in my neck.

I moved away from him, off the bed, before I could change my mind—no matter how much I wanted that heat, now was not the time. *Maybe it would never be.*

At that thought, my gut twisted.

"Please don't." I backed away from the bed. "What you did in the forest—what you're doing now, and—and last night…I don't know what—" I tucked hair behind my ears.

What had I been thinking last night? Even this morning, in his arms, surrounded by his warmth and scent, I'd been delusional. We couldn't afford to be distracted by Lust. We had an egg to find and a dragon to slay.

If anything were to happen between us, it would have to wait.

At his look of confusion, I said, "Never mind. There are more important things. Tell me about the Golden Effect and the Romantica's theory."

"Ivy—" Pain flitted across his face, then it was gone just as fast. His jaw tightened. "You're not going to like it."

"Just tell me."

"The Golden Effect, as you call it, happens when a power defeats the Forces, whether it's a monster or a curse like the one we broke yesterday."

"What power?"

Zach ignored my interruption. "The Romantica began to develop this theory about seventy-five years ago, when they started finding…patterns. They noticed that whenever a curse was lifted by the Royal's Kiss, three more curses in other villages would pop up within the span of a moon's cycle."

"Coincidence."

"And if the villages were right next to each other? Ivy, try to hear me. This Golden Effect…its magic is ten times more powerful than any Kiss. If we hadn't broken the amulet, then these villagers would never have properly healed. They may have even died from another curse that would have taken its place."

It took me a moment to understand what he was saying, and once I did, I felt sick.

On one hand, I could not dispute the facts I had seen with my own eyes. On the other, I refused to admit that the Royal's Kiss was truly pointless—because…because that would mean all this time—all these years…

Zach was suggesting the Kiss caused more curses and monsters to pop up. That it was actually *evil*.

There was no way. *No.*

"There were more instances as well," Zach continued. "Trolls' caves that the Royals took down with their magic turned into a breeding nest for dark serpents. From the dead earth where dwarves were slaughtered a wraith emerged… There are hundreds of examples."

"Do you have any proof?"

Zach gritted his teeth. "That I could show you right now? Of course not. I'm only telling you how our theory started. Believe what you want, as you always have. All we know is that when we began fighting monsters *without* Royals, we were able to clear areas that *stayed* clear."

My stomach rolled. I grabbed the edge of the dresser to keep myself from swaying. I didn't believe him. There was no way I could. "You told me the gold happens because of a power. What is it?"

Zach took a deep breath, looked me in the eye, and said, "Love."

I pounded my fist against the dresser. "That's not funny."

"Am I laughing?"

"You're saying we broke the curse on the amulet through Love? Zach, that's—"

He stood and seized my arms. "Down in those waters, when your mother almost shut the door on you, and I held your hand, what did you feel?"

I stared up at him, speechless.

"I'll tell you what I felt when you promised you'd be with me. I was happy. I wasn't so lonely that I felt like I could've just disappeared. I felt lov—"

I tried to escape his iron grip. "We got through the enchantments. That's why the jewel broke!"

"*How* did we break through the enchantments?"

"S-strength," I stammered.

"If that's what you want to call it—fine. Then what about the griffin?"

"What *about* the griffin?"

"What power defeated it? Caused it to disintegrate into gold dust?"

"I don't know!" Anxiety crawled up my throat, choking me—it was like I was back in that cursed well water again. "It had to be magic."

"Magic from *who*? There was no one else in that forest."

"You don't know that. It was all such a blur—you jumped in front of me and saved me, and that's when it burst into gold."

Zach stared two burning holes into me, willing me to understand. Waiting for me to put the pieces together.

When the griffin's talons buried themselves in his chest, saving me but sacrificing him, what power had been released then? What triggered the golden magic? Was it Zach himself? Maybe the question was *why* he had leaped in front of the griffin's talons when it was sure to kill him.

Because he…

CHAPTER TWENTY-FIVE

DENIAL

"You don't love me," I whispered.

Zach backed up and sank onto the bed. He rested his face in his hands and his elbows on his knees.

We were silent a long time.

I licked my lips, pushed back the curls that had escaped from my braid. *Breathe, Ivy.* "Zach, you *don't* love me."

"You don't think I've tried to deny it?" He jumped to his feet, the muscles in his neck and arms tight, strained. "To tell myself it's just Lust? For all the girls for me to fall in love with… It had to be the one who completely denies Love's entire existence. The most Royal of them all."

He crossed to the window, lifted one arm and rested it and his forehead against the glass. He laughed bitterly. "Isn't the irony hilarious? The girl I love begging me to kiss her every day, and I have to refuse. And I *have* to. Not just for my own beliefs and this golden theory, but for my own sanity. Because a kiss would mean *nothing* to you, while it meant *everything* to me."

I couldn't speak. I could barely breathe.

I didn't believe in Love, but Zach *did*, and he believed he had fallen in…

At last, I managed to rasp, "But…but you barely knew me."

He shook his head, his hair brushing against the glass. "I knew you enough. I met you, and you were beautiful with your freckles and talk about strawberries. Then you were demanding that we should be partners and, even when I told you no, you showed up on the battlefield. You were fierce and strong and brave, and I admired you." He turned away from the window, walked back to the bed and sat down. "Then after your mother slapped you, and I walked you back to your room… I don't know. Maybe it was then."

"Why then?"

"I heard you crying," he said softly, eyes focused on the floor. "You cried like your heart was being ripped in two. Every Royal I'd met always cut off all emotion, but you let yourself feel something. And then you showed up at the Council meeting, eyes a little red, like nothing happened. But something *had* happened, and I worried about you. I haven't stopped since."

His words had me trembling. *Sacred Sisters, what is this prince doing to me? I believe every foolish word.*

He held out his hand and slowly rotated it, studying the Mark of Myriana. "You asked me why I didn't just go search for the dragon myself with my Sense. The answer is…I couldn't let you go alone. Or with anyone else. You wouldn't be safe with someone like Amias. Someone who wanted you only as a weapon. To make themselves stronger by using you." He looked up, then repeated the same words from the enchantment. "They wouldn't make you feel wanted for just being you."

Oh, don't say that.

With his marked hand, he took mine and pulled me closer, to where I stood between his legs. Zach was tall enough to only have to tilt his face upward to be inches from my own. "Tell me I'm wrong. Tell me you would've been better off with a different partner."

I couldn't. His hands moved into my hair as our breathing synchronized.

A knock on the door sprang us apart. I swiveled around, and with hands still trembling, rushed to the door. Millennia stood in the doorway, holding two steaming mugs, and Bromley was behind her with a basket of food.

Millennia cast a look from Zach to myself, then strode in, handing me a mug. I accepted it, trying not to spill any tea.

Bromley smiled at me, but it quickly faded when he noticed my hands shaking the mug. He glanced at Zach, and I subtly shook my head.

Millennia took a long sip from her tea then squinted at me over the rim. "So, princess, what's in those mountains?"

"Um—what?" My mind was still too full of Zach's confession to comprehend what she was asking.

"Don't think that I didn't notice what you said yesterday—that the fate of the kingdoms rested on you two." Millennia flicked her wrist at both of us. "You're after whatever is brewing in the Wu-Hyll Mountains, aren't you?"

Zach still sat on the bed, staring at the floor. I remained silent, my brain moving at a snail's pace.

Irritated, she snapped her fingers. "Hello?"

I set the mug of tea on the dresser, rubbed my forehead, and sighed, trying to refocus on our mission. What Millennia had said last night had a ring of truth to it. If she had a Master Mage who recognized the dark signs like the magical thunderstorms and the sparrow harpies, it wouldn't be hard to decipher that *something* was growing in the Wu-Hyll Mountains. But given the Romantica mages' lack of access to our archives, it made sense why they didn't know *what* was forming. The question was, did I trust her enough to tell her? She *had* saved our lives with the serpents *and* helped us find the amulet—she may be a Romantica, but like Zach, she wasn't evil. And if she truly wanted us dead there would've been plenty of opportunities. So I told her.

"Great wisps on the Seas of Glyll," she said, "a Sable Dragon. I'd expected something terrible, but not…" She took a steeling breath. "This is it then. She really means to raze the world with this dragon, doesn't she?"

Her words struck a chord inside me, and for a moment, I couldn't respond. This whole time I'd known that the Sable Dragon would destroy the Legion if let loose, but without the Legion, the rest of the world would surely follow. All she would have to do is stand back and let her dragon wreak havoc, and with no more humans in the way, her monsters—her children— would inherit the earth.

Millennia turned toward the door. "Well, we better get moving."

"What?" Brom, Zach, and I said in unison.

She blinked. "I'm coming with you."

I gaped at her. "After what I just told you…you want to join us?"

"Absolutely. You need my help. Especially since the Royal's Kiss is no use to either of you."

I dug my fingernails into my palms. Maybe I believed Zach thought he loved me, and maybe I couldn't deny that *something* was different about the Golden Effect and the Royal's magic, but to completely throw out the one power we had to defeat the dragon—no, that was too dangerous. Despite the Romantica's theory, we were still going to use a Kiss. It was the *only* way to kill it for certain.

"Slaying a Sable Dragon isn't like breaking a cursed amulet. There is no other way this time. And it's really none of your business what goes on between me and my partner."

Millennia raised an eyebrow. "Oh? And how has your luck been with the Royal's Kiss so far?" She pointed a slim finger at Zach. "From what I can tell, he's refused to participate."

Zach was now staring out the window, still quiet.

"You want to help," I repeated slowly.

"Before, I thought you were mindless followers of the Legion, but I was wrong." Her tone was soft, similar to when she had been braiding my hair last night. "I meant what I said, Ivy."

Zach wasn't any closer to Kissing me. If anything, he was farther away. Especially now that I knew all his reasons for saying no.

His belief that a kiss shouldn't be used as a weapon.

The Romantica's theory that the Royal's Kiss didn't truly work.

And the fact that he loved me and I would never return feelings that could not exist.

So, even though I knew the Royal's Kiss—along with the spell I'd been studying the whole trip—was the only chance at destroying the egg, I had to face the facts: Zach was nowhere close to giving in, and there'd be even more vicious monsters in the mountains. At least during the mountain leg of the journey, it would be helpful to have a mage at our side.

With a sinking feeling, I realized not only did I still have to convince Zach to Kiss me, but I also had to convince him that what he felt for me was merely Lust, not Love. That seemed even more impossible than killing the dragon.

"Yes, we could use your help," I told Millennia. "I'll meet you downstairs after I change."

Satisfied, Millennia left, but Brom lingered, probably sensing something was wrong. I wondered if I wore the same expression I did whenever my mother left me broken.

"Go." I shoved his arm gently, giving him a reassuring smile. "I'm coming."

Brom turned to leave, glancing over his shoulder with

narrowed eyes in a way that told me he blamed Zach for my state. Well, he wasn't entirely wrong.

Zach waited until Millennia and Brom were well down the hall before he said, "You sure this is a good idea?"

"Not really, but she's got a point," I said. "You won't Kiss me, and it's only going to get more dangerous. If she wanted to kill us, she could've let the basilisk vipers do their job. And honestly? I could use someone who isn't against me at every turn."

"I'm not against you."

"Well, you're not entirely with me, either."

"I just told you why," he said, his voice low and weary.

I bit my bottom lip. "I'm sorry, Zach, it's just hard for me to…"

"Believe me. I get it. If you don't believe in my feelings for you, then at least consider the Golden Effect and the Kiss. I need you to just think about it, Ivy."

My hands quivered again, and I clutched them behind my back. "Zach, what you think you're feeling for me, it's not—"

"*Don't.* Please don't tell me what I'm feeling isn't real. You have no right to tell me that." He turned away, rubbing the back of his neck, and swore colorfully under his breath. "That's exactly why I didn't want to say anything. But if it makes you feel any better—if it's what you want—I'll keep trying to get rid of these feelings, or at least ignore them."

With that, he left, his footsteps resounding in my brain.

I should've been relieved. But instead I felt a strange void in my chest. A hollowness I hadn't been expecting.

I stood over the threshold of the doorway for a moment longer, still thinking of his words. Of all the reasons he'd given for loving me. Freckles and strawberries and fierce and strong… something shifted in my chest. Almost like a small seed. A small flower blooming, turning its petals to the sun.

It was warm and wonderful and made me feel lighter than air.

I changed out of the borrowed dress and into my tunic, vest, and pants, which had dried overnight. The sunlight was coming in low now, and it caught something in my bag, creating a glint of light that made me squint. My magic compact.

Master Gelloren!

I scrambled to the sack and fumbled for it, my breath in short gasps. How could I have forgotten this treasure? This link that connected me to my Legion? The one thing in the world that made sense to me.

I sank onto the bed and stared at it for a few moments, reveling in its cool silver and sleek surface. I closed my eyes and thought of Master Gelloren, then clicked open the compact, and the mirror's surface pulsed with soft amber light.

"Ivy?"

"Master Gelloren," I breathed in relief.

His face shimmered into view like tiny bits of light congealing together. "Ivy! I've been trying to reach you for days. I was about to send out another party to find you."

"I'm so sorry, Master, time escaped me," I said, squeezing the compact.

"Great seas, princess, what have you been through?"

Perhaps it was the worry and anxiety so evident in the dark circles under my eyes, or perhaps he was confused as to why I had waited so long to contact him—a mystery I would never dare to explain. How could I tell him my attention had been captured by a certain swordsman?

"After the griffin, we encountered an entire horde of basilisk vipers, but a female mage who goes by the name Millennia saved us. Do you know her?"

Gelloren's beard twitched as his mouth set into a deep scowl. "I've heard her name, yes. She's a new young mage with incredible power and discipline. She's from Raed, and she's wanted for slander against the Legion. She's a Romantica, Ivy."

"I somewhat gathered that. Do you know anything about her master?"

Gelloren paused. "She's rumored to have one, but I never caught the name. Romantica and Royal mages obviously don't travel in the same circles."

Though rare, it wasn't unheard of for apprentices to become more well-known than the masters themselves, especially when one came around as young and talented as Millennia. But not knowing her master still made me uneasy.

"You need to stay away from her and keep moving," he continued.

I almost laughed. I'd just told her she could join us. Merciful Queen, what had become of me these past few days? Me, direct descendant of Myriana Holly, traveling with two Romantica.

"Where are you? Are you to the mountains yet?"

"No, but we're not far. We're in a village north of the Galedral Forest."

"You must hurry, Ivy, you don't have much time left."

"We're about to leave, but we were delayed. The Curse of Venera had been cast on this village, Master."

Master Gelloren lowered his gaze and sighed. "That is a tragedy."

"We were their only hope. We had to stop and help them."

"Ivy, I understand. But the counter-curse is greatly taxing—"

"No, it's not that. It's..." Explaining that we broke the curse by destroying the amulet could lead to a lot of questions I wasn't sure I could answer. If I admitted Zach was a Romantica and had refused to Kiss me, Gelloren would tell me to come home at once, and everything—our entire journey—would have been wasted.

"We managed to break the curse without the Kiss. With the

help of the mage," I quickly added. "The results were quite remarkable. Have you ever heard of showers of gold?"

Gelloren's brow furrowed. "Just rumors. *Romantica* rumors."

I chose my words carefully. "They might not be just rumors." I quickly explained the golden rain's effects and the Romantica's theory behind it.

Gelloren's image flickered within the small compact mirror. When his face came back into focus he looked furious. "Ivy, tell me you don't believe this nonsense."

I thought of the griffin, of Zach's breath on my neck, the look in his eyes when he told me I wouldn't be safe with anyone else, of the villagers weeping with joy, of the decayed, dead earth left after the monsters died by Kellian's glowing blue blade.

"No, of course not. I'm just curious. It's important to know our enemy, Master. You taught me this."

The muscles in Gelloren's face relaxed. "Remember, Ivy, your power is the only thing that can save us from the Sable Dragon. So you must hurry."

I nodded again, mouth dry. "One more thing, Master. Do you remember that village Kellian and I cured with my Kiss about two moons ago?" The Curse of Jecep had plagued the poor village with poisoned crops. All it took was one poisoned plant, then when it was pulled its roots spread, multiplying the poison. "How is it? I mean, is everyone recovering properly?"

Gelloren sighed. "I'm sorry to say, but the Curse of Resinda descended a few weeks ago, and we were too late. I—"

I closed the compact on Gelloren's deep, bass words.

"If we hadn't broken the amulet then these villagers would never have properly healed. They may have even died from another curse that would take its place."

I tucked the mirror into my bag and stood, picking up the

mug of tea Millennia had brought me. I tried to take a sip to calm myself, but my hands trembled so hard I spilled some down the front of my shirt. I squeezed my eyes shut, clutching the mug tight in my hand.

Then I whirled and threw it. The mug smashed through the window and flew into the village square.

Silence followed the shattering glass.

I walked to the broken window and stared out at the rising sun and multicolored sky, where only yesterday golden rain had fallen in buckets because...because why?

Love?

I dug into my bag for a handful of coins and placed them on the bedside table, leaving more than enough to replace the window glass and shattered mug.

CHAPTER TWENTY-SIX

A TREASONOUS BALLAD

With the horses unable to handle the mountain terrain, we decided to leave them at the village and continue on foot. It was hard saying good-bye to Lorena. She was more than just a horse to me. She'd saved me during countless battles and gotten me through a hundred patrols. But horses would slow us down, and Rochet said she'd personally take care of them, so I gave Lorena a handful of orange peels and kissed her snout, muttering, "I'll see you soon." I felt Zach's gaze on me and remembered when he said he liked oranges as well. Would he later be able to smell the citrus on my hands? Not that I expected him to be close enough to smell them any time soon.

After a day's walk, we reached the end of the Galedral Forest at the edge of the Wu-Hyll Mountains and came to the base of the monstrosities themselves. There were still some trees here and there, but mostly the ground was covered in stone. It was beautiful, though, and I couldn't help but be in awe of them. Not only because of how big they were, and how majestic, but the idea that this was where it all began for my ancestor.

The Wu-Hyll Mountains were where it was said the dwarves' caves had been, where Myriana and Saevalla and

Raed had their battle against the dwarf, where the first Kiss had been born. In those caves was where Myriana's first heir had been taken and turned into the Evil Queen, so it made sense the Sable Dragon egg would be found here. It made me shiver thinking I could be in the very spot where Myriana and her sister had first encountered the huntsman, Raed.

Though I'd never been to these mountains, many of my ancestors had traveled to the caves, rooting out the dwarven clans and exterminating them like ants in their dirt tunnels. Now, only goblins, wraiths, griffins, and trolls wandered these mountains. Dwarves never came here anymore, probably because it reminded them of the slaughter of their ancestors.

The sound of trickling water interrupted my musing, and I followed it to find a fresh stream. It ran along the side of the mountain pass, so we decided to camp there and then make a fresh start into the mountains the next day.

Millennia was very useful. With a flick of her wrist, she started a fire. She was even able to guide water from the stream into our flasks, which was a spectacle in itself. Bromley was amazed to watch the rivulets of water twist and turn in midair as if they flowed down an invisible tube into the open flask.

When she offered to take the first watch, I insisted we do so in pairs. "It's more dangerous in the mountains, and we can make sure both of us stay awake," I said, sitting next to Millennia.

But it was only an excuse. I couldn't forget Gelloren's words, *"You need to stay away from her."* Since I'd already agreed she could accompany us, I could at least keep an eye on her.

Zach raised an eyebrow but said nothing. The last words we'd shared had been him still trying to convince me he'd fallen in love with me.

How do you talk normally after that?

Once Brom and Zach were asleep, I turned to Millennia. "So you're from Raed?"

Millennia frowned. "How did you know that?"

I'd forgotten that Gelloren had told me, and she hadn't mentioned it. "Zach said your accent sounded Eastern."

"Hm. And I thought I hid it pretty well. Yes, I am from Raed."

"My mother just came from there. She said there'd been a sighting of the Evil Queen."

The firelight cast a strange glow on her eyes, and her frown deepened. "I wouldn't put much stock in those sightings."

"Why? Because they're from the Legion?"

She didn't reply, and I wondered if I'd struck a nerve.

I let a few moments of silence pass before I tried again. "I understand why you wouldn't like the Legion, but we're honestly trying to win this war, to save *everyone*, even the Romantica. Why wouldn't you trust our efforts to get rid of the Evil Queen once and for all?"

Millennia snorted. "I'll never really trust them, just as I can never forgive them for what they did."

Fearing the worst, I hugged my cloak tighter. "And what was that?"

Millennia looked back at me and opened her mouth, then her gaze darted to the side, as if she was considering something. "I can't believe I'm about to tell you this…"

"Tell me what?"

"Do you believe in True Love?"

Odd that two different people asked me that same question within the same number of days.

Remembering the look on Zach's face, I couldn't answer.

Luckily, she didn't wait long. "It's fine. I didn't think you would. But I know you feel *something*." She glanced over at Zach's sleeping form, and my face warmed. "Whether or not that something is Love, I don't know, but whatever *it* is, it's there." She kept very still, like her muscles suddenly seized up. "I'm in love. Tarren was my childhood friend. Nothing could compare to the kisses we shared. The ground shook, the stars fell, and the waves of the far-off oceans crashed down on us.

"In Raed, the Romantica and the Royals had an… understanding, I guess you could say. They enjoyed our music and stories. My troupe was especially popular. I wasn't an entertainer, but Tarren was, and he got invited to the palace to sing. I didn't want him to go. He'd just proposed to me that very day, and I was worried. But he told me he'd make his song count."

Millennia took a deep, shuddering breath and lifted her head to look at the stars. "He sang of Love. He told the Romantica tale of Myriana and Saevalla, and the Council was furious. A blasphemous song in their sacred castle? They seized him and took him away to probably labor away at some mine. The next day I was told he'd been taken away in service to the Legion. I tried to break into the castle to look for him, but my earth magic wasn't strong enough, so that's when I set off to find a master." She clenched her fist. "To get stronger."

"Millennia…I…I'm so sorry."

I truly was. Even though the punishment was clear for heresy in the Royal Legion…it was just a song.

I remembered Jiaza's story and how furious I'd been. Now I couldn't find it in me to care as much. Maybe it was all this confusion about what was right and wrong and beliefs and emotions I didn't think existed—I just knew the pain in Millennia's voice made me want to help her. Even if that was treasonous thinking.

Millennia shook her head. "I don't want your pity, princess."

"It's not pity, it's…regret. I've been taught that True Love doesn't exist. You can surrender to Lust, you can care for someone and develop a bond, but this all-powerful thing called Love doesn't exist. I mean, it can't. It's impossible to give your heart to one person. Our emotions are too fragile to remain constant—it's why the Legion teaches us to lead and make decisions without them. But then…I listen to you about your Tarren, and to Zach about his parents, and…" I shrugged. Not to mention the fact my own mother wanted to run off with a man whose name I didn't even know. It was a story I'd never thought much about before, but now…I had to wonder…could Dahlia have thought she'd been in love with that man?

"I just don't know anymore."

It was the first time I admitted it out loud. That my faith was wavering, that for the first time in my life, I was confused, curious even, about this *illusion* in which these Romantica believed so passionately.

She rubbed her brow. "My master told me I should be going after the source of the Darkness within the mountains, and don't get me wrong, I do want to help. But I have to admit, I had hoped that if I helped you, maybe you'd be able to free Tarren for me in return." Millennia stared so hard at the ground I wondered if she was trying to melt the rock with her eyes. "It's barely been two months without him and I already feel like…like a part of me is missing. Like I'm missing an entire limb."

For a while, I was silent. Her words were illogical, driven by emotion so strong I could barely fathom its depths. But she was finally truthful with me. Whatever other reason she'd had—her master wanting her to find the dragon, or just helping people along the way—I could tell *this* was why she really wanted to join us. At least she didn't try to pretend her crusade was only for some noble purpose.

She simply wanted her "love" back.

Millennia reached for a lock of her hair and twirled it

once between her fingers, her gaze straight ahead. "And some days…I miss him so much…the pain is so bad that I wish I could get rid of it somehow. If I could just forget him or cut out all this…" She let go of her hair and hugged her shoulders, sighing. "Sometimes I think it might be easier if I were a Royal. And I couldn't feel anything, like you."

I didn't argue, because I knew she was in pain. But it wasn't true what she said. I *did* feel things. All the time. Too much sometimes. The difference is that Royals, like with our Sense, learned to bury it. To push it aside and not let emotions rule us.

"I promise I'll do whatever I can," I said softly, holding out my hand.

Millennia smiled and grasped my hand, squeezing it tightly. A firm shake.

Shaking hands with a Romantica. Promising to free a heretic. Maybe I was becoming more like them every minute and less like the princess my mother wanted me to be. The princess I'd set out on this journey to prove I could be.

"Which way?" Zach asked me as he stomped out the flames from our campfire the next morning.

Drifting away from our little area at the base of the stones, I reached out with my Sense, the wind blowing through me as I closed my eyes. I felt it then, small but steady, in the pit of my stomach, growing like an infection, spreading into my gut and shoulders. I pointed in the direction where I felt the darkness the most and opened my eyes. It was west, over some rough boulders.

Millennia raised her blue hood and frowned at the direction. "We shouldn't stray far from the mountain path. It could get very dangerous."

"But we can't just *not* follow Ivy's instinct," Zach countered. "We'll get farther from the egg, and it'll take too long to get there."

"Then we'll make our own path somewhere in-between. I'll be able to tell if we stray too far from it," I said.

With our packs shouldered, we started on our way, picking out our own trail, moving somewhere between the stony feeling in my gut and the stone-carved mountain path.

CHAPTER TWENTY-SEVEN

OVER THE EDGE

The mountains of Wu-Hyll were the epitome of beauty. The stone swirled with gray, cream, indigo, and lavender. When the sun hit the rocks, they glimmered like diamonds. Trees dotted the mountainside, and occasionally we came across deer grazing on plateaus before they leaped off in graceful bounds down the slopes, kicking up loose pebbles.

I tried my best to lead the way, keeping the regular mountain path in the general line of sight while drifting more westward. We climbed over boulders and jumped over thin streams trickling on smooth rocks worn by hundreds of years of the water's steady pulse. Bromley stayed behind me, while Millennia and Zach picked up the rear.

We stopped midday, and despite the chill of the mountain air, we were sweating. I led them to the gentle stream we'd been following. Dropping my bag by my feet, I heard a small clunk of metal against stone. I paused for a moment, remembering the compact in my bag and my last conversation with Gelloren.

The look on his face when I mentioned the Romantica's theory was still clear in my memory. Like me, he was unlikely to believe anything he had not seen, especially something that could contradict hundreds of years of Royal history.

But was it possible for it all to be true?

The thought paralyzed me. Like when Zach had first brought up the theory of the Golden Effect, I felt nauseated again. So I just stood there, staring at my bag and the magic mirror resting in the folds of its fabric, waiting for the feeling to pass.

A hand lightly touched my arm. Millennia stood above me with a concerned brow, then she motioned her head toward the stream. I followed her there, leaving Brom and Zach to rest in the shade of a small cliff.

"You're doing a good job," Millennia said as she pulled down her hood and gathered her black hair off the nape of her sweaty neck.

I washed my hands, which were coated with rock dust, and shrugged. "It's not so hard, and the added power of Zach's Sense helps. What's difficult is repressing the Sense during a battle. Without proper training it could paralyze you. But the Legion taught me how to suppress it when I need to."

Her shoulders stiffened as she bent to splash water on her face and rub some on her neck. "That's good, then." She returned to her pack for lunch.

I stuck my hands in the stream again. Even though I felt like we'd been able to make some progress from our conversation last night, she still hated the Legion, meaning that she couldn't completely trust me. Yet, for the sake of her fiancé, she was willing to try. Though I didn't understand the primitive tradition of marriage the Romantica upheld, I knew they took it very seriously. She must believe she loved Tarren deeply to turn to the enemy for help.

The enemy. *Fields of Galliore, I'm calling my own people the enemy now?*

I stood, but the rocks were slippery, and I lost my footing, falling backward into the stream. Though it was shallow, the icy water brought me back to the well's enchantment, and panic, like claws, gripped my throat.

Seconds later, I was lifted out of the water.

"Troll's breath," Zach swore next to my ear. "What were you doing?"

Relieved, I rested my head against his chest and breathed deeply. "C-clearing my head." His heartbeat thundered in my ear.

"It looked like you were trying to drown yourself."

Surprised at the tremor in his voice, I looked up and saw how pale he was. Like black lightning splitting apart the frozen ground, the look on his face struck me, breaking open the very foundation of who I was. It made me realize that whatever he felt for me, I didn't understand, but I wanted to.

That single thought. That horrible, blasphemous thought — suddenly wanting to understand Love — made my whole body shudder.

Last night, sitting next to Millennia, I'd admitted I was confused, but now I actually *wanted* to understand the heretical teachings of True Love. I might as well burn my Legionnaire cloak now.

Holy Queen, have I forsaken you?

"You're shaking." Zach stepped out of the shallow stream and knelt on the rocks. "But warming you up has its perks," he said with a smile, and hugged me tighter to his chest. Then he called for Millennia to start a small fire.

I could hardly feel the chill in my bones, only the mad struggle between wanting to run back to Myria, fall at my mother's feet, and confess that I really wasn't worthy to be her heir — that she'd been right all along — or bury my face in Zach's neck.

I gave in to the latter and pressed my cheek to his collarbone. Despite everything, I was smiling.

"I believe you."

"What?" Zach dipped his head to hear me over the running stream and my chattering teeth.

"I believe you."

There was hesitation, then, "About what?"

Did I believe in his feelings, the Romantica theory, or both?

Even I didn't know in that moment.

I placed a hand on his cheek and brought his face to my lips. Shockingly, he didn't pull away. Kissing his cheek gently, I said, "Thank you, Zach."

Zach blinked, then his lips tugged to the side in a half smile. He pressed his forehead against mine. "My pleasure, princess."

Millennia walked over and held out a small flame around my damp clothes, letting it warm me. Brom watched me with wary eyes. But was it from my dip in the stream? Or the way Zach held me?

What would my best friend think if he knew I was starting to believe Love actually—*maybe*—could exist?

"So are you going to tell me what's been going on with you lately?" Brom loaded an arrow he'd just sharpened for the tenth time into his crossbow and lifted it to rest on top of the boulder we hid behind.

"I'm not sure where to start," I said, twirling an arrow's feathers between my fingers. We'd been sitting behind the boulder for the better part of an hour, waiting for a herd of small mountain elk to pass through. We'd found their droppings this morning, and Zach and I both agreed that a little hunting would be a good idea, considering we didn't know exactly how long we'd be stuck in these mountains where game was scarce. So we'd paired off, Brom and I following fresh tracks that led to a grazing area on the side of the mountain, while Zach and Millennia investigated another set of tracks.

"There's just…so much," I said finally.

Brom just shrugged and peeked over the boulder again.

I searched for the right words to continue our conversation. Until just a moment ago, Brom had been silent as we'd waited for the elk. At first I thought his silence was because he was being moody—upset that I hadn't confided in him yet. Brom was like my brother. He was *always* there for me, as I was for him. He was probably hurt that I'd left him in the dark since the cursed village. In truth, it wasn't because I didn't want to talk to him. It was more because I was ashamed to put these conflicting—heretical—thoughts into spoken words.

"Does it have anything to do with Zach's fuss about us splitting up?" Brom said.

"No. Well, maybe a little."

My palms suddenly felt clammy, as if the very mention of Zach set my entire body on edge. Zach had wanted to stay with me, but I told him that out of all of us, I'd have the most warning thanks to my Sense. It was logical for a powerful mage and swordsman stuck together to watch each other's backs. With a frustrated groan, he'd reluctantly agreed.

I chewed on my lip, not sure how much I wanted to keep secret. Though Zach hadn't come right out and "declared his love" for me in front of Millennia and Brom, I wondered how much Brom had figured out for himself.

"Can we just not talk about him?" I said.

Brom raised his eyebrows. "Okay…then how about this: why did you let Millennia join us?"

I hadn't expected that. "She's proven to be a powerful mage. If Zach still refuses to use the Kiss, then we might need her."

"Does that mean you're giving up? Trying to use the Kiss, I mean?"

I sighed. "I don't know, Brom. I've been studying the spell you copied for me, almost every night, so I still have to hope, but honestly? After what happened with the amulet, I don't see Zach giving in. Everything is... It's so confusing. I mean, the Royal's Kiss has worked for five hundred years, why should I doubt it?"

He frowned. "What do you mean?"

I relayed to him what Zach had told me about the Golden Effect.

Brom stared at me with wide eyes. "That's amazing," he whispered.

I shot him a look. "Amazing?"

He turned back to look over the boulder. The herd was still nowhere in sight. "I'm sorry, Ivy. I know it goes against everything you were taught but..."

"But what?"

"Even though this could change everything, and it would mean that all this time Royals have been wrong, wouldn't it also mean that Love really exists? It's just a nice thought, that's all. That an emotion, a force, could be so powerful as to stop all the evil in the world. Any normal person could use it. They wouldn't have to be... I mean anyone could protect whoever they..."

He kept his gaze focused on the tall rippling grass.

I understood what he was saying. It was the same issue as the night of the storm in the forest, when he'd wanted Zach to stay and protect me because he knew he couldn't.

In his eyes, Zach was a powerful swordsman, I was a powerful princess, and Millennia was a powerful mage. And he was just...well, Brom wasn't *just* anything. Not to me.

What he didn't understand was how much he really did

protect me. Every day.

I wrapped an arm around his shoulders and tugged him close. "Bromley, I owe you my life, you know."

He let out a snort of disbelief, his crossbow sliding down the rock as he surrendered to my hold.

"Down in the well, one of the enchantments we had to overcome was loneliness. I saw my childhood—my childhood *before* you. You saved me back then, Brom. When I was shipped from Freida to Myria to start my training, I had been suffering from loneliness for a long time. I barely knew my sisters. And my mother…well, you know my mother. Then later you were assigned to me. I'd never have admitted it then, but I relished your company. You were always with me, and I never felt lonely again."

Bromley stared at the mountains, his eyes narrowed as the breeze blew his hair back.

"I wish you wouldn't say you can't protect me. Because you do. You always have. I wouldn't know what to do with myself if you weren't here with me."

"Well, of course I'd be here," Bromley said. "You're my sister."

At this I threw my other arm around his shoulders and hugged him tightly. My chest glowed with warmth. I felt safe, just like I had when Zach had taken my hand down in the well, when he broke the enchantment. If Zach claimed Love had been the force that broke through the amulet's curse, then was what I felt for Brom…also love?

It wasn't the same kind of Love that Zach felt for me. According to the Romantica, there were two different types of Love: Romantic Love and Familial Love. I knew what I felt for Brom wasn't Romantic. I'd always thought this feeling was just the family bond that united all Royal lines. But what if it wasn't just a bond, but a force? An all-powerful force that could move mountains?

Again, more heretical thoughts. I almost laughed. What would my mother say?

Squeezing him tight, I breathed in his scent of home—of brucel wood and shassa root—and wished I was back in Myria where things were simpler, where I knew what was up and what was down.

"Please, Ivy, you're choking me."

I relinquished my hold and turned to the meadow. "Do you think the elk will come back before dusk?"

"I think they will eventually. There's not a lot of grass on these mountains."

I rubbed my eyes and leaned against the rock, staring up at the passing clouds. "I'm sorry for all this, Brom. I know I need to be sure of myself. Especially right now. Maybe my mother was right. I'm too weak to—"

Brom bumped my shoulder. "Forgive me for saying this, milady, but your mother is an old crone."

I choked on a laugh. Maybe Zach was rubbing off on him.

My page flushed. "Sorry, that was out of line. But it takes a strong person to admit when they're confused, especially if it means questioning everything you've ever known."

Smiling broadly, I bumped his shoulder back. "You're right. She is an old crone. But she's still my mother, and I want to please her. Even after everything."

Brom said nothing for a while, then, "But *why*?"

"I don't think I ever told you this, but when I first arrived at the Legion in Myria, at six years old, a dragon attacked the outer wall. It was unlike anything I'd ever seen, Brom. It was pure bronze, with scales that gleamed like topaz. My mother was bringing me to Myria from Freida to officially crown me. When the dragon attacked, she shoved me into the arms of one of her attendants and placed a Kiss on my forehead. It was a

Kiss of protection. She'd never done anything like that before. Then she raced off with her partner. I watched under the cover of a wagon, encased in a glowing red protective shield, as she performed the most powerful Kiss I'd ever seen. Her partner sliced off the dragon's head in one blow. And I thought then, *I want to be her.* Powerful enough to take down an entire dragon.

"Even as mean as she is to me, as cold as she is, how can you not admire someone so strong? So noble? Especially when that someone is your own mother."

Brom said nothing. He simply gripped my hand.

"But it doesn't matter what she thinks anymore." My gut twisted at the truth of the words.

"What are you talking about? How could it not matter now?"

"I'm thinking of turning my back on everything she stands for, Brom. On the Legion's teachings. On everything. I keep obsessing about it—what would she think about me traveling with two Romantica and wanting to understand what Love is? That would be it, Brom, she'd truly hate me. She'd even try to disown me—get rid of me as a pure descendant."

"You're right," he said in a low voice, "she probably would. But what if you manage to defeat the dragon *without* a Kiss and figure out how to end this war? Then *you'd* be the one to admire."

Leaning my head against the rock and closing my eyes. *Now* that *would be a miracle.*

Brom suddenly twisted around at the sound of hooves. "They're coming. Finally." He held out the crossbow to me, but I pushed it back to him.

"By all means. You tracked them."

Brom smiled and propped himself up on his elbows, getting into position just as the herd leaped into view.

...

The evening chill settled early in the mountains. By sunset, it was nearly freezing, and Brom, Zach, and I had to turn to our heavier cloaks as we moved across the rocks. Millennia seemed perfectly fine in her thick blue robes. She was, however, considerate to our thinner clothes and conjured up a small flame to follow us.

Zach gave the flame a wary glance. "When it gets dark, you'll have to extinguish that."

Millennia tugged her hood farther over her face. "Whatever you say, prince."

"It's one thing to have a fire when we're stationary and vigilant, it's another to have one when we're traveling and exposed," Zach continued.

"Oy, I'm not arguing with you," Millennia said, glancing over her shoulder at the sound of a rock Bromley had knocked loose with his boot.

I climbed over a particularly large boulder then stopped to look down. "We may as well camp there." When all three of them were behind me, I pointed to the dimly lit expanse below.

Bromley let out a low whistle. "I have a feeling what we've been through doesn't count as real mountains."

He had a point. Below us was a steep ridge that could be climbed down, given careful maneuvering, and beyond was an entire valley of stone walls. They weren't too steep, but the valley itself was huge—perhaps a whole mile of just rocks.

Because there was nowhere to go but down, we started our descent. For the most part, we were able to move along without one another's help, but every once in a while, when Millennia wasn't too exhausted from climbing, she would wave her hand, and the rocks would form a rough staircase.

By the time we reached the valley floor, the sun was already gone and we were able to see the first signs of stars. Millennia produced a small fire and, without a word, passed out on a flat rock, using only a small bundle for a pillow and her heavy robes for covers.

"I'll take first watch." Zach headed upward around a pile of rocks to get a good vantage point.

Bromley didn't need telling twice. He unrolled his bed and covered up with a cloak, facing the small flickering fire.

I took my time getting situated. Occasionally, I would gaze at the stars and watch as the smoke from our fire drifted into the heavens like a hazy gray river. The moon and stars were so close it looked like I could reach up and snatch them out of the sky. At finally hearing Bromley's breathing turn deep and rhythmic, I placed my hands flat on the cold rock and stared at them, thinking hard.

Did I dare go to Zach now?

Though every muscle in my body yearned to venture closer, the cold mountain air allowed me to keep my wits. *Don't go, Ivy.*

What would happen if I went up there?

I clutched the sheet of paper with the spell I'd finally memorized. Gelloren told me to stay away from Millennia, a Romantica. They told lies. I'd always been taught that. But I'd seen the Golden Effect with my own eyes, so how could that be a lie? It didn't mean Love was the trigger, though. So what *was* the trigger? Why, then, had the griffin burst into golden light when Zach sacrificed himself for me? Was it the sacrifice itself or the *reason* he'd done it?

I crumpled the paper.

Because he loved me.

I slammed the ball of paper on the rock and tried to smooth it out, my hands trembling. I had to stop thinking like this. I had to stop being swayed by him. Where was the princess who'd do anything, who'd Kiss anyone to stop a monster? To win?

I'd always been devout in my beliefs.

But I believed in Zach, too. I believed him when he said he loved me. But how could I believe in both things? Wasn't that hypocrisy?

The spell words on the paper blurred, and I gritted my teeth. I stuffed it into my bag and stood.

I was tired of being confused and tired of being tugged in both directions. For so long I'd been able to ignore the Romantica and their beliefs, because they'd never been a part of my life. But now I had one who seemed to be taking over my every thought. Maybe I owed it to my partner to try to understand what he meant when he said he loved me.

Maybe that's what was so frustrating about it all. I didn't *know* enough about Love and the Romantica to make an educated decision about what I really believed. In a way, that was the most logical—the most *Royal*—thing to do. If I gathered all the information, I'd feel confident in whatever I chose.

Not like now, when I felt like I was teetering over a large abyss.

I needed to know what was down there before I stepped over the edge, or stepped back to safety.

The breeze picked up, and a strong gust loosened my hair and nearly blew out our fire. I threw some wood onto the pile and walked toward Zach, stepping to the edge.

He sat on a flat, elevated rock that allowed him total view of the valley. He saw me approach but made no move. I hovered above him, remaining standing, and looked at the valley below, thankful for the moon and stars that illuminated the mountain floor.

I shivered as another gust blew through us. "Aren't you freezing?"

Zach had his arms crossed. He hadn't yet looked at me.

"I'll survive a chilly night."

I pursed my lips. "How was hunting with Millennia?"

He smirked, gaze still focused ahead. "Jealous I was alone with another woman?"

I stared at him, then sat down next to him, hugging my knees. "Maybe a little."

His gaze snapped to me, lips parted in surprise.

It was true, though I'd felt only a slight stab of irritation, knowing she'd get to spend time with him when I didn't.

Zach's lips twitched. "You don't have anything to be worried about."

The moment he said those words, a rush went through me like I'd never felt before, and I ducked my head, determined not to show it. Yes, I blushed, but it was more than that. It was...a *thrill* that started in my spine and made me grin so wide my cheeks hurt. It was happiness in the strangest form.

When he caught me smiling, he took my chin and lifted my face to his. "Are you happy about that?"

The smallest smile played on his lips as he waited for me to answer.

"M-maybe a little," I repeated.

It was possible that Zach hadn't expected the same reply, but whatever the reason, something had rendered him speechless. With his fingers still holding my chin, we stared into each other's eyes until I could no longer take it and turned my head away from his grasp.

I cleared my throat. "Did you and Millennia talk about anything interesting during your watch?"

Zach didn't take his eyes off me. "Not particularly. She asked me about Saevall. My first mission as a member of the Legion. Wanted to know why I had never agreed to a partner before and"—he paused and finally glanced away—"why you were the exception."

I swallowed and raked hair behind my ear. "And you said?"

Zach grinned, a full-blown smile. "None of her business."

I laughed, now enjoying the cool wind on my hot cheeks. "For the record, I'm glad you agreed to be my partner."

Zach raised a skeptical eyebrow. "That's a load of griffin dung."

It was understandable that he didn't believe me—I hardly believed it myself, since it was only a few days ago when I was screaming at him for tricking me.

I smiled and shook my head. "It's true."

"Okay, I buy that you may not hate me anymore. But I'm still not going to Kiss you, and that's the whole reason you wanted me as a partner...so what changed?"

"I—" My voice caught, the giddy happiness I'd had rapidly transforming into bouncing nerves. I closed my eyes to make sure I couldn't see him when I said, "You were right."

"About what?" he asked, his voice close.

"You said...tell me I'm wrong. That I'd be better off with someone else. And you're...you're *not* wrong."

Without warning, Zach's hand wrapped around my ribcage, while his other slid under my hair and cradled the right side of my neck.

"You're not making this easy." His hot breath tickled my neck for a moment before his lips made contact with it.

I inhaled more slowly than a gasp with ten times more tension in my lungs. My eyelids fluttered as the muscles in my back contracted. He held on to me, moving his lips across my skin in deep, sensual kisses.

Somewhere, in the back of my mind, I thanked the Sisters that Zach didn't seem to know that a Kiss could be placed anywhere, lips to skin, and the magic could still be triggered. But I didn't dare try anything. For one, I wouldn't have even been able to *think* of a spell, but more than anything else, he would've never kissed me like this again. And I...I wanted him to.

I brought a trembling hand to his shoulder and pressed my fingers into his strong muscles. His hand on my neck moved gently over my skin, the base of his palm coming to rest on my throat. His kisses moved up to the corner of my jaw, right below my ear.

I'd heard other girls describe the feelings of Lust before — that it felt like hot flames were licking your body. Or that Lustful kisses were like fiery scorch marks all over.

But I disagreed. Zach's kisses didn't burn me in a way that fire would. Instead it was like being out in the snow and practicing with your sword until your hands were numb, then placing them in a basin of warm water heated by coals. The moment your fingers touched the heated water, all you wanted was to plunge your entire frozen body in. You were desperate to feel the warmth spread to your body and shiver with the pleasure it brought.

As his lips passed over my throat and back to the edge of my jaw, a sound escaped me. I was desperate for more. My hands groped at the back of his shirt as he tilted my head upward, kissing at the base of my throat and moving toward my clavicle and farther down. His hand that rested on my shuddering lungs traveled down my hip and onto my thigh.

There was nothing that could keep me up now. I lowered myself down to my elbows and he followed, his lips now kissing my shoulder, fingers tugging down my sleeve to allow more bare skin for his kisses to travel over.

Without thinking, simply following the signals from my own body, I twisted under him. I didn't even have to guide him — my hands simply brushed across his neck, and his face came up to meet my own. His breathing was low, labored, and hot against my lips.

My fingers curled into the fabric of his shirt.

I should've seen his reaction coming.

His eyes snapped open, as if finally waking up from a trance. With a groan, he rolled off me, smoothing back his hair. "*Troll's breath,* Ivy." He dragged one hand down his face and covered his mouth. "You're more dangerous than the vipers."

For a moment, I was dumbstruck and still basking in the glow of that warm, heavenly bath. Then I shook my head, clearing it. "I didn't initiate...*that.* I just came up here to talk."

To try to understand Love, I'd told myself. Had that just been a pathetic excuse?

"Ivy, don't patronize me." His gaze landed on my bare shoulder. "You know how I feel about you. You came up here and told me... What did you *expect* to happen?"

I couldn't answer that, not when I wasn't sure myself. "I should go to bed."

He stared at me for a few weighty moments then turned his gaze back to the stone valley. "Yes, you probably should."

I stood, wobbly, and climbed off the rock. I was halfway to the fire when I heard Zach unsheathe his sword.

The Swordsman Prince must've had better ears, or his brain was much clearer than mine, because he had already recognized the crumble of loose pebbles and the hiss of goblins' tongues.

CHAPTER TWENTY-EIGHT

"GALLEEK OKK AK YAWK."

I cursed myself over and over. *This* was why I had promised myself I wouldn't surrender to Lust. Why I'd keep my focus on our mission. If I hadn't been so distracted by...*other* feelings, I would've been able to sense them sooner.

But I didn't have time to dwell on my mistakes. I ran to wake Millennia and Bromley.

"Attack!" I screamed, my voice echoing through the rock valley.

Goblins—three-foot-tall creatures with big heads and skinny limbs—climbed down the side of the cliff like spiders. From the look of it—close to thirty in all.

The moment my shout cut through the night air, the first two goblins leaped off the rocks toward Zach. He raised his sword and, with a flash of silver, sliced one down the middle, dust flying up and disappearing in the darkness. He pivoted just in time to slam his elbow into the side of the other goblin's head. The creature went down, bouncing off the rocks.

Bromley jumped to his feet, awake and shaken. But, bless him, he had quick reflexes and tossed me my sword, then began loading his crossbow. Millennia, too, had woken quickly, neither bleary-eyed nor frightened. She was already running past the fire and into the battle.

Zach took on four at once. Swinging, dodging, and cutting, he tore through the goblins. The goblins drew back, snarling and muttering curses in goblin tongue under their breath. Unlike trolls and dwarves, goblins used only their claws and curses for weapons, making them difficult to dodge but easy to cut down.

"Don't let them hit you with a curse!" I yelled, remembering Kellian's comatose form lying in a bed in Myria. Another wave of the creatures jumped off the rocks. Zach had taken out five, but there were still at least twenty left.

Bromley swung up his loaded crossbow and fired arrows with pinpoint accuracy. He took down two, and with piercing shrieks, they fell to the rocky floor. I darted forward to finish off any that survived, swinging my sword into an upward cut on the first goblin. With an arrow sticking from its shoulder, it tried to twist away from my swing, but my strike was true. As my sword sliced open the tiny chest of the goblin and its shriveled gray skin crumbled into dust, I froze. Something was familiar about that goblin's face.

Before I had time to consider it, sharp claws scratched my back from behind, and I yelled and twisted around, slashing down and killing my attacker. Pivoting to my right, I swung my sword in a great arc, lopping off another goblin's skinny arm before it had time to cast a curse on Zach. The little beast screamed something in goblin tongue and struck me, its long nails managing to cut only the fabric of my tunic.

With the creature so close, I got a good glimpse of its twisted face, and my muscles locked in place, my breath freezing in my chest.

I knew this goblin.

Like all goblins, it was short, bald, with wrinkly gray skin, red eyes that blinked like a serpent's, forked tongue, and long fingers and toes. But this one's face was scarred.

And I knew by what. Because I'd seen it happen.

From its forehead, through its eye, and down to its jaw, there was a deep, long purple scratch that turned its eye a bright pink instead of the normal crimson. Through Minnow's memories I had seen Kellian make that same scar.

Right before he'd killed it.

"Ivy!" Zach roared, throwing a dagger into the goblin's head, just as it had been about to rip into my stomach with its claws. "Pay attention!"

I gasped and blinked, whirling to face the battle. *Focus, Ivy. It could've been a mistake. A trick of shadows. A coincidence, even.*

Not thirty paces away, a tight tunnel of wind surrounded Millennia. Captured in the tunnel were three more goblins, screeching and howling. She jerked her arms upward, and the tornado arched into the sky and opened, spitting them out to the ground with a sickening crunch.

Still on the rock, Zach engaged in a heated battle with five new foes. He would've killed them all within a minute, maybe two, if not for their curses. Zach was able to lash out only when he wasn't busy dodging the curses that arced out of their fingers like lightning.

Brom and Millennia battled the last few goblins on the ground as I scrambled up the rocks to help Zach with the remaining five. Reaching the edge of their battle circle, I struck at a goblin with my sword. It managed to dance away from my blade and then turned on me, raising long fingers and licking its shapeless, shriveled lips with its forked tongue.

When my gaze landed on its reptilian face, I choked.

It was the same. The same face as the other one. The same face as Kellian's goblin.

I saw the green lightning shake Kellian's body all over again—his scream filling my head. How could I forget this last memory of Kellian and his fate? Through Minnow's memories

I had watched him kill it. With the power of a Kiss, his body pulsing with blue battle magic, Kellian had driven his blade into the goblin's chest. It had dissipated into smoke. It had *died*.

Yet here it was. Alive. Miles away from the place he had killed it, only three weeks later. And there seemed to be... copies of it?

I turned to look at the goblins Zach was battling. The ones Brom had shot with his arrows. The ones Millennia had in her wind tunnel.

So I hadn't been imagining it. How could there be so many of the same goblin?

I couldn't move. I couldn't *breathe.*

The goblin lunged for me.

Thankfully, Millennia saved me, hurling a rock into the side of its bald head and knocking it down. I darted around the rocks to where the goblin had fallen.

The beast was barely conscious, but I waited until Millennia and Brom joined me.

"Hold it down," I told the mage.

Casting me a sideways glance, Millennia raised her hand and curled her fingers. The rocks on either side of the goblin crumbled and reformed around its hands and feet, pinning it to the ground. Its body twitched and struggled against its stone bounds.

I knelt down, ignoring the ache in my knees as the rocks dug into them, and pulled out my dagger. "Kellian killed you." I lifted the blade over its chest. "I know he did."

The goblin hissed, "*Galleek okk ak yawk.*"

Enraged, I drove the dagger into its chest all the way to the hilt. The goblin didn't even have time to scream before it crumbled. The dust flew in my face, sticking to my wet cheeks, catching in my eyelashes, and flying into my hair.

"What did it say?" Brom whispered behind me.

It was Millennia's voice that answered. "Yet I live again."

CHAPTER TWENTY-NINE

HATCHING A NEW PLAN

We plunged on into the mountains, regardless of the darkness. If there were more creatures coming, we had to put distance between them and us. I was thankful for the travel, though. It allowed at least part of my mind to stay sane. The other part of it pounded with the same horrid thoughts, and no matter what look anyone gave me or what anyone tried to say, nothing penetrated my outer shell.

I had shut them all out.

I wished to curl into a ball and disappear, then reappear in my bed back in Myria, with Colette and Robin begging me to tell tales of my adventure.

But this wasn't an adventure. This was a nightmare.

How many creatures had my Kisses helped slay, to later be brought back to life?

And somehow then multiplied?

Had everything I had done, everything my comrades had sacrificed—I thought of Minnow, Tulia, and their princes, and Telek and Kellian—all been for nothing?

I spent a long time staring at Zach's mark on my hand, realizing with horror that it could mean nothing. That my own mark perhaps was only a mark of death.

When dawn crested over the peaks, I led us to a stream.

My companions left me alone, having seen the toll this awful truth had taken on me. They said nothing when I went to sit by myself and pick at an orange with my fingernails. I was thankful for it, because they had no idea what I was going through.

My very existence was questioned. My own birth was unnecessary. The Royal's Kiss seemed to only make things worse—or it wasn't helping at all. So what was the point in breeding more Royals? What was the point in creating a powerful descendant of Myriana?

But more than that…what did it mean for the Legion's future? Did it mean the Romantica's theory was correct?

Was the secret actually Love?

I dug my fingernails into the orange, and juice dribbled down my hand. All I knew was the Royal's Kiss wasn't working. I couldn't think of alternatives anymore.

No more magic. No more solutions that I didn't fully understand.

Chucking the rest of the fruit across the stream, I stood and walked back to Zach, Millennia, and Brom, who were toasting bread, elk meat, and cheese over a small fire.

I dug into my pocket for the worn, crumpled sheet of paper with the Sable Dragon spell on it, and then I tossed it into the flames.

All three of them stared up at me.

I sat to join their circle. "All right. No Kisses. Now what's the new plan?"

It took them only a couple of moments to process what I said.

Zach gave me the biggest, dopiest grin I'd seen on him yet.

"Does the egg have any weaknesses?" Millennia asked, her fingers over the flames, encouraging it to rise a little higher.

"The shell itself is made of a substance stronger than iron. It's said there's not a blade—or person—strong enough to break it." I sighed. "That's where the Kiss came in. Unfortunately, as long as the dragon is in its shell, it's safe."

"So what could break it?" Zach asked.

"That's the thing...we can't. But..." I hesitated, because now they were going to think I had truly lost it. "We could accelerate the hatching."

Millennia blinked. "Um, correct me if I'm wrong, princess, but wasn't your whole mission to defeat the Sable Dragon *before* it hatched?"

"I know it sounds crazy, but think about it—if we can't destroy the egg, then we have to destroy the actual monster," I said. "We accelerate the hatching by using fire magic to heat it, *then* we kill it. Don't get me wrong, even right out of the egg, the dragon will be more powerful than all the creatures we've ever faced combined, but it's our only shot at killing it without using the Kiss."

Millennia and Zach shared a look, then they glanced back at me. Brom shivered and moved closer to the fire.

Millennia shrugged. "Doesn't look like there's any other option."

Zach's lips twitched into a tiny smile. "Sounds like the challenge I've been waiting for."

I glanced up at the mountains and placed a hand on my chest. I could feel the darkness welling inside me. "Then let's go hatch an egg."

We moved through the mountains at a breakneck pace, and I was glad to be too tired to think about how this new plan was practically suicide. The sick feeling on my shoulders and at the bottom of my ribcage was growing exponentially stronger. We were close. Perhaps only a day's travel.

But by afternoon I was mentally and physically exhausted. Bromley, who had been traveling next to me, caught me under the arms when I slipped on some rocks and lowered me to the ground. "Milady, are you all right?"

I nodded and tried to stand, but then swayed dangerously to the side. In an instant, I was swept up into Zach's arms.

"I'm fine," I said meekly. It was pathetic, really.

"You didn't get any sleep last night, and we've been charging around like deer in a stampede. We need to quit for today."

"I'm fine with that," Millennia said. "Better to stop now before we enter the ravine."

The stream we had been running parallel to fed into a large river, which had, over time, carved out a giant ravine in the middle of the mountains. It was steep and dangerous, but still beautiful, and perhaps a half mile ahead, almost hidden from view by twisted stone spires and boulders forming the base of mountains sloping on either side.

Zach carried me to a small cave cut off by the mountainside, offering only a bed-sized space of shelter. Because of last night's goblin attack, I wasn't crazy about Millennia and Zach leaving to scout the area. But it was for exactly that reason that I had to let them.

Bound in my bed wrap, I curled next to Bromley, resting my head on his shoulder, and closed my eyes.

"Milady…are you sure about this?" Bromley asked me as sleep pulled at my consciousness.

"Absolutely not," I said. "But that goblin shouldn't be alive, much less have thirty doppelgangers. I *saw* Kellian give it that gash on its eye and kill it before it managed to curse him." I shuddered and burrowed deeper into my bed. "What if we kill the dragon with the Kiss and it comes back to life, bigger, and worse, and with ten more dragons at its side? They would destroy us all, Brom. I wish I could believe in the Legion and the history I've been taught all my life, but I'm not sure I believe in anything anymore."

I'd been asleep for maybe an hour or two before a violent pain in my chest woke me. It was so sharp I had no trouble recalling the sensation. I had felt it once before on a patrol. It was the feeling of absolute evil closing in—of a creature that was created from the darkness itself—a wraith.

I tore away from my bed wrap and sat up with a start. Zach jumped to his feet—he must've been on watch yet again—his hand going to his sword on instinct.

"A wraith," I rasped through the stinging pain.

"How close?" Zach asked. There were dark circles under his eyes.

"Very."

Millennia pulled herself up. Brom, who was still next to me, was already reaching for his crossbow.

"Think we could get ahead of it?" Millennia asked.

"It's worth a shot. I don't want to fight a wraith," I said, remembering what they had done to my comrades on patrol. Only half of us returned unscathed. A quarter didn't return at all.

But if we did have to fight it, it was possible we stood a chance. All our bladed weapons were pure silver, the only metal that could truly wound a wraith. Another reason why the rowan deer and their antlers were so sacred.

We set off at practically a run, springing over rocks and reaching the ravine just as the sun was setting. Water splashed on our boots as we treaded across the slippery stones. The shadows stretched on through the ravine, allowing rays of sunlight to bounce off the water, creating rainbows.

An arrow of pain pierced my chest, and I stumbled, slipping on the rocks. Brom caught me again as the rainbows turned to shadow, and all light was sucked from the ravine. Two forms, as black as a cave's depth, slid down the ravine's steep sides like waterfalls.

Two wraiths.

My body went numb. *Five* Royals had had trouble with *one*.

We froze, dropped our packs, and raised our weapons.

The wraiths hovered by the rocky slopes on each side of the ravine, their bodies a twisting mass of black smoke. I glanced at the one closest to us, on the left side of the ravine. The wraith's head was merely a shape that flickered between amorphous smoke and a scorched, grotesque skull. Its body was made up of tendrils of darkness woven into a tattered cape. The hands appeared skeletal, fading in and out of human vision.

"It's immune to most elemental magic except fire. If it touches you too long, you'll die from overexposure to the cold. Its fingers are as sharp as knives, and it usually kills with its hands," I rattled off under my breath, in case Millennia, Zach, or Bromley needed any reminders.

"I'll take one, you three take the other," Zach said, the silver of his sword gleaming even in the gloom.

"Don't be ridiculous," I whispered, eyeing the wraith across the river. "This isn't the time to reject help again—"

"It's *not* that, believe me. I've fought one of these before and survived. Hopefully I can do it again."

So comforting. I bit my bottom lip and glanced at Millennia and Bromley. The three of us combined probably didn't equal another Zach.

"No time to argue." Millennia nodded to the wraith next to us as it drew breath, and all the warmth in the air got sucked into its churning black body.

That was Zach's cue. He took a few running steps and then leaped over the water, his sword raised over his head. Landing, he brought the sword down in a swift cut, slicing through the air where the wraith had once been. Millennia had once compared Zach's movements to a wraith. I understood why. He was unbelievable. I watched him—if only for a split second—spin and slash at the shadowy creature, twisting and turning with a flash of silver at each movement.

The other wraith regarded us for a few seconds then darted forward. Brom's silver-tipped arrows passed through it. Millennia conjured up a wall of fire, and it stopped at the blazing inferno—not fearful, but wary. The creature could not pass through fire, but it knew a mage could not hold up magic like that for long.

Drawing on every lesson I'd ever had, I made a short jab with my sword through the flames. The wraith was more than quick—it was clever and had anticipated my attack. It grabbed my sword and pulled, jerking me toward the wall of flames. Millennia barely had time to drop it before I would've been scorched alive. Pulling me, the wraith wrapped its hand around my wrist, cutting into my skin as its daggerlike fingers squeezed. I screamed as the cold flew into my body, drawing all the warmth from my blood.

An arrow passed through its head, and a knife flashed by its ear. The wraith let go and shrieked, annoyed. I cradled my bleeding wrist that had turned a blackish blue from the cold, and picked up my sword. Next to me, Millennia conjured a flaming whip and twirled it around her head. She snapped it at the wraith, and the creature screamed again, seemingly in pain this time. Taking it as an opening, I switched the sword to my other hand and darted forward, slashing downward and slicing its arm. Another painful screech issued from the wraith as darkness exploded around my blade. It was like getting hit in the face with an ice storm.

Darkness whirled around me and threw me into the ravine wall. Pain exploded down my back, while circles of light danced in my vision. I was barely able to throw my arms in front of me to break my fall. On the ground, achingly long moments passed before my vision cleared, but my limbs still refused to move. So Bromley took up the fight.

Brom was more skilled than I had ever given him credit for. In fact, he was quite incredible. He was smaller, which allowed for speed and agility, and those two qualities meant everything against a wraith. I had seen him use only a sword and crossbow, because that was what we usually sparred with, but now he held two silver daggers and used them like they were an extension of his hands. He dodged and ducked, swung and punched. The wraith moved faster than a blink, but if I wasn't mistaken, Bromley seemed to get in a jab or two.

I struggled to my feet and raised my sword again. As I started forward, I heard Millennia muttering something—then my sword ignited. As did Bromley's daggers. The wraith shrunk away from the flaming blades, hissing and shrieking. With renewed confidence from my fiery sword, I swung low at the wraith. It twisted away, but just barely escaped the inferno.

Together, Brom and I attacked the monster, forcing it to dodge not only the silver, but also the flames.

It felt natural, fighting with Bromley. We had practice-fought against each other so often that we knew each other's style. We worked as one, and it was brilliant. Bromley ducked and sliced his daggers out, sweeping his arms in an arc, and in the same movement I went high and swung my sword for the wraith's head. Unable to dodge both of us, the wraith shrieked, its body sliced clean through with fire and silver. It crumbled to dust.

As the wind carried the remnants of the creature away, Millennia collapsed into a pile of billowing blue fabric. She was visibly shaking, no doubt from the cold and fatigue. I was about to run to her when I saw what was happening across the river.

Zach still fought the other wraith.

And he was losing.

The swordsman was skilled, but he was still only human. He probably hadn't managed more than a few hours' sleep in the past two days, and he couldn't keep up.

Millennia was practically unconscious, unmoving on the ground. She would be no help. I ran to the stream and was about to jump across, when Bromley stopped me. "Stay back," he told me, "you're losing too much blood."

I glanced at my wrist, and I could scarcely believe the amount of blood that coated my sleeve. It was practically dripping, and I recognized the dizziness from blood loss.

Then, before I could stop him, Brom had jumped across and joined my partner against the wraith. With Brom's help, the tide turned slightly, and Zach was able to get his second wind. Once the two warriors had the wraith against the ravine wall, Zach made a valiant strike. The shadow creature screeched and recoiled as Zach plunged his sword into its side.

But the move came at a cost. The wraith grabbed Zach's arm and he screamed. I knew what that explosion of cold felt like. Zach staggered away—and I knew—he'd reached his limit. The monster saw it, too, and went for the final blow.

Something burst in my chest. The cry ripped through my gut and into my throat. I tried to jump over the stream, but my coordination was shot. I fell into the icy water, and it swallowed me. I pushed off the slippery rocks at the bottom, and my head broke the surface just as the wraith moved in. It reached for Zach's heart with five daggers disguised as skeletal fingers.

I was too late to stop it—but Brom wasn't.

He stopped the wraith's hand with his knife. The sound of silver clashing against metallic bone echoed through the ravine. Chest heaving, Brom swung back with his free arm to go for the creature's throat. But the wraith had the same idea.

And it was much faster.

This time I couldn't scream as Brom fell to the ravine floor, blood pouring from open wounds on his throat and collarbone. All breath, all sound had been knocked out of me.

Zach lunged over Brom's fallen body and hacked away at the wraith like a thing possessed. Bits of smoky darkness were tossed into the air, transforming to dust as Zach sliced and cut with a fury I'd never seen.

Once the wraith was nothing but tiny particles of darkness, Zach turned back and fell to his knees next to Bromley.

With numb limbs, I pulled myself out of the stream and crawled, sopping wet, to Bromley. My knees and hands collided with a pool of blood, and at the touch of the warm liquid, I shattered.

Bromley. *Brom.*

He shook on the cold stones, his eyes wide and alert and… knowing.

He tried to talk, but the wound on his throat only leaked more blood.

"Sh-shhhh." I sobbed, my voice strange to my own ears. "No, Brom, please, I can't do this without you. *Please.*"

With trembling fingers, I gripped his hand and squeezed. It was freezing, nearly lifeless.

But I could save him. I still had the *Royal's Kiss.* So what if it was evil? So what if it created more monsters? I would pay *any* price for Brom's life, no matter what the cost—a thousand more wraiths crawling the earth if that's what it took.

I reached for Zach across Brom's shivering body, trying to conjure up the spell in my mind. Trying to think with a desperate sense of clarity. I couldn't fail this spell.

Zach took my hand in his, and I knew he wasn't going to deny me this time. Not now. Not for Brom.

But he didn't have to. Brom did. With his remaining strength, with the life draining from his eyes, Brom pulled me back. Blood pooled at his neck. His mouth was open but no sound. Subtly, so subtly, he shook his head.

I was willing to pay any cost, but Brom wasn't.

My brave Brom. *My Brom.* I didn't care what the Legion said—what I felt for Bromley was so much stronger than friendship. He was my family. My brother. Bond wasn't a strong enough word for what I felt for him. It was a force, a magic that defied all reason and logic.

Love was the only thing strong enough to describe him to me.

I loved him with all my heart. All my soul.

I gave a strangled moan, hunched over him with my forehead pressed to his, and sobbed.

Tears ran in rivulets down my cheeks and splashed onto Brom's face, rolling down his cheek and mixing with the steady stream of blood.

Then...a spark of gold.

As more of my tears rolled down his neck onto his wound, gold shimmered, covering the terrible crimson and replacing it with...

I gasped and reeled back. Light, beautiful light, shone in the darkness of the ravine, rolling off Bromley in waves. Sparks and dust danced over him, whirling around him in a tornado of sheer gold.

Everything, everything was gold.

Gold light splashed onto Zach and me, showering us with the strange magic. My wrist tingled and, without even looking, I knew it had healed.

It was so bright I had to close my eyes.

When I opened them, Brom was staring at me, wide-eyed, through the clearing golden mist. His neck was completely healed. Our astonishment lasted just a moment before we threw ourselves into a tight embrace, tears still flowing.

We sat on the cold, wet ravine floor, holding each other just like the time when I was ten and Mother had come and gone from Myria without asking to see me once. I'd been devastated. Bromley held me tight that day, and I clung to him.

And together the world had looked much brighter.

In fact, it had looked golden.

CHAPTER THIRTY

LOVE IS...

The four of us stayed at the bottom of the ravine in a small cave for half the day. While Brom and I had sat locked together, Zach had crossed the river and helped Millennia back to our side. She was still pretty out of it, so Zach carried her until we found our tiny cave. After the battle with the wraiths, it felt like a palace.

We built a fire the old-fashioned way and threw our bed wraps over Millennia. Though Brom had assured me that physically he felt fine, nearly dying had taken its toll on him mentally, so I pressured him to sleep, and in no time, his head was on my lap and he was snoring lightly.

At his snoring, Zach and I looked at each other and shared a smile.

Zach prodded the fire with a stick and gestured to Brom. "I owe him my life."

"Stand in line," I said with a soft laugh.

"What's the story between you two?" he asked. "Most Royals don't care so much about their pages."

"We're family. He was assigned to me when he was very young, after he lost his parents. So he might have actually seen me as more of a mother back then, even though *technically* he was supposed to take care of *me*." I brushed some hair away from his forehead and smiled. "One of his first nights as my page, he developed a bad cough. It had been from crying himself to sleep the night before. I stayed up that night with him, giving him honeyed lemons. After that, he followed me around wherever I went. He was there for me when my mother never wanted to be. I...I don't know what I would've done if he'd... I was foolish to let him come."

"From the sound of it, I doubt you could've stopped him."

"Probably not." I bit my bottom lip and looked at Zach. "It was Love, wasn't it?"

He almost smiled, then he dropped his gaze to the fire. "You tell me, Ivy Myriana."

I wasn't a witch or a mage. My only magic came from my Kiss. For all I knew, I did not have magical tears, for I had cried enough to know.

"I know nothing about Love, Zach, so *you* tell *me*."

He looked up, brows raised. "You said you knew what Love was."

"Only the Legion's version of Love. Something tells me it's different than yours."

I thought he would've been happy to talk about the force he believed so strongly in. Instead, he looked uncomfortable. "It's complicated."

"I'm starting to understand that, but please try," I said quietly, running my fingers through Brom's light brown hair.

"Well, there's Love between friends and family—Familial Love." He tilted his chin at Brom. "Some people say that's the best form of Love. It's universal. Even Royals accept it— without calling it that. They understand it, because it helps them preserve strong bloodlines."

I nodded, plenty familiar with that already. It was the Royal "bond" that I thought I'd always shared with Brom. Now

I knew, it wasn't strong enough to describe what I felt for him.

"But Romantic Love…" Zach shook his head. "It's completely and utterly irrational. It can't be understood, and it can't be explained. It's unreasonable—which is probably why the Legion doesn't want to believe it exists. It's falling for someone even when you know they can't love you back." At that, his eyes drifted to my face, and I looked away, my pulse spiking.

"Love is sacrifice. It's painful. It's wishing that you could have one more day together, one more minute, one more *second* together, and hoping it lasts a lifetime, and then believing maybe it could." Zach was whispering now, watching the sparks in our tired fire die.

"That sounds absolutely foolish—"

He frowned. "Well, maybe but—"

"—and completely wonderful."

He looked up, and his eyes widened.

I wasn't sure what kind of expression I was making, because I'd never remembered feeling this way before. I lifted my hands to my mouth and sucked in a quick breath, holding back a tide of emotions. Terrified, excited, sad, and happy all at once—swirling inside me.

His mouth pulled up into a small half smile, and he looked at me with what I could only suspect was…well, love.

"How did you fall in love with your fiancé?" I asked Millennia later.

She stopped, and the stone steps she'd been raising crumbled. After a long rest for both her and Zach, we'd finally picked up the trail to the top of the ravine. While I'd been trying to focus on the path ahead, my mind kept going back to my conversation with Zach hours before.

Her blue eyes narrowed. "What do you mean—how?"

"I honestly want to know. I don't talk to many Romantica. I don't know how Love…happens."

Her shoulders relaxed a little, and she stared off into the distance, as if lost in a memory. "That's the thing. It just does. No reason at all. Or maybe it's all the reasons."

She was about to continue when Zach peeked his head from the top of the ravine's wall we'd been climbing for the past hour. "Hurry, ladies, you have to see this."

Glancing at each other, Millennia and I dropped our conversation and picked up the pace. She lifted the stone steps back up for me, and in no time we were at the top.

I saw why Zach was excited. We were very high into the mountains, but the stone had given way to life. Grass, trees, and other greenery decorated the side of the mountain we were now traversing. It was a nice change to see green rather than gray, and I was grateful for it. In a few months, this would all be snow. How lucky we were that it was late spring. Passing under a few trees, I found the pain in my chest and the weight in my shoulders barely tolerable, and rested against a large trunk.

Millennia stopped next to me, checking my face, then called up to Brom and Zach, "Go on. See what's ahead. We'll catch up." She turned back to me, handing me her water flask.

"Thank you," I said, then guzzled down the water. I handed back her flask. "You were saying about Love?"

She smiled as she took the water. "Where was I?"

"The reasons," I urged.

She was quiet for a moment, flattening the grass with her boot in a small circle. "You find yourself looking at his faults, looking at yours, comparing them over and over in your head until you realize you just don't care. For me…Tarren and I grew up together. We were childhood friends, and it just grew into something more, naturally. Not that it wasn't hard sometimes. I once thought he was cheating on me, and I became so jealous."

She paused, squeezing her eyes shut as if it hurt to bring up those memories.

Then after a few minutes, she opened her eyes and continued. "It turned out he was being secretive because he was trying to buy me a ring." She shook her head and laughed, then her smile crumbled, and tears swam in her blue eyes.

I took her hands. "Oh, Millennia, I'm sorry. I didn't mean to upset you."

"No, it's all right. I just miss him." She hurriedly wiped tears away, then looked back at me with a hardened gaze and held out her hand in front of my face. On her ring finger was a gorgeous band of braided silver. The ring Tarren had given her. "But it forces me to keep going."

I couldn't find any words to reply as we started back down the path.

Another sharp pain split my side, and I winced, drawing Brom's attention from staring up at the great mountains ahead of us.

"You feel it more up here, don't you?" Brom asked, sidling closer to me.

I scowled. Of course he noticed. Zach had, too. They had both been slowing down for me and taking more breaks since we'd left the ravine. Both could tell the pain in my chest grew worse and worse. Zach in particular kept hovering around me, the same expression of guilt he wore when he'd first learned I'd taken his Sense from him.

"I'm fine." I kneaded my side, and the pain eased slightly. "Just tired of sitting in the same position for three hours."

Brom rolled his eyes and rested his folded arms on his knees. "And yet you've never complained during watch before."

Ignoring him, I turned my attention back to the sky. The stars and moon were no longer visible. Instead it looked like a dark charcoal blanket had been placed over the world. "The sun should have risen by now…"

My gaze focused in on the horizon. A cluster of black clouds had emerged between two peaks where the sun was supposed to be. With a jolt of horror, I realized they weren't black clouds. They were sparrow harpies.

I jumped to my feet, my heart racing like I'd just run up the side of the great ravine. While sparrow harpies feasted only on the dead, I'd never heard of a swarm this size. A swarm that blocked the sun.

"Sparrow harpies. Everyone up. MOVE!" I yelled.

Millennia and Zach were up in seconds. We scrambled for our gear and raced toward the rocky outcrops, searching for shelter. Brom was the one to find the first cave. It was a small entrance, barely big enough for Zach to fit through, but he squeezed in between the rocks just as the buzzing sound reached our ears. In no time, the sound grew to the magnitude of a torrential downpour. It was like a tornado was whipping through the mountains, shredding the very stones.

On instinct, we backed farther into the cave, our boots slipping on the pebbles and loose rocks. Millennia produced a small fire, and its light bounced around stone walls, illuminating stalagmites and stalactites that stretched toward each other almost like the teeth of a great monster in the Seas of Glyll.

Brom leaned against the cave wall. "How long do you think we'll have to stay in here?"

"However long it takes for the swarm to pass." I cursed. "I just hope they stay in the mountains."

"But sparrow harpies don't feed on the living," Millennia said.

I shook my head. "That doesn't mean they're harmless. There's no telling what a swarm that size could do."

Zach nodded. "We need to find that egg."

As a particularly loud buzz echoed through our cave, Brom slipped from his stance against the wall and fell with a surprisingly loud crash of…metal?

Confused, Zach, Millennia, and I converged on Bromley. Millennia held the ball of fire in her palm, casting its orange glow at his feet. Scattered across the cave floor was an array of ancient-looking mining tools and a slew of small glittering gems. The magical firelight danced over the jewels' surfaces, making them look liquid.

I bent and touched a rusty pickaxe then winced as the blade nicked my finger. Still sharp. Only dwarf tools and weapons could remain that sharp after all these years.

"Dwarf mine," I whispered under my breath, a little excited. This could've been the cave where the dwarves of the story had dwelled, guarding their jewels and luring unsuspecting humans to trade and double-cross—sometimes murder. Could this be the legendary cave where the hunter Raed was cursed into a beast and fled to Maid Freida's cabin? It was a silly thought—there were so many caves in these mountains.

"I'm not surprised," Millennia said, lifting her fireball higher to give the room a wider glow. "According to legend, these caves had been full of them long ago."

"Yes, but they also should have been cleared out by Royals hundreds of years ago. After the dwarves stole away the first heir, Myriana and Raed personally led an army to these mountains and tore apart the mines."

Zach shrugged. "There must've been hundreds. Maybe they missed one."

I didn't reply. Something…something felt strange here. For the past two days my Sense had been pulling me in a certain direction. It had been strong and painful, barely able to ignore or push down. But the moment I'd stepped into the cave, my Sense had been...muffled. Almost like someone had placed a pillow over it. It was there, ever-present, but muted. I'd never experienced anything like it before. That alone made me insatiably curious.

I moved deeper into the cave, seeing more relics strewn about that had been tested by time. Most of them were jewels and mining tools, and others were tablets with dwarven curses carved into the stone.

Millennia suddenly gripped my arm tightly. I turned to look back at her, and her eyes looked strangely...purple in the firelight.

"We shouldn't venture far," she said, her voice low and heavy.

I pried her hand away and turned deeper into the tunnel. My Sense was almost entirely deafened now, replaced with a strange inner toll. It was like when I was in Myria Tower and its bells pealed over the kingdom, sending vibrations into my bones.

We entered a room much bigger and cleaner, as if someone had cleared away all loose rock and pebbles, but it held more dwarven items. Large symbols were carved into the stone, and against the far end of the room was a full-length mirror, more symbols lining the edges, like a decorative frame.

The mirror was dusty and tarnished, but I knew, without a doubt, that this was where the vibrations inside me were coming from. I moved toward it, not even sure what I wanted to do, just knowing I had to find their source, like the bells in the tower back home.

"Ivy."

I flinched at the sound of my name, and looked over my shoulder to see Millennia standing there with wild eyes. They were back to being blue, but she clutched her head like she was in terrible pain, as if a wedge had been driven into her skull.

"Ivy, don't. What are you doing?" she whispered.

Her voice was frightening, in a way that made me both scared of it and scared *for* her. I looked behind her to see Zach and Brom, both staring at me, completely mystified.

"Ivy, what is it?" Zach asked. "Talk to me."

"It's a magic mirror. It has to be. And I feel something strange, like…like bells or…"

Millennia gripped her head, her hands buried deep into her raven black hair, her breath coming out in wheezes.

I looked back at the mirror, close enough now to see the symbols clearly, and I realized that what I had thought were dwarven symbols were actually spell words, more specifically, the words of shared memories.

Don'na illye min'na.

"*Ivy*," Millennia hissed, "back away."

Zach, Brom, and I stared at her in surprise. Her voice was like a viper's hiss, unnatural and…and evil.

I glanced back at the mirror. What did she so desperately not want me to see? "You know what this is," I muttered, finally recognizing what I saw in her eyes—fear.

She said nothing, but her shoulders were tense, her hands clenched at her sides. The flames that she'd once held now danced across her knuckles, turning her hands into two glowing balls of fire. But her long sleeves did not catch. Perhaps a strange thing to notice, but seeing the crazed look in her eyes, I knew there was no way she was fully concentrating, so why was her fire so controlled?

Like I'd suspected from the beginning, Millennia was too skilled for someone her age. I'd chalked it up to a natural-born talent, but even that was farfetched for her level of control. It was too strange…impossible, even.

Then there was the place she'd said she came from: Raed.

The forests of Raed. It was where my mother had said there'd been a sighting of the Evil Queen—she had asked to send troops to investigate the sighting.

It was too much of a coincidence, and it all came down to one important question.

"Millennia," I breathed, taking a backward step toward the mirror. "Who...who did you say your master was?"

She lunged for me, as I somehow knew she would, but I flung myself at the mirror and collided into the glass.

"Ivy!" someone screamed. Zach, or Brom, or maybe both. They sounded far away.

Amber light poured around me, sucking me into the world of the mirror.

CHAPTER
THIRTY-ONE

SHARED MEMORIES

"The world of the mirror, my child, is a place you should never enter. It holds the memories of its owners, including their thoughts, hopes, and dreams. Spend too long within the shared memories of a magic mirror and you will begin to lose yourself and forget that these memories…are not your own."

Gelloren's words from a childhood lesson came back to me in the glow of the brilliant amber light. It seared my eyes and made my head scream in pain, as if it was about to split open. As quickly as it came, the pain faded, and a scene swam into view.

I recognized the Hall of Ancestors, half-built, with the roof still still open to the sun and clouds. The arches had yet to be joined in the middle or the carved faces added to the walls.

The details of the memory were crisp, as though whoever it belonged to had retained it from that morning.

A handsome man, with dark brown hair and a clipped beard, wore fine clothes and a cloak that was such a deep red it reminded me of Weldan's. He stood in the center, arguing with a group of other men plainly dressed. He gestured wildly and shook his head, finally raising his voice to the nonexistent ceiling, "I don't care what they all think. This is the end of the discussion."

"But King Raed—"

Raed. That means the magic mirror holds the memories of…

Anxiety flowed through me as I stood watching Raed, *my husband*, argue with those from the village.

"I said *no*. Now leave. I must talk to my queen." His gaze shifted back to me.

As the scene transformed into shades of amber light, the people and the half-built hall contorting, I tried to hold on to who I was—I was Ivy, not the owner of these memories. But I already felt unbearable sadness flow through me like white-water rapids, pulling me under until I couldn't separate my own self from the memories that now surrounded me.

I was in a bedroom, curled in the sheets, sobbing, a pool of blood between my legs.

"Darling," a soothing voice called to me from the end of the bed, "you should let them clean you up. Don't worry, we can keep trying."

At Raed's voice, I sat up and swallowed back more tears, preparing for the same argument we'd had months ago, after the last miscarriage.

"We have to stop this, Raed. We have a beautiful daughter already. Daisy." I wrapped my arms around myself and took another breath. Each one was a struggle. "Why can't we just make love like we used to? Why do we have to keep trying for another baby? We know the dwarves' curse worked. I can no longer deliver a pregnancy to term. We *know* this."

Speaking the words echoed the pain of losing the child all over again. Losing another precious baby who could grow up to be just as gorgeous as the one I had now. It was unbearable. Like knives cutting into my useless womb. With every lost child, the knives stabbed deeper.

Raed looked at me, the stress and worry on his face showing in the creases around his eyes. "The town council is convinced the power that allowed me to turn back into a human and to defeat the dwarf flows through our veins, and that we should produce as many heirs as possible who will allow the power to continue. Myri—" He walked over and cupped my face in his hands. "They believe in us. They want us to protect them. If we have the power, shouldn't we try? I mean, this power could be heaven-blessed."

I recoiled at the word "blessed." I'd heard they had begun to build a chapel in the village to offer me prayers, as if I were a living god. The thought repulsed me. I was just a girl. A new mother. Nothing more.

"I can't…I can't do this anymore. Please." I leaned in to him, yearning for a kiss that would assure me he still loved me, believed in our love, believed in the power of us together.

He turned his head. "I'm sorry, Myriana."

The scene shifted again, Raed and the bed filled with the blood of a child who would never be, dissipating like smoke from a candle. The colors swirled, and I was briefly allowed my own mind and my own memories again. This was Myriana's memory. Her real life. Not history transcribed from a Royal archive book or a tale around a Romantica bonfire, but the truth. *Her* truth.

The revolving colors solidified into a door. I was shocked at the detail of this door. At the knots and grooves of the wood. The door would be forever ingrained in my—*Myriana's*—mind.

I threw open the door and saw what I knew I was going to see. Then slammed it shut and started to run.

As I ran, I struggled to become Ivy again, to separate from this horrible, heart-shattering memory.

A strong hand grabbed my wrist. I turned and looked at my husband in disgust. He hadn't even had the decency to get fully dressed. He was bare-chested and wore only trousers.

"Myri," he breathed.

"So, this is your solution? To put an heir into my sister?" My voice was taut with emotion. "My *sister*?"

Raed's face turned to steel. "It's the solution the town is looking for. Saevalla has your blood. We can continue to rule if we produce heirs with our power. Myri, this is for—"

"I don't *want* to rule," I screamed, wrenching away from him. "I want to be with only you. I want to raise our daughter. I want to forget what I just saw."

The memory dripped with shadows. Raed's face and voice faded, and I curled into a ball on the floor.

Saevalla. My beautiful, tender sister. How could she do this to me? We shared everything. Even our love for Raed, but this…this…*no*.

No, I am not Myriana. I am Ivy.

I fought to keep my sanity as memories flew by, attacking my soul and heart and eating away at everything good inside me. Saevalla giving birth…Saevalla giving birth a second time… watching them grow.

Then one scene grew into such sharp focus that it felt like needles were pricking every inch of me.

I drew my black cloak around me and stood in a huge cave, purple fire sconces lining the rounded wall. A stone altar stood before me, wet with the blood of animals the dwarves had sacrificed.

"I want you to cut it out."

The dwarf's smile stretched. "So you've told us, Your Majesty. And you don't care what we do with it afterward?"

"What concern is it of mine? Just make it stop."

"Then please." The dwarf gestured to the altar, and I climbed on top of it and lay down, staring up at the domed ceiling.

The chanting began. Haunting and wild. Dark and twisted. Echoing and terrible.

The dwarven clan surrounded me, and the one I'd made the

deal with loomed above me, holding the beautiful dagger that Raed had given me as a wedding gift. Its blade was engulfed in black flames.

He plunged the flaming dagger into my chest.

I screamed, screamed, *screamed*. The pain was too much. I'd never live. I'd never survive. But that was okay. I wouldn't have to live with the jealousy and hatred anymore for my own sister and my beloved who betrayed me. It would all stop.

With this last thought, the world was ripped from under my feet. It was like I was floating away. I saw my body—no, Queen Myriana's body—on the altar.

Again, the memories became amber shades spinning and distorting into a similar scene. Dwarves still circled the stone altar coated in dried blood, chanting, but instead of Myriana, a new girl lay on the table. She was young and beautiful—raven black hair and snowy white skin, just like Myriana—but with different facial features.

My—*no, the girl's*—eyes snapped open.

They were the color of a dark amethyst—violet and haunting. And familiar.

The dwarves' chanting reached a powerful crescendo as they each raised an arm holding a gleaming dagger. Then they drew them across their necks. One by one, the dwarves fell, each one's blood flowing in steady rivulets to the altar where I—the girl—lay. The blood traveled up the altar, seeping into my clothes, my hair. Their blood was hot, steaming against my skin.

I knew what to do with this blood.

I lifted my hands, and a ball of crackling purple energy formed at my fingertips, convulsing and pulsing with power. Purple flames rolled over my arm. I held out my hand and studied the burn.

It was a mark. My mark. The Mark of Myriana.

I smiled.

This. This would be my legacy. *My Hydra Curse.*

"Ivy!" A voice was screaming. Screaming a name. My name?

I wrenched my eyes open, although my lids felt like they weighed a thousand pounds, and found myself leaning against the mirror as if I'd never left it.

In reality, I knew I hadn't. Like entering the amulet's enchantment, time was irrelevant in the world of the mirror. I may have been encased in the amber glow of the mirror for mere seconds while I could experience an entire lifetime in the glass.

But time was now moving again and so was Millennia, her hands closing around my throat and thrusting me against the mirror so hard the glass cracked behind my back, shattering and spider-webbing.

Zach screamed my name, but a wall of purple flames erupted behind Millennia and me, preventing Zach and Brom from getting close.

Her hands squeezed my throat, nails digging into my skin. Gasping for breath, I stared into the familiar deep-violet eyes.

I rasped one word. One name. "*Myriana.*"

CHAPTER THIRTY-TWO

THE QUEEN'S HEART

It was as if I'd uttered a sacred spell. At the mention of the Holy Queen's name, Millennia ripped her hands from my throat.

"You...you saw. You know." She stared at me, her violet eyes wide with horror.

I rubbed at my throat. Zach screamed for me through the wall of purple flames. I wanted to yell at him to run, to leave me. Because I knew that who was standing before me would never let any of us walk away alive.

"You're Myriana," I whispered. "You're the Evil Queen."

Even though I'd seen it—no, *experienced* it—I couldn't believe my own words. It couldn't be true. The Holy Queen, my beautiful, powerful ancestor, couldn't be the Evil Queen. It would mean everything, *everything* was a lie. The Royal's history was wrong. It hadn't been the first heir. The Romantica's tale was wrong, too. It hadn't been Saevalla, either.

The Evil Queen had been Myriana Holly all along.

Millennia, or Myriana, whoever she was, gripped the sides of her head, pulling at her black hair, her face contorted in both pain and fury.

"I'm *not* that pathetic weakling," she hissed through

clenched teeth. "I'm the part of her that she couldn't live with."

My gut twisted with revulsion, remembering the dagger plunge into Myriana's chest, her begging the dwarves to remove it, then the young girl on the altar with the glowing purple eyes.

And I knew. I knew what she was.

"You're her Heart."

At my words, Millennia let out an inhuman shriek, and her shoulders and arms burned with purple fire as she threw herself at me. But I was prepared this time. I grasped a shard of the broken mirror she'd slammed me against, and when her fiery arms lunged for me, I stabbed the shard deep into her thigh. She gave another shriek, and the flames separating us from Zach and Brom weakened. Zach took a running jump over the inferno and was by my side, sword drawn, in seconds.

"What *are* you?" he snarled to Millennia as I fumbled to draw my sword.

She dug her fingers into her temples and drew heaving breaths while blood trickled from the piece of mirror lodged in her thigh. Through a curtain of black hair, she stared at me, this time her eyes a beautiful shade of cerulean.

"I...I can't... Run. *Run,*" she moaned.

Millennia was still in there somewhere, fighting to keep the Evil Queen at bay. Like the young girl upon the stone altar in the world of the mirror, Millennia was nothing more than a victim—a host for the Queen's Heart. She was possessed. But Zach had no idea, so when he darted forward with his blade, he believed he was attacking someone wicked—a witch maybe, but not an innocent girl possessed by the Evil Queen.

Without thinking, I lunged in front of him, parrying his blade with my own, our swords clashing in a resounding metallic echo.

"What're you doing?" Zach yelled at me.

What *was* I doing? I should let Zach kill her while she was weak, while the possession didn't have hold of her. But then… then we'd be killing an innocent. Someone we were sworn to protect. Someone who was willing to do anything for the sake of the person she loved.

Before I could answer, Millennia gave another howl of agony, and the violet flames in the cave flickered out, throwing us all into darkness.

"Brom!" I screamed.

"I'm here!" he yelled, his voice close.

"That blasted mirror." A haunting voice echoed in the darkness as if the Heart of Myriana was in the very air, rather than the body of an innocent girl. "If my other self hadn't been so weak, so scared her precious prince would find out what she'd done, she would've never removed all her memories of me and trapped them in one of the dwarves' mirrors." Her voice was raspy and labored, as if every word was an effort to speak—and maybe it was. I didn't know how much power it took for a full possession of a soul. Underneath her words, there was shuffling. What was she *doing*?

"Too late now. It would've been so much easier if my last body had survived creating my son's curse, then I wouldn't have needed to go traipsing all over these mountains looking for him."

Horror ripped through my gut, making me nauseated. *Her last body.* Sacred Sisters, she's been moving from body to body. *She's possessing innocent girls. Poor Millennia.*

"Alas, what's done is done." Her voice was farther away now. "I *had* hoped I'd be able to use your helpful little Sense to reach my son, then kill you both, but it looks like I'll have to get this stubborn body there on its own."

Another shot of crippling panic made my limbs lock. She'd been edging around the wall in the darkness so she could get out…

"No matter. You'll die here anyway." At her last word a great rumbling shook the cave. Her elemental mage magic. The Evil Queen had been using her control of Millennia's magic all along, and now she was going to use it to bury us.

An arm pulled me to the cave wall and pushed me flat against the stone, and I knew without a doubt Zach was shielding me with his own body. Rocks rained down and their crash made the earth beneath my feet tremble. But Zach still held me under him, protecting me. I could hear his heart pounding in his chest and feel his breath on top of my head. Terrified that he could once again get hurt from protecting me made me want to throw him off, but I didn't dare, in case I pushed him into falling rock. This time there was no gold magic to bring him back to me—this was no monster with sharp talons. No matter how much Zach loved me, his sacrifice against nature wouldn't save him.

Miraculously, once the rocks settled and the mountain stopped shaking, Zach's chest still rose and fell above me. Cautiously we lifted our heads and blinked through the dust. The rockslide that Millennia—or rather, Myriana—had caused had created an opening in the cave ceiling, allowing sunlight to pour into the cave. Zach moved aside as I scurried out from beneath him, heart racing.

"Brom!" I called. *No, no, I can't lose him again.*

"I'm okay." A pile of rocks shifted to our left, and Brom emerged from the rubble, shield in hand. The clever boy had used his shield against the cascade of rocks.

I stumbled toward him and hugged him tight. "Thank the Sisters," I breathed into his dusty hair.

"This doesn't look good." Zach's voice came from the direction of the cave entrance, and with a sinking feeling, I guessed what he was going to say.

"We're trapped." The entrance of the cave was completely

sealed by massive boulders, probably too large and heavy for any of us to move. But that didn't stop Zach from trying. Placing his shoulder against the wall of rubble, he pushed, his boots slipping and losing grip on the loose rocks under his feet. Brom and I joined him, but after what seemed like an hour of pushing, we backed away, breathing heavily. Zach rubbed a dirty hand across the back of his neck and let out a string of curse words I'd never heard him speak before.

"Well that's not budging anytime soon," he said when he'd finally exhausted all his swears.

I gripped my hands to keep them from trembling and took calming breaths, leaning my head against the wall of the cave and closing my eyes. I tried to keep my thoughts at bay, but they came crashing onto me like the rocks had, pummeling me and breaking me. I bit my lip as my eyes filled with tears.

It was all hopeless.

Everything I knew, everything I'd ever been taught had been a lie. Myriana hadn't been blessed. She hadn't been a new race of humankind with the ability to defeat the Forces of Darkness. She'd just been a girl. A scared girl with the weight of an entire growing kingdom on her shoulders, and when the person she loved most betrayed her, she'd broken. She'd given in to the darkness festering inside her, and rather than moving on and dealing with the pain in her heart, she had the dwarves…cut it out.

My breaths came in rapid succession as I slid down the wall to my knees. And even though I was breathing, I couldn't get enough air into my lungs. I was drowning again, but this time without water. And that thought only made it worse. I'd seen this happen before to a few young Royals before their first battle—a panic attack, the older ones had called it.

My breaths came faster, a new kind of pain squeezing my chest. It was different than my Sense—crushing my whole torso like a troll standing on top of me, and I couldn't breathe because my lungs were collapsing.

Just when I thought I'd suffocate, I felt hands on either side of my face, and Zach's forehead pressed against mine, his nose touching mine, his cheeks touching mine, his lips... hovering above mine. My breath stopped—my heart skipped several beats, one right after the other. I didn't move, didn't try to breathe, just reveled in the warmth of Zach's breath on my cheeks, on his rough fingertips burrowing into my hair. Losing my breath completely somehow reset everything. I took one solid gulp of air, then another, and blinked slowly, our lashes so close they almost touched.

"Tell me what you saw, my love," he whispered gently.

My heart almost jumped into my throat at his words. *Please don't let this be the last time he calls me that.*

I told him and Brom everything—of the memories I'd seen in the world of the mirror.

Throughout the whole story, Brom and Zach listened with rapt attention, and when I stopped talking, when my voice felt hoarse from all the words and the rock dust, Zach placed a gentle kiss on my forehead.

"You learned the truth, Ivy." He said it in a way that felt like praise, and I glowed with warmth.

I lifted my gaze to the blocked cave entrance. "But it's too late. Millennia—er—Myriana is surely going to hatch the Sable Dragon."

"I don't understand," Brom said, also staring at the caved-in rocks with a frown, "if she's really the Evil Queen then how come she hasn't already made the dragon hatch? Why was she traveling with us? Shouldn't she know where it is?"

"It's because the Evil Queen is possessing Millennia's body," I explained, quickly recapping what Myriana had said about her last body not surviving the curse that created the Sable

Dragon egg and the mirror's shared memories of Myriana's first host.

"You mean she didn't retain the memories of the girl before her?" Brom asked.

I shook my head. "Even if she did retain them, this mountain range is huge. It could've taken her forever to find the egg on her own, and it doesn't seem like she has the same Sense that Royals do."

Zach snapped his fingers. "Maybe not as *Millennia*."

"What do you mean?" I asked.

"Well, look at how weak she was. Instead of trying to kill us directly, she used her earth magic to try to crush us. What if the reason she was so weak is because it was the first time she had attempted to fully take over her host's body? What if she didn't have enough power to control both Millennia's mage magic *and* her body the whole time?"

"Which would mean…" I started, my mind racing, "that the Millennia we've been traveling with is still the real Millennia." That thought gave me a surge of strength. Millennia was still there. She'd been there all along—probably fighting the Evil Queen the whole time—battling with an entire other consciousness causing insurmountable pain.

"Right. It would've been too difficult to control her *and* lead her to the Sable Dragon," Zach said.

"But now that she's fully possessing Millennia, she'll be able to locate the egg," I breathed.

"But it'll take her forever to get there." Brom pointed to a dark spot on the rocks that looked like drying blood. "You wounded her, right, Ivy? If she's weak *and* injured, it's going to take her some time."

Zach inspected the light coming through the crack in the ceiling. "Time is all we need. That opening up there isn't too high. Brom, do you think you can fit through?"

Brom squinted at the light, frowning. "I can try," he muttered, standing and dusting off his trousers.

After some coordinating, and shifting as many movable rocks as we could to form a platform, Zach stood on the rocks, and Brom stood on Zach's shoulders. I watched and prayed the whole time, to whom, I was no longer sure, but it made me feel better anyway.

Too many tension-filled seconds of swaying and reaching passed before Brom was able to grab the lip of the opening. I scrambled up next to Zach, and together we pushed Brom's feet up. With a shout of triumph, Brom slipped his shoulders through the crack, then the rest of him followed. Lying on his stomach, he looked back down at us. "All clear. Sparrow harpies are gone, too," he called. "The crack's a lot bigger than you'd think. I'd guess you can both fit through."

Zach and I breathed a sigh of relief. Grinning, Zach waved him away. "See if you can find our packs in the front of the cave. I've got some rope you can throw down here."

"Got it. Be right back." Brom's face started to move away.

"Brom!" I yelled.

His face came back. "Yeah?"

"Please be careful," I begged.

He smiled in return. "Of course, milady." With that, he disappeared from view.

"He'll be fine, Ivy," Zach said, knowing how worried I was—with wraiths and goblins and sparrow harpies and who knew what else out there. "The kid's strong and skilled. I wouldn't have been able to kill that wraith without him."

I knew he was, but that didn't stop me from worrying—nothing ever would. My knees buckled, and I dropped to the little stone platform we'd raised. Wordlessly, Zach sat next to me and wrapped an arm around my shoulders.

"I know," was all he said.

I turned to him and buried my face in his chest, his arms enveloping me. As worried as I was for Brom, the events of the past hour came to me in full force, and I almost couldn't breathe again. I clawed at his shirt, squeezing the fabric in my palms, wishing we were anywhere but right here. I wished we were back at the village on that bed, or in that forest with the golden sunlight, or at the Romantica's bonfire.

"Myriana loved him, Zach," I whispered, my voice muffled in his chest.

Zach didn't reply, just ran his hands up and down my arms.

I tore myself from his chest to look at him. "But he betrayed her. Did Raed love her? Did he love Saevalla? Or did he just love his new kingdom?" I pressed my palms into my eyes. "I don't understand Love. It's not logical, it doesn't make sen—"

The words died on my tongue. Love wasn't logical. It was the opposite of everything the Legion taught. The Legion taught us to rule without emotion, to base every decision on reason and lead others to do so. Could that be because Love led to the very emotions that Myriana had fallen prey to? Anger? Hate? Jealousy? Revenge? Did the Legion teach us only of Lust because we needed to prevent the powerful, irrational emotions that accompanied Love?

If that was the case, then I could understand *why* the Legion had claimed it didn't exist. Love was dangerous. It was a risk.

"It's worth it," Zach said.

I looked at him, jolted by his words even though they were soft, calm. "What?"

"I can tell what you're thinking. You get that look every time I talk about Love. You're thinking Love is the reason Myriana's heart surrendered to all those dark emotions."

"Well, isn't it?"

"The Legion thinks opening your heart to someone and

trusting them with it is too much of a risk—well, I'm telling you, it's worth it." He grazed his knuckles against my cheek, and flipped a curl behind my ear. "You're worth it."

I swallowed hard, my skin hot from his touch. "And if I hurt you?"

His hand moved onto my neck, and with his thumb against my jaw, his gaze captured mine. "Even if you burned me to ashes, Ivy, it'd be worth it. That's the beauty of trees, remember? They grow back."

"You're not a tree, you fool," I said.

"But don't you think I bear a remarkable resemblance?"

At this, I finally laughed, and Zach ducked his head to kiss my cheek and jaw. "I love your laugh. I love—"

I placed a hand over his mouth, stopping his beautiful yet confusing words. "Don't."

I'd told him I believed him, and I meant it. I believed he loved me. I even believed Love existed, but I couldn't let him say it to me again. Not when I couldn't say it back to him. It would've been easy, *too* easy, to tell him the words he wanted to hear…but I couldn't, not after he told me what Love really was, what it truly meant.

Love wasn't manipulation. It was honest, trusting, open. How could I tell him I felt the same way he did when I didn't fully understand it?

I knew I loved his goofy smile and loud laugh. His cocky shrugs and tender gazes.

I knew I loved the way he held me and the way he ran his fingers across my arm.

I knew I loved that he had stood in front of the Master Mages, my mother, and the Saevallans, and told them he wanted to be my partner.

But I didn't know if I loved *him*.

More than anything, knowing that Love had inadvertently

been the reason Myriana's heart had turned evil and cold, I was terrified. Zach said it was worth it—worth the danger, the risk, the heartache…but I wasn't sure, especially when I still didn't know if these feelings were Love or just the intense effects of Lust.

"Don't say it," I pleaded.

Zach took my hand from his mouth and traced the mark with his lips. "I *want* to say it. It's what you do before going to fight evil queens and deadly dragons: you confess."

I drew away my hand. "No, you want me to say it back. *That's* why you told me."

He leaned his head back against the rocks. "Can you blame a fellow for trying?"

My hands curled into fists on my lap, my shoulders hunched, like I could somehow make myself smaller. "Oh, Zach," I whispered, my voice echoing in the confines of the small cave.

"I want so much more than your lips, Ivy. I want your heart." Zach leaned close and brushed his lips against my hairline. "Because I love you…*desperately*."

Desperately. My fingers loosened from a fist as I remembered the night he told me about his parents, the night he swept me up in a beautiful story.

"Zach, I—"

He cut me off by kissing under my ear, and I shivered in response. His hold on me tightened. "I know you want me, but do you love me?" His hand slid onto my neck, and his thumb rested on the base of my throat. "After all this, I'll want your answer. So we've got to survive."

Once he released me, I instantly missed his arms, but his words pulled me back to reality.

First, get out of this cave. Beat Myriana to the egg. Defeat the dragon. Survive. Then think about all this later. That's all

I could promise him at the moment and—bless him—that's all he was asking for.

"Okay. After."

What felt like hours later, Brom showed up with the rope. Climbing out of the cave went surprisingly smooth. Zach's shoulders scraped against the rock, but it wasn't anything some shassa root salve couldn't fix.

I wondered, as we maneuvered over rocks on our way back to the mountain path, if Myriana had just been a normal girl, then why did her heir and Raed's and Saevalla's heirs all possess the power of a Royal's Kiss? Zach had said the Romantica believed it did more harm than good, but I couldn't begin to understand how that was possible, unless it was similar to the Curse of Jecep where a poisoned crop multiplied once pulled from the roots and...

I tripped on a stone and scraped my palm catching myself, making both Brom and Zach stop in their climb.

"Ivy?" Brom asked.

He asked me something else, but I didn't hear him clearly. My brain was speeding through the memories I'd seen in the mirror. The last thing Myriana's Heart remembered was something called the Hydra Curse. What if that glowing ball of purple energy hadn't just been the queen's power manifested?

"What if all the Royals are cursed?" I whispered, staring down at my injured hand now seeping blood. Droplets ran down my wrist, coloring the stag antlers of Zach's mark with crimson.

"It's why every time we use our Kiss, the creatures we defeat are multiplied, and more curses spread. Because our blood—our blood is cursed." My hand started shaking so hard my whole arm trembled. It was like the mountainside was crumbling under my feet. Like I was falling with no hope of ever hitting the bottom.

Zach reached for me, probably to steady me over the sharp

rocks, but I recoiled from his touch.

The mark on his outstretched hand was exactly the same as the burn from the hand of Myriana's first host once she touched the curse.

Our marks were physical evidence of the curse. And Zach, with the Mark of Myriana, was now the most cursed of all. *Oh Sisters, I cursed them.* My partners, my Kisses—nothing but tools to spread more darkness. Perhaps the irony was the worst part of it all.

Brom took my hand and doused water over it, making the scrape sting. I barely flinched.

I stared at Zach, all hope that he'd given me in the cave snuffing out like a candle. "How can we defeat someone who has literally put her curse, her own power, in our *blood*?"

And if it was in our blood, maybe that's how the Sense worked. The evil that called out to me—resonating in my chest—connected to the Hydra Curse that lay within us.

I clutched the front of my tunic as if I could somehow rip out the darkness tainting my lungs. In a way, I was one of the Queen's creatures—born from her wickedness. We all were.

The wind whistled in my ears, carrying over the mountains and whipping back our hair and cloaks.

Zach tore his gaze from me to stare at the gray scenery before us. "The Hydra Curse works only through our Kiss. So we just...we can't Kiss."

I already knew we couldn't Kiss, but it didn't seem as simple as what Zach made it out to be. We still had no concrete plan of defeating her if she reached the egg before we did.

If only she had a weakness. Something to exploit.

Again, I turned to her memories. Was there something in there...something I had missed that we could use? What had crippled her heart so much that made her want to cut it out?

Had it been Raed sleeping with Saevalla?

No, surprisingly, I didn't think that was it. I'd *been* her. I knew what had killed me the most and it had been…

The miscarriages. Losing the babies, one after another. Feeling them grow inside me, then losing that second heartbeat.

It made me want to rip out my own.

I felt Brom wrapping my injured hand with a clean bandage, but he seemed so far away. Everything felt disconnected from me. For a moment, I was Myriana again.

The idea of losing a baby was all-consuming. There was nothing else in the world that mattered except protecting a new life.

"It's babies," I whispered.

Brom leaned close. "What?"

I looked up and focused on Zach. "That's her weakness. Babies."

As soon as the words were out of my mouth, I realized that I had proof. Solid, indisputable proof that the Evil Queen would go to any length to protect an unborn child—like weaving spells into her creatures and curses to prevent them from harming a woman with child.

"Rochet," Zach and I said at the same time.

In the cursed village, Rochet had been pregnant and the only one not to have any symptoms of the curse, even though she'd been drinking the well water like everyone else. A witch's power was derived from the Evil Queen's Forces of Darkness, so her Curse of Venera hadn't affected Rochet or her unborn child.

"Patrice, too," I said, grabbing Zach's arm in an iron grip. "The griffin attack. She'd been pregnant and was the only survivor."

"And the pregnant girl in the burning house—at the attack at the wall. She'd survived a burning, collapsing house," Zach said, breathless.

There was no way they were all coincidences—all miracles.

Zach and I shared a grim smile. It wasn't an all-powerful Kiss or even mage magic. But it was *something*. We could work with something.

When the stars were just beginning to wink at us, the pain in my chest grew so heavy I struggled to stay upright. At one point, I staggered forward, and Zach lunged to catch me.

But I'd found it.

As Zach steadied me, I pointed up the mountain's face. It looked like a few hours' hike to a large cave. Even at night, the darkness congregating at the mouth of the cave was almost tangible. Like an army of wraiths could step out of it at any second.

We camped roughly a mile from the cave, then woke up to a sky of pink and red, as if predicting the blood that would be spilled.

No, don't think like that, Ivy.

But it was hard not to. I thought about the swarms of sparrow harpies, the horde of doppelganger goblins, the wraiths, and the devastating magical storms with black lightning that froze the earth. And those were only the *omens* of the Sable Dragon, not the beast itself.

Putting aside the fact that we would have to battle Millennia if she'd managed to reach the egg, we still had to defeat the dragon without the Kiss. And now without a mage to help us. Neither Zach nor I had talked about what we could do, because deep down we realized there was nothing *to* do except wait for the egg to hatch then defeat the dragon somehow. Even if that meant collapsing the whole mountain. So how could we possibly survive?

With a terrible clench in my stomach, I realized we probably wouldn't.

Two hours later, we approached the entrance of the cave. We paused and looked over the edge of our climb. From this angle we could see the vast distance we'd traveled over the past few days—the deep ravine and the stone valley far off to the south and, at the very edge of the world, the trees from the Galedral Forest and beyond. The sight was breathtaking. If we didn't succeed, this entire world and all its people would be nothing but seas of ash. That was why we had to win. Why we had to fight.

CHAPTER THIRTY-THREE

LAIR OF THE SABLE DRAGON

Entering the cave was like driving a blade into my chest. The darkness hit my Sense so powerfully that I fell to my knees, clutching my shirt and fighting for a breath. I'd never felt evil such as this. Tangible. It hung in the air and entered my lungs with each breath I drew.

Zach and Brom both dropped next to me. I waved them away. "I'm fine," I wheezed.

"Clearly, you're not," Brom said.

Now that I knew the darkness from the cave was reacting with the darkness that was already inside my blood, it wasn't sheer will that allowed me to push down the Sense, it was anger. I wasn't going to let this stupid curse slow me down. I wouldn't let that old crone turn my own body against me.

Squeezing my shirt in my palm, I opened my eyes and got to my feet. "Let's go."

Zach took my hand. I glanced at him, and we shared a smile.

The cave was dank and dark and curved to the right, the tunnel disappearing into the darkness. It didn't matter if there were intricate tunnel systems in this cave, because I'd be able to find the egg regardless. The problem was getting back out.

"Plan ahead," Brom said, as if reading my thoughts. He

took out bright red berries I hadn't even noticed him gathering along the way and smashed them against the cave's walls, leaving a crimson stain.

We lit a torch, the dry wood bursting into orange flames, creating flickering shadows that reached into the tunnel's depths. With a stab of pain that had nothing to do with my Sense, I missed Millennia. She would've been able to light it with just a wave of her hand.

We carried on for some time, occasionally coming to forks in the tunnel. Brom smeared more berries, and I pointed us down the path that brought more and more pain to my chest.

As we walked, I watched the shadows dance across the walls, remembering the way the firelight and smoke drew Zach and me into our own mystical dance the night at the Romantica camp. How the same intoxicating feeling had consumed me when he kissed my neck and shoulders out on the rocks. My heart pounded from the memory.

How could I know if this was Lust or Love? All I did know was that I never wanted to let go of his hand. I wanted our time together to stretch for eternity.

I sucked in a breath.

Brom and Zach stopped. "What?" Brom asked, his voice taut with tension.

"Nothing, just the pain," I lied.

I wiped my brow with my other arm and concentrated on my breaths. In and out. Pushing down the Darkness. *Focus on what is important.*

Finally, we came to a halt when I couldn't stop a fit of coughing. I let go of Zach's hand, covered my mouth, and coughed and coughed. I'd never coughed so hard before in my life, hacking as if there was something in my lungs that needed to come out. Suddenly it did. I drew my hands away from my mouth and caught sight of what looked like ink.

It was as though I had coughed up darkness in its liquid form.

"Fields of Galliore," Zach whispered. "It's killing you."

"It's because we're here." Brom touched his torch to an extended ledge on the cave wall, and a spark ignited. As the purple flames rose, my stomach lurched painfully, remembering the fire that had danced across Millennia's shoulders and had separated me from Zach and Brom.

The purple fire spread through the cave, following the ledge that encircled the large cavern. From where we stood, the flaming ledge extended all the way to the other side, engulfing the room in purple light. Ominous shadows flickered in the gigantic domed ceiling. In the center, seated on a round slab of rock like an altar, carved with special symbols of the language of the dwarves, was the egg.

"Fields of Galliore," Zach repeated.

It was gigantic, rising maybe thirty feet tall. Its shell was a swirl of purple, black, dark blue, and gray, resembling the marble in the Hall of Ancestors back in Myria Castle. We stared up at it, entranced by its beauty, yet terrified of the horror within. Then my gaze dropped to the stone altar and what lay before it.

I recognized the altar immediately. It was the same one where the dwarves had cut out Myriana's heart, the same one where the first girl had received the Heart. I also recognized the heap of azure robes at the altar's base.

Millennia.

I started to cough again, the fear of seeing Myriana—of being too late—escalating as I coughed up more black liquid. But the egg's shell was intact. If Myriana had released a five-ton dragon, surely we would've known by now.

We slowly drew our weapons. Brom notched an arrow into his crossbow then withdrew a silver dagger. Swords out, Zach and I crept forward.

"Millennia?" I called.

The pile of robes didn't move. I shot a look at Zach. He frowned and gripped his sword, the leather grinding in his tight grasp.

"Millennia?" I tried again as we inched forward. Every now and then I'd glance up at the giant egg, hoping for some clue—some sign as to what was going on.

No movement—from the egg or Millennia. Could she be dead? And if she was, did that mean the Evil Queen had died, too? Or simply moved on to her next host?

When I was about twenty paces from her, something glimmered at my feet, catching the light of the purple torches flickering at the perimeter of the room.

It was a piece of mirror drenched in blood.

The shard I'd driven into her thigh. I bent and picked it up with trembling fingers.

"I had hoped that mirror had been lost to time."

Startled, I dropped the shard, and it shattered.

Millennia lay on the ground, facing me, with her head resting on a pile of her gorgeous black hair. Her eyes were wide open, but they were not blue as I'd hoped they'd be. They were violet.

"But I should've made sure of it, just as I should've made sure you died in that cave." Her lips moved to form the words, but her voice was not Millennia's. It was Myriana's. Stronger. Deeper.

Whatever happened to her between the last cave and this one, her possession had gotten stronger. But she was still too weak to attack us yet. That much was obvious from the body lying twisted on the ground.

I looked to Zach, and he nodded. Swords drawn, we raced toward her. Halfway there, we hit an invisible wall and flew backward, skidding across the cave floor. Rocks and loose pebbles cut into my skin. The two of us groaned and blinked through the dust at the shimmery purple dome surrounding Millennia's body, now visible.

I cursed. A protective *Illye* circle.

She moved her head toward her dragon egg and laughed. "Give it time, my dear descendant. I'll be ready to fight you soon enough. Thanks to your little move with the mirror shard, I had to heal this leg."

I picked myself up, and so did Zach. I dared not look behind me, but I prayed Brom wasn't there, that our charge had not been in vain and Brom had been allowed to get into position.

Slowly, she sat up, her black tresses falling across her face like a curtain. "Curse this body," she growled. "You have no idea how painful it was, listening to my host encouraging you to not use the Royal's Kiss, but I admit, controlling her mage magic was difficult enough."

"And yet…" She sighed, her shoulders rolling back in satisfaction as the *Illye* circle crackled overhead. "It was so *easy* to enter her heart."

I closed my eyes briefly. *Oh, Millennia. You were heartbroken at losing Tarren. It's not your fault.* Sadly, it would've been too easy for the Evil Queen to take hold of a devastated, angry girl who hated Royals.

The *Illye* shield surged with energy, purple lightning arcing over the dome and striking the cavern's wall, sending large pieces of stone to the floor.

"Don't do this, Myriana. You don't understand what you're doing," I said, my knees trembling from the Sense, from the fear—from both.

Her violet eyes flashed to a color so dark it looked almost entirely black. "*I* don't *understand*?" Her red lips twisted down into a grimace of pure loathing. "I don't want to hear that from *you*." She raised her hand and stroked the language of the dwarves carved into the side of the altar. The symbols pulsed purple under her hands, glowing like amethysts under firelight, and the *Illye* circle fizzed with power. She was gaining strength from the altar—the egg—the very air laden with darkness.

"You," she snarled, "a princess who *denounces emotions*. Who denounces *Love*."

At her last word, *Love*, dripping with disdain, I realized that the creature that stood before me wasn't just all the darkness in Myriana's heart. It was her love as well. Though it had been twisted by all the other dark emotions—the hatred, rage, jealousy—they had turned her love into something poisonous.

And suddenly I did understand. I understood everything.

"That's why Myriana established the Legion. Because she'd literally cut out all her emotion," I said, "she cut out *you*. She had nothing but logic and reason left—"

"I'll KILL you!" she screamed. Myriana twisted her hand and the *Illye* shield dropped as a tendril of darkness suddenly burst forth from the egg's shell, reminding me of how the enchanted water in the well had lashed out and dragged me into its depths. The tendril hit a spot just to the left of Zach and me like a whip, cracking the cave floor open.

Instinctively, I searched for Brom before I remembered where he was supposed to be. *Just find a good spot, Brom, and be patient*. I imagined him hiding behind a rock, crossbow poised, just like when he shot the mountain elk.

"Myriana!" I yelled, before she raised another hand, ready to strike again. "Please stop! Listen to me—"

My words were lost on her.

Zach and I pushed away from each other as the tendrils

struck the ground where we'd been standing. We landed hard on our backs, the wave of residual darkness sweeping over us like a sandstorm, driving more evil into our noses and throats. I turned over and vomited black liquid as thick as ink. Zach was choking on it, too.

"Stop calling me that!" she screeched, "I am *not* that weakling who couldn't kill Saevalla. The sister who *betrayed* her. I was so close to smothering her with a pillow—the same pillow my beloved slept on when he was with her."

Her voice was hysterical—shrieking—the words of a heart tortured by centuries of hatred and anguish.

"I'll kill them all, though—I swear this to you, princess. My son will burn this world to the ground, and I will create a new world. One without magic Kisses. And Royals. And *fools* believing that a new race of mortals walked among them."

The members of the town who had pushed Raed to produce heirs with Saevalla. She wasn't just extracting her revenge on Royals. She wanted *everyone* to pay.

"My *real* children will survive. And no one will ever have to suffer the pain of knowing love and loss. They will find peace in the afterlife…as I never could. As *you* will."

Myriana flexed her wrist, and another tendril of darkness lashed out, the *Illye* shield dropping once more. This time it would've hit us, but Zach was too fast. He picked me up and leaped out of the way, the darkness hitting the stone floor with the force of a black lightning strike.

We dropped to our knees, my heart pounding, and watched in horror as Myriana wiggled her fingers at us. "So close. What a fast prince you are."

Then she raised both arms, and before another strike of energy could be unleashed from the *Illye* circle, I screamed the words I'd been practicing in my head for an entire day.

The only spell I knew to stop her.

"You'll hurt the baby!"

Myriana froze. Her violet eyes wide with shock and…fear?

"What?" Her voice was hoarse from her screams.

I cradled my stomach. "Please, Myriana," I begged. "My child. Please spare my child," I sobbed. At this point, it wasn't hard to cry.

Zach pulled me into him protectively, shielding me, like the perfect father would.

Myriana stared at the two of us, darting from my face to Zach's then back again. Her arms trembled above her head, ready to unleash another deadly strike that neither Zach nor I would be able to survive.

But our bluff had worked.

It was the one weakness we could exploit. Make her hesitate. She was willing to burn down the whole world, but she couldn't kill a baby—the one thing she'd loved with all her heart.

Burn down the whole world, but save one pregnant woman? It didn't make sense.

But then, Love didn't make sense.

Her face twisted into a mixture of worry, anguish, and rage as she lost her focus, and the *Illye* shield dispersed in a final crackle of energy. "You're lying—"

Her words were cut off by the sharp release of an arrow and her own scream of pain. An arrow had lodged itself in her shoulder, a hair's breadth from her neck.

Pride blooming in my chest, I followed the arrow's trajectory to where Bromley stood on top of a fallen piece of stone, aiming his crossbow down at the Evil Queen.

"Rest in peace, you witch," he said.

CHAPTER THIRTY-FOUR

POSSESSION

The idea had come from our fight against the griffin, only this time Zach and I had been the bait while Brom had lain in wait for the perfect moment when both the shield and her guard were down.

Millennia convulsed, her body shaking like she was having a seizure, and she fumbled to pull the silver-tipped arrow's shaft from deep in her shoulder. Wrenching it out, she threw it on the ground, the arrow clattering on the stone floor, blood dripping everywhere.

She glared at Brom and then mounted the stone altar, thrusting her hands onto the egg.

Darkness rolled over the open wound on her shoulder, already beginning to heal. Then the darkness flowed into the egg, pooling at her hands, swirling and growing like the Queen's and the dragon's powers were converging somehow.

"Brom, get down!" I screamed just before the effect hit me—as if someone twisted a blade buried in my chest. I coughed up more thick black liquid and stumbled, trying to stay up. Zach reached for me, but as his hand grazed my wrist, the mountain shook.

Darkness came from every corner and crack and seeped

into the stone altar. Inky black tendrils like vines crawled along the egg's shell.

I couldn't scream. I could barely even breathe. The darkness was sucking the oxygen out of the air.

The mountain shook again, and the stalactites trembled. I cried out as Brom dropped from the rock and rolled onto the floor. He didn't move—I prayed he was only knocked unconscious and nothing worse.

Zach raised his sword and sprinted toward Millennia. She lifted a hand, curling her fingers like a claw, then thrust it to the side. Zach's feet swept out from under him as an invisible force knocked him into the cavern's wall. I screamed for him and tried to run, but my legs were heavier than lead, and I fell to the floor. The darkness was collapsing on top of me. My lungs were filled with it.

I was drowning again. Like I had when my mother raged at me. Like I had in the well. I remembered the way the cursed water had pulled my body, twisting my muscles and making them scream in agony.

What had saved me?

Zach.

His name came to me as it did then. He said he was going to protect me that night by the fire. I believed it with every ounce of hope I had left inside me.

I crawled toward him as the cavern floor shook under my hands and knees, praying to every star I knew that he was still alive. I barely registered that the egg's shell began to crack. Whatever star was listening answered my prayer—Zach shifted on the floor, groaning and shaking his head.

A surge of strength flowed through me, and I managed to get to my feet. He was alive. That…that was all that mattered. If he was alive, I could figure out something else. We could still defeat Myriana. As long as he was still alive.

Zach was the secret strength that had saved me in that well, just as he saved me now by giving me the strength to keep moving. If Zach did that to me, then what would the thought of Tarren do to Millennia—her one true love?

With great effort, I changed course, stumbling over loose rubble from the craters in the floor. Millennia was still in there—I just had to reach her.

I walked toward Myriana, aware of the cracks in the eggshell growing, the mountain shaking around us, and Zach struggling to his feet behind me.

I stopped a few paces from the Evil Queen.

"Myriana!" I screamed over the booms coming from the egg.

Myriana twitched but didn't look in my direction. Darkness flowed from the air into her body then out through her hands, entering the shell like she was some sort of conduit, feeding the Sable Dragon the energy it needed to hatch.

"You didn't fail them!" I yelled.

She looked over her shoulder at me, her violet eyes blazing.

I spoke the words I knew that somewhere, deep down, she needed to hear. Underneath all that evil. All the hate. She was a mother.

"Those babies. The ones you couldn't have—you didn't fail them. It wasn't your fault."

She wrenched her hands from the egg and lunged for me. Her hands wrapped around my neck with such force that I fell to the ground. The stone collided with my back and rattled my bones.

Straddling my stomach, Myriana's hands began squeezing the life from me. "*Don't talk about them.*"

I struggled to form words. My vision blackened.

"Y-you d-didn't fail Tarren, either."

Myriana's hands froze on my neck.

"Just because you couldn't rescue him on your own—you can't blame yourself, Millennia," I whispered through the rasp in my throat. "It wasn't your fault."

The queen's eyes burned a violet so deep they turned indigo. "I wasn't strong enough."

Millennia. I tried to shake my head, though her hands still held a viselike grip around my neck. "Yes, you are. You're plenty strong. He gives you strength, doesn't he?" I gripped her wrists and squeezed gently. *Because it's what Zach gives me.*

The violet in her eyes flickered to a deep blue. There was something there.

"That's what Love does, right? It makes you feel pain, but courage, too."

Millennia's hands twitched, barely loosening their hold.

"The Legion is wrong." I forced the truth out of me as if I were cutting into my own skin and baring all. "We've always been wrong. We put power and blood and logic above everything else, when we should've been ruling with our hearts."

Hearing myself admit this was like making another incision into my skin. But I couldn't stop. I had to keep going so I could sew the wound back up tight. So that it could heal properly.

"Love *does* exist. I saw it in the way you talked about him. You still love him. You always will. And it makes you stronger. You're not weak like her, Millennia. You didn't cut out your heart or abandon your feelings—you embraced them." I grabbed her hands, feeling Tarren's ring on her finger. "Why else would you still wear this ring? I know you can push her out. Please, *please* don't let her win."

She blinked. Blue irises.

Overhead, a crack in the egg splintered. The loudest *boom* yet shook the floor as the black tendrils reached the top and seeped into the open cracks.

"Remember Tarren." I tore her shaking hands away from

my throat and threw my arms around her, squeezing tight. "Come back to him, Millennia. Come back," I cried as the egg gave a gigantic tremble.

Millennia's eyes cleared into her beautiful ocean blue as Zach caught up, standing over us. "Tarren…" she whispered.

From above, a great claw the color and texture of obsidian broke through the shell, sending a fragment flying into the cave wall and shattering.

The Sable Dragon was awake.

Millennia's face twisted in pain. "Ivy—I can't hold her back—Myriana—"

She held on to me—held on for dear life. I opened my mouth to respond, to tell her to fight back, feel the love she had for Tarren. To drive the Evil Queen from her heart.

"Kill me, Zach." The words were barely out of her mouth before Zach had the blade of his dagger pressed to her throat.

Shocked, I couldn't move. The Queen was still inside Millennia, and if we killed Millennia, then we would kill the Queen. It had been the plan all along, but…

Around us, the mountain was crumbling. Rocks and stalactites fell from the ceiling. The obsidian claw scraped against the shell from within, causing more pieces to fall like giant boulders.

"Kill me—hurry!" Millennia cried, tears running down her pretty cheeks, bringing red blotches to her face.

Zach's hand shook. He stared at Millennia in horror, but the dagger pressed deeper into her neck. Droplets of blood gathered at the edge of the blade.

Logic said to kill her. The *Legion* said to kill her. *Perish emotions and vanquish doubts. Lead by example.*

I tugged on his wrist. "Don't—please, don't."

I couldn't let him. How could we kill an innocent girl whose only crime was loving someone too much?

"Do it. I don't want her to use me as a puppet. I want her out, even if that means taking her with me." Millennia tried to shove me away.

I held strong. "Then get her out. Get rid of the feelings that make her stronger."

"I—I c-can't." Millennia pitched her head forward, sobs shaking her body. "I'll never stop hating the Legion. I can't let these feelings go."

"Then change them." I grabbed her shoulders, just as another dragon claw broke free. "Forgive the Legion. Forgiveness is harder than giving up. I won't let you give up like she did, Millennia. Tarren would want you to love."

Millennia stared at me through her tears. Zach jerked his blade away, his face a mixture of doubt and anguish. He couldn't do it and, for the first time, I felt so grateful for what I always thought was his weakness—his faith in Love.

Millennia collapsed into my arms.

I held on to her until Zach jerked me back. I almost fought his grip, but then I saw why he'd ripped me away. Purple flames bloomed from Millennia's chest and spread, dancing over her shoulders and neck. She gazed upward, cheeks streaked with tears, her face calm and peaceful.

"I'm sorry, my love."

With her words, screams ripped through the cavern, echoing louder than the booms of the egg that shook the mountain.

I'd heard these screams before.

They were the screams of Myriana when the dwarves had cut out her heart.

As the screams echoed, the purple fire rose off her and disappeared into thick smoke, a twisting mass of shadows and fog—the warped heart of Queen Myriana. Then, as quickly as it rose, it burst into golden dust. It was as if the Heart could not withstand Millennia's pure act of love—forgiveness.

Millennia passed out in my arms. Who could blame her after holding an evil spirit inside her for months?

About twenty feet away, Bromley stirred on the ground, groaning. I tried to call to him, but my words were drowned out by a gigantic *crack* as loud as thunder. The three of us looked up.

A single red eye stared down at us through a break in the shell.

CHAPTER THIRTY-FIVE

HATCHED

The rumbling had stopped. The booms were gone. The mountain was still once again. But that didn't mean it wasn't about to be torn apart by the dragon.

We were in no shape to fight. I was still coughing up blackness. Zach blinked hard and shook his head a few times, as if he was fighting to stay conscious from a concussion or worse. Brom had just woken up and likely also suffered a concussion. Millennia was out cold, and powerless at that. And here we were—the baby Sable Dragon about to break free of its shell.

Myriana was right—this would be our end.

Still gripping Millennia, I stared at the red eye. It blinked slowly as if it was trying to focus on us. Then the claw scraped down the side of the egg, and half the shell fell with an earth-shattering *boom*, forcing us to our knees. I swear all of the Wu-Hyll Mountains trembled. Half its scaly black body emerged, and a wing dripping with black ooze twitched. With that one twitch, the rest of the egg shattered, and pieces flew everywhere.

Zach pushed both Millennia and me flat, ducking as a shell fragment flew over our heads.

The Sable Dragon stretched toward the cavern's ceiling. It

was easily fifty feet tall, even as a hatchling. The scales on its face, neck, shoulders, and tail extended outward like flower petals, each one sharper than the last, glittering like the bones of a rowan deer. Its black wings spread out, still covered in slime, and its body shimmered obsidian. Just like the ancient text had said it would.

The ancient text… I struggled to remember what I had read in the library that day. The day I'd searched for the spell for a Kiss to destroy it.

Its only vulnerable spot is its mouth, where the very flames are produced.

The cave shook as the dragon gave a roar, revealing row upon row of glistening teeth sharper than a sword's tip, stronger than steel.

"I've got an idea—do you trust me?" I said in Zach's ear.

Zach met my gaze. "With my whole heart."

Despite everything, I smiled. How he could still make me smile in a situation like this, I'd never understand.

Bromley was already limping to us. I pulled him down, hugging him, then drew back to admire my brave little brother…maybe one last time. What I saw on his face was love. And unconditional faith. "Brom, if this fails, if Zach and I…if we don't make it, I need you to take a message back to Myria. Tell them about the Hydra Curse. About Myriana. Everything. Make them believe it. Do whatever you have to. Can you do that?"

A muscle in his jaw ticked. He nodded.

I leaned forward and kissed his forehead. "Find shelter and watch over Millennia. Zach and I have a dragon to slay."

Brom grabbed my hand, kissed it, and whispered, "Milady." Then he stooped and hoisted Millennia before limping behind a large shell fragment as big as a boulder.

Fighting back tears, I let Zach help me up, and together

we faced the dragon, arm in arm.

"What's the plan?" Zach said, as the dragon swished its neck from side to side, testing its jaw, smoke already curling from its nostrils.

I opened my mouth to tell him when the dragon decided it was done being ignored. The great beast jerked the rest of its body out of its shell, and the other half crashed to the cavern floor. Only this time, the floor didn't hold its weight. The rock crumbled under the force of the marble shell, and the floor caved in, falling into what were probably dwarven mine shafts.

Zach grabbed my waist, and the two of us clung to a stalagmite that managed to stay upright as the rest of the floor tilted. Rocks and bits of marble rolled downward to the giant crater where the altar and egg had once been. The dragon was so massive that it barely noticed when the floor caved in. It shook its hideous body and got down on all fours, huffing smoke from its nostrils.

"We have to get closer," I yelled over the sound of sliding rock.

Droplets of sweat and blood rolled down the side of Zach's face as he quickly inspected the newly slanted floor. It was full of cracks opening to the caverns below and sharp rocks that could skewer us as easily as the dragon's claws and teeth could.

"I see a path." He pointed to a large slab of rock—what I realized was the destroyed altar—almost directly under the dragon's chin.

It would be the best spot for what I had planned.

Zach gripped my hand tightly. "Ready?"

"Yes."

As if the dragon heard us, it lifted its spiked tail and whirled it around—Zach and I dove, the tail slamming into ground where we'd just been. More rock crumbled away, falling into the black abyss.

Still holding hands, we slid down the stone, picking up speed as the incline grew steeper.

"Zach!" I screamed as we sped toward the altar—a giant outcrop of stone that jutted out of the floor. He'd seen it. Zach stabbed his dagger into one of the many cracks littering the stone floor. It sparked, and the blade snapped, but it had stalled our descent enough to help us get to our feet and jump onto the rock altar instead of smashing into it.

We stumbled onto the altar that was covered in the egg's black ooze.

Steadying each other, we looked up to see the dragon's head tilted toward us, watching our progress.

"Might be a good time to clue me in on that plan, princess," Zach muttered, his eyes locked on the dragon.

How could I tell him what I had planned next for us? I swallowed. "The most vulnerable part of the dragon is inside its mouth."

"Ivy, are you suggesting we get eaten?"

"If only," I whispered, as the great beast arched its neck toward Zach and me. It seemed mildly impressed by two puny mortals standing in front of it without screaming.

I took his face in my hands, forcing his gaze away from the dragon. "The flames will burn *slowly*. If we can withstand the fire and get into the mouth…"

Zach detached my hands and gave my fingers a tight squeeze. "We can run it through."

"It's going to be excruciating. Every evil, dark emotion will eat away at us in physical pain."

"Oh, is that all?" He pulled me close, wrapping one strong arm around my back.

"But we'll…" I couldn't make myself say the words. In the background I could hear the dragon draw breath, preparing its flames.

"I don't care," Zach whispered against my temple.

"Zach—" I gasped. I didn't know what I wanted to say. But I didn't want our lives to end this way. Just then, what I regretted the most was that I hadn't been able to give him my answer.

"I never meant it," Zach said over the rumbling within the dragon's long neck.

"What?"

He drew his sword. I placed my hand over his on the hilt, covering Myriana's mark, staring into his eyes.

"I lied when I said I'd try to stop loving you. I didn't try once. And I doubt I'll ever stop."

Like everything else when it came to Zach, it was completely unexpected and unbelievably inappropriate, given the situation. Here we were, about to be burned alive, and I was…happy. Beyond happy. Beyond reason and logic happy.

Then the black flames engulfed us.

It wasn't just being burned alive, it was every terrible emotion I could've ever thought of—anger, pain, hate, jealousy, loneliness, and suffering, so much suffering.

Suffering of a thousand tortured souls, writhing forever in eternal darkness.

But even that was nothing compared to the ugly emotions I felt and connected to. Real-life pain that I experienced and lived with every day.

Fear for going up against the Evil Queen and the Sable Dragon. Fear I wasn't ready to defeat them and I'd doom the rest of the kingdoms…times ten.

Guilt for surviving while Kellian and my other partners had not…times a hundred.

Shame when my mother lashed out at me or hit me or looked at me with disgust in her eyes…times a thousand.

My flesh was searing hot and burning cold at the same time. My insides thrashed in agony as if needles were stabbing into my veins and forcing poison into my bloodstream. Both my head and heart were splitting in two—physically and emotionally—betrayal, devastation, jealousy, hatred. Emotions so strong it made me want to cut out my own heart and give it to dwarves—sealing away my pain so I could never feel again.

Just to make it stop.

Maybe Myriana had been right to get on that altar surrounded by dwarves. *Make it stop.*

Then something under my hand twitched.

Zach.

I focused on that one sensation. That I still had hold of someone.

Someone who stood with me, hands on a sword, burning in black flames, to save the kingdoms.

Someone who loved me when I cried.

Someone who loved me even if I yelled at him.

Someone who loved my freckles, my imperfections.

Someone who *wanted* to love me, and did.

I couldn't use words to give him my answer. He'd never hear me. But I could show him.

Once, just once, before we burned and drove the sword into the dragon's mouth and probably died, I would have that kiss—the kiss I'd craved since the Master Mage joined our hands...for reasons I hadn't realized then.

I stood up on my toes. Somehow, through all this pain, I was able to move. I touched his cheek. Flames licked our bodies—nothing could compare to this agony. Razor teeth loomed over us now, the very heart of the fire only feet away.

And I kissed him.

His lips weren't soft or full. They were rough and chapped. He smelled like smoke and sweat and blood.

Still, it stopped time. It pulled the sun from the sky and tossed the stars into the sea.

Or maybe it was all in my head. It didn't matter. Nothing mattered except this kiss.

Zach dropped the sword and wrapped both arms around me, pulling me tighter, kissing me back.

I let the sword fall from my fingertips as well, lost in his kiss.

The mountains moved. The sick were healed. The flames stopped.

The flames…*stopped*?

A small part of me realized *that* was not in my head. It was real.

As our lips briefly broke apart, a breath away from each other, I vaguely noticed Zach and I were both encased in gold.

Shining, gleaming, shimmering in pure, beautiful golden light like we were children of the sun.

As Zach shifted his lips against mine, deepening our kiss, letting our breaths mingle as one, a giant cascade of gold like a tidal wave washed out of the cave, dissolving the dragon into a thousand orbs of congealed light.

When Zach released his hold on me, letting me slide out of our kiss, I finally looked up, blinking through all the golden light and dust.

The dragon was gone. The shell fragments were gone. The darkness in my chest was gone.

I looked back at Zach, my mouth open in shock.

Clearly just as surprised, he blinked, and slowly, his lips spread into a grin.

"Looks like I have my answer."

CHAPTER THIRTY-SIX

LEAD BY EXAMPLE

Even as we picked our way through the tunnels, back out to the light of day, all of us now healed thanks to the Golden Effect, or rather the magic of True Love, I could not escape Zach's smugness.

So maybe I was in love with him.

And maybe our kiss had killed the dragon and sent a golden wave through the cave that could've spread our magic over an unknowable distance.

But he needn't seem quite so full of himself.

Of course, I couldn't keep from smiling the whole way, either.

Millennia stretched out her arms and sighed, her face lifted toward the sun. She wasn't as pale now, with rosier cheeks and her eyes less of a deep-blue and more of a gray-blue. I wondered how much of the queen's spirit had altered Millennia, physically and otherwise.

"I haven't felt so light in months," she said.

"Do you remember how she possessed you, Millennia?" I asked.

She frowned and tilted her head. "I remember going into the forests back home right after I'd tried to save Tarren. Then the next few days were blurry…" She shook her head. "I just remember waking up and knowing I had to leave Raed. It feels like the last few months have been like that. I decided to do something, but I never remembered the thought process of the decision. But…I was still…me."

Her face clouded over as she talked, as if she was worried she had done terrible things while being possessed and was suddenly remembering them all.

I placed my hand on her shoulder. "It doesn't matter. You're free now."

She tackled me with a hug. I laughed and wrapped my arms around her shoulders.

"If you hadn't reached me back there," she said, her voice right next to my ear, "that evil old hag would've been eating at my soul for eternity."

The two of us pulled away. "That was you. I can't imagine how you could forgive the Legion, but I'm glad you did."

"I was able to forgive them only because I met you, princess. When you asked me about Tarren, and about Love, you proved to me that Royals aren't cruel. Just ignorant." She gave me a wink.

I squeezed her hands. "It's true. We have a lot to learn. But I promise, we'll get Tarren out of the dungeons."

With tears in her eyes, she kissed my cheek.

"So can you still do magic?" Bromley asked, sitting with his back against a tree, also enjoying the sun after the darkness of the cave.

Millennia shook her head. "I haven't tried. I'm not entirely sure I want anything to do with it anymore. I'd much rather sit and listen to Tarren sing every night."

Zach looped his arm around my shoulders like it was the most natural thing in the world—I tried to stop myself from blushing. "Not that I don't think spending every night in a theater is a wonderful thing, but I wish you'd reconsider. You're a good fighter. Something tells me that wasn't all the Queen in there. We could use your skill against the Forces."

Millennia squinted up at the blue sky. "I'll think about it. Maybe once Royals and Romantica finally see eye to eye, but who knows when that will happen."

"It may take some time, but it *is* going to happen. It has to," Zach said. He turned his hand over, studying the Mark of Myriana that still remained. "We have to assume that if our marks are still here, then the curse on the Royals still exists. But now that we know the truth of the Kiss, we can finally gain the upper hand."

For the first time since our kiss only hours ago, anxiety crept back in.

"I'm going to get some water," I announced, brushing off Zach's arm and walking away from the cave's entrance, toward the stream running down the mountainside.

Millennia's and Brom's voices, talking about the events of the battle and the dragon, faded and were soon replaced by the sound of the little waterfalls cascading over rockslides. I dipped my fingers into the icy stream. It felt heavenly. Cupping my hands, I sipped from the clear brook.

Soft footsteps came up behind me, and I didn't move as Zach reached over and filled his own hand with the refreshing water. "I know what you're thinking, Ivy."

"Can you blame me?"

"No, but—"

"It's impossible."

"That's what you said about Love."

I brushed back strands of hair with my wet hand, leaving droplets across my cheek. "This and that are different."

Zach knelt in front of me and took my cheeks in his hands, his thumb brushing away the water. "Only a little. Getting the Legion to believe in Love won't be as difficult as you think."

"You obviously don't know the Legion."

"And you're underestimating Love again."

I opened my mouth to argue, but then closed it.

Did I really need a reminder of how powerful Love was after what we'd just been through?

I smiled. "I guess I am."

"You have to be the one to tell them, though. No way am I breaking the news to those stubborn geezers."

"Zach!" I jerked back and splashed him.

"Cold!" He laughed then caught my wrists and pulled me close. His breath tickled my cheeks. Water clung to his bangs and eyelashes.

"You know," he said softly. "I think I'd like to kiss you without the excruciating fire all around us."

Nerves bounced in my stomach then leaped into my throat, only so I could swallow them back down. "Oh?"

A smile tugged at the corners of his mouth. "Would that be all right?"

"Only if you promise not to use a spell."

Zach chuckled, tilting his head to rest against my forehead. I laughed, too, and closed my eyes, leaning in to his touch.

My laughter was cut off by his lips. He captured my mouth fully with his and drew me in tighter. I succumbed to his kiss, all laughter gone, leaving nothing but a sensation that filled me—a sensation of such warmth and desire and pleasure and pure...*happiness* that I felt as if I were going to burst.

Unlike all my other kisses, instead of draining me of magic, this seemed to pump me full of its own.

I never wanted it to stop.

When Zach released me, our breaths were labored.

"Definitely better without the fire," I muttered, his forehead still resting against mine.

He grinned and kissed me again, much softer than before.

Still blushing, I took his hand, stroking my fingertips against the Mark of Myriana. I wondered if Zach wanted it removed, since our marks were the very symbols of the curse we carried in our blood. A constant reminder that we could spread darkness with just one wrong Kiss.

"I'd like to keep it," Zach said. As usual, he seemed to know what I was thinking.

"Are you sure? Even knowing what it means?"

"It can mean whatever I want it to mean," he said. "And it means I'm yours."

I wanted to bury my face in my hands out of embarrassment, even though I didn't remember ever being so happy.

Zach took advantage of my shyness to lean in and kiss the spot below my ear, then my neck, then my collarbone.

Before I managed to lose *all* thought, I pushed him back with weak hands. "All right, you've made your point, but it still won't be easy," I said, "making the Legion believe in Love."

"Don't fret, my princess." His lips brushed my temple. "We can change things."

I raised an eyebrow. "And what makes you so sure we can break five hundred years of tradition and beliefs? An entire institution?"

"Well," Zach said, gripping my hand and kissing the back of it, "I've heard it's best to lead by example."

For five centuries, the Legion has ruled with every good intention and a passion to protect the weak and innocent. We have ruled with logic and reason but persecuted those who thought differently, namely those who believed we should lead not only with our minds, but with our hearts. Today is the day we change. Today, we learn how to love once again. Today, we unite with the Romantica, and face the Darkness together…with Love to light the way.

Excerpt text from *Queen Ivy Myriana*

EPILOGUE

THREE YEARS LATER...

A small hand knocked the bottle of ink across the letter to the Council of Raed I'd just spent an hour working on, splattering the paper—and the front of my dress—with great big splotches of black. I closed my eyes, letting the irritation roll off me.

I gently clutched the wandering fingers and looked down at the child nestled in my lap. "What did I say, Tania?"

The toddler's bright green eyes stared up at me, fixed in that wide-eyed look of wonderment and innocence children always had.

"Help you," the little girl protested. "You run out."

I curled my legs up in the chair, pushing Tania's tiny body closer to my chest. "Thank you, my little wisp." My kisses danced, light as feathers, across her cheeks.

She squealed with delight and threw her arms around my neck.

"There you are." An exasperated Millennia stood in the doorway of my office, hands on her hips. Her dark hair was gathered elegantly at the nape of her neck and various wildflowers were nestled in her braids.

"Tania, what did I say about disturbing Queen Ivy?"

The little girl pouted in my lap. She tried to hide behind my knees and looked up at me with a look only a toddler could pull off—adorable innocence. "Do it?" she tried.

I burst into laughter as her mother plucked her off my lap.

"I'm sorry, I thought you knew where she was," I said, placing the now-ruined letter into the wastebasket.

Tania played with her mother's hair but grinned sneakily as if she and I shared a secret.

I'd made good on my promise to free Tarren almost as soon as we'd returned to Myria. Millennia and her childhood love ended up staying in Myria so Millennia could train under Master Gelloren. She was growing more and more adept at her elemental magic. They had also chosen to raise their child in the castle, since they had played an integral role in the effort to unite the Royals and the Romantica.

"Oh, I wasn't talking about this little deviant." Millennia bounced her daughter on her hip. "I was talking about *you*. It's almost time for the wedding! Why aren't you dressed?"

"What are you talking about? I have plenty of ti—" I stopped, glancing up at my clock, then clapped a hand over my mouth. "But I promised Brom I'd check on his new battle strategy today," I protested. Where had the time gone this afternoon?

"Ivy, I think the war can take a break for just this one evening. The Commander will understand. Have you forgotten how important this wedding is?"

She was right. It was the first wedding among Royals in Myria, and in the past year, the war had been going remarkably well. In fact, it was barely a war now, more like small skirmishes on the outskirts of the four kingdoms, pushing residual Forces from villages.

It had taken much time, even more effort, and many lives to make it so.

The first year had been the worst. Many, many people had died.

While the True Love's Kiss, Zach's and mine, had destroyed several dark creatures in the northern sector of Myria, there were still innumerable monsters to defeat. After returning to Myria's Crown City with news of the Hydra Curse, it took months of convincing. Months of battles where I would search for proof of the Royal's Kiss's true nature and treachery, but it was Master Gelloren who finally supported my claim. From there, the Legion slowly started implementing new battle tactics, removing the Royal's Kiss completely and retraining troops in the art of combat. Women were taught swordsmanship, and everyone in the villages willing to take up arms was called to the castle to train.

In the first few major battles following the removal of the Royal's Kiss, too many bodies littered the field, including the bodies of good friends. When I found Tulia lying with a cursed blade in her stomach, staring up with blank, unseeing eyes at the sky full of sparrow harpies, it was the first time I questioned whether or not we were doing the right thing. Were we too eager to get rid of the Kiss? Were we too weak to survive without it?

Zach held me that night, and I'd cried in his arms for hours. I'd cried for Tulia. I'd cried for fear of leading my people to their deaths. But as they always had, Zach's arms enveloped me, gave me strength, and reminded me why we were doing this in the first place.

"Ivy." Millennia slammed her hand on my desk and I jumped out of the past and back to the present. "If you don't get dressed now, I will have Tania do your hair. Now go."

I scribbled a note on my desk to rewrite the letter to the Council of Raed and stood. "Yes, all right. How is the bride, by the way?"

Millennia scowled. "She'd be doing a lot better with her best friend there."

I winced. "You've made your point. I'm going."

After giving them both kisses on the cheek, I hurried out of my office and turned down the spiral staircase of the west wing, toward the bride's rooms. My fingers trailed over the decorations of beautiful white and gold wildflowers tied with ribbons and ivy hanging from the stone walls. It reminded me of the gardenia flowers that had hung from the walls when Zach had first arrived in Myria.

I knocked softly on the door and a shaky, "Come in," sounded in response.

I stepped in and shut the door behind me, turning to admire Minnow in all her beauty. She wore a pale yellow dress with fine lace trim and a sheer silk veil rimmed with a crown of yellow wildflowers. Her golden hair hung in curls with intricate braids entwined in white ribbons.

A maid stood next to Minnow, adjusting the trail of her wedding gown and veil, while Matilda, dressed in a beautiful light blue dress, sat on the edge of the bed sipping a glass of gingerberry wine. She gave me a disapproving eye roll. "At last, the queen graces us with her presence."

"I know, I'm sorry," I said, shooting Minnow an apologetic smile.

It wasn't two minutes before the maid descended upon me. She unwound my thick hair from my usual tight bun and pulled a few strands back, entwining them with light blue ribbons while I sat still and admired Minnow.

She was indeed a beautiful bride. Her mother had made the dress, insisting on the color yellow. When I'd asked her why the dress would not be in Romantica white, she replied, "Seems to me the color of Love is gold, isn't it? Besides, my Minnow looks lovely in yellow."

I couldn't argue with her there.

"Oh, Minnow," I breathed, "you're breathtaking. Roland won't know what to do with himself."

Minnow beamed, practically glowing as bright as the sun in all that yellow. "I hope so. I adore telling him what to do."

We were so busy laughing, we didn't even hear the knocking until the door clicked and swung open. My friends' laughter faded, and I turned to see who'd come in.

Mother.

While everyone else chose soft, gentle colors for the wedding, my mother wore her usual dark, striking fabrics. Her hair was wound up tightly on her head, and jewels glittered around her neck.

Queen Dahlia strode into the room and stopped just in front of me. There was a time not long ago when I would've flinched when she got so close. Not anymore. Things had changed.

Her dark eyes were fixed on me. "May I have a word, Ivy?"

I could guess what she wanted to talk about. The letter to the Council of Raed would've included *her* battle strategy for the goblin hordes escaping from the Fields of Galliore into the eastern forests. It was always something having to do with the war, but that was okay. If this was the way we could understand each other, as warriors, I was fine with that.

When my mother had heard our story of the Hydra Curse and the truth about Myriana's heart, she had said very little to me. But over the course of a year, she began to slowly change.

She attended all of my battle strategy meetings and ripped them apart mercilessly, but then stayed with me for hours afterward poring over maps, discussing tactics. I didn't try to get more from her than that. I'd defeated the dragon and Evil Queen, done everything that I'd hoped would get her to say she was proud of me—and maybe she was, somewhere deep down, but she saw no need to tell me.

And I saw no need to ask.

It was enough to have her presence night after night, working with me, next to me.

"Of course, Your Highness," I said with a nod, then turned to Minnow. Kissing my friend on both cheeks, I wished her luck, and left with my mother.

We walked in silence for a while, before I finally grew impatient. "If it's about the letter to Raed, I'm almost done with it. I can send it tomorrow."

My mother paused, pursed her red lips, and glanced out the window. "No, Ivy, it's not about the letter." She reached into the folds of her dress and pulled out a white velvet box, covered in black ink fingerprints.

My hands trembled as I took it from her. It was the box in one of my saddest, loneliest memories—I'd recognize it anywhere, even fifteen years later. I opened the box and stared at the simple but beautiful silver band.

When I did nothing but stare at it, Mother plucked it out of the box and slid it onto my ring finger. "It fits," she said softly.

"What is this, mother?"

"Someone…someone very dear to me gave me that. It was a symbol of…of how much he cared for me."

Even though she wasn't saying it in words, I understood what this ring was. After working with the Romantica for three years, I knew a wedding band when I saw one. "But"—I swallowed—"why are you giving it to me?"

"Because…" Mother took a deep, shuddering breath. "Because you gave me back what it meant. And that…is far more precious than a band of silver."

I covered the ring with my other hand, my eyes stinging.

"Everything I've ever done was to protect myself. I am a selfish woman, Ivy Myriana, and I'm sure you know that. I had no desire to feel the pain of losing someone I...someone close to me ever again."

If there was one thing I understood about Love now, it was that it didn't make sense. If my mother had tried to protect herself from losing someone else she loved to the Forces by constantly pushing me, critiquing me, yelling at me, and distancing herself from me...I couldn't blame her for that.

Nor had I ever.

"I understand," I said.

Dahlia turned and started walking down the corridor, back the way we'd come. "Don't forget to change your dress. You can't attend a wedding with ink all over you."

I glanced down and grimaced at the ink splotches courtesy of Tania.

My new chambers were four times as big as my previous one, with an extra room where I "received" guests. I'd known it was going to be more extravagant when I'd been given the title of Queen, but I hadn't expected all the extra space. Zach had refused the title of King—a Romantica through and through—so he still resided in a smaller room, though it hardly mattered. He spent most of his time in my chambers anyway.

I entered my rooms to find Zach standing in front of my full-length mirror, tugging on his shirt cuffs.

"—Will you...no, no." Zach sighed and scratched the back of his head, grumbling something.

Then he took another deep breath and said, "Ivy, will you do me the honor of..." He ran his hands down his face and groaned. "Ivy, will you—"

"Will I what?" I asked.

"Troll's breath!" Zach jumped, turning so quickly he knocked over a vase filled with gardenias that Tania had picked for me yesterday. Being the legendary swordsman he was, he caught the vase, but the water and flowers spilled everywhere.

I walked over, stifling a few giggles, and bent to help him pick up the flowers. "Sorry, I didn't mean to scare you."

"I thought you'd already gotten ready," he said, avoiding my gaze as he gathered up the extraneous petals. Zach's face was a brilliant shade of red—like a strawberry.

Maybe it was the idea of him and strawberries, or maybe it was the scent of gardenias, so reminiscent of the day he first came to Myria, but before I could stop myself, I grabbed his shirt collar and kissed him. It was rougher than I planned, and he hadn't been expecting it, so we both fell backward, Zach's back planted firmly against the mirror.

Though he'd been surprised, he quickly caught up. His lips and breath and hands moved in a familiar rhythm that made my head dizzy. My hands traveled from the collar of his shirt to his broad shoulders, and my pulse climbed when his hands on my thighs moved upward to rest on my hips. Our kiss lasted a few moments longer before Zach pulled away—or as much as he could. His head was still against the mirror.

"What brought that on?" he asked, removing my hands from his shoulders and squeezing.

"I don't need a reason." I smiled. "But if you must know—I haven't a clue."

Zach grinned and tucked a strand of hair behind my ear. "I can live with that."

"But it's probably because I love you," I said, momentarily reveling in the rush I got whenever I used those words.

Zach's smile faltered, and his expression was a little more serious than moments before.

"Hearing you say it…every time…there's nothing in the world like it." He lifted his face back to mine, showing me that familiar devious smile.

"What?" I asked.

Zach brushed his hand across the freckles on my cheek,

revealing the faded Mark of Myriana from under his shirt cuffs. "I want you as my partner. For love this time, as my wife. Forever."

I want you as my partner. The same words I'd used that morning, after I'd seen him fight for the first time, after realizing that our Kiss could change the world. I had been right about that. In a way.

I leaned in for another kiss, echoing his reply from years ago, "I thought that had already been decided."

ACKNOWLEDGMENTS

I'll never forget the words of my critique partner, and one of my favorite people in the whole world, Melissa Jackson, when I told her the concept of this book and she responded with: "So they're like…making out on a battlefield?"

As crazy as this idea is, and as impossible as it was to describe without cracking up, Melissa didn't try to dissuade me from it. Instead, she was its golden champion. Thank you, Mel, for reading it, editing it, obsessing over it with me, and being a pillar of support while I dissolved into tears and incoherent text messages throughout my book journey.

Thank you to Judi Weiss for finding my tiny #pitmad tweet among literally thousands of amazing pitches and believing in it. I can never thank you enough. And of course, to my brilliant and sweetheart of an editor, Lydia Sharp, whose never-ending patience, dedication, and expertise helped make this book something I could be proud of. All of the hugs and cupcakes in the world couldn't express how grateful I am to you.

To everyone at Entangled Teen, y'all are rock stars and deserve to rule the world.

A special thanks to Vicki L. Weavil for her ongoing encouragement and feedback. Your prose is so gorgeous I could cry sometimes. Thank you for the introduction to my agent, Frances Black, at Literary Counsel. You are both spectacular women.

A huge shout-out goes to my local critique group made up of some of Baton Rouge's greatest writers. Season, Russell, Nick, Lee, Bridget, Andy, and Sean—because of y'all I can look forward to Mondays. Paula, thank you for spending every Sunday editing with me, while watching me consume a hundred green tea frapps and listening to me freak out over the latest round of edits.

To my darling Meaghan Mulligan, with whom I spent hours walking up and down the aisles of Barnes & Noble only the second time we met because we could not stop talking about YA books—you are a perfect, wonderful, precious treasure. You somehow knew this book would be published way before I did.

To all of the book bloggers, internet/twitter friends, beta readers, critique partners, author mentors—every single lesson I learned and step I took in my writing and publication journey can be traced back to you. I speak for debut authors everywhere when I say that we couldn't do this without your sharing, tweeting, teachings, and support. The writing community is truly magical.

I owe one of my oldest and most precious friends in the world, Bridget Clark, a debt I can never hope to repay for being my first writing partner and making me realize that *this* was my true passion.

Jason, my big brother, thank you for starting me on the road to becoming one of the biggest geeks on the planet. Watching cartoons, reading graphic novels, and playing video games with you since childhood has cultivated and inspired the imagination I have today.

Finally, how can I begin to thank the two people in my

life who pushed me day after day, rejection after rejection, to pursue my dream no matter what? Thank you, Mom and Dad, for everything you've ever done and everything you will continue to do even after I told you stop like a million times.

And to Mim and Pap, you both are the reason I know True Love exists.

Grab the Entangled Teen releases readers are talking about!

Bring Me Their Hearts
by Sara Wolf

Zera is a Heartless—the immortal, unaging soldier of the witch Nightsinger. With her heart in a jar under Nightsinger's control, she serves the witch unquestioningly. Until Nightsinger asks Zera for a prince's heart in exchange for her own.

No one can challenge Crown Prince Lucien d'Malvane… until the arrival of Lady Zera. She's inelegant, smart-mouthed, carefree, and out for his blood. The prince's honor has him quickly aiming for her throat.

So begins a game of cat and mouse between a girl with nothing to lose and a boy who has it all.

Winner takes the loser's heart.

Zombie Abbey
by Lauren Baratz-Logsted

Everyone in Porthampton knows his or her place. There's upstairs, downstairs, and then there are the villagers who tend the farms. But when a farmer is killed in a most unusual fashion, it becomes apparent that all three groups will have to do the unthinkable: work together, side by side, if they want to survive the menace. Even the three teenage daughters of Lord Martin Clarke must work with the handsome stable boy Will Harvey because, if they don't, their ancestral home of Porthampton Abbey just might turn into Zombie Abbey.

RISEN
BY COLE GIBSEN

My aunt has been kidnapped by vampires, and it's up to me to save her. Only…I had no idea vampires existed. Then there's the vampire Sebastian, who, yes, is the hottest being I've ever come across, but there's no way I can trust him. He swears he's helping me get answers, but there's more to his story. Now I'm a key pawn in a raging vampire war, and I need to pick the right ally.

ASSASSIN OF TRUTHS
BY BRENDA DRAKE

The gateways linking the great libraries of the world don't require a library card, but they do harbor incredible dangers. And the threats Gia Kearns faces are the kind that include an evil wizard hell-bent on taking her down. Gia can end his devious plan, but only if she recovers seven keys hidden throughout the world's most beautiful libraries. The last thing she needs is a distraction in the form of falling in love. But love might be the only thing left to help Gia save the world.

8906

entangled teen

an imprint of Entangled Publishing LLC